P9-CFO-085

DISCARDED

DISCARDED

LIFE:
AN EXPLODED
DIAGRAM

LIFE:
AN EXPLODED
DIAGRAM

Mal Peet

12/11

CANDLEWICK PRESS

This is a work of fiction. Names, characters, places, and incidents are either products of the author's imagination or, if real, are used fictitiously.

Copyright © 2011 by Mal Peet

Interior photographs: copyright © 2011 by Edwin Dalton Smith/
The Bridgeman Art Library/Getty Images (pages viii–ix);
© Corbis (pages 228–229);
© Dorling Kindersley/Getty Images (pages 350–351)

All rights reserved. No part of this book may be reproduced, transmitted, or stored in an information retrieval system in any form or by any means, graphic, electronic, or mechanical, including photocopying, taping, and recording, without prior written permission from the publisher.

First U.S. edition 2011

Library of Congress Cataloging-in-Publication Data

Peet, Mal.
Life : an exploded diagram / Mal Peet. — 1st U.S. ed.
p. cm.
Summary: In 1960s Norfolk, England, seventeen-year-old Clem Ackroyd lives
with his mother and grandmother in a tiny cottage, but his life is transformed
when he falls in love with the daughter of a wealthy farmer in this tale
that flashes back through the stories of three generations.
ISBN 978-0-7636-5227-2
[1. Family life—England—Fiction. 2. War—Fiction.
3. Social classes—Fiction. 4. Coming of age—Fiction.
5. Norfolk (England)—History—20th century—Fiction.
6. Great Britain—History—Elizabeth II, 1952– —Fiction.] I. Title.
PZ7.P3564Lif 2011
[Fic]—dc22 2010042742

11 12 13 14 15 16 BVG 10 9 8 7 6 5 4 3 2 1

Printed in Berryville, VA, U.S.A.

This book was typeset in Fairfield.

Candlewick Press
99 Dover Street
Somerville, Massachusetts 02144

visit us at www.candlewick.com

For Bernard and Hilary

CONTENTS

PART ONE

PUTTING THINGS TOGETHER

1.

NORFOLK, EARLY MARCH, 1945

R UTH ACKROYD WAS in the garden checking the rhubarb
when the RAF Spitfire accidentally shot her chimney pot
to bits. The shock of it brought the baby on three weeks early.
"I was expectun," she'd often say, over the years. "But I wunt
expectun *that*."

She'd had cravings throughout her pregnancy, ambitious
ones: tinned ham, chocolate, potted shrimp, her husband's
touch, rhubarb. Rhubarb was possible, though. Ruth and her
mother, Win, grew it in the cottage garden. They forced it,
which is to say, they covered the plants with upended buckets
so that when new tendrils poked through the soil, they found
themselves in the dark and grew like mad, groping for light.
Stalks of forced rhubarb were soft, blushed, and stringless. You
could eat them without sugar, which was rationed, and Ruth
wanted to. So she'd waddled out into the garden on a rare day
of early-spring sunshine to lift the buckets and see how things
were doing. See if there was any chance of a nibble.

Win had said, "You put that ole coat on, if yer gorn out. There's a wind'd cut yer jacksy in half."

Ruth hadn't seen George since his last leave, when, silently (because Win was sleeping, or listening, a thin wall away), he'd got her pregnant. Now he was in Africa. Or Italy, or somewhere. There was no way she could imagine his life. He might even be dead. The last letter had come in January:

The last push, or so they say . . . Cold as hell here in the nights . . . Hope you and the little passenger are well.
Love, George

Probably not dead, because there'd have been a telegram. Like Brenda Cushion had got, six months ago.

Ruth had gone down the garden path with her huge belly in front of her. She was frightened of it. She had little idea what giving birth might involve. Win had told her almost nothing; she was against the whole thing. Knocked up by a soldier: history repeating itself. Nothing good could come of it. The baby had grown in Ruth, struggling and undiscussed. An unspeakable thing. A wartime mishap. The two women had sat the winter out in front of dying fires of scrounged fuel, listening to the wireless, grimly knitting, not talking about it.

Washing blew on the line: tea towels, Ruth's yellowish vests, her mother's bloomers ballooned by the wind, their elasticated leg holes pouting.

There were two rhubarb clumps, a rusty-lipped bucket inverted over each. Ruth had leaned, grunting, to lift the first one when all hell broke loose above her head.

The air-raid siren had not gone off. The air-raid siren was a big gray thing the shape of a surprised mouth, mounted on a wooden tower behind the Black Cat Garage, more than a mile away. It made a moan that turned hysterical, then stopped, then started over again, rising in pitch, driving the local dogs mad. Throughout the summer of 1940, it had wailed day and night as the German planes came over, and Ruth and Win had spent terrible long hours in the darkness under the stairs, waiting for it to stop. Or for the riot in the skies to fall upon them and kill them. (Sometimes Ruth couldn't stand it and had gone outside, despite her mother's prayerful begging, to watch and listen to the dogfights in the sky, the white vapor trails scratched against the blue, the black trails of planes falling, the awful hesitations of engine noise that meant one of ours or one of theirs was falling, a man in a machine was burning down.) But on this occasion, the siren remained silent. There had been no German air raids for eighteen months, after all. The war was over, bar the shouting.

So Ruth was terribly surprised when the chimney pot exploded and the German plane came from behind the elms and filled the garden with savage noise. The machine was so low that she was certain it would plunge into the cottage. She fell backwards with her knees in the air and saw, with absolute clarity, the rivets that held the bomber together and its vulnerable glass nose and the black cross on its fuselage and the banner

3

of fire that trailed from its wing. One of the Spitfires in pursuit was pulling out of a dive. Its underbelly was the same blue as the heavy old pram that Chrissie Slender had lent her. The sound of the planes was so all-consuming that the fragments of the chimney tumbled silently into the yard. Inside their wire run, the hens frenzied.

2.

THE HEARTBROKEN NAZI

YOU'LL THINK IT fanciful, I suppose, but I blame that German plane for my lifelong dislike of surprises and loud noises. It's an unfortunate dislike, really, because the world, during my long stay in it, has got noisier and noisier. And more and more surprising.

It so happens that I know who flew that Junkers 88 over Bratton Morley, at little more than tree height, on March 9, 1945. Forty years after his suicidal flight, I was in Holland, doing research for a picture book about what were called doodlebugs, the German rocket bombs launched upon England during the last year of the Second World War. In Amsterdam I spent almost a week in a thin and lovely old building full of books and maps and documents and photographs. It was like being in an immensely tall bookcase. On my last day, one of the librarians brought me a book entitled *Our Last Days*. It was a collection of first-person accounts by German servicemen and civilians of their experiences during the final desperate stage of the war they knew they had lost. I flicked through it and saw the words *RAF Beckford,* which was the name of the Norfolk air base four miles from where, in an untimely and messy fashion, I was born. I licked my finger and turned the pages back. The piece was a badly written (or poorly translated) story by a former Luftwaffe sergeant called Ottmar Sammer.

I struggle to tell you how I felt when I read it. A bit like looking in a mirror for the first time in years, perhaps.

Here, in my own words, is Sammer's story.

He'd spent the last two years of the war in charge of the ground crew of a squadron commanded by Oberst Karlheinz Metz. Metz was, as a pilot, both brilliant and fearless. He'd joined the Luftwaffe at the age of eighteen, and by the time he was twenty, he was dropping bombs on Spanish democrats, thus helping to inspire Picasso's *Guernica.* During the blitzkrieg on Britain, he'd flown more raids than any other officer. Once, he'd flown his crippled bomber back from Plymouth with all his crew dead. He'd won so many medals that if he'd worn them all at once, the sheer weight of them would have made him fall flat on his face. (That was the nearest that Sammer came to making a joke.) Metz was also a passionate Nazi. There was a photograph of him in the book. The odd thing was that no matter how long I studied it, I forgot what he looked like as soon as I turned the page. He was weirdly ordinary-looking.

In March 1945, Metz's squadron was stationed in western Holland. His situation was quite hopeless. American and Canadian forces were less than fifty miles from his airfield.

He had not flown, nor received any orders, for more than two weeks. Of the twenty-two planes he'd originally commanded, only seven still existed. Of those, only three were airworthy. He had, despite his demands, only enough fuel to get one plane to England and maybe back. On March 7 he received a signal from Berlin telling him to destroy his aircraft and retreat his squadron eastward to the German border.

Metz did as he was told, almost. On the morning of March 9, he assembled the surviving members of his squadron and made an inspirational speech about the defense of the Fatherland. His men raised their hats and cheered him; then they put explosives in all the aircraft except one and blew them up. Imagine that: a row of machines, which had known the inside of clouds, going bang and slumping their flaming arms to the ground. Sammer said that Metz kept his face straight while he supervised it but that tears ran down his face. (I suspect that Ottmar was gilding the lily there.) Metz then ordered his men into trucks and watched them drive away. Not all the men, though. He'd kept Sammer and the armorer and another man behind. Metz got them to fuel up the surviving 88. He also got them to load the belt-fed machine guns, despite the fact that there were no gunners. At this point Sammer realized what the Oberst was intending to do. He claims that he tried to talk Metz out of it but was ignored.

When the plane was ready, Metz led the others to the squadron headquarters, which was a low building made of concrete blocks, its curved corrugated-iron roof covered with camouflage netting. Most of the floor space was the operations room, in which metal chairs were arranged in front of a blackboard and a map easel. Metz instructed his men to bring four chairs through into his personal quarters, which was not much more than a dimly lit cubbyhole containing his camp bed, a wardrobe, and a chest of drawers. A slightly garish color-tinted photograph of Adolf Hitler hung on the end wall. On the chest were an almost-full bottle of Cognac, six glasses, a framed photograph of a handsome young Luftwaffe pilot with dark hair flopping almost to his eyes, and a windup gramophone with a horn like a huge brass daffodil. Metz told the others to sit, then served them generous measures of brandy. He cranked the gramophone and lowered the needle onto the disc. The four men sat and listened to a piano sonata by Beethoven, the *Appassionata*. During its quieter passages, the gasping and collapsing of burning aircraft was clearly audible. During its turbulent finale, Metz, his eyes closed, made vaguely musical gestures with his fists. When it was over, he remained in his chair for several long moments, seemingly mesmerized by the blip and hiss of the gramophone. At last he got to his feet and deliberately dragged the needle across the surface of the disc, ruining it. The brass daffodil screeched in agony. Metz then stood to attention in front of the Führer's portrait, jabbed his right arm out, and said, or rather yelled, *"Heil Hitler!"* The other men hastily, if less enthusiastically, followed suit.

The Oberst picked up the photograph from the chest, tucked it under one arm, and led Sammer and the others briskly out to his plane. The radiance from the white-hot aircraft carcasses wobbled the air. He shook hands with each of the men in turn, wished them good luck, and climbed up into the cockpit. When the engines were firing steadily, Sammer pulled the chocks away from the wheels and Metz taxied bumpily onto the runway.

Metz's last orders to Sammer had been to take his— Metz's—staff car and catch up with the rest of the evacuated squadron. Sammer disobeyed. As soon as the Junkers was airborne, the sergeant returned to the Oberst's room and stripped the sheet from the bed. He attached it to a tent pole, and with this white flag of truce sticking out of the front passenger window, he and his colleagues drove south, not east. They surrendered to the first Canadian troops they came across, who apparently treated them as a bit of a nuisance. I was a little surprised that Sammer jovially admitted to all this in his memoir, which ends at this point. I've patched together the end of Metz's story from other sources, one of which is my imagination.

Metz flew extremely low over the North Sea in an effort to sneak under British radar. At first the weather was on his side: it was very murky. It cleared, however, just before he reached the coast of East Anglia, and he was spotted by a coast-guard station just north of Great Yarmouth. (He could hardly have been missed; he nearly took the station's radio mast off.) Seven minutes from his target, he came under attack by three Spitfires.

That target was RAF Beckford, and Metz's plan was simple: he would dive his plane onto the damned place and purge it with fire. That he himself would die was no matter. To all intents and purposes, he'd been dead for almost two years already. This had to do with the photograph that he'd propped up in the copilot's seat, the beautiful young flier with the tumbling hair. The boy had joined the squadron in the autumn of 1942, and for six months Metz had experienced an agonizing happiness. He'd felt a need to nurture and protect that went against the grain of himself. The friction had been delicious.

Then, in May 1943, the boy had been killed. Metz, frozen at the controls of his own plane, with his flight engineer screaming in his headphones, had watched it happen. Had watched the two British Hurricanes following his darling's smoking machine down like frenzied sharks following a blood leak, triangulating the bullets in as if there were an infinity of bullets. Had watched the boy's plane do a half cartwheel into the sea and simply cease to exist. Joy and love gone, bang, just like that, swallowed into the crinkled gray texture of the English sea. The Hurricanes were from RAF Beckford; Metz intended to end his war with a vengeance.

Flying solo, he had no way of defending himself from the Spitfires. Flying at so ridiculously low a height, he had very limited options for evasive action. So he stuck grimly to his course, watching the Norfolk landscape race toward and under him while his plane took an absurd number of hits and disintegrated around him. Just before he overflew a hamlet called Bratton Morley (did he glimpse a bulbous woman lifting her shocked face and falling over?), his starboard engine caught fire.

Metz didn't make it to Beckford, although he got close. Two miles from the air base, he plunged, burning, into a sizable tract of forest known locally as Abbots Wood. He had almost certainly died by the time the ancient and heavy English trees ripped the wings from his fuselage. Jolting in the smoking cockpit, he tobogganed through the woods and plunged into a stretch of water called Perch Lake.

The woods were wet and sullen after the long winter. It didn't take long for the crews from Beckford and Borstead to hose and beat the smoldering out. They hadn't the equipment to lift the remains of the plane from the lake, so Metz was left sitting next to the shattered photograph of his lover under fifteen feet of silty water. Four months later, a courting couple were put off their stroke when his black and gassy body parts bobbed to the surface.

3.

LABOR

THE VIOLENT OUTRAGE overhead went away and was replaced by human noise: Win, howling Ruth's name, punctuated by the various aliases of God. Ruth tried to call back, tried to say that she was all right, but found that she had no voice. The next thing was the banging of the gate and young Tommy Slender running to the back door, going, "Gor, bogger! Missus? Ruthie? You seen that? That Jerry? Come over just now? That near on took our chimbley off!"

Ruth got her elbows under her and looked down the garden path. The boy was running circles on the rough concrete between the kitchen door and the outside lavatory. He had his arms stretched out and was making shooting noises; they mixed strangely with Win's howling.

"*Fadda fadda fadda!*"

"Ruth! Dear God, Jesus Christ!"

"*Brahahaaa! You seen our boys come arter him? Bogger!*"

"*Sweet Lord! Ruth!*"

Then Chrissie Slender was looking down at her.

"You all right?"

"Yeah."

"You dunt look it. Can you get yerself up?"

"I dunno," Ruth said.

"Wait you there, then," Chrissie said, and went away.

She came back with Win, who was white-faced and fluttery, and Tommy, who had one ear pinker than the other because it had just been slapped. They pulled and pushed Ruth to her feet. The moment she was upright, a pain the shape of lightning went through her and she cried out. She thought it might be the pain of the child dying; for all she knew, violent noise might kill babies in the womb.

After a moment or two she could walk.

In the kitchen, she perched her backside on a high stool; for some time now she'd been unable to sit comfortably on a chair. Win was useless. She walked in and out of the room, clapping her hands together, looking up at the ceiling, and mumbling stuff from the Bible. Chrissie put the kettle on the stove and made a pot of tea. She found a damp residue of sugar in a crumpled blue paper bag and spooned it all into Ruth's cup.

"Drink it," she told Ruth. "Yer've had a shock. That'll settle you."

Ruth took a couple of sips.

"Thas it," Chrissie said. "Thas brought the color back to yer cheeks already."

Ruth had, in fact, gone quite red in the face. But it wasn't recovery. It was shame. For some reason she'd let go of herself. Her lower parts were a hot flood.

Tommy said, "Mum, she're wet herself!"

"No, she hent," Chrissie said. "And mind yer bleddy manners. Ruthie, I reckon yer waters hev broke. D'you know what that mean?"

Ruth shook her head. She had a hot wet cup and hot wet legs and didn't know what to do with any of them.

"That mean baby's ready to come," Chrissie said. "You got to get upstairs. Tommy, get you home and get the bike and fetch Nurse Salmon up here. Thomas! You hear what I say?"

"Yeah."

"Then dunt stand there lookun like a bleddy fish. Do what I told yer."

Tommy ran the thirty yards home pretending that the sky was full of Nazis and that he was dodging their bombs. His mother's bike was leaning against the wall of the outside lav. It was a woman's bike, without a crossbar. Tommy was too short to sit on the seat and reach the pedals, so he rode it standing up with his face almost level with the handlebars, machine-gunning everything that crossed his path.

District Nurse Salmon had retired in the summer of 1939. Bad timing. Ten months later, the Cottage Hospital outside Borstead started to fill up with damaged soldiers and airmen, and she found herself called upon to tender to the needs of the civilian population. The local doctor, a depressed and alcoholic

Scot, steadfastly refused to visit civilian patients who could not pay his fees (in guineas). So instead of gardening and reading and walking her fat little terrier, Miss Salmon spent the first six years of her retirement cycling hither and yon, dealing with fevers and earaches, tweezering gravel out of boys' knees, dressing ulcers, lancing boils, strapping up broken wrists and fingers, dabbing antiseptic on dog bites, stitching cuts, blitzing head lice, and, very occasionally, delivering babies. When she was paid for her services, it was usually in kind: a dozen eggs, half a week's ration of tea, a rabbit (unskinned), a bundle of carrots, a bottle of parsnip wine. She lived in a tidy little Victorian house a mile and a half from Bratton Morley, set back from the Cromer road. The house suited her; it was plain but slightly posh, as she was. She was in the kitchen frying a slice of belly pork for her lunch when Tommy Slender pounded on her door. She didn't get to eat it until ten hours later.

Ruth had imagined any number of fearful things about what they called labor. Chrissie had told her it would hurt. ("Thas like havun yer top lip pulled up over yer head.") But she'd had no idea that it would go on for hours and hours, the pain rolling through her time after time. Even so, it was not the physical agony that almost unhinged her brain; it was the embarrassment. Lying there, spraddled and heaving, with Chrissie holding her down, and old Nurse Salmon peering and poking at the parts of her that not even George had ever had a close look at. Her own language shocked her. When the pain roiled in, she swore and blasphemed in a voice that didn't seem hers. It was like she was possessed by some raging, goaty old Satan.

Her mother used this as a pretext to excuse herself from the proceedings.

"I ent gorna stay here an lissun to any more of yer language, Ruth," Win said. "If you can't get ahold of yerself, I'm off downstairs."

In truth, Win was more frightened than offended. She noisily cleared up the soot and shards of chimney pot that had spilled from the fireplace, then busied herself in the garden. When it got dark, she sat in the living room with her fingers in her ears, humming hymns. At eleven o'clock, she was shaken awake by Chrissie Slender, who said, "Win? Come you upstairs an say hello to yer grandson. He're had a helluva struggle gettun here."

Win followed Chrissie up the stairs. Ruth's bedroom smelled of sweat and disinfectant. Nurse Salmon was putting things into her leather bag. A stained sheet was bundled at the foot of the bed. It would need a salt-and-soda soak, Win thought, and even that probably wouldn't do the job. Ruth's face was yellow and slick in the lamplight. The child lay on her chest, wrapped in a towel. From where she stood, Win could not see its face.

"So. How're yer doing, Ruth?"

"Dear God," Ruth said, "I ent gorn through that again."

"I should hope not," Win said.

In accordance with George's wishes, Ruth named the baby boy Clement, after Clement Attlee, the leader of the Labour Party. Win thought it was absurd.

16

4.
WIN LITTLE

AS FAR AS Win was concerned, men were coarse and troublesome when you didn't need them and gone when you did.

She was the youngest of five children. The others were all boys.

John, the eldest, died of diphtheria before she was born.

James—Jimmy—was a dark-haired unruly boy. His love for his little sister, which was awkward but genuine, took the form of teasing, of comedic tormenting. He would carry her to the top of the dark staircase and leave her there. Then he would creep into the understairs cupboard and make spooky noises while scratching his nails against the underside of the treads. Not long after Win had started to sob in terror, he would emerge and bound up to her, saying, "Blas' me, Winnie, if there ent a big old wolf come and et up mother! But dunt yer worry;

I'll save yer." He'd scoop her up and leap, whooping, down to where lamplight and safety and a scolding awaited.

Jimmy fought with their father. Verbally and then physically. One night in 1902, when Win was four and fast asleep, Jimmy kissed her good-bye. He had blood on his teeth, which left a smear on her chin. Then he walked all the way to Lowestoft and got work on a trawler. He was fourteen years old. Five years later, he wrote a short letter to his family from Nova Scotia, in Canada. They never heard from him again.

The next boy was Albert, who was born with his brain askew. As a baby, Win would be laid for her daytime naps in a pulled-out drawer of a chest in her parents' bedroom. Albert would go up there and watch her sleeping. Then he would put something he'd found outdoors—a snail, a special stone, the part-rotted corpse of a bird—next to her and push the drawer back in. He'd coffin her. Death interested him. Not long after Jimmy set off for the coast, Albert did something to another little girl and got taken off to an institution the other side of Norwich.

Then there was Stanley. He was a year and a half older than Win. She wore his hand-me-down nappies and jumpers. Later, she walked with him to school, holding his hand until they met up with other children along the lane. Then he'd let go of her and join the other whooping boys, throwing stones at gateposts or stamping on horse-chestnut shells to expose the unready conkers nested within.

School was a room behind the church. The teacher was Miss Draper, who had a mustache and was usually angry about nothing that Win could understand. Once or twice a week, the vicar came in and talked to them until he was as angry as Miss Draper, then blessed them and went out in a swirl of coattails.

Strangely—unnaturally, almost—Win quickly learned to read. She helped her elder brother with his lessons, which were mostly passages from the Bible. She moved her finger along the text while he stumbled across words that had no meaning for either of them: epistle, foreskin, Jericho, abomination, deliverance.

Stanley looked like his mother: soft and pale and worried.

The father of these ill-starred children was a small, hard, bearded patriarch called John Sparling. He was the head stockman for the Mortimers, who owned that part of the world, including the cottage the family lived in. Sparling wore brown leather boots and gaiters, which his wife cleaned and oiled every night before going to bed. He smelled of cow. (Until she died, Win would picture him whenever she got a whiff of manure.) The death, disappearance, and madness of his first three sons shamed and angered him. The gentleness of the fourth dismayed him. He blamed his wife: some wrongness in her bloodline or a crookedness of her womb. The late birth of a daughter was a sort of irrelevance, a mishap. But, surprising himself, he came to love her. Winifred was sharp and watchful, like himself. By the time she was four, she was standing on a stool alongside her mother, peeling potatoes at the sink with the second-best knife. She ran to greet him on his homecoming, asking after the sick calf he'd spoken of the night before. In the parlor, after dinner, Stanley would say, "Tell that rhyme we learned at school terday, Win."

And she would recite it, word-perfect, and Sparling would take her on his knee and say, "Yer smart as a whip, gal. Smart as a whip."

But Win grew away from him. She got older before he wanted her to, before he'd noticed. By the time she was ten, she had outgrown his rough advances. She had sided with her mother, had come to regard men as A Cross to Be Borne. She was keen on chapel, singing clearly and accurately the hymns her father mumbled.

In 1914 John Sparling died of what was then called farmer's lung. His persistent light cough had deepened during the autumn of the preceding year. By Christmas he was spitting blood into his handkerchiefs, and he died just before Easter.

His wife's fear was greater than her grief. The cottage was tied, which is to say that it came with her late husband's job. The possibility—the very real possibility—of becoming homeless made her sick with dread. So when she saw Edmund Mortimer awaiting her at the cemetery gate, she faltered and gripped Stanley's arm.

Mortimer removed his black hat and held it in front of him by its brim. Win observed the nervous way his fingers toyed with the sleek fabric. It meant that he was embarrassed to be giving them notice, and she was glad.

"I'm deeply sorry for your loss, Mrs. Sparling."

"Thank you, sir."

"And I share it," Mortimer said. "John was as good a man

with livestock as any in the county. I scarce know what I shall do without him."

Win's mother kept her head lowered. "Nor dunt I," she said. It was as bold a thing as Win had ever heard her say.

"No. I . . ." Mortimer cleared his throat. "What I wanted to say, Mrs. Sparling, is that I don't want you worrying yourself about the cottage. I'm putting Sam Eldon in charge of the stock, and he and Mrs. Eldon are well settled where they are. So I've no need of your place. It's yours for as long as you want to stay. The rent is something we might talk about some other time."

At this point Mrs. Sparling wept for the first time in a week. She snuffled her gratitude, almost choked on her relief. Stanley made an awkward humming noise that was perhaps meant to be consoling.

Edmund Mortimer looked discomfited and tried to be jocular. He glanced a smile in Win's direction.

"Besides," he said, "from what I hear, your lovely daughter might not be single for that much longer. It wouldn't do for her to be without a place."

Win was not such a fool as to be unable to read the message in that remark. The family would not be homeless, but it would need a man, a breadwinner. And that would not be Stanley. Still working out his apprenticeship to a baker in Borstead, his pay was a pittance. Bread maker, yes, almost. Breadwinner, no. Mr. Mortimer was referring, slyly and benignly, to Percy Little.

Percy was a year older than Win and had been a nuisance

for most of her life. As a boy, he'd been a ringleader of the small mob who'd pelted acorns and snowballs at her. He'd put a toad in her school desk. He'd darted sticky arrowgrass at her skirts, untugged her hair ribbons. Over the years, Win's tormentors had dwindled away, attracted by younger, softer targets or repulsed by her icy disdain and wicked tongue. But Percy had persevered in his pursuit of her. Gradually his harassment had softened into a rough courtship. When he was thirteen, he'd persuaded Win to kiss him on the mouth. She'd thought the experience peculiar and not worth repeating. Later Win had started to fill her clothes in a way that she found troubling and Percy found interesting. He wanted to touch her in particular places and she wouldn't let him.

When he left school, Percy had gone to be a stable-lad for the Mortimers. He discovered he had an affinity with the huge, placid cart horses and plow horses. He loved the careful way they placed their feathery, iron-shod feet on the earth. When they were not working and needed exercise, he led them past the Sparling cottage and hoisted squealing Win up onto their backs. She found it thrilling to be so high off the ground, perched atop half a ton of warm and muscular architecture.

During the winter, when her father was dying, Percy made repeated efforts to put his hands inside her clothes. She wouldn't let him.

He'd said, "If we was married, Win, yer'd hev to."

Walking with Stanley and her mother back from the graveyard, thinking about what Mortimer had said, Win understood—

or thought she understood—what the framework of her life had to be.

So the next time Percy put his hand on her leg, she said, "Not till we're married, Percy."

"Yer'll hev me, then?"

"If yer behave yerself," she said.

Afterward she realized that she'd be called Win Little. A foolish name.

Their engagement was accelerated by the First World War. Magnificent recruiting sergeants addressed gatherings on village greens and in church halls, speaking of Heroism and Duty and the Vileness of the Huns. From behind them, vicars and squires and chairmen of parish councils glared into the audience, daring cowards to meet their gaze. Men started vanishing from the countryside, marching away accompanied by faltering music. On one Saturday afternoon, six of Mortimer's men went off and joined up; they came back from the recruiting office beery, puffed up, and boastful.

Win thought that Percy might not go if he was married.

The wedding took place five days after her eighteenth birthday. Stanley gave her away, fumbling it. Percy moved into the cottage, sleeping with Win in the bedroom that Jimmy and Albert had shared.

She kept him safe for a whole year. He showed no sign of wanting to fight, and because he was a newlywed, he was not condemned for it. No one handed him a white feather, that soft and silent accusation of cowardice.

Two days after their first wedding anniversary, Percy was conscripted. He went to Thetford for six weeks' basic training, then came back to her, a stranger in a manure-colored uniform, his eyes unfamiliar beneath the peak of his cap. He insisted that they have their photograph taken before he went to France. They walked to Borstead, from where they took the train to Norwich. The photographer's studio was on Prince of Wales Road. They had to queue; other men in uniform with their wives and fiancées were there ahead of them. They posed in front of a painted backdrop of a garden with a fountain. Afterward they had tea and cake at a café in Tombland, in the shadow of the cathedral.

He came home once more after that. Then in 1918 he was shot in the belly and drowned facedown in a Belgian meadow that battle had turned into a smoking and bloody swamp.

Win was very angry. She was angry with him for getting killed. She was angry with Edmund Mortimer, who could've told the Conscription Board that Percy was an essential agricultural worker. She was angry because she was pregnant. She was angry because there'd been no pleasure in getting that way. (How would there have been? She was a prig; he was unsubtle.)

When the baby was born, she called it Ruth. A biblical name. Also a word that meant sorrow and regret.

5.
DNA

I'M SENTIMENTAL; I admit that. No, not *admit*; I *proudly declare* that. After all, what's so great about being unsentimental? What are the synonyms for *unsentimental*? Hard-eyed, hard-nosed, hard-hearted, hard-boiled. Realistic, phlegmatic, unfeeling. Do any of those appeal to you? Fancy sporting any of those on your T-shirt? Besides, scratch a cynic and you'll find a sentimentalist beneath the paint. That's as true here in no-nonsense New York as it is anywhere else. Maybe more so. Take my immediate neighbor, for example. She has the awkward name Agnetha Ogu. (The *h* is silent, the second *g* a sort of gulp.) She's a second-generation immigrant. I find it difficult to guess her age and even more difficult to ask. She's trim and brisk and works in some sort of IT business. The second time we met, I made a cautious inquiry about her origins.

She said, "I don't have a past. I have a future."

A few weeks later, when Christmas was looming, I invited her in for a drink. She looked around, trying to conceal her disapproval. (Most of my place is devoted to my work, so it looks like an explosion in an art-supply shop or a library. Agnetha's apartment is clinical.) The blown-up and framed photograph of Win and Percy caught her eye.

"This is nice," she said. "Who are these people? Do you know?"

I suppose she'd assumed that I'd bought the print in Greenwich Village or somewhere. I told her that they were my grandparents. I told her about Percy and the horses and the war. I told her about Win being widowed before my mother was born and how she'd spent her working life in a laundry. I guess I sounded very matter-of-fact—I was busy fixing our drinks. So I was surprised when I saw that Agnetha was touching the picture with the tips of her fingers and that she had wet eyes.

"I don't have anything like this," she said.

Sentimentality and nostalgia are closely related. Kissing cousins. I have no time for nostalgia, though. Nostalgics believe that the past is nicer than the present. It isn't. Or wasn't. Nostalgics want to cuddle the past like a puppy. But the past has bloody teeth and bad breath. I look into its mouth like a sorrowing dentist.

In the photograph, Win is sitting on a wicker garden chair and Percy is standing slightly behind her with his hand on her shoulder. She was proud of her long brown hair but knew that this was a vanity. So she wove it into a tight plait and pinned it severely to her head. She's wearing a pleated floral blouse that fails to conceal the fact that she has a generous bosom. The expression on her face is hard to read. Consider, after all, that she had recently and reluctantly married; that she had traveled to a nearby city for the first time; that her husband was a foolish soldier; that although she'd thought this would be a very special moment, she'd waited in line for it; that the photographer was the first foreigner she'd ever encountered (an Italian called Delmonico); that she had been told to smile. She looks blank.

Percy is in the uniform of a private in the Norfolk Regiment. Presumably, he could have chosen to take the cap off, but he kept it on, perhaps because it made him look taller. I wish he'd taken it off. I try to imagine what he was feeling. He was a cocky farm boy who'd experienced the crushing brutality of military training. He has a possessive hand on the girl he'd pursued since childhood. He is wearing the king's uniform and no doubt feels himself to be part of an important historic project. He is almost certainly scared, because, daft as he was, he knew that death is the soldier's trade. He would have practiced bayoneting, stabbing sandbags hung from gallows. The peak of the cap shadows his eyes. Like Win, he is expressionless. The pair of them stare into the muzzle of Signor Delmonico's camera, like people trying to maintain good manners in the face of some obscene species of horror.

I'm reading all this into the picture, obviously. Maybe they didn't feel anything like that at all. There's sentimentality for you.

On the other hand, there's the fact that Percy is part of me. He's woven into my DNA. We share cellular structure. He might be responsible for the shape of my nose, my dislike of cats, the color of my hair. He might have some genetic say in the kind of people I'm attracted to and the people who were attracted to me. And therefore he might be to blame for my failed marriage. Likewise, I might owe him my success, such as it is.

Win, too, of course. Her thorny string of cells is just as much a part of me. But I knew her; I never knew Percy. And, like Win, I am angry with him for marching off into oblivion. I deal with my anger by making up stories about him. By imagining him. By bringing him up a lost country lane between two vast peaceable horses, his hands between their bridles and their hot flat cheeks, to where my young grandmother leans on a gate.

I stole the photograph from my parents' house in 1978, after Win's funeral. It took them three months to notice it was gone.

6.
RUTH

WIN BROUGHT HER daughter up closely. In Bratton Morley, this was not difficult. The place consisted of nine cottages, nine families knitted together by intermarriage and employment by the Mortimers. Threads of connection reached out to the other clusters of dwellings on the estate; nevertheless, at the time of her marriage, Win could have written on a single sheet of paper the names of everyone she had ever met.

Edmund Mortimer was a kindly employer. He did not stop a man's pay when he was off sick. When his pigs were slaughtered, the lesser cuts—trotters, half-heads for sausage, thin end of belly for streaky bacon—were distributed among his people. His windfall apples were there for the taking. At potato-lifting times, women walked home from the fields with bulging aprons.

Mortimer's instinctive kindness toward his employees had been intensified by a deep sadness. The Great War had shocked and depressed him. He had listened to the patriotic bombast with intense unease, had read the triumphalist reports in the *Times* with utter dismay. Of the twenty-three of his men who had gone off to fight for the king—the kaiser's cousin—only ten had returned, some of them maimed. He had walked to greet them home and shake their hands, if they still had them. He wrote notes to bereft mothers and young widows on black-edged paper.

After the war, it took him eight years to get his farm back to full strength, eight years during which many of his fields lay fallow and women and awkward boys did the work of experienced men who had died. The landscape itself seemed to grieve. In the untilled fields, poppies proliferated like a million droplets of blood. Doggedly, he'd got things back to something like normal. He had not paid much attention to the Sparlings. He'd fixed the rent on their cottage at a guinea—twenty-one shillings—a year, payable on Lady Day, March 25. Win or her mother had queued to pay it, in hoarded coin, to Mr. Hedge, Mortimer's moonfaced young steward. Hedge marked it down in a ledger using a pen dipped in black ink, counting the money into a metal cash box with an ironical flourish, because most of the money had come from Mortimer in the first place.

Win and her mother were glad of Edmund Mortimer's casual generosity, or neglect. Without a man's wage coming in, they were poor. (Shortsighted and slow-moving Stanley had moved into a room above the baker's. Walking to Borstead from Bratton at five in the morning to knead bread dough had proved beyond him. His rent and board more or less canceled out his wages.) The two women lived off their garden produce, the eggs from their dozen hens, and seasonal fieldwork.

To Win's satisfaction, Ruth was plain. She attracted no particular attention. She was a quiet, almost solemn, child. The only problem was her hair, which was ember-red and rather beautiful. Win recognized the danger of it and kept it cropped into a short bob. Win's sentimental mother protested, weakly, but Win cited head lice and other horrors and snipped away with the kitchen scissors.

When Ruth was five, she went to school. For the first week, Win walked her there. Then, astonishingly, she announced that she had found herself a job at the new Borstead Steam Laundry. Win was made of sterner stuff than Stanley; she set off for Borstead at six thirty the following Monday with her head lowered into an early autumn drizzle.

Win made that walk twice a day, six days a week, for the next three years. In all that time, she missed only four days of work, when deep snow made the road impassable. (Those days were deducted from her wages, of course, so she returned to work as soon as the snow turned to icy slush. In old age, when walking became a burning agony to her, she loudly regretted it.)

Then, in 1926, her mode of travel to work changed, and this change echoed down Ruth's life. In that year, the laundry acquired two electrically powered delivery vans that resembled the milk floats that had recently appeared in Norwich. The drivers' cabins were blunt, open-sided wedges with a single seat.

Steering was by means of a handle like a boat's tiller. Behind the cabins, the floors of the vans were just large enough to carry ten large laundry hampers and six small ones. The tin sides of the vehicles were painted a smart maroon with the legend BOR-STEAD MODERN STEAM LAUNDRY painted in curly yellow lettering. It took very little skill to operate these machines, so one of the driving jobs went to the weirdly cheerful Willy Page, who happened to live in Bratton Morley. He was some sort of cousin to Win and was gormlessly in love with her. At the end of his working day, Willy was allowed to drive his van home. So it made sense for him to hang around, smoking hand-rolled cigarettes, until Win finished her shift, then let her hop into the back. Equally, it made sense to drive her to work in the mornings and take Ruth to school at the same time. Mother and daughter sat in the back of the slow, jolting van, trying to ignore Willy's chatter, watching the road and sky unfurl their seasons.

All of which meant that Ruth arrived at school before the other pupils. It was not the same school that Win had attended. Saint Nicholas's Elementary School was the converted chapter house of Saint Nicholas's Priory on the outskirts of the town, on the road to Yarmouth. It had a door for boys and a door for girls and a contested outdoor lavatory. The teacher was no longer the angry and mustachioed Miss Draper. She had been replaced by Miss Selcott, a sensitive and somewhat despairing young woman from the Home Counties. Ruth had no idea where or what the Home Counties were. She pictured a distant place bathed in warm light and populated by happy families. A place from which Miss Selcott had been tragically exiled, perhaps by

Romance. So, out of kindness, during the hour or so before the other pupils arrived, Ruth formed a bond with Miss Selcott. While Ruth moved silently among the desks, distributing exercise books and filling the ink pots, she listened to Miss Selcott reciting the verses of Elizabeth Barrett Browning and Thomas Hardy. At the ends of the days, between the departure of the other children and the soft whine of Willy's van, she would do likewise. In this way, Ruth acquired something of her teacher's voice and learned that love was a form of distress.

Arithmetic, however, was neat and unambiguous and had nothing to do with love. Ruth developed a talent for it. When Miss Selcott filled the left-hand side of the blackboard with chalk numerals and, with a challenging flourish, drew the equals sign, Ruth's mind ticked like a cooling tractor. Miss Selcott surveyed her gawping pupils with a tragic patience. Eventually, inevitably, she would say, "Ruth?" And Ruth would stand up and walk between the desks to the blackboard while the boys hissed and sniggered at her. Then she would write the answer in white on the mysterious space at the right of the blackboard. Blushing and costly moments of triumph.

When Ruth left school, it was Miss Selcott who found her a position—junior bookkeeper—with Cubitt and Lark, Corn Merchants and Agricultural Auctioneers. The firm's offices were the upper two floors of a sober-faced Georgian building that kept watch over Borstead's marketplace. Ruth worked at a high desk in a back room with a view over the churchyard. Old Mr. Cubitt flirted with her; young Mr. Lark sought to find fault with her work. Neither had any success. After three years, the word *junior* disappeared from her job title, and her wages went up to fifteen shillings and sixpence a week. She spent her half-hour lunchtimes with Stanley. In the winter, she'd walk the short distance to the bakery and share a pie with him in his tidy, monastic little room above the shop. He'd fuss over the spilled crumbs. On warmer days, he'd bring the pie to the churchyard, and they'd eat on a bench with a congregation of sparrows at their feet.

Ruth Little became a tall, athletic young woman. In passive defiance of her mother's wishes, she let her hair grow long; it fell in soft red billows onto her shoulders. In bright light her brown eyes held flecks of bottle-green.

She began to accompany Mr. Lark to livestock auctions, sitting at the small portable table behind and below his lectern, recording the sale of animals. The men gathered around the sale ring looked at her as if assessing her breeding potential. But few ever approached. Once she heard a man say to another, "Cawd, no, boy. You wunt get nowhere with that mawther. Thas Win Little's gal, that is. She anythun like her mother, she'd hev yer nuts for mince."

Mrs. Sparling—Ruth's grandmother—died in 1935. *Congestion of the heart,* Dr. McVicar scrawled, messily and meaninglessly, on the death certificate. And now Ruth had something she'd never previously experienced: short periods of solitude. They came in the mornings. At the window, cupping her hands around her tea mug, she watched Win hoist herself into Willy's van and disappear backwards, holding on to her lacquered black straw hat as if walking pace were a reckless speed.

Ruth had an hour. She locked the doors.

She went to her bedroom and reached for the shoe box hidden at the back of the top shelf of the wardrobe. She carried it to the dressing table and took out the things she'd bought, fearfully, from Griffin's, the chemist's. Lipstick, face powder in a gold-effect compact, mascara. A bottle of scent called 4711. A chocolate-colored eyeshadow called Temptation. She made up her face, not really knowing how. She looked, thrilled, at the clumsy tart in the mirror. She kissed a dark invisible Gypsy lover with her ruby lips.

She stripped to her ribbed vest and knickers. The silk stockings felt lovely, sliding them on.

The only way she could see all of herself in the mirror was to stand in the bedroom doorway. She posed in its frame.

Were her legs too heavy-looking? Would her breasts get bigger? Did breasts stop growing at the age of eighteen? She lifted a shoulder and flicked her long hair behind it. She pouted. She imagined Mr. Lark licking his lips, his trembling fingers reaching for her. And now she imagined—oh, God, it made you weak at the knees, and it was like aching for a wee but different—that she was undressed like this and swanning around the sale ring with all the men looking at her and burning for her and yelling out mad amounts of money and then—

And then the downstairs clock chimed the three-quarter hour, and Ruth hastened to clean her face and dress in the pleated skirt and white blouse and lace her brown shoes. Tied her hair back out of the way. Wheeled her heavy bicycle out of the shed and pedaled toward her ledgers.

Win was no fool. She'd found the box, had nosed the Babylonian wickedness within. But she was undisturbed. She had filled her daughter with the fear of men, and there was no cosmetic that could cover that. Or that's what she thought until George bloody Ackroyd came along.

7.
A WINK IN THE BARLEY

THE HARVEST HOLIDAY went back a long way. Centuries. When wheat and oats and barley plumped and hung their heads, schools and businesses closed. Weavers and wives and itinerants and children flocked to the fields. Pale clerks and awkward teachers went to blister their hands on pitchforks, to gather in and glean. At harvesttime, Edmund Mortimer delighted in the presence of half-forgotten members of his community in his fields. The coarse lunches and murmured courtships in the purple shade of his hedges. The tang of horse sweat, the swirls of chaff against the reddening sky.

He could not summon enough people to the harvest of 1942, so he telephoned the army camp at Northrepps. By luck, the captain he spoke to was himself from a farming family. The following day, a three-ton army lorry jolted down the track to the first of Mortimer's nine fields of barley. The ten volunteers in it were under the command of a sergeant of the Royal Engineers, who was awaiting a posting. His name was Ackroyd. Hedge, the steward, greeted them skeptically.

The soldiers were all townies and clueless. But they were also cheerful and cocky and excited by this relief from routine. Within an hour, they were loudly competing at the work, pushing one another aside to lift sheaves from the binders. Their language was a horror, but their daft energy lifted the day. By noon the hazy cloud had dissipated, and Ackroyd's men, ignorant of country niceties, had stripped to their waists, and the local girls were rolling their eyes at one another. When Hedge blew his whistle to signal the lunch break, Ackroyd and another man went to the truck and lifted out a crate of India Pale Ale. They went between the narrow shades of carts and trees, insistently distributing bottles. A sweaty young clown from the Royal Fusiliers tried to pour beer into the horses' mouths.

Late in the afternoon, when the teams of horses were being changed, George Ackroyd went to relieve his bladder behind the three-tonner and lingered in its shade to smoke a cigarette. He looked up into the huge and faultless sky in which crescent-winged birds circled and swooped. He blinked away memories of other birds, in another country, picking human meat from the husks of burned machines.

A black car, a long Riley saloon, pulled up alongside the gateway to his left. Three people got out. The driver was a somber man with thinning hair who, despite the heat, wore a brown suit and a stiff collar and a striped tie. He opened the rear door and held it while a smiling older man in a blue collarless shirt emerged. The other passenger was a young woman who was wearing a belted floral-print dress. George observed the fullness of her figure and her long flame-red hair. He parked his cigarette in the corner of his mouth and sauntered after them into the field, watching the shift of her hips as she carefully placed her feet in the rutted earth.

Hedge bustled toward them, saying heartily, "Mr. Mortimer!"

"Herbert," the older man said. "How goes the day?"

"Very good, sir. Very good." Hedge turned to the somber man. "We're expectun a good yield, Mr. Lark, all things considered."

Lark sniffed, nodding.

Mortimer surveyed the glowing field. The cut portion of it was stitched with stooks of grain aligned with military precision.

"And how are our gallant volunteers getting on, Herbert?"

Hedge looked blank. George trod his smoke out and stepped forward.

"The lads've enjoyed themselves, sir. They're not trained for this sort of thing, but I hope they've made themselves useful."

Mortimer smiled at him. "So you'd be Sergeant Ackroyd, I presume?"

"Sir," George said, and made as if to salute, but Mortimer stuck out his hand, and after a tiny hesitation, George shook it.

Ruth, standing a pace or two from the men, studied Sergeant Ackroyd in stolen sideways glances. His braces hung loose at his sides, and his pale khaki shirt was unbuttoned. She had not seen a man's torso since a bank holiday trip to the seaside in 1938. Ackroyd's was lean; you could see how the muscles worked. His face was narrow, unusually symmetrical, and, like his throat and forearms, deeply tanned by something fiercer than an English sun. His black hair was cut short at the sides but fell in a sweaty tumble onto his right eyebrow. Ruth had heard north-country accents only on the wireless: comedians doing jokes and songs that made her mother scowl. Perhaps for this reason, she thought there was cheek in the way Ackroyd spoke. Mockery. He had a narrow mustache, like a movie star. She wondered for the first time what it would be like to be kissed on the mouth by a man with a mustache. As she was thinking about it, Ackroyd looked directly at her and winked. Winked! Ruth looked away, feeling her whole body blush.

Two days later, Ruth left the office at five fifteen, and there he was, right outside, sitting on a brown-painted motorcycle, smoking. She was shocked to a standstill. He was wearing the same light fatigues, but this time, thank God, his shirt was buttoned. She could see that he'd come from Mortimer's fields; there were sweat stains at his armpits and chaff on his boots.

"Ayup, lass," he said. "Fancy a ride home?"

He'd bundled a jacket or something into a rough cushion and strapped it to the metal pillion.

Ruth's eyes skittered around the square. People were looking. Of course they bloody were!

"Dunt be so soft," she managed at last to say. "I ent gettun on that thing. Anyhow, I're got my bike round the corner."

Ackroyd regarded her, considering.

"Suit yourself," he said, and flicked his cigarette away. He eased the motorcycle backwards off its prop and kicked it into life.

She turned left at Black Cat corner onto the lane to Bratton Morley. After a minute, he drew level with her, throttling the engine back until its beat matched the chug of her heart.

"Go away!"

He laughed. She saw his white teeth. He reached over and put his hand on the small of her back and accelerated, propelling her forward at a speed too great for her feet to stay on the pedals. She cried out in thrilled alarm, and after fifty yards he relented, releasing her. She braked and came to an unsteady halt. She stood with her feet on either side of the bike, feeling hot and inelegant and angry and fearfully excited. Ahead of her, he turned the motorcycle around, maneuvering with some difficulty in the narrow lane, and pulled up alongside her. They were in the deep shadow of a big elm tree; everything outside it was too bright to be visible. When he killed the engine, the silence overwhelmed her.

"Sorry," George said. "You liked it well enough, though, eh?"

"I could're come off," Ruth said. "You mad sod."

"You should report me, then. I'll bring you the form."

From somewhere close by, a pheasant uttered a raucous laugh.

"How'd you know where I work, anyhow?"

George tapped the side of his nose with a forefinger. "Military Intelligence."

"What?"

41

He looked around cautiously. "MI6. Spies."

Ruth looked around, too, anxiously. "What?"

"I'm pulling your leg. How many knockout redheads work for a man called Lark in Borstead, d'you reckon?"

(There are phrases, casually spoken, that worm through time. Fifty-three years later Ruth would surface, briefly, from her coma and mumble the words "knockout redhead." And Clem, sitting by her hospital bed, would hear them as "Got out of bed yet?" Reliably, he misunderstood her to the very end.)

George Ackroyd pursued Ruth Little for two weeks. In the stifling nights, she dreamed about, or imagined, a clumsy red deer harried by a lean and lupine shadow.

She forbade him to come anywhere near her work. As in all country towns, Borstead's pulse was gossip. So he waited in the shade of the elm. She dreaded these encounters yet came to yearn for them. The utterly familiar lane became strange and perilous; she was terrified of being seen with him. Willy and her mother did not come home this way—he took the main Cromer road and turned off at Bratton Cross—but her neighbors often did.

Half a mile beyond the elm, the lane cut through Skeyton Woods. And eventually, fearfully, she led him into the trees.

And then he was gone. For two afternoons, Ruth pedaled slowly beneath the spread of the elm, then waited by the rotting five-bar gate that opened into the wood. On the first of these afternoons, when it became clear to her that he was not going to come, she felt something that might have been relief. On the second, she filled with hurt and was astonished to find herself, for the first time since early childhood, crying.

The following Tuesday morning, she found an envelope on her desk. It was addressed to MISS R. LITTLE, C/O CUBITT AND LARK, THE SQUARE, BORSTEAD, NORFOLK. She looked at it, alarmed, as though it were something ominous or sinister: a spider on a slice of cake, perhaps. She had never in her life received a letter. When she found the courage to pick it up, it felt fragile. The paper was thin; she could almost read the writing through the envelope. (She worried that somebody might already have done so.)

The handwriting was fussy and tilted, almost italic.

Dear Ruth,

I expect youll be wondering where I got to. I hope so anyway! Well I got a posting with only 10 hrs notice. I hoped to see you but I could not get away. I can not tell you where I'm going for obvious reasons. (EG I would get shot!) I will think about you Ruth and I think you know what I mean (!) As you know I am a city boy born and bred but from now on I will think of trees and country side etc in a new way.

I dont know when I'll be back but I will be back. We have not known each other long Ruth but if your so inclined I ask you to wait for me. When I come back I will come down there and ask you a very serious question. I think you know what that question is.

I will think of you Ruth as I say. I hope you will think of me too.

Go careful on that bike!

Yours sincerely,

George (Ackroyd)

8.
THINGS RUTH DIDN'T KNOW
ABOUT GEORGE AT THE TIME

HE WAS ONLY a couple of months older than her. (She thought it was more than that. She considered herself a girl and him a man.)

He was born in Sheffield, the eldest of four children. He left school at the age of fourteen, in 1932. It was not a good time. Unemployment was rife. Men waited at factory gates on the off chance of a day's work. With his mates, George went on the cadge: gleaning spilled coal, running betting slips, a bit of petty theft. The pressure was on him, though. His younger siblings were waiting for his clothes and his bed.

A week after his uncelebrated fifteenth birthday, he joined the army. He went from short trousers into full uniform. He signed up for fifteen years.

He was sent for basic training to Catterick, where he showed some aptitude for mechanics—inherited, perhaps, from his father, who had been a lathe operator—and was attached as a trainee fitter to the Royal Engineers.

He had five good years, learning his trade, and how to drink, in postings up and down the country. He once, years later, spoke fondly to Clem of an army-versus-civvy mass punch-up in Yeovil, Somerset, in 1937.

He was genuinely astonished by the war; he hadn't been paying attention. Hitler had been a sort of joke in the newspapers and newsreels. Then everything got insanely hectic, and he found himself in France, a corporal, meaninglessly bossing people around and being slapped on the back by elderly Frenchmen. On May 30, 1940, he lost control of his bowels on the beach at Dunkirk when German dive-bombers howled down and sand admixed with body parts exploded all around him. He was ashamed, so when he'd blundered into the sea, he struggled out of his soiled pants and trousers before being hauled, bare-arsed and half drowned — he was a poor swimmer — into a gaily painted launch from the Isle of Wight called the *Anne-Marie*.

He was rewarded for his gallantry by a week's home leave.

There was nowhere at home for him to sleep, so he stayed around the corner in Palmerston Street, at his mate Jacko Jackson's house. Jacko had joined the merchant navy six months earlier, and his bed was spare. The city was blacked out at night; George, awakened by the sirens, stood at the window watching the thin fingers of searchlights groping for German bombers. He would not go to the shelters; he had a great fear of being crowded into confined spaces. (Which meant he was not ideally suited to marriage, as Ruth would later discover.) In the half-light of dawn, the street would fill with women, head scarves knotted on their foreheads, their arms folded beneath their bosoms, clattering garrulously to the factories. On the penultimate night of his leave, he inexplicably got into a fight at a pub called the Hounds in Hand. He was in Jacko's bed, sopping the blood from his mouth with a thin towel, when Jacko's sister Muriel came into the room to see if he was all right. To make sure that he was, she got into the bed with him.

"When this is all over," she said, before it was all over, "I'll be waiting for you, George."

Whether she was or not, he never troubled to find out.

By Christmas 1940, he was in North Africa, promoted to sergeant, in charge of a tank support unit and suffering from dysentery. He was to spend a good deal of his war squatting in tented latrines, smoking. The habit of lingering in the lavatory remained with him for the rest of his life, although usually he was in search of solitude rather than relief.

9.
EGG AND SOLDIERS

ON CLEM ACKROYD'S third birthday, he got his first car and met his father. These two momentous things—especially the car—ensured that the day remained his earliest memory.

He awoke to see his mother looking down at him.

"Happy birthday, Clem," she said, then lifted him from the bed. Gusty rain prickled the window. Ruth held his little penis while he sleepily peed into the enameled chamber pot.

Down in the kitchen, his grandmother was busy at the stove. Ruth settled him into the tall chair and pushed it up to the table. Then Win brought him his favorite breakfast, a fried egg on a slice of bread and margarine. She cut it up into pieces that he could eat with a spoon.

"If thas hot, blow on it," she said.

He watched the yellow juice of the yolk slither over the margarine and leach into the bread.

Ruth tested a cup of warmed milk with her little finger.

"Eat that up, Clem, an then we'll open yer presents."

Win had knitted him a sleeveless jumper, brown and yellow stripes, with the wool from an unraveled prewar cardigan. His mother helped him into it. Even over his pajama top, it was itchy. He looked like a giant wasp with a human head and arms. Then Ruth put a parcel in front of him, a shoe box wrapped in stiff brown paper. She helped him tear away at it and lift the lid.

The box was half full of little metal soldiers. Ancient wars had peeled the uniforms from some of them. Others had been disarmed; they made threatening gestures with tiny empty hands that had once held swords or muskets. Hidden within this ragtag army was a pink sugar mouse with a string tail. Clem held it uncomprehendingly, so Ruth moistened its nose with her lips and put it to his mouth.

From the lane, Willy Page tooted, and Win put on her long black coat, sighing.

A little later, there was a *Coo-ee* from outside and Chrissie Slender and Tommy came in, damp, and sang "Happy Birthday to You."

Then Chrissie said, "Go you on, then, Tommy. Give Clem his present."

It was a painted tin monkey attached to a string between two sticks joined by a spring. When Tommy squeezed the sticks together and released them, the monkey spun head over heels.

It dawned on Clem that today was different from other days. His bafflement took on a happier coloring. He sucked the mouse and watched Tommy work the monkey. The grown-ups stood by the stove, drinking tea, talking. He picked up words: *George, ration book, bacon, teeth.*

Then his mum lifted him out of his chair.

"Right, then, young man," she said. "Les go an see whas in the parlor."

The parlor door was closed, which was a thing Clem hadn't known before.

When they were facing it, Ruth said, "Close yer eyes. Tight. Are they closed?"

Clem nodded. He heard the door open. An anxious thrill ran through him and lodged in his bladder. A small dampness warmed his pajama bottoms. He felt his mother's hand take his and lead him in.

"Open yer eyes," she said.

He didn't know what it was, of course. He'd never seen such a thing before. It looked very big. It took up most of the space between the two armchairs on either side of the fireplace. It worried him, because it had not been there at bedtime the night before. It was beautiful, though: green, and very shiny. And because this strange morning had taught him this, he knew that it was his.

He looked up at his mother's face.

"Thas a car, Clem," she said. "D'yer like it?"

By the middle of the day, Clem had started to work out that pushing the pedals with his feet—like walking, but sitting down—made the heavy thing move. Ruth guided him back and forth the short distance between the kitchen door and the front door, leaning over him to work the steering wheel, which he couldn't get the hang of.

In the early afternoon, the rain died off and a pallid light filled the garden. Ruth carried the car outside and set it down on the concrete. Clem climbed into it, bundled up in his winter coat. She steered him around the corner of the lav and onto the brick path that led down to the gate. His knees went up and down in a way that didn't belong to him. He turned the steering wheel randomly.

On the third trip to the gate, he became aware that his mother's hand was no longer on his back. The car stopped, and he looked up at her. She had her hands to her face, which had changed color. She was looking at something beyond him. There was a man standing on the other side of the gate. Clem's eyes climbed up him, from the wet-edged brown shoes to the legs and jacket of the gray suit to the suntanned face that was divided in half by a black mustache. The man wore a gray hat and carried over his shoulder a huge long bag with white lettering on it. Between the stranger and Ruth a silence stretched above Clem's head, like a sheet hung on the washing line.

The man put his bag on the ground and took off his hat. His hair was as black as the gloss on a beetle.

"Correct me if I'm wrong," he said, "but you'd be Clem, right? Is that your name?"

"Yes," Clem whispered. The man's voice was not like other men's voices.

"Aye, I thought so. That's a right handsome car you've got there. Would it be a birthday present, by any chance?"

Clem wasn't sure that he could get out of the car by himself. He looked to his mother for help and saw that she was crying. It frightened him. Then she walked past him as if he weren't there. And she was saying, "Bloody hell, George. Bloody hell."

She pulled the gate open and let the man put his arms around her. Let him bury his fingers in her hair.

10.
A HOME FIT FOR HEROES

"**GOD, GEORGE,** I nearly died," Ruth said, setting the kettle on the stove. "The fifteenth, you said. Next week."

"I wangled an early. The demob officer was a bloke I'd been in Africa with. I thought it would be nice if I got here today."

"Is that where you're come from? Africa?"

He laughed. "No. Aldershot. Mind you, it took about as long. The ruddy trains. The buggers treat you like dirt."

"Do they? Clem, let go of my leg; there's a good boy."

"He don't know who I am," George said. "He's scared of me."

"He'll be all right. That'll take a bit of gettun used to."

"Palestine," George said.

"Palestine?"

She half remembered it from a newsreel. Her and Chrissie in the dark of the Regal, fag smoke wreathing in the beam of the projector. A huge hotel with its side blown off by a bomb. Jewish terrorists. How could there be Jewish terrorists? They were all skeletons. The main feature had been *The Best Years of Our Lives.*

George lit a cigarette with a brass lighter that flipped open to the flame.

Dear God, Ruth thought, who was he? He was different, somehow. Like he could get angry any minute, or something. She would have to sleep with him tonight. With her mother listening. She couldn't do it. She wasn't ready. The thought of it made her feel faint.

"Jerusalem," he said. "Bloody mad hellhole."

To her, Jerusalem was a song. A sort of hymn.

He could not persuade his son to sit on his lap. Ruth poured weak tea. The cup trembled in her hand, chinking against the saucer.

"So, love, where'd you get the car?"

She blushed, not knowing why. "I'll tell yer later." She lowered her voice. "That ent exactly new. Painted up."

"Nowt wrong with that," George said. He looked at his son. "Now then, young man. I've got a present for you, too. Would you like to see it?"

Clem looked up at Ruth for guidance.

"Another present, Clem! Thas nice, ent it?"

George pulled the kit bag to his chair and untied the complex knot. He rummaged theatrically inside it.

"Is that it? No. Is that it? No, that's not it neither. Ah, here we go."

He produced an oddly shaped package wrapped in newspaper and tied with string. He held it toward his son, who still lurked behind his mother's skirt. Ruth picked her child up and carried him to the table and sat him down on her lap.

"Whatever can this be, Clem, that Dad're brought yer? Shall we undo it?"

The newspaper had photographs of foreign-looking men on it, and the writing was black wiggles and dots that looked a bit like music. Ruth imagined, madly, that her husband must be able to read it.

George's present for his son was an exquisitely carved wooden camel.

"It opens," George said. "See?"

The camel's hump was brass-hinged. George reached across the table and lifted it, revealing a hollow slightly larger than an eggcup.

"See? You can keep your sweets in there. Or money."

Sweets, Ruth thought. Clem dunt know what they are.

George fished in his trouser pocket. He brought out a silver sixpence and dropped it into the hump.

"There you go, lad," he said. "That's got you started. It'll all add up."

"What is ut, Mum?" Clem asked.

"I've got something for you, as well, Ruth," George said, reaching into the bag again and producing a small soft package.

"What is it?" she asked stupidly. She was like a child, too.

"Well, why don't you open it and find out?"

It was a silk shawl, diaphanously white, embroidered along its edges with green and silver threadwork. At each of its four corners was a tiny seashell. It was perhaps the most useless thing you could give to a red-haired woman who lived in Norfolk and was saving her clothing coupons for a new winter coat.

"I spent a whole afternoon haggling for that with a nig-nog in Cairo. I wore him down in the end, though."

"Thas beau'iful, George."

She held it against her face and wept. It smelled whorishly of foreign parts.

"Now what are you crying about, lass?"

"Nothun. Sorry. I'm sorry, George. Just I wunt expectun you. You give me a shock."

She'd planned things for his return. A sign on the gate saying, WELCOME HOME GEORGE. A strip wash at the sink, then a touch of makeup and her better set of underwear. Clem in his Sunday clothes. A bottle of beer or two. She'd been more or less promised a half shoulder of pork. And he'd mucked it all up.

She wiped her face on her sleeve.

"It's just we hent got nothun in for tea. Our rations all run out yesterdy, and we can't get nothun till tomorrer. All we're got is two eggs and the last of the bread. What mother'll say when she get home I can't imagine."

"Don't worry yourself. Look here."

From the bag he produced two shiny canisters, unlabeled two-pound tins.

"One's Spam; t'other's corned beef. I can't rightly say which is which."

* * *

Later, Clem turned fretful.

"Thas all the excitement," Ruth said untruthfully. "I'll take him up. Say night-night to yer dad, Clem."

The boy clung to her and tried to hide his face in her shoulder. George wondered if he should kiss the child's head; while he hesitated, Ruth turned away toward the stairs.

"Good night, Clem," he said cheerily. "Sweet dreams."

Left alone, George made a recce of the home he'd never lived in. Thorn Cottage was smaller and darker than he'd remembered. It was permeated by the heavy, sweetish fumes from the sinister-looking paraffin heater that stood in the hall. The kitchen, like the rest of the downstairs rooms, had electricity, but the cooking was still done on a black cast-iron range built into the brick fireplace. The floor was covered in green linoleum, worn so thin that it seemed no more than a cracked coat of paint over the slate slabs beneath.

The front room—the "best room"—was a grim and crowded museum of Victorian furniture. A framed photograph of a young woman and a soldier stood on a heavy sideboard next to a threadbare stuffed squirrel inside a glass dome.

The parlor had only two armchairs, one on either side of the hearth. On each sat a ball of wool transfixed by knitting needles.

It seemed to George that every mark in the place—every scar on the skirting boards, every nick and chip in the stair treads, every dent in the dull brass doorknobs—was a trace of dead people he had never known and wouldn't have wanted to. Dim presences to whom he had no connection. Who frightened him. This place was old and poor. It was not the bright new world he had been told he was fighting for. He had come home to the past, a past that wasn't even his own. He felt, suddenly, panicky and claustrophobic.

He went out into the back garden. The colder air went to his bladder, and he pushed open the outhouse door. It clattered against an obstacle, a galvanized metal bath hung on a hook. A speckled spider had spread her net within it. Relieving himself, he noted that the bog roll was newspaper scissored neatly into rectangles the size of ten-shilling notes and hung on a nail.

He went to the end of the garden and surveyed his new and awful domain. The hedge had grown wild. Things he presumed were edible protruded from weeds. A fork with a broken handle angled into black soil. Two rusted upturned buckets.

He lit a cigarette. The last of the sun slanted onto the roof. The thatch was ragged and greened by moss; below and to the left of the half-ruined chimney, a sheet of corrugated iron had been slid in to slow a leak.

He pulled on the ciggie and straightened himself.

Discipline. Drill.

"Men all present and correct, Sarn't?"

"Yes, sir."

"Ready to kick the shit out of Jerry, Sarn't?"

"Yes, sir."

"Excellent. Carry on."

Men in burned-out tanks who'd come apart like overcooked chickens when you tried to pull them out. You threw up and then you dealt with it.

"Burial detail! Over here!"

They'd fought—he'd fought—for sex. To capture the brothels of Benghazi and Tripoli from the Italians, the Germans. Then take the tricks learned there home to wives and girlfriends who were starving for it. Unless the ruddy Yanks had been there first.

Ruth had got heavier; there was no denying it. She'd slumped, somehow. Having the boy, presumably.

Two months ago—no, three now—he'd been in a back-street bar in Cyprus, being served miraculously cold beer by a gracious Egyptian prostitute wearing see-through trousers and a spangled bra.

"You'll not be getting much of that in Norfolk, lad," he told himself—correctly, as it turned out.

As the light died, he heard footsteps on the path. His mother-in-law, a shade or two darker than the gathering dark, came around the corner of the lav.

"Ayup, Win," he said.

She turned, lifting a hand to her chest and stumbling as if a sniper had got her.

"Who's that?"

"It's George, Win."

She peered as he walked toward her.

"George who?"

"George your son-in-law."

"What're you doing here?"

He flicked his cigarette away and said, "It's nice to see you, too, Win."

* * *

The can that Ruth opened was the Spam. She fried slices of it in a bit of lard with an onion and served it with a boiled potato each and tough garden cabbage.

Win said, "You're cut that Spam thick, Ruth. That wunt see us out the week at that rate."

At ten o'clock, Ruth pretended she needed him in the kitchen.

She said, "I'm gorn up to bed, George. Give us five minutes."

He went outside and smoked another cigarette. When he went back indoors, the cottage was intensely dark and utterly silent. He groped upstairs, clutching the wounded banister. In their bedroom, the light came from an oil lamp the shape of a faded yellow tulip. Clem was asleep in a cot within reach of Ruth's arm. She wore a flannelette nightdress buttoned almost to her throat. Her glowing hair aroused him. When he began to unbutton his trousers, she turned the lamp out.

(This became their unvarying nightly ritual: she would go upstairs and get into bed while he smoked a last cigarette. In almost forty years of marriage, he would never see her completely naked. And, in time, he grew glad of it.)

In the morning, Clem stood in his cot, gazing with baffled horror at the dark stranger in his mother's bed.

11.

THE PERFUME OF AXLE GREASE,
THE WHIFF OF HALITOSIS

FOR A WHILE George Ackroyd dealt with his mounting fear, the hostility of his mother-in-law, the coyness of his wife, the reticence of his son, the implacable hugeness of the sky, and his awful sense of having been somehow tricked, in the only way he knew how. He sought to impose regimental order and efficiency. He went about bringing manliness to this unmanned household.

In the skewed and decrepit garden shed (built by John Sparling half a century earlier), he found ancient tools and restored them. With the oiled and sharpened shears, he straightened the hedge. With a rusted hammer, he nailed new boards onto the roof of the chicken coop while the birds regarded him with yellow and baleful eyes. Under Ruth's direction and Clem's silent gaze, he dug the vegetable beds. He rehung the washing line, jabbing stones into the ground to steady the uprights. He replaced the broken hinge on the kitchen window, using infinite patience and the wrong screwdriver. He gave the inside of the lav a new coat of whitewash.

After a fortnight, this persistent odd-jobbery had brought Win to the verge of distraction.

The following Sunday, she came back from chapel with the news that there was a job going at Ling's. The announcement didn't distract George from the *News of the World.*

Win pulled free the long pin that fixed her hat to her hair and stood holding it, looking at him.

Ruth was at the sink, peeling potatoes. After half a minute of awful silence that pinkened her neck, she said, "That might suit you, George. Thas your line of work."

He looked up at last. "Oh, aye? Why, what's Ling's? A Chinese tank regiment?"

In fact, J. W. Ling and Son, of Borstead, were — as announced on a wrought-iron sign that spanned the wide entrance to the yard — SUPPLIERS AND REPAIRERS OF AGRICULTURAL MACHINERY. George leaned Ruth's bike against the wall of a brick building that looked as though it had been, once upon a time, a pair of farm cottages. On one of the doors there was a stamped-metal sign reading OFFICE. The room had two desks, one with a typewriter on it. Apparently, a gale had swept through the place, scattering paper. One wall sported no fewer than eight calendars, all of them topped by a picture of a tractor, none of them turned to the month of April. On one of the desks there was a push-button electric bell with a woven two-wire cable that trailed away into the gloom. A handwritten card next to it suggested that he RING FOR ATTENDENCE. George pressed it experimentally and heard, from some remote distance, a faltering tinkle. Several minutes later, a short, burly man stuffed into a one-piece overall came in and immediately went out again and started shouting.

"Look, bor, I dunt give a monkey's. Do what I say. You weld the bugger up an I'll tell him thas the best we can do. If he want ut by Wensdy, thas up to him."

He came back into the room and picked up a piece of paper, apparently at random, and scowled at it. Without looking at George, he said, surprisingly formally, "And what can I do for you, sir?"

"I was told you had a job," George said.

The man grunted a laugh. "Job?" The small word had at least three vowels in it. "Bleddy right, I're got a job. The job I're got is gettun them buggers out there to lissun to a bleddy word I say."

George concentrated hard, trying to discover the meaning of Ling's words beneath the thick blanket of his accent.

"I meant a job going," George said. "A position."

The man put the paper down and turned to him. He had blue eyes inside plump little purses of skin. The bald dome of his head rose out of a thicket of graying and unkempt curls. He surveyed George's demob suit, his collar and tie.

"Ah. Thas right, I do. Sorry. Yer Win Little's son-in-law, just come home?"

"Yes."

"So you'd be George, er?"

"George Ackroyd."

"Bill Ling. Howja do."

He held out his right hand, which was black and lacked half of its third finger.

"Yer dunt hevter shake ut if yer dunt want to."

"No," George said, gripping the other man's hand. "There's nowt wrong with axle grease. I'm partial to the smell of it."

Ling grunted humorously again. He took a tin of tobacco from his overall and rolled a cigarette. George lit it for him with his American lighter.

"So, then. Win tell me you was in the Engineers. That right?"

"For nine years, after I joined up. Then the REME from forty-two — Royal Electrical and Mechanical Engineers."

"What was that all about, then?"

"Tanks, mostly. Half-tracks, Bren gun carriers, armored cars. That sort of thing."

Ling picked a shred of tobacco from his lower lip. "We dunt get a lotta them come in."

"No," George said. "I don't suppose you do."

"Tractors, reapers, balers, harrers. Go all over the place sortun out threshun machines, things like that. Lot on ut is donkey's years old. Patch up an bodge. That dunt sound like what yer used to."

"No. But a machine is a machine. An engine is an engine."

Ling lifted his eyebrows and nodded as though this were a novel piece of wisdom.

"So yer reckon you might pick ut up, do yer?"

64

"I should think so."

Ling looked around the office as though help or advice might materialize from its shadows.

Eventually he said, "Well, I do need a man what know his arse from a gasket. Things hev got busy, this past year. I tell yer what, George. Why dunt we try ut for a month? See if the work suit yer? How do that seem?"

"Sounds fair enough to me. When d'you want me to start?"

"Lessay Mundy." Ling grinned, displaying a random collection of teeth. "There ent no hurry. I daresay you an Ruth hev still got a bit of catchun up to do, arter all this time."

George would work for Bill Ling for twelve years. The other men never grew to like him. They never addressed him by his first name; they called him Sarge, and behind his back, they imitated his brisk and upright manner of walking. When there were breaks from work, they would isolate him by retreating inside the slow, thick moat of their impenetrable dialect.

George remounted Ruth's bike and pedaled the three-quarters of a mile to Borstead. The trees and hedges along his route were misted with the green of early spring. The town was silent. He passed a pub called the Feathers, turned back, and wheeled the bike into an alleyway that led to the rear entrance. There were only three people in the bar: two elderly men, who sat silently in front of their pints, and an elderly woman perched on a bar stool, reading a newspaper aloud to her glass of stout. George took the stool farthest from her and, after several minutes had gone by, took a two-shilling piece from his pocket and tapped the counter with it. A woman with lips painted close to her nose emerged from a curtained doorway and reluctantly drew him a pint of bitter.

Later she drew him another. Drinking it, George felt the absence of joy pierce him like a bayonet.

He did not want to go home—*home?*—so he rode the bike in the opposite direction. He passed through the dripping gloom under the railway bridge and, on a whim, turned right onto a narrow road he had no memory of. He found himself alongside an extensive playing field, in the middle of which was a pavilion, a gray stone and white-gabled house, like something pictured in a fairy tale. The field was divided into a number of football pitches, and upon three of them, boys in shorts and motley shirts were charging after a ball, massing and hallooing like huntsmen. Beyond them, the railway embankment, its flank darkly patched by brambles.

George rode slowly along the low beech hedge, watching the games, and above his head the moody clouds split open. Sun, in beams as clearly defined as searchlights, straked the sky. As if in celebration, something sounded a long fluting whistle. A clanking two-carriage train, gusting smoke, ambled into view. A goalkeeper turned and waved to it and, with his back to the play, conceded a goal. George laughed. He took his hands from the handlebars and applauded.

The playing field ended in a line of poplars like huge upended besoms. Here, the lane forked. George turned left and was astonished to find himself in a newer, braver world.

He pedaled slowly past a long row of new, cement-rendered, and white-painted semidetached houses. They looked solid, modern, confident. Fresh. Each one had a slate-roofed porch over the front door. Each one had a small lawn, separated from its neighbor by a ruler-straight privet hedge, still only knee-high, and separated from the road by a tarmacked pavement. At the end of the row, the road turned smartly right. At the corner house, a woman was cleaning her windows, standing on a kitchen chair. Her buttocks swung with the work, and her calves were muscular. George rang the bell on his handlebar, and she turned and waved to him as if she knew him. Or wanted to. He rode right and left and right and left again through a grid of new suburban roads that were named after poets: Chaucer, Donne, Browning, Arnold. The names meant nothing to George. He rode, admiring it all, to its limits, attracted by the chug of a cement mixer and the growl of machinery. Beyond Marvell Road, an acre of raw and muddy earth had been dug into trenches into which men were slumping barrowloads of concrete.

George dismounted and lit a cigarette. Before he was halfway through it, a car—a black Morris—drew up. Its driver clambered out. He was wearing a suit and had a clipboard in his hand. He balanced the clipboard on the roof of the car and leaned back inside and produced a pair of Wellington boots. With his backside perched on the bonnet of the car, he bent to unlace his shoes.

"Excuse me," George said.

The man looked up, frowning.

George, smiling nicely, said, "What's all this, then?"

"Pardon me?"

"I mean, what's all this going to be? More houses?"

"Er, no. This is the new Millfields Primary School."

"Ah," George said.

The man pulled off his left shoe and, surprisingly, sniffed its interior.

"This will be where your children go to school, Mr., er?"

"Ackroyd."

"Yes. We estimate, on a ten-year projection, a minimum of one hundred and ten children on the estate. You chaps back from the war have already been busy, if you know what I mean. Quite right, too."

George stood on his cigarette.

"Estate?"

The man looked at him quizzically.

"So these are council houses," George said.

"Yes, of course. Sorry, I assumed you lived here. You're not a tenant, then?"

George cycled back into Borstead—the playing fields were silent now—and leaned Ruth's bike against one of the two trees in front of the town hall. He waited almost an hour before he was ushered into the presence of the housing officer, who was, according to the gold-effect lettering on the little black nameplate on his desk, Mr. G. Roake. He stood up to shake hands when George entered. Even from across the desk, his breath was rank. He had thin colorless hair greased over the top of his head, and he did not convincingly occupy his clothes. His eyes, magnified by his spectacles, took up a disproportionate amount of his face. His hand, in George's clasp, was bony.

"Take a seat, Mr. . . . "

"Ackroyd. George Ackroyd."

Roake wrote George's name on a piece of paper, not checking how it was spelled.

"How can I help you, Mr. Ackroyd?"

Roake's accent was not Norfolk. George could not identify it.

'Those new council houses. Up off the Aylsham road."

"Millfields?"

"Yes. I want to put my name down for one."

Roake gazed for a moment. "Yes. Well. We can do that for you. Have you applied for council housing before? Here or elsewhere?"

"No."

"I see." Roake shifted a knee and opened a drawer. "There's a form to fill in, of course. Always a form." He put sheets of stapled paper on the desk but left his hand resting on them. "There's a waiting list, as you'll appreciate."

"Is there?"

"Oh, yes."

The way he said it started something cooking inside George.

"How long's this waiting list?"

"Well, that's hard to say. It's not so much the length of the list. More a question of when a house becomes vacant and which families on the list have priority. According to the number of children, and so forth. The quality of their present accommodation. Amenities. That sort of thing. There's an assessment process."

George clasped his hands together and stared at the linoleum between his feet.

After a moment or two, he said, "D'you mind if I smoke?"

"I'd rather you didn't, actually."

George nodded, slowly, and without lifting his head said, "I've been in the British army for fifteen years. I came out a month ago. I survived Dunkirk. With seven other blokes and only a Thompson submachine gun and a rifle between us, I marched two thousand Italian prisoners out of Benghazi. I had dysentery and had to stop the whole ruddy column every time I needed a shit. I was at El Alamein, and a German 88 hit the unit next to us and the blood came down on us like rain. In forty-six, when the heroic ruddy conscripts came home to parades and free beer and women, I was sent to Palestine. I was sitting with my mates in a bar a hundred yards from the King David Hotel when the bloody Irgun blew it up. We spent forty-eight hours digging stinking bodies out of the rubble. The flies were unbelievable. I've come home to a . . . a *hovel* I share with the wife and our three-year-old son and her evil mother. It's got no running water, no light, and stinks of paraffin; the roof leaks, and we pay rent to a ruddy farmer who lives in a manor house and owns half the flamin' county. It's like I've fought a war and ended up living in the Middle Ages or summat. What does the G stand for?"

"Pardon?"

George leaned forward and tapped the nameplate. "G. ROAKE. What's the G stand for?"

"Oh, right. It's Gordon, actually."

"Give me a new house, Gordon. I fucking deserve it."

Roake rested the lower part of his face in a cup of skeletal fingers.

"Yes," he said, "you do." He slid the form across the desk. "Fill this in, Mr. Ackroyd. I have to tell you, however, that, of itself, national service does not give you any special advantage."

"It doesn't?"

"No."

George folded his arms and sat back in the chair.

"How about you, Gordon?"

"Sorry?"

"The war. Were you in it?"

There was a sneer in the question.

Roake blinked at him through his spectacles.

"Yes. However, unlike you, Mr. Ackroyd, I didn't see a great deal of action. I spent almost three years in Japanese prisoner-of-war camps. Well, labor camps, to be accurate. In Burma, mostly."

"Ah," George said, embarrassed, enduring that familiar feeling of being outranked and outflanked. He cleared his throat. "That would've been tough, I should think."

"Yes," Roake said, "I think it would be fair to say that. Of the one hundred and eight men under my command, only eleven survived. Not all of us are glad of it."

He held out the form.

"Fill this in, Mr. Ackroyd. I'll do my best for you."

"Thanks," George said, adding, out of habit, "sir."

It took George almost a month to deliver the form back to the town hall. For reasons he did not want to share with himself, he had decided to keep it secret. He filled it out, carefully and only slightly mendaciously, at his bench at Ling's during the second week of his work there. Then, when he thought it was done, he discovered that he would also have to produce his marriage certificate and Clem's birth certificate. He had no idea where these were and could think of no plausible reason to ask. So in stolen moments he hunted through the nooks and crannies of Thorn Cottage. He found his marriage certificate in the front room, his mother-in-law's dark museum. It was scrunched up double in a drawer in the coffin-black sideboard, behind a canteen of cutlery that had not conveyed food to a human mouth in a century. Evidence of his son's birth was harder to find. In the end, in bed, he asked Ruth where it was.

"Why, George?" Sleepy question.

"I've never seen it."

"He's a lovely boy, George. Don't you worry. That'll be all right."

The next morning, in the kitchen, yawning, she handed the certificate to him. Win saw it.

"What yer want that for?"

George put the paper into his overall pocket and smiled at her.

"Forms to fill in, Win. National Insurance. The welfare state. What we voted for. Everything down on paper, fair and square."

Win looked at him, drying her red hands on her apron.

"Welfare state, my arse," she said.

12.
GOOD-BYE TO ALL THAT (NEARLY)

WHETHER OR NOT ex-Captain Gordon Roake interceded, George waited only two years and a bit for his council house. The letter arrived on a bright June morning in 1950. Win had already left for work. (Willy's electric road-boat had been replaced by a petrol-engined van, which Willy drove as though it were a high-spirited and unpredictable stallion, never trusting it enough to risk third gear.) Clem, as a treat, had been allowed to eat his porridge sitting on the back step in the sun. George used his bread to wipe the marge from his knife and slit the envelope open.

Ruth watched him, holding her cup with both hands. Outside of birthdays and Christmas, the postman paid rare visits to Thorn Cottage. She suspected trouble.

"What is it, George?"

He didn't answer her but read the letter through again, then handed it to her. She studied it, squinting. (Soon, she will be able to read only through round-framed National Health glasses, which will make her look owlish and somewhat foolish.)

"Whas this mean, George?"

"It means, Missus Ackroyd, that in three months we are going to be out of this dump. That we'll have a place of our own."

"You put us down for a council house?"

"Damn right I did. That's the least we deserve."

"Whyever dint yer say nothun?"

George shrugged. "There's a waiting list. It might've been years. I didn't want to get your hopes up."

Ruth sat down. "Bloody hell, George."

He grinned at her.

"Where's 11 Lovelace Road, anyhow?"

"The Millfields estate. Off the Aylsham road."

"What, in Borstead?"

"Of course in ruddy Borstead. You noticed a new council estate in Bratton Morley?"

She gaped at him. "You expect us to move to Borstead?"

He put his cup down. "No. I don't *expect*. There's no *expecting* about it, Ruth. There's a nice new house waiting for us. It'll be ours from September, and we're going to go and live in it. I thought you might be pleased, to be honest."

"Well, I . . . Thas all a bit sudden, George, is all. I dunt know what mother'll make of it."

"It's nothing to do with her."

"Of course that is, George. She're lived here all her life."

He smiled hugely. His mustache stretched itself toward his ears.

"Well," he said, "she can live here the rest of it an' all, as far as I'm concerned. If you take another look at that letter, you might see that 11 Lovelace Road is down for Mr. George Ackroyd and his dependents. Who are, if I remember correctly, Mrs. Ruth Ackroyd and Master Clement Ackroyd. No mention of a Mrs. Win Little."

"George, you can't mean . . ."

He finished his tea and stood up.

"George, we can't leave mother here all on her own."

"Why the hell not? Listen, it'll be the happiest day of her life when I walk out of that door for good. She'll hang flags out. Mind you, she'll miss having me to bitch about."

"George!"

Clem had turned to watch them, licking his spoon. Ruth saw and rolled her eyes at George, who understood. He took the letter from her, folded it, and put it in his overall pocket. He went and sat on the step next to his son, ruffling the boy's hair. He laced up his work boots and then, whistling, walked down the garden path. At the decrepit shed he stopped and studied it as if it were a man improperly dressed on parade. Smiling, he stepped forward and kicked the door until it was reduced to kindling.

Clem, thrilled and frightened, turned to his mother. "Whas Dad doing that for, Mum?"

In stolen moments and in muted voices, Ruth and George argued throughout that summer. George, most of the time, maintained a dogged, bland resolve. But on a Saturday night in early August, he lost his temper. They were at the end of the garden, splashed by the moonlight spilling through the elms. He aimed his finger at her face.

"Listen," he said, "this is bloody stupid. This is our chance to have a life. I didn't fight a war to live with your ruddy mother. I didn't marry you to live with your ruddy mother. I was in charge of men who died, in case you've forgotten. What I went through you can't even imagine. And I end up back home being treated like something she trod in. I won't have it, Ruth. I won't sodding have it, you hear me? You and me and Clem are going to have a life of our own whether you like it or not. And that's an end to it."

"Thas all very well for you to say, George, but she's my mother. I can't just—"

He'd heard it all before and couldn't bear it again, so he hit her. He slapped her face. The sound was a wet *plop*. She turned her face away and stared down for several seconds, as if she were inspecting the rows of vegetables close to her feet.

"Ruthie," George said. "I . . ."

Then she looked up, her eyes silvered by tears, and hit him back. It was an awkward upward swing of her fist that surprised the corner of his jaw, and he staggered backward and sat down among the carrots. He gawped up at her and she began to cry. He got to his feet and moved toward her. Ruth retreated.

"Dunt you touch me," she said, thick-voiced.

She wiped her eyes on the backs of her hands.

"I hent never hit anyone afore in my life. I can't believe the first person I do hit is my own husband."

She sobbed horribly.

George's self-pity expanded until it included her, and he put his arms around her.

After a while she said, "I'll tell her tomorrer, after she come home from the chapel."

"Right," George said.

"And you make yerself scarce. I can't stand the thought of you and her tearun inter each other. Take Clem round to Chrissie's or somethun."

"Why would I take him to Chrissie's?"

"I dunno. Think of some reason. Thas not like she ent always pleased to see you."

He smiled. "You reckon she fancies me?"

"Chrissie fancy anythun in trousers, as well you know."

"I'll take 'm off before I go, then."

Ruth snuffled a sort of laugh. The back door opened and a rhombus of mean yellow light fell onto the yard.

"Ruth," Win called. "Ruth? Whatever are yer doin out there? I thought yer'd gone to make the Horlicks."

While Ruth stumbled through her rehearsed speech, Win stood as still as a monument in her chapel clothes, at the sink, holding the tea strainer out in front of her like a pessimist's begging bowl. Her black Sunday hat on the draining board. Her back to her daughter.

Eventually she said, "An when's this, then?"

"First of September, Mum."

"What, *this* September? Next month?"

"Yes."

Win inhaled deeply. "Yer kept this quiet, Ruth. How long're you known?"

"Not long, Mum. It come up sudden. Thas nice, though, 'cos Clem'll be able to start up at the new school."

It sounded feeble. Ruth felt sick.

"You seen this house?"

"No, but George say they're very nice. Up off the Aylsham —"

"I know where they are. Two of the mawthers at work live there — Dorothy Eldon and Jane Whassername, who ent no better than she oughter be. Always gorn on about how they're got the indoor toilet, as though thas somethun to be proud of, doin your business insider the house and stinkun it up."

Ruth said nothing.

"Breed like rabbuts up that estate, by all accounts," Win went on. "Dorothy moan about how she can hear next door at ut, the walls are that thin. An thas a laugh, seeing as how she're up the spout agen herself."

She banged the strainer against the side of the sink, dislodging the tea leaves.

"I're lived here aller my life, Ruth. Born an grew up here, like my father and his father. Back beyond that, I dunt know. This come as quite a shock. I ent sure I can just up and move to Borstead jus like that."

"Well, Mum," Ruth said, "we . . . I mean . . . That ent . . . You dunt . . ."

Win turned and surveyed her primitive kitchen.

"Nemmind, though. My Father's house hath many mansions. We stay who we are, no matter where we go. I can walk to work from the Aylsham road. That'll save me heven to listen to Willy Page's squit mornin and night. Though I dunt know how we're gorna get everythun there. Hev George thought about that?"

Ruth gazed at her mother, stricken.

"Mum," she said, "the house ent . . ."

She made an enormous effort to say what had to be said.

"Mum. You dunt hev to come. You can stay here if you want. George . . ."

"No, Ruth," Win said. "Thas all right. I daresay that'll be all right. That can be a struggle livun here. I can see how for Clem and gettun to work that might be better to be in Borstead. I'll get used to ut. I ent so stuck in the mud as you think I am."

Defeated, Ruth hung her head.

The gate banged against its post.

She heard Clem say, "Tommy said I could, Dad. Why can't I?"

Then they were all together in the kitchen, which suddenly felt as small as a shoe box.

George looked from one woman to the other. Win smiled at him. It was a shocking event.

She said, "Well, yer a dark horse, ent yer?"

Ruth wouldn't meet his eye. She looked down at the floor, and he knew.

The first of September was a Friday. Bill Ling gave George the day off and lent him the flatbed Morris lorry. George spread a tarpaulin over its oily floor and drove to Thorn Cottage. It took an unimaginable amount of time to dismantle the cast-iron beds and bring them down the narrow staircase. The stuff from the front room weighed a ton. He didn't want any of it; he wanted them to lie on bare floors, eat off bare floors, until he could afford new things, modern things made of bright metal and plastic and Formica that had no miserable history. At midday Willy turned up, grinning, at the wheel of the laundry van, and they loaded that, too, with sheets and towels and table shrouds and the Sparling dinner service, the pieces clad in newspaper, like gray abandoned nests.

They unloaded it all at 11 Lovelace Road just before the weather changed. George drove the lorry back to Ling's yard and collected his bike. Rain fell as yellow beads from a sallow sky. He rode back into Borstead and stopped at the Feathers. He shook himself in the entry like a wet dog.

The landlady lifted her painted eyebrows at him and said, "The usual, George?"

"No," he said. "A whiskey. Make it a double."

"Celebrating, are we?"

"Aye," he said. "A new life."

He lifted the glass and drained it.

The landlady expressed mock disapproval.

"If I'd're known it was that important, I'd're joined you."

George pulled a half-crown out of his pocket. "Do, then," he said.

She poured two more drinks but refused his money, laying her fat hand on his.

"Thas on the house, George. Cheers. Here's mud in yer eye."

* * *

When he got back to Millfields, the rain had drifted out to the
North Sea, leaving the sky a tipsy festival of russet and bruised
purple. He got off the bike and admired his new house from the
other side of its glossy wet hedge. Its bland face was drenched
in evening color. His young son was standing on the path. He
picked the boy up and planted him on his shoulders.

"What say, young Clem? You like it here?"

The child said, "When're we gorn home?"

He carried the boy to the front door and found it locked.
They went around the back. Ruth was at the kitchen sink, rins-
ing unpacked plates. There was a faint roaring from somewhere.

"Clem," she said. "Come'n feel this! Hot water from
the tap!"

George jockeyed Clem to the foot of the stairs and paused
to look into the larger of the two front rooms. It had been turned
into the Sparling Museum. Win, with a yellow cloth duster in her
hand, stood inspecting it: the glass cabinet of grim ornaments;
the mausoleum sideboard surmounted by the long-dead squirrel; the murky oleograph of Christ as *The Light of the World;*
the squat occasional table obdurately awaiting an occasion.

On Monday a man from the council came to see that they were
settled and to hand over the rent book. From him Ruth learned
that *Lovelace* was pronounced, correctly, as "Loveless."

13.

THE BEST OF ROOMS, THE WORST OF ROOMS

I **LIVED IN** that house for the next thirteen years, and in all that time I spent a total of maybe ten minutes in that front room. For some reason, Win lit a fire in its grate every Christmas morning; otherwise, it went unheated. In the bitter Norfolk winters, the room radiated cold like the exhale of a grave. Eventually, George rigged up a heavy curtain on a pole over its door, sealing Win's past more firmly in its modern exile.

Gradually, as I made cautious friendships on the estate, I came to realize that almost all the other houses had front, or "best," rooms similar to ours. And always the same one — on the right as you came in the front door. (Not that anyone used the front door; in accordance with rural custom, we were a backdoor community. A knock on the front door was always an occasion for alarm.) One or two families did not conform. The Rileys, fecund Roman Catholics, notoriously used their front room as an extra bedroom. As did the Moores, but they had a son with polio who had an iron frame on his leg. The Parkers, around the corner from us on Dryden Road, actually spent evenings in their best room. We'd see light seeping from the edges of their curtains and wonder what they could be doing in there.

Best rooms were museums. But unlike conventional museums, they did not commemorate the past. They denied it.

The inhabitants of the Millfields estate—with only a very few exceptions, among them my father—belonged, and knew it, to the rural working class. We had been, until comparatively recently, peasants. The world we lived in was still recognizably feudal, and we knew our subordinate places in it. So, if our best rooms had been museums in the traditional sense, they would have contained hoes and spades, jars of hoof oil, yokes for carrying pails, cracked boots stinking of dung, unworn christening gowns, wonky milking stools, superstitious medicines, rusted bayonets, crutches.

But they didn't. Like ours, the best rooms on the council estate contained items of ponderous furniture, embroidered platitudes and biblical quotations in wooden frames, brass fireside companion sets, elaborately vulgar vases and ceramic shepherdesses, loud clocks, bone-handled cutlery in boxes lined with imitation velvet, black-edged plates printed with Prince Albert's likeness, poufs stuffed with horsehair, out-of-tune musical boxes. Superfluous, boastful things that properly belonged in the homes of people from a social class above our own. Best rooms announced that we had those things, too, thank you very much. Yet they were quarantined, permanently, in the best room. And for a particular reason: if we had actually used them, if we had incorporated them into our daily lives, we would have been pretending to be better than we were. We would have been getting Above Ourselves.

Getting Above Yourself was a heinous and peculiar sin. It attracted vicious censure. Win, among others, had exquisitely attuned antennae for detecting the faintest whiff of it. For example, when, in 1961, our ambitious neighbor Maureen Cushion summoned the doctor to a home visit instead of walking to the surgery, Win was scandalized. From behind the curtains she watched the car arrive at the house and the doctor hurry in with his black bag.

She said, "Chuh! That Maureen, she think she're got everyone at her beck and call, now she're got the tellerphone."

The fact that Maureen suffered a miscarriage two days later cut no ice with Win; she paid her cold courtesy ever after.

It must have been a torment to Win that her daughter's husband was Above Himself from the word go, having been a bloody jumped-up noncommissioned officer. And later, when I got way, way Above Myself, she could only cope by pretending that I was mad, or a changeling, or invisible.

But I get ahead of myself, which is nearly as bad as getting Above Myself.

Now and again families would update their best rooms. Out would go the sullen black sideboard; in would come its perky modern replacement, a veneered plywood affair with splayed and spindly legs and sliding doors with recessed handles. It would stand abandoned among the glowering old stuff, as incongruous as a stripper at a Presbyterian funeral. A modern picture—an Asiatic woman with a green face, a stylized child with photo-realist tears running down its cheeks, a racing car taking a bend—would be hung above the mantelpiece. Tiled fireplaces would be boarded up and electric fires installed; families would stand and admire the way the curled elements reddened, then switch them off, wary of the demand on the meter, and close the door.

Our best room never went through such transformations. It remained as immutable as a Sicilian grudge. George lived with it in a state of blank denial, like a murderer whose victim is buried under the cellar floor. Later, and to Win's immense irritation, he and Ruth developed a passion for redecorating. Every three years or so, they would hang new wallpaper in the living room or hall, paint the picture rails an adventurous shade of muted pink, the door panels duck-egg blue or primrose yellow. I remember them being almost in love at such times. Once I came home from school to find Ruth tiptoe on a chair, lining up a roll of pasted wallpaper on the living-room wall, the furniture herded onto the rug. George was pretending to support her, both his hands on her broad backside. They hadn't heard me come in.

"Stop that, George," she said. "I can't concentrate. I'll get this all wonky."

Yet there was happiness, naughtiness, in her voice.

No, there I go again. Sentimentality. Maybe it wasn't like that at all. Maybe she was just annoyed.

They never redecorated the best room. It stayed just as Win had re-created it, for almost thirty years. After she died, George and Ruth waited three weeks, then phoned a man called Cooper, who did house clearance. Cooper came and looked around the room. He pushed his cap onto the back of his head and made a sad noise through his plump lips.

"How much?" George asked.

Cooper shook his head. "I dunno. Say twenny quid?"

"Fair enough," George said, and took his wallet out of his pocket.

Cooper raised his eyebrows but took the money. He'd meant that he'd pay George twenty pounds, but you don't look a gift horse in the mouth, especially one from an uppity northerner. He came back the following Thursday and loaded it all onto his lorry and drove Win's family's history to an auction room in Norwich.

Within a month, the best room had been papered in Regency-stripe wallpaper and recarpeted. Its windows were rehung with curtains (patterned side to the street, of course) that matched the wallpaper. Chintz-covered "cottage-style" furniture was installed. The woodwork was painted a shade called *dawn*. Ruth and George admired their work, feeling, I imagine, a spring tide of relief and liberation. It's just possible they stood in the doorway holding hands, or almost.

All the same, they never had nor found a use for the room.

One night—in 1980 or thereabouts—after my parents had gone to bed, I smoked a joint in there. Just for the lonely naughty hell of it, and with the paint-stiffened window opened as wide as it would go.

14.

1956: THE CLOCKWORK OF HISTORY TICKS

THE HEADMASTER OF Millfields Primary School was an over-weight, kindly, bespectacled man with a face that was always a bright pink. His name, by happy coincidence, was Mr. Pinkerton. He was a romantic socialist whose ambition was to instill in his charges a love of those rich things—poetry, art, Russian achievements, music, the beauties of the natural world—that might console them during lives that would almost certainly be poor, coarse, and disappointing.

Early in the summer term of 1956, he eased himself smilingly into Mrs. Pullen's classroom with a large, fat envelope under his left arm. The children stood up. He bade them, pinkly, to be seated.

"Boys and girls," he said, "as you know, you will—I am sorry to say—be leaving us at the end of term. We—I—shall miss you. You were among the first children to come to this brand-new school, and you will be among the first to leave it. You will be going to secondary schools, where you will learn new skills and how to be grown-ups."

Clem, seated in the third row, paid only intermittent attention to this speech. His eyes were fixed, sidelong, on Hazel Cork, who could be relied upon to have a fit when anything out of the ordinary happened. Hazel's fits threw her from her seat onto the floor, where she would writhe and swear and try to eat her ponytail and display her knickers. Clem was unsure whether he wanted this to happen or not.

"Today," Mr. Pinkerton continued, "you are going to sit quietly at your desks and do a test. There's no need to be frightened of it. It's just a way to help us decide which kind of secondary school will suit you. But I want you to concentrate and do your best. And Mrs. Pullen and I will be watching to make sure you do not copy answers from your neighbors."

Mr. Pinkerton smiled to soften this stern injunction.

He sat in Mrs. Pullen's chair while she heavily yet softly patrolled the room. He was not at all sure what he thought of the eleven-plus examination, or "the Scholarship," as it was commonly known. On the one hand, it offered working-class children such as these a troublesome route to betterment. The brightest among them might, just might, claw their way to positions in life that their parents could not imagine. His own heroes had done exactly that and changed the world. On the other hand, the eleven-plus was designed to sort the sheep from the goats. It was socially divisive. (Even though there was no reason to suppose that sheep were superior to goats. Or vice versa.)

Mr. Pinkerton entertained an idea—more exactly, a dream—of a system in which all children, boys and girls, were educated together and in which their particular talents were nurtured and equally valued. The details of such a system evaded him. They were beyond his imagining.

He surveyed his harshly barbered and unkempt flock. It was unlikely that any of them would pass, anyway. And as far as the boys were concerned, that might be just as well. Newgate Grammar School represented all that he found deplorable. God help a boy from a council estate who found himself there. Lamb to the slaughter. Kid to the slaughter. One or the other.

Someone in the back row farted, audibly, setting off a susurration of titters.

"Boys, girls," Mr. Pinkerton said as sternly as he was able, "please."

Seven weeks later, George Ackroyd came home from work to find his wife in a state of high excitement. She waved a sheet of paper at him, wobbling the pink hair rollers under her head scarf. She'd had a home perm; the kitchen was full of its rank and acrid stink.

"Clem're passed the Scholarship, George! He're got a place at the grammar school!"

"What?"

He read the letter, still wearing his bicycle clips.

"Ruddy hell."

He read the letter again at the blue-flecked Formica kitchen table.

"Where is he?"

"I dunno. I told him, and he went off on his bike."

Win came in from the garden, wearing her laundry whites.

"He go to that Newgate," she said, "he'll start to think his shit dunt stink."

George's feelings about the matter were complicated, as were his feelings about his son generally. His first thought was that there had been some sort of mistake. Clem was a quick little reader, and he was a dab hand at drawing. God only knew where he got it from. Other than that, he was not noticeably different from the other boys on the estate. He had the same yokel accent and rough manners, the same scarred knees resulting from bike accidents, the same obsession with climbing trees. He was hungry all the time. He ruined his clothes in bloody, muddy, and unruly games of football in the local park. And now this!

George lit another Player.

A couple of years earlier, he'd noticed that Clem's drawings were mostly of war machines: tanks, planes, and imaginary monstrosities that spat flame and bullets, all rich in technical detail. This pleased George; he thought he'd found something, a common interest, that would span the silent distance between his son and himself. That Christmas he'd bought the boy a Meccano set, and the two of them had spent the long and dreary December afternoon building a dockyard crane, George's fingers nimble with the fiddlesome nuts and bolts. Clem's initial enthusiasm for the task had soon waned. He'd been more interested in the plans and diagrams than in constructing the machine. George had finished the job unaided, had experienced a childish pleasure winding the crane's little winch to hook the lid off the mustard pot. Then Clem had spent much of cheerless Boxing Day drawing ever more madly complex Meccano plans, numbering each component and providing a number key. He'd covered the blank side of half a roll of leftover wallpaper. The set itself was never used again. George had been disappointed in his son, just as he had become disappointed with everything else. But here was a thing, now: passing the ruddy Scholarship!

George felt himself to be a cut above the rest of the estate. Rather than join the beery crowd watching Borstead Wanderers boot a ball about, he spent his Saturday afternoons doing jobs around the house, keeping it dress-parade smart. He wished others would do the same. The Leggetts had turned number 16 into a one-family slum. He'd seen a rat in the street the other night, and he was pretty sure where it'd come from.

There were three wages coming in, now that Ruth had her part-time job at Griffin's, managing the till and checking the prescriptions. In all but name, he was the foreman at Ling's. His wages went up a pound a week every year. They were doing all right. George was proud of the fact that his wife had a new washing machine that gurgled itself empty via a ribbed gray pipe into the sink. He'd bought himself a new bike. Secretly, he nursed plans to rent a television set. His son getting a place at

Newgate seemed part of . . . it. What "it" was, George couldn't rightly say. Change? Progress? Socialism? Well, that hadn't lasted long. Bloody Tories were back in. Short memories people had. As soon as they could put bacon and cheese in their sandwiches again, they'd gone and voted Conservative, like the idiot sheep they were. "It" was a better life, though, no matter what. The future he'd fought for. He'd imagined love, respect, comfort, pranky sex. "It" hadn't turned out to be that, though. Quite the opposite. But his boy had passed the Scholarship.

Suddenly and urgently George wanted to know if any of the other kids on the estate had passed. He hoped not, by Christ.

Sundays, in the 1950s, were days of fathomless boredom and infinite silence. Clem hated them, numbly. His grandmother's power over the household had diminished since the move to Borstead, but in accordance with some deal or treaty he had not witnessed, she still held sway over Sundays. In fact, since she had fallen out with the chapel and joined those Brethren loonies, keeping the Sabbath holy had got a lot worse. Clem was not allowed to play football or ride his bike or go down to the park. Nor read comics, which gave off a satanic aroma that only Win's subtle nose could detect. There was no proper breakfast because there would be a Big Dinner. The Big Dinner was mince-and-onion pie with potatoes and sprouts. The house brewed the smell of it through the morning. He had to wear Best Clothes, which, on this hot summer day, consisted of a clean Ladybird T-shirt and long khaki-colored shorts that bloomered out below a snake belt. In the afternoon, while the grown-ups snored to the wireless, he swung himself back and forth on the front gate, pushing himself away from the post with his left foot until the hinge groaned and sent him slowly forward to the post again, with a *clonk*. And a *clonk*. And a *clonk*. The sun burned his cropped head.

Something moved at the edge of his dazed vision.

"Wotcha, Ackroyd, you skunkwhiff."

Goz Gosling, perched on his almost-motionless bike. Goz lived on Milton Road, on the far side of the estate from Lovelace. He was something of an outsider. In part this was to do with his odd looks. Goz had black curly hair that sat on top of his head like a nest that had landed there without him noticing. He had darkish skin and a long nose that widened at the end like a spoon. (It was a belief shared by Win, among others, that a Gyppo had once spent the night in the lower branches of the Gosling family tree.) Goz was strange in other ways, too. He had funny ways of talking, as if he hadn't settled on a voice of his own. He laughed at things that no one else did. He didn't like football. He was, however, the estate's undisputed champion at slow biking. It took him ten minutes to cover the twenty yards from the corner to Clem's gate, and when he got there, he held the bike stationary, jigging his shoulders and twitching the handlebars to keep his balance. Then, with a tragic wail, he fell sideways and clutched the gatepost.

"Orright, Clem? Hot enough for yer?"

Clem shrugged. "Nah. Call this hot? My dad says when he was in the desert, if yer wore a tin helmet —"

"Yer brains'd be cooked in quarter'n hour an you'd go mad an die. You told me."

"Did I?"

"Yeah. Twice."

Clem pushed himself away from the gatepost, and when he clonked back, he said, "What're you doin?"

"Nothun. Thas bloody Sundy, ennet?"

Goz switched his voice to posh, like an officer in the films.

"So I thought I'd undertake a spying mission deep into enemy territory. Loaded the jolly old transmitter into the saddle-bag. Codebooks in my pants, where Jerry'd never think to look. Cunning, eh? Sewerside pill on my tongue, see?"

He stuck his tongue out to reveal the Polo mint, sucked thin as a wedding ring but still intact, on its tip.

"Wanna come for a ride?"

"Yeah, but I can't."

Goz sighed, got off his bike, and dropped it into the hedge. Clem saw that he was barefoot, which was amazing. Goz sat on the curb with his naked feet on the hot road and his back to Clem.

He said, "I hear yer passed the Scholarship."

"Yeah," Clem said after a pause.

"So've I," Goz said.

"You hent."

"I hev."

A long silence. Then Clem said, "Hev anyone else? Woodsy, or Cush, or any of them?"

It was a monumental question packed with fear.

"Nah," Goz said. "Not as I know of, anyhow."

He turned and looked up at Clem.

"So thas just me an you, then, ennet?" He grinned, displaying his buck teeth. "We're gorna get some stick, young Ackroyd."

George's pride in his son's achievement flipped into outrage when he received a packet of information from the grammar school. The first item was a grudging letter of congratulation on headed notepaper and signed by Miss A. D. Withers, Secretary to the Headmaster, Lieutenant Colonel B. O. Bloxham, MBE. The second was the school brochure in a buff cover featuring an ink drawing of Newgate's splendid Jacobean frontage.

The Sir Henry Newgate School, George read, *was founded in 1606 by Sir Henry Newgate, Bart, the grandson of Sir John Newgate, appointed Sheriff of Norfolk by King Henry VIII. Originally (and properly) known as the Sir Henry Newgate School for the Sons of Gentlefolk, the school's values emphasized, and continue to emphasize, academic rigor, discipline, and Christian values. The school chapel, completed in 1621 . . .*

George took up the third item. It was a list of what Clem would need when he went to Newgate. Everything was, helpfully, costed and could be procured, exclusively, from Treacle and Phipps, School Outfitters, of Cathedral Plain, Norwich.

"Hell's bells," George said, looking up at Ruth. "The blazer is five quid, and the badge is ten bob on top of that, sew it on yourself. And he's got to have *house tabards* for sport, whatever the hell they are. Stone me."

Ruth scanned the list. "That all come to more than thirty-five pound, George." She'd gone rather pale. "An thas not countun shoes. He'll need new."

George ground his cigarette out in his saucer.

"I thought education was meant to be free in this ruddy country," he said.

That evening Win went up to her bedroom and returned with four five-pound notes in her hand. She handed them to her astonished daughter, along with a heavy sigh.

"I dunt spose we can hev the boy gorn off to the grammar rag arsed," she said sorrowfully. "Thas a good job some on us hev put somethun away for a rainy day insteada spendun it all on newfangled contraptions."

And she turned and smiled at George with implacable sweetness.

Also in the year 1956, a rockabilly American singer called Carl Perkins released a song called "Blue Suede Shoes." Being a song about fashionable footwear, it left the people of Norfolk largely unmoved. As did "Hound Dog," by Elvis "the Pelvis" Presley. However, in Norwich, two so-called coffee bars played the songs incessantly on their jukeboxes, and in full sight of passersby, black men from the nearby American air base jived with white girls. The police were summoned.

A film called *Rock Around the Clock,* featuring a fat-faced man called Bill Haley, who had a curl pasted onto his forehead and a band called the Comets, provoked young people to get out of their seats and dance in the aisles of the Norwich Odeon. The police were summoned.

That summer, six Teddy boys and their girlfriends appeared on the seafront at Cromer. The young men wore jackets — lavender, powder-blue, and pink, with black velvet collars — that hung to their knees. Their black trousers were tight on their skinny legs, and they wore suede shoes with thick soles. They sported Elvis hair, Brylcreemed into waves that met and slumped onto their foreheads, and long sideburns. Their girls wore tight sweaters over brassieres like the noses of jet aircraft, and loose skirts. They were surrounded by curious locals and photographed eating chips by the *Eastern Daily Press*. (The photo was published above the characteristically witty caption *The Teddy Boys' Picnic*.) The police were summoned. The Teds were arrested on suspicion of Causing Excitement and put on the next train back to London.

Politicians and bishops and newspaper editorials thundered dire warnings about the pernicious effects of that latest vile import from America, *rock 'n' roll*.

It would also be the subject of Lieutenant Colonel Bloxham's stern address to Clem's first Newgate School assembly, in September.

The salesman at the school outfitters (it might have been Mr. Treacle himself, considering the slithery sweetness of his manner) got the measure of Ruth and Clem as soon as they entered the premises. He'd had a good many Scholarship boys through the doors that summer. Ruth was wearing her best clothes and spoke in her best Miss Selcott voice, but he smelled the anxiety coming off her, sharp as ammonia. When Clem was kitted out and staring, appalled, at his reflection in the full-length mirror, Treacle coughed behind his freckled hand.

"If I may suggest, Modom?"

Ruth blushed at him. Her head was full of panicky arithmetic, knowing exactly what was in her purse. And the price of the leather satchels.

"Boys," Treacle said, "have the regrettable habit of *growing*. Especially at this particular age. They can't help it, of course. One minute they are four foot six; the next they are five foot two. You purchase a pair of shoes, size seven, and by the time you get home, his feet are size nine. What is one to do?"

Ruth waited fearfully for enlightenment.

"I normally recommend buying larger sizes, Modom. A blazer of this quality is a considerable investment, after all. It would be not unreasonable to expect it to last two years." He considered Ruth's tired footwear. "Or even three. The cap is probably fine. In my experience, boys' heads grow more slowly than the rest of 'em."

Clem's soul iced up. The cap was the worst thing imaginable. It was, like the stupid blazer, a pukey shade of green. It had a stupid button sort of a thing on the crown, from which four lines of gold braid descended, north, east, south, and west. Above the cap's blunt peak, the embroidered badge —

something like a dragon peering through a bunch of flowers —
looked like a target a Nazi sniper might aim at. If only. Given
the choice, Clem would have preferred his brains splattered
over the mirror rather than be seen wearing the bleddy thing on
the estate.

So when, on the first morning of the new term, Clem waited for
Goz to come down the street, he wept.

"You look a right twot," Goz said, stationary and upright on
his bike.

"So do you," Clem said, wiping his face with the overhang of
his sleeve, pretending his tears were snot or sweat.

"I know. These caps're a form of cruelty."

"I'm not gorna wear it. Round the corner, I'm gorna stick it
in me saddlebag."

Goz nodded like a judge. "My spies tell me," he said, "that if
we're caught not wearing them, we get our arse thrashed. And
that it hurt."

"Bollocks."

"Yeah. Them an all. Ready, then?"

As soon as they turned onto the Aylsham road, they were
ambushed by their former comrades, dressed in hand-me-down
Secondary Modern uniforms. Clem and Goz crashed through
with their legs kicking right and left, their brown leather satchels bouncing against their backs. A hail of stones and unripe
conkers fell just short of their bikes, but the taunt reached
them, echoing in the tunnel of the railway bridge:

*"Grammargogs! **Grammargogs! GRAMMARGOG** BASTARDS!"*

Later that same week, Edmund Mortimer suffered his first heart attack. Luckily, he was holding the telephone at the time—he was trying to get through to his son, Gerard, in Canada—and when he fell, he dragged the instrument off the desk. The crash brought his housekeeper hurrying to the morning room.

And in November of that momentous year, a boat called *Granma* departed the coast of Mexico and headed for the island of Cuba. It contained eighty-two hairy revolutionaries—among them Che Guevara—led by a man called Fidel Castro. Their lunatic ambition was to liberate Cuba from the American-sponsored dictatorship of a man called Batista. Improbably, they would succeed, and Fidel Castro would make a significant con-tribution to twentieth-century history and to Clem Ackroyd's yet-undreamed-of loss of virginity. Clem would, no doubt, have been interested to learn this, but at the time his mind was on more urgent matters. When the *Granma* slipped into the Gulf of Mexico, he was in a tearful agony of dread. He and Goz had been bushwhacked by the Sec Mods again, and Brian Woods had thrown Clem's cap into the back of a passing lorry loaded with beets. His dad was going to go mental.

15.

AN UNSENTIMENTAL EDUCATION

I'M NOT GOING to bang on about my suffering, my brutalization, and my salvation at Newgate. Those long seven years. (Well, eight, if you count the missing year.) Lord knows, bookshop shelves already creak under the weight of Misery Memoirs and Teen Novels that might as well all be called *My School Hell*. I have no desire to add my small pebble to that avalanche of unhappiness. In any case, looking back at it from this distance, it seems mostly funny. Tragedy does sometimes look like comedy to the survivors. And I survived. There's scar tissue, but after a while you stop seeing it in the mirror. Believe me. I know a thing or two about scar tissue.

So, briefly:

You walk through the school's wrought-iron gates. (Which are massive. And there's a carved griffin or some such thing perched on the stone posts at either side.) The original School House, three hundred and fifty years old, autumn-yellow creeper clambering up its russet face, is, actually and truly, beautiful. Between you and it there is a huge and immaculate lawn circled by a gravel path.

Rule 7: No one, other than the headmaster and his immediate family or guests, may set foot upon the school lawn.
Rule 8: Pupils walk clockwise around the school lawn, on pain of death. Only staff and prefects are permitted to walk anticlockwise.

(It occurs to me that I could convey the nature of my school experience simply by reproducing *The Newgate Rules*. I kept a copy for years, but I lost it somewhere between my divorce and my emigration to America. It was a little hardbacked book with a blue cover, the first book we were issued with. We were told to learn it by heart, and we did.)

For most of its history, Newgate had been a boarding school dedicated to turning the superfluous sons of moneyed families into military officers or, failing that, into the kind of brave, loyal, and gormless chaps who were the worker ants of the British Empire.

When Goz and I arrived, slack-jawed and fearful, many of Newgate's ancient and honorable traditions were still in place. They included ritual humiliation, physical bullying, incessant sarcasm, public undressing, violent games, caning, snobbery, ferocious patriotism, and the singing of the national anthem on the least pretext. (Such as the Duke of Kent's birthday or the

anniversary of the Battle of the Nile.) There were still boarders. They lived—for want of a better verb—on the top floor of
School House, accessed by a formidable back door.

*Rule 13: The rear entrance is forbidden to all boys other
than boarders.* (We all had a good snigger about that
one.)

Most of the rest of School House was the generous living
quarters of the headmaster, B. O. "Stinker" Bloxham, and his
family. Since this family consisted only of the old tyrant, his
fat strident wife, and his daughter (a rarely glimpsed teenager
whose eyes aimed in two different directions simultaneously),
they must have had little difficulty in avoiding one another. One
huge room was the Head's study. I was inside it only once, for
an arse caning in 1958. Another was the Nelson Library, named
after Norfolk's best-known adulterer, which only sixth-formers
were allowed to use. The real school, where actual teaching
took place, was concealed behind School House: a ramshackle
collection of ugly buildings surrounding the playground.
"Playground" is what it was called, but the word suggests
something inappropriate. Not much playing went on. Imagine
it, rather, as the kind of bleak area vibrating with tribal hostility
and potential violence that you see in American prison movies.

The boarders were there not on merit, like me and Goz, but
because their fathers (military men, to a man) paid fees. They
were generally, therefore, a bit thick.

But only sixth-form boarders could be prefects or house

captains — or the Gestapo, as they were jovially called. Goz and I came up against the Gestapo on our first day, at lunch.

(*Lunch.* What a social litmus paper that word was! At Millfields Primary, we'd had "school dinner," which we ate, uncritically, in the middle of the day. In the evenings, when fathers came home from work, we had "tea." On weekends we had dinner at twelve o'clock on Saturdays and one o'clock on Sundays. We'd never heard of *lunch,* which was, it turned out, short for *luncheon* and rhymed with *truncheon.* We'd gone to a new school and discovered a meal we never knew existed. And we ate it in a room we'd never heard of: a *refectory.* There's upward mobility for you.)

I was scooping pudding — semolina with a splot of thin red jam on it, like a clot from a nosebleed — into my mouth when Goz nudged me. I looked up and saw that a line of, well, men, blokes, was leaning against the oak-paneled wall of the refectory, looking down at us new boys. *Men* in *school uniforms.* Uniforms the same as ours, except that they all had long trousers (we wore chafing flannel shorts) and wore yellow waistcoats under their blazers. And they all carried bendy little cane walking sticks, like the one Charlie Chaplin had in the old silent movies. The one nearest us had a faint rabbit-colored mustache.

He said, "Well, Matthews, what are these, would you say? Worms or Maggots?"

Rule 32: Fee-paying first-year boarders are "Worms."
First-year Scholarship boys are "Maggots."

The Gestapo called Matthews studied us and sighed. "Mainly Maggots, by the smell of 'em, Shipton. Seems to be mostly Maggots, these days, worse luck."

Shipton said, "See anything you fancy?"

Matthews made another survey. Then he leaned forward, and, to my horror, placed the tip of his cane under Goz's chin and used it to lift Goz's face toward him.

"This one," Matthews said, "is slightly interesting."

"He looks like a Jew or something," Shipton said.

"Are you, Maggot? Are you a member of the tribe of Israel?"

I sat there frozen, with a spoonful of gloop just below my gape.

Then Goz said something that doomed him to years of suffering and in the same moment secured my respect forever and ever, amen.

He said, "Piss off, you great poofter."

The masters at Newgate were men who'd had the Time of Their Lives (good, bad, ugly, or all three) during the Second World War, or, in some cases, the First. Several of them were homosexual. (I use the term deliberately. Back then, *gay* still meant "energetically happy" or "brightly colored." Moreover, it could not have been applied, accurately, to the tweedy, closeted buggers that taught us.) While it was puzzling that it needed three masters to supervise the boys' showers after PE, I'd like to put it on record that I never witnessed any sexual abuse. (Some of them may still be alive and in touch with their lawyers.) And, as I recall, the homosexual masters were rather more kindly than the other sort, but I may be sentimentalizing. All masters wore black academic gowns that gave them a batty appearance. They smoked incessantly, even in class.

On Wednesday afternoons, they transformed themselves into army officers, the prefects turned into sergeants, and we boys became their toy soldiers. We wore itchy uniforms that were too big for our bodies, black berets too big for our heads, and incredibly heavy black boots. The playground became the parade ground. Assembled on it, we looked like rows of thin brown mushrooms that had been dipped in ink at either end. We were marched up and down and back and forth for half an hour while the Gestapo screamed incomprehensible orders and abuse. Then we were marched, shouldering disabled First World War rifles that were longer and heavier than we were, to the school playing fields, where we attacked one another. One miniature platoon, bleating cries of bloodlust, would attack the long-jump pit while another would defend it. The masters/officers would spin wooden football rattles to simulate the sound of machine-gun fire while smoking their cigarettes or pipes.

I survived these inglorious battles, and others. In large part, I owe this to the art master, whose name was Julian Farrow. (School nickname: Jiffy.) Which is odd, really, because we never greatly liked each other and he was usually disappointed with my work. Jiffy was a small, intense Welshman whose bird-bright gaze glimmered at you from beneath tangled luxuriant eyebrows. He always wore harsh clothes in shades of murk. Bristly tweed jackets the color of cow flop. Dun flannel trousers, brutal shoes like dead dogs' noses. He dressed that way, I now think, because at Newgate, art was seen as a mimsy, girlish subject and he was desperately determined not to look effeminate. ("Bender" Bendick, the geography master, often wore gay cravats, but that was okay, because geography was a manly subject with military implications.) Inside Jiffy's coarse carapace dwelled a passionate heart that pumped paint. He was a lover of violent color. The gods he worshipped were Cézanne and van Gogh and a Russian painter called Chaïm Soutine. Jiffy showed us the improbable colors—purple, rose, orange—that Cézanne found in a perfectly normal French landscape. He waxed lyrical about the slathers of thick paint that van Gogh used to depict the streetlights outside some café. He relished the sickly yellow, lurid red, and bilious green flesh tones in Soutine's distorted portraits.

I didn't get it. My favorite artist was Frank Bellamy, who did the *Dan Dare* strip on the front page of the *Eagle* comic. Bellamy's art was clean and bright and hard-edged and knew what it was doing.

Jiffy would say, "What is Cézanne/van Gogh/Soutine telling us, boys?"

And I didn't know.

I loved, love, the surfaces of things. What things actually look like. Or, rather, what they would look like if we were looking at them for the first time. Or if we had been suddenly cured of blindness. Back then I believed (and on my good days still do) that art explains the things that words can't manage, merely by delighting in them. Fire flame reflected in the brown belly of a teapot. The echo of the eye in a spilled tear. Warped reflections in a car's chrome fender. The shadow of Dan Dare's heroic jaw as he contemplates the burning of a galactic battleship in a Venusian eclipse. The soft textures of a girl's breast in furtive sunlight.

I fumbled and fought against Jiffy's nurturing until the term we did Still Lifes. On Fridays he would give us the History of Art, closing the art room's curtains and talking us through slides he slid onto the wall via an Aldis projector. We got about two minutes per image. Longer than that, and the projector's lamp would melt the slide. In Year Four, we looked at Spanish and Dutch still-life paintings from the seventeenth century. Jiffy was sniffy about Still Life. He was all about what he called the "latent energy" of things. Objects that just sat there being themselves were not his cup of tea. (Whereas I was very interested in how difficult it was to draw a cup of tea.) So he taught Still Life in terms of composition. How the artist had used triangles, parabolas, and other geometrical devices to shape the painting. How light and shade were patterned. How these techniques might be used to paint something more worthwhile.

I sat there ravished, breathless, gazing at the treasures cast upon the wall. Hands and eyes that were now less than dust had painted things that were packed with life. The gleam in a pewter jug, the gloss on a dead bird's wing, the mellow curve of a clay pipe, the silver glitter on the scales of a fish, the dash of pigment that became winter light on a wineglass. It was incredible. It was almost frightening.

One of the slides was a painting by a Spanish monk called Juan Sánchez Cotán. Bear with me while I describe it. Or try to describe it. My hobbling and pigeon-toed prose can't do it justice, I know that. And, in fact, Cotán's subject matter sounds pretty unexciting. All the same, I've stood in front of the painting—it's in San Diego, California—on several occasions and spilled tears of envy every time. It's a picture of five things: an apple, a cabbage, a melon, a pinkish slice cut from the melon, and a cucumber. They are exquisitely, almost obsessively, realistic, yet they look not merely natural but *super*natural. The apple (actually, it's a yellow quince, I later discovered) and the cabbage dangle on lengths of coarse string on the left-hand side of the painting. The cabbage is lower than the quince. The melon, the segment cut from it, and the warty cucumber sit on what looks like a stone window ledge, protruding slightly from its edge. But the window—if that's what it is—is utterly and intensely black. Blacker than any night sky in the darkest part of the universe. Darker than death. The whole middle of the painting is a terrifying void. But the fruits and the vegetables, those humble and edible objects, have their backs to that void. They bathe in the brevity of light, casting their modest shadows onto the stone. They say, they *insist,* that they briefly exist.

"Here we are," they say. "Death is the default. There's no

avoiding it. It's the background into which we will inevitably melt. We will rot and so will you. But in the meantime, eat, see, smell, taste, listen, touch. Look how commonplace and how beautiful we are."

And they really were. Are.

I wanted to tell Jiffy all this, but I didn't know how. Didn't have the words. I was only fourteen, after all. And the other boys would have called me a pretentious prat, and worse. But old Brother Juan Sánchez had set me on my course. I've made my living these past thirty years painting and drawing things exactly and intensely as they *are* and letting them speak for themselves.

In time, and reluctantly, Jiffy recognized that I wasn't going to become one of his inspired splatterers. He even praised (and, to be fair, greatly improved) my technique, even though he used the word *technique* as if it were a sad and regrettable impediment. He never gave me a mark higher than B. So I was just a bit pleased when I passed my O level with a grade A. My best piece of exam work was a pencil study of my grandmother's hand resting on our table next to an orange. I was terribly proud of it. Hands are difficult. Textured globes aren't exactly easy, either. I liked the way the surface of the orange was echoed in the skin of Win's work-coarsened, sixty-two-year-old hand. She was a patient model. She sat for hours with her Bible in the other hand. She could have memorized the book of Job in the time it took. Perhaps she did.

* * *

I have a framed print of the Cotán painting here in my apartment. It hangs opposite the photograph of my young grandparents. I keep meaning to move it. Because when I look at it, I see Percy and Win reflected in the glass, hovering in the eternal darkness at the heart of the painting, just to the right of the apple — Sorry, quince.

16.
NORFOLK FROM THE SKY

EDMUND MORTIMER'S KIND and faulty heart finally gave out on a crisp October morning in 1960, a week after he'd presided over his forty-ninth Harvest Festival. (Which turned out to be the last Harvest Festival celebrated in the great Tithe Barn at Bratton Manor Farm. Gerard Mortimer did not share his father's fondness for outmoded rustic customs, nor did he care for the expense involved.)

According to the old man's wishes, his coffin was carried to the cemetery on one of the farm's wooden carts, which happened to be the same age as himself. The cart was pulled by his last surviving pair of shire horses, Titan and Magnus, who were somberly but splendidly kitted out in gleaming black harness and plumes of black feathers. The route took them through Borstead's market square, which was crowded with respectful onlookers and astonished children.

Inside the leading car of the funeral cortege, the atmosphere was prickly. Gerard Mortimer was embarrassed and deeply irritated. It was typical of his father to dictate that this occasion be turned into some sort of damned . . . parade. The *horses,* for God's sake, as if he were royalty. All these people ogling them, the men taking their hats off and bowing their heads, the women wiping their noses with handkerchiefs. Ridiculous. Gerard's wife, Nicole, had allowed herself to be carried away by it all. She'd started lifting her hand to the crowd like the queen mother until Gerard had reached across and seized her wrist. Françoise, his troublesome fourteen-year-old daughter, squirmed and pouted between them, as if wearing a black skirt and knee-socks was a form of cruel and unnatural punishment.

Gerard leaned back in the leather seat. It was all right; it would soon be over. Then he could start, at last. He'd been waiting one hell of a long time.

On the second Saturday after he'd stowed his father in the family crypt, Gerard Mortimer drove his dark-blue Humber into Ling's yard. George greeted him.

"Morning, Mr. Mortimer. I'm sorry for your loss. We all thought very highly of your father. A real gentleman."

"Yes. Yes, indeed. Thank you, George. How are you getting along with the Ferguson?"

"Well," George said, "we . . ."

"Show me."

Concealing his surprise — and his anxiety — George led

Mortimer over to where the tractor stood semi-eviscerated in one of the lean-to workshops.

"The main problem is the oil pump—" George began, but Mortimer cut him off.

"I want to talk to you, George. Not about this piece of junk, and not here. What are you doing this afternoon?"

"Well, I . . . nothing much, I suppose."

"Good. I'll pick you up after you've had your lunch. Say, two thirty? Lovelace Road, isn't it?"

George stood rubbing his graying chin stubble, watching Gerard depart. The man was a rum'n. Not a bit like his father. Harder. Impatient. Not a trace of the old man's buttery Norfolk burr, either. Touch of a Yank accent. His men, behind his back, called him Zherrah, mimicking the way his wife pronounced his name. French, or French-Canadian, or whatever she was. Uppity posh foreign crumpet. What the hell did he want to talk about that couldn't be said here?

George watched the big car pull smoothly away from the gates and wondered what he'd done wrong.

At a quarter to three, Ruth ducked away from the living-room window.

"He's here," she stage-whispered.

"Tuh," Win muttered bitterly. If having Gerard Mortimer turn up outside the house in his bleddy great car weren't getting Above Yerself, what was?

Ruth hastily pulled off her pinafore and touched up her hair. It was a wasted effort. Mortimer didn't come to the door. He sat in the Humber and sounded the horn, twice, and George, shaved and in his Sunday best, hurried to the summons.

In Norfolk you don't need to build very high to have a commanding view of your territory. So when, in 1780, the Mortimers commissioned the architect van Wyck to design a new home a short distance from their rambling Elizabethan farmhouse, he settled for a mere three stories under a shallow-pitched roof. (Usefully, this meant that the servants, who lived in the attics, acquired the habit of stooping.) The problem was, van Wyck quickly realized, that visitors to Bratton Manor would be able to descend from their carriages and walk directly to the front door. And this would never do. The Mortimers would need their guests to *ascend*. So he had the low slope in front of the site leveled for a forecourt, and he extended a grand terrace from the front of the house. That was a far better arrangement; now visitors would have to climb a splendid balustraded staircase onto the terrace in order to gain admittance.

George tried to seem unimpressed as the Humber approached the house. They'd not talked much on the way there. Gerard had driven with exaggerated care, but slightly too fast. Once or twice he'd belched, and George had caught the whiff of alcohol. They passed along the flank of a high-walled garden and then drove through a Victorian archway into a cobbled courtyard surrounded by brick-and-flint outbuildings. The car was immediately surrounded by a small pack of thrilled and noisy spaniels. George, who disliked and feared dogs, hesitated with his door part-open.

"Oh, don't worry about this lot," Gerard said. "Too bloody useless to actually bite anybody. They're the wife's. She's dog mad."

He led George through the furry maelstrom into a large room containing an extraordinary number of boots and coats, as well as a distinct reek of horse. A low, heavy door gave on to a dim passageway.

"This way, George. We'll talk in the morning room. The females know not to come in there."

He shoved open a door on the left and led George in. The room was lit by mellow and angled sunlight. It seemed to be both a library and an office. A wall of shelves slumped under the weight of books, box files, and ledgers. A desk strewn with papers stood in front of the tall bay window. A pair of tapestry-covered armchairs sat like plump old ladies at either side of the fireplace.

"Sit," Gerard said, gesturing, and marched over to a mahogany cabinet. "You a whiskey man, George?"

"Ah . . . now and again."

"Excellent."

Gerard brought two heavy glasses and a decanter to the fireplace and sat down. He poured the drinks.

"Cheers."

"Ta," George said. He shuddered as the Scotch burned down his gullet.

Much of the wall opposite the fireplace was covered with eight-by-ten-inch black-and-white photographs pinned together into a complex single image. Gerard saw George looking at them.

"An aerial view of the domain, George. We'll come to that in a minute. First things first."

He swallowed a glug of malt and leaned back in his chair, resting one foot on the ankle of the other.

"I've been talking to Bill Ling about you. He says you're the best man he's ever had."

He raised his free hand, halting whatever it was that George might have been about to say.

"We're talking man to man here, George. No bull."

"Fair enough."

"You were in the REME. North Africa. That right? Heavy armor support?"

"That's right."

"So you know all about tracked vehicles? Tanks and half-tracks? Bulldozers? Heavy equipment?"

"It was a long time ago."

"A skill is a skill, George. I doubt that you've lost it."

"Well . . ."

Gerard leaned to top up George's glass.

"You probably know—well, everybody knows everything about every other bugger's business in this part of the world—that I was in Canada for several years. 'S where I met my wife. Montreal. But I spent a good bit of time in Saskatchewan. The prairie. Looking at farming. It was a revelation, George;

an absolute *revelation*. Flat as a pancake, Saskatchewan." He stumbled over the word this time. "A bit like Norfolk. But that's where the resemblance ends. Because over there, they've got fields two miles long and a mile across. Straight fields, George. Rectangles. Can you imagine? They plow using four huge half-track tractors side by side, cutting ten furrows apiece. Four men can plow a square mile in a day. Straight up, straight down, nothing in the way, you see? Harvest, same thing. Four, maybe more, big combines, line abreast. Incredible sight. And the yields are *fantastic*, George. Now, come over here."

Gerard led George over to the aerial photographs of the Mortimer fiefdom. The composite image was rich in detail. The shadows of trees and hedges and church towers suggested the pictures had been taken early in the morning.

"Here's where we are," Gerard said, tapping the roof of the manor.

Peering, George saw that the Humber was parked in the rear courtyard, exactly where they'd left it ten minutes earlier. He experienced a brief warping of reality, a moment of dizziness. The whiskey, probably. *Go steady*, he warned himself.

"Up here, see, the outskirts of Borstead. You're, ah . . . no, you're not quite on it. And way over here is the edge of the airfield. This is the road to Gunston and Norwich. Got your bearings?"

"Aye, I think so. It's, er, pretty impressive."

Gerard snorted. "Impressive, eh?" He took a swig from his glass. "You know what I see when I look at this? I see mess. Chaos. Higgledy-piggledy anarchy. Eh?"

George was perplexed. Etiquette, the rules of class distinction, obliged him to agree, but he had no idea what he would be agreeing *with*. So he nodded without speaking.

Gerard tapped his estates again where a square had been marked out with some sort of blue pencil.

"Look here. This is a square mile, give or take. How many separate fields are there in it? Go on, count 'em. No, don't bother. There're seventeen. Seven-bloody-*teen*. Nine separate field entrances off four different lanes. Ridiculous. Approximately fifteen percent of land area is bits and bobs of woodland and hedges that never run straight for more than a furlong. Four of the fields have been plowed. D'you see?"

George did indeed see that four irregular patches had been combed. They looked like the whorls and volutions of a giant's fingerprint.

"Hardly a straight furrow to be seen, is there? Because the tractor had to swerve away from this lump of hedge, here, then around this little bit of woodland, here. The thing is, what're those trees *doing* there? What are they *for*? What are the *hedges* for?"

George was alarmed. Mortimer had worked himself up, or down, into a state of angry depression.

He managed to say, "I've never really thought about it."

"Ah!" Gerard's exclamation was a pounce. "Of course you haven't! Most people haven't! God knows, my father didn't. Or wouldn't. But I have, George. I've thought about it a lot. Come and sit down. Top you up?"

"I'm fine for the minute, thanks."

"Suit yourself. Cigarette?"

"Don't mind if I do." (He'd been gasping for one.)

The light was ebbing from the room now. The tobacco smoke rose in flowering blue tendrils.

"Agriculture is a business, George. And like any other business, it's all about *efficiency*. I tried to get the old man to see that, but . . . well, mustn't speak ill, and all that. But he was . . . sentimental. 'The land is a *resource*, Father,' I'd say. 'We have to maximize our gain from it.' And he'd smile and pat me on the head, like I was one of Nicole's bloody spaniels."

The intimacy of this image discomfited George, who took a cautious sip of whiskey.

"And it's not just gain, profit. We've got a growing population in this country. More and more mouths to feed. And we're not going to do it using farming methods that are a hundred years out of date. I saw the future in Canada, George. It's *mechanization*. Mechanization on a grand scale. Plus"—Gerard held up a finger—"*agrochemicals*: fertilizers, insecticides, herbicides. You can't bloody *weed* a square mile, y'know."

"I don't suppose you can, no."

"No. But the problem facing me is this: you can't apply modern methods to country like that."

Gerard waved his cigarette at the wall of photographs.

"That was designed for horse-drawn plows. Harvesting with scythes. Potato-lifting by hand. A dozen sheep per field. It's medieval, basically. So, if we're going to modernize farming,

George, we've got to modernize the landscape. Straighten it out. Rationalize it. Get it machine ready. Turn this part of Norfolk into clean prairie. That's my vision."

Mortimer tossed his cigarette end into the fireplace and sat back in his chair. He smiled.

"And you, Mr. Ackroyd, are wondering why the hell I'm telling you all this, seeing as how you're not a farming man. Am I right?"

"Well, yes, to be honest."

"Of course you are. So let's get down to business. In various places up and down the country, there's a lot of stuff that's been lying idle since the end of the war. Ex-military stuff. Tracked bulldozers and so forth—things they used for building airfields and coastal defenses and whatnot. I'm buying up a lot of it. And I'm having some damn serious agricultural equipment shipped over from America. The locals will have their eyes on stalks when they see it, by God. But I'm going to need someone who knows big machinery. Someone who knows how to work it, maintain it. Someone who's not scared of it. Someone like you, George."

From somewhere deeper in the house came the faltering sound of a piano.

George hung his jacket carefully on the back of a kitchen chair. Ruth was in an ecstasy of curiosity, and he knew it.

"George?"

He loosened his tie and pulled it off over his head.

"George!"

He grinned, relenting. "He offered me a job."

"What d'yer mean, a job? What sort of a job?"

"He's buying in a whole ruddy fleet of machinery. Big stuff. And he wants me to look after it all. Full-time."

"Oh, my God, George. Whatever did you say?"

"I told him I'd think about it. Then he offered to pay me double what Bill's paying me. Plus a car. So I said yes."

Ruth put both hands to her face, shocked. After a second or two, tears of delight rolled onto her cheeks from behind her spectacles.

It wasn't a car, as it turned out. It was a smartened-up ex-army Land Rover. It was instantly the talk and envy of the neighborhood. And three weeks later, two men from the GPO turned up to install a telephone. Win refused, absolutely, ever, to have anything to do with it. If it rang when she was alone in the house, she'd cover her ears and shout, "He ent here!" at it. She went to her grave (actually, it was a plastic urn) without ever speaking to someone she couldn't see. Other than God, of course.

17.

THE END-OF-THE-WORLD MAN

BORSTEAD OFFERED LITTLE in the way of amusement, so Enoch Hoseason always attracted a small crowd on Wednesday and Saturday afternoons.

At the western corner of the marketplace there stood a narrow archway leading into an irregular space called Angel Yard, named after a tavern long since demolished. For well over a century, Angel Yard had been occupied by little businesses and workshops specializing in agricultural services: harness makers, twine merchants, seedsmen, and the like. Hoseason's great-grandfather had built a forge there and had prospered as a blacksmith. But by 1960 that business, like the others, was fast becoming obsolete. Horses — and their shoes — were on the way out. Enoch had turned his hand to sharpening lawn mowers, repairing garden tools, and, now and again, to hammering out wrought-iron gates and railings.

In social and religious terms, the Hoseason clan had always been awkward, harsh, thorny. They were Methodists for a while, but found Methodism a bit slack. They joined the Baptists, but found them a bit wet. Eventually they formed their own sect, calling themselves simply the Brethren. The men grew beards and tyrannized their women. Their instinctive response to more or less anything was to rail against it. The delights of the flesh, in particular, got their backs up. They bitterly regretted the pleasure involved in the conceiving of children, and chastised their young because of it. Way ahead of their time, they were the Taliban of north Norfolk. And like all prophets, they were lonely and scorned.

Then Enoch had a vision. It appeared one evening in his furnace and revealed the purpose of his life. Two terrible and beautiful angels of flame foretold him the end of the corrupt and mortal world. God, they confessed, had tried to purge the world with water, but sin had refused to drown. Now it was the turn of fire. All sinful flesh would melt, burn, vaporize.

"We speak of fire from the fire," the male angel said, "yea, even unto a man that worketh with fire."

"Hallelujah," Enoch cried, dropping his tongs and falling to his knees.

"Know that the earth shall be like unto thy furnace."

"Amen!"

"Know this, also: the seed of the fire is already in the hands of men. It shall become a mighty tree that groweth up to heaven, and all shall be consumed in the leaves and branches of its burning."

Enoch's eyes were wet with joy.

"When, angel? When will this come to pass?"

The female angel smiled at him. Her uplit breasts were perky under her flame-resistant robe. She spoke without speaking.

"The revelation is in the Book."

This answer came as no surprise to Enoch Hoseason, who came from a long line of biblical fundamentalists. As soon as the angels faded back into the glowing coals, he reached for the Good Book with a trembling hand.

The end of the world is almost as old as its beginning. In chapter one of Genesis, the first book of the Bible, God spends most of a week creating the earth and all that is in it; then a mere six pages later (in Enoch's dog-eared copy), He destroys it all in a flood, the only survivors being, of course, Noah and his family and their floating menagerie. So it's hardly surprising that for thousands of years people have been predicting another End. The Apocalypse. Armageddon. The Day of Judgment. Again. Nor is it unreasonable. Consider our brutal, bloody, and filthy history, our nasty habits. If there was ever a species that deserved purging from the surface of the planet, it is humanity. We are, or should be, a temporary infestation or infection, a smart virus awaiting its divine antidote. The prophets of the Bible return to the theme over and over again. Enoch was keenly aware of this. He had spent countless hours studying them. He was particularly interested in the book of Hosea—naturally, since the name was the seed of his own. The trouble was that the book of Hosea was almost impossibly difficult to understand. It was also drenched in sex. It began with God commanding Hosea to marry a prostitute:

The LORD *said unto Hosea, Go, take unto thee a wife of whoredom and children of whoredom: for the land hath committed great whoredom, departing from the* LORD.

Did this mean, Enoch had often wondered, that his own mother (long since gone to her reward) had been a whore? Well, yes, sadly. All women, from snake-fancying Eve down, were; this truth was the very foundation of God's Word. Satan works his wiles through women. Salome, Jezebel, Delilah, the Whore of Babylon. But Hosea, like the other prophets, promised universal cleansing.

Therefore shall the land mourn, and every one that dwelleth therein shall languish, with the beasts of the field, and with the fowls of heaven; yea, the fishes of the sea also shall be taken away.

That last bit pleased Enoch. He'd always had problems with the Flood. If all things were sinful, it seemed odd that fish, not to mention ducks and seagulls, for example, had got off so lightly.

But the female angel (whose breasts still troubled Enoch) had said, "The revelation is in the Book." She was clearly directing him to the book of Revelation, the Bible's violent and visionary climax. He was already deeply familiar with it: the Lion of Judah, the blood-soaked Lamb, the seven seals, and the seven candlesticks. The four horses and the seven plagues were constant visitors to his waking and his sleeping. But now he returned to the book looking for something precise: a date.

Enoch knew, of course, that previous prophets of the End had come unstuck by getting the date wrong. Because the book of

Revelation gave the number of the Beast as 666, there had been widespread panic, and rapture, toward the end of AD 665. But the following year had passed without incident, as far as global destruction was concerned. Then the idea took root that mankind's term on earth was a thousand years. So Christendom was seized by terror and joy in the year 1000. There was anarchy, in fact. Lawless mobs roamed Europe, looting and pillaging and raping on the grounds that they were doomed anyway, so what the hell. But the sun rose, as per usual, on the first day of 1001. (The Muslims, who worked to a different calendar, laughed up their sleeves at the foolish Christians.)

Nevertheless, the dread of dates with zeroes in them persisted. (Enoch's younger brother, Amos, was among many who came to believe that AD 2000 was the cutoff date. He became a vegetarian in the hope that he would live long enough to be a witness to the cataclysm. To his great disappointment, however, he would die in 1998.) Other dates had come and gone. The American prophet William Miller had announced that the Last Day would occur in 1843. When annihilation failed to occur, the date was revised to 1844—October 22, to be precise. October 23, 1844, eventually became known as the day of the Great Disappointment.

Despite all this, Enoch Hoseason believed that the recurrence of particular numbers throughout the Bible, especially those in the book of Revelation, would, as the angel had promised, give him a date. The fact that earlier prophets had got it wrong did not daunt him. That men had failed to discover a thing did not mean that it did not exist. Australia, for example, had been there all the time. So, neglecting work, food, and rest, he made abstruse calculations on sheet after sheet of paper. Eventually he came up with the five numbers 2, 8, 10, 6, and 2: October 28, 1962. Soon. Very soon; hence the urgency of the vision. Hosanna!

The date of the End, the search for it, had not blinded Enoch to the other message of the Scriptures: that there are those who will be saved, those whose penitence and purity of heart will pluck them from the fire and seat them upon the white pews surrounding the eternal throne of the Lord. Obviously—because the angels had appeared in his, Enoch's, forge—the Brethren were the Chosen. While this was joyous, it was also a problem. Should they be told? If they knew, might they become complacent? Might they cease to spread the word, cease to labor in the sour fields of sin, sowing the seeds of salvation? Might they—God forbid—slacken into sin themselves?

Enoch prayed energetically for guidance, but none came. He was not disappointed; he understood that the vision brought with it hard responsibilities. So at last he summoned the Brethren to his house and shared the revelation, swearing them to secrecy. Their joy and their fierce resolve assured him that he had done the right thing. Amos wept glittering tears of delight and beat upon his breast repeatedly. Jonathan Eldon uttered inspired words. Win Little rocked in her seat, hugging her stout old body, thanking the Lord for releasing her, at long last, from slavery and whoredom. Not to mention a bleddy uppity son-in-law.

Enoch Hoseason was a big man. Not tall, but wide and power-ful; a compressed giant. On the Saturday after he'd shared his vision with the Brethren, he carried the massive anvil from his forge, hugging it to his chest, and set it down in the archway facing the marketplace. Those who happened to witness the feat were mightily impressed. He was accompanied by Amos and Jonathan. Each carried blackboards painted with ominous passages from the Scriptures. They positioned them on either side of the arch. Enoch began to preach to the small but swell-ing crowd of onlookers. He punctuated his sermon by smiting the anvil with a heavy, long-handled mallet.

"Ye shall die. Be certain, ye shall die."

CLANG!

"And sooner than ye think."

CLANG!

After a month or two, Enoch also started setting up his iron altar on Wednesdays, early-closing day. As on Saturdays, he always attracted a jovial crowd.

"Less see yer lift that thing agen, bor!"

"How nigh is that enda the world, Enoch?"

"I do hope yer gorna finish my gate afore that come, Enoch!"

"Mock ye, yea. Let mockery be a comfort unto thee. For the seventh seal shall be opened, and death shall not be an ease unto thee."

CLANG!

18.
WIN'S MELLOWING

GEORGE, **WITH HIS** back to the bed, buttoned up his pajamas and said, "What's up with your mother, Ruth?"

"What d'yer mean?"

"You must've noticed. She's been different lately. She's stopped bitching at me all the time."

"Shush, George. She'll hear us."

He grinned. "I doubt it. She's gone a bit deaf, I reckon."

He took his socks off and looked at himself without pleasure in the mirror. How had he got so old? When had his hair started going Absent Without Leave? He got into the bed, and Ruth clicked them into darkness.

He spoke to her broad back. "You know what I mean. Instead of moaning at me all the time, she's gone all sweetness and light. Don't tell me you haven't noticed. Like last night, when I got in late. What I usually get is 'Yer'll hevta scrap around if yer want somethun, 'cos we had our dinner the usual time.' But no. She goes, 'I're put yer dinner in the bottom of the oven, George.

The gravy hev gone a bit thick in the saucepan, but that'll be all right if you heat it up.'"

"That was nice of her, George. I don't see why you should get upset about it."

"I'm not *upset*. I'm not saying that."

"So what are you sayun, then?"

"I dunno. Just that it's a bit strange, is all."

"She's gettun old, George. Thas all it is."

"No," George said. "It's something else. I don't trust her. It's like she's looking at me, saying, 'I know something you don't.'"

Ruth laughed, shuddering her bulk.

"Dunt be so daft, George. Go to sleep."

19.
THE STRAWBERRY FIELDS,
EARLY SUMMER, 1962

CLEM AND GOZ wheeled into the field and dismounted. They eyed the other bikes leaned against the hedge.

"Shite," Clem said. "There's hundreds here. All the good pickun'll be gone."

"Nah. We'll be all right, comrade."

They marched over the hot hard earth to the weighing tables and took six empty punnets apiece from the stack. There was a queue of pickers waiting to have their fruit weighed. Cushie Luckett was one of them.

"Orright, Grammargogs?"

"Orright, Cushie. Good pickun?"

Cushie shrugged. "That ent bad. I're made twelve shillun already."

Goz grinned at him. "I thought you had a proper job, Cushie. Whassup, the abattoir run out of pigs?"

"I'm orf sick," Cushie said. "And you hent seen me, Gosling."

"As far as I'm concerned," Goz said solemnly, "you have always been entirely invisible."

They made their way across the top of the field to where Mortimer's watchful foreman stood. He looked up and raised an arm.

"Over here, you boys!"

"Hardly a necessary instruction," Goz murmured.

"Right, you boys. Set you onter the bottom of these two rows here."

The foreman had a hand-rolled cigarette attached to his lower lip by some magical adhesive. It bobbled as he spoke but did not fall.

"How many baskets you got there? Twelve? I shunt think yer'd be needin aller them."

"Oh," Goz said, all disappointment. "Why? What time are you knocking off?"

"Six, sharp."

Goz had a watch on his wrist and he looked at it. "That's a good hour and a half away. I reckon we'll need another dozen, don't you, Clem?"

"At least."

"Hah bleddy hah," the foreman said. "We'll see. Now, you go all the way down the bottom of the row afore you start. And lissun—"

"Clean the plants," Goz said.

"Clean the plants." The foreman frowned, puzzled to find himself an echo. "You get all that fruit orf, other than the green uns, 'cos I'll be along behind to check up. And dunt you even think about slippun stones into them baskets. Orf you go, then."

Clem and Goz had picked strawberries every summer since they were toddlers. They considered themselves experts. Pickers were either kneelers or stoopers, depending on their age. Older pickers, mindful of their backs, shuffled along the rows on their knees, like sinful pilgrims. It took two kneelers to work a row, because in that position you couldn't see the fruit on the other side of the plants. And you were likely to miss the pick of the crop: the small, firm, and intensely sweet berries that lurked under the straw between the rows. You would most likely feel the sad squelch of them under you before you found them, and go home with stubborn gritty stains on your knees.

Clem and Goz were stoopers. They straddled a row apiece, easing the straw aside with their feet as they moved up, uncovering the fruits that had snuck out into the sun. Their hands busily riffled the dark green leaves. Their fingers automatically assessed plumpness and ripeness, passed quickly over the hard dimples of whitish berries, recoiled from the gray fur on those that had gone to rot. Perfect strawberries pulled away from their stalks with a crisp little pop.

The late sun scorched their backs. Not quite impervious to temptation, they gobbled only one strawberry every ten minutes or so, choosing it according to some selection process they could not have explained. A quickening of aroma, perhaps, or a perfection of shape in the hand. Slipping them quickly into their mouths without looking up. Most of the other workers were women accompanied by small children, whose mouths were smeared with juice like clumsy lipstick. Gossip and low laughter drifted on the warm air. There was a scattering of younger pickers, too; like Clem and Goz, they'd changed hurriedly out of their school uniforms and pedaled the mile and a half from Borstead. Twenty yards ahead of the boys, Doreen Riley's ample backside was aimed right at them. Goz caught Clem gazing at it.

"Ah, c'mon. You can't be that desperate."

"Wanna bet?"

Goz grinned. "It's the heat."

They went into one of their little routines, doing *Goon Show* voices from the wireless.

Clem: "It's the heat!"

Goz: "The heat, by God! The drums! The flies! The native women!"

Clem: "It's enough to drive a white man crazy, I tell you!"

Goz: "Steady, old chap. Steady. Remember, you're British. Think of the queen."

A punnet held four pounds of fruit. Six punnets earned you two shillings. Not in hard coin, though. At the weighing table, so long as you made the weight, or exceeded it, the cashier tore four tickets from a thick reel. Each was printed MORTIMER ESTATES LTD and 6*d*. At the end of the day's picking, you queued again to have these sixpenny tickets exchanged for cash that was brought in brown bags from the estate office late in the afternoon. It was a system based on distrust; one wouldn't want a load of money sitting all day in a field full of quick-fingered casual workers. It had the added advantage of keeping them there until the end of the day.

In less than an hour, Clem and Goz had filled their twelve punnets. Forty-eight pounds of fruit. Goz straightened up, wiping his face on his sleeve. Gold straw dust glittered on the damp hairs of his forearm.

"Are we done?"

"Yep, reckon so. Look at this un."

Clem held up his pick of the day: a big, glossy, flawlessly scarlet berry. It was too good to eat.

"Boo'iful," Goz said. "The size of a dog's heart."

They headed up toward the head of the field.

"Not if it was a Pekingese," Clem said.

"Nor a Jack Russell. I was thinking more like a Labrador."

"Norfolk lurcher."

"Speak for yerself," Goz said.

They shuffled forward in the queue, pushing their punnets with their feet. The weighed strawberries were being loaded onto a trailer. One of the loaders was a girl neither of them had seen before. She had very dark hair that swung against her face and neck as she moved. She wore an old blue-checked shirt that was too big for her — a man's shirt — its tails bunched into a knot at her waist. When she stooped to lift, you could see down into it, where white crescents could be glimpsed. Her jeans stopped at the calves of her slender legs. They were unlike the slack, cheap denims that the boys wore; they fit her. Clem could not help noticing the seam that curved down from her waistline and vanished under her bum. She was not used to the work. Her mouth was set in a pout, and she seemed to have some invisible barrier surrounding her, defying contact.

A rough male voice awoke him.

"Oi! D'yer want them strorbries weighed, or what?"

Clem dragged his gaze away from the girl.

"Sorry," he said, and stacked his load onto the scales.

He stood aside while Goz collected the tickets.

"What d'yer reckon? Do another six?"

"Yeah," Clem said. "Might as well. I'll get em."

He went to the pile of emptied punnets. He was closer to the girl now. He watched her lift filled ones; his own were on top. She carried them to the trailer, hoisted them up, then paused, reaching out. When she turned around, she was holding a perfect strawberry delicately in her fingertips. It was Clem's dog's heart. She turned it, examining it. She raised it toward her mouth.

"You aren't gorna eat that, are yer?"

He was more surprised that he'd spoken than she seemed to be.

"Pardon me?"

Her face was too small. No, it wasn't that. It was that her eyes were so big. And dark, but full of light under rather heavy black eyebrows. Her mouth was wide. Below the full lips, her chin was a soft little triangle. She looked Spanish, Clem thought, not really knowing what that meant; perhaps that he'd seen her in a painting projected onto Jiffy's wall.

He had to say something. "You'll get told off."

She stared at him without expression. Or maybe a smile refusing to be seen.

"I really don't think so," she said. A posh voice. Mocking him?

Clem glanced to his left. The foreman was walking in their direction, his face red and slick with sweat beneath his flat cap.

"Clem," Goz said. A warning. But Clem couldn't stop looking at the girl. She put the strawberry into her mouth, its plump tip first, and bit it in half. She closed her huge eyes.

"Mmmn. God!" Mumbling it.

A thin rivulet of juice ran from the left corner of her mouth onto her chin. She turned her head and wiped it away on the shoulder of her shirt. She looked at Clem, swallowing.

"You think you've got sick of them, but every now and again you get one that's too luscious to resist, don't you?"

It seemed to Clem that the world had gone entirely dark for an instant, but he hadn't blinked.

"Yrrng," he said, then cleared his throat. "Yeah. I picked that one."

"Thank you," she said, apparently seriously.

The foreman came alongside the trailer. He glowered at Clem, then saw the girl. He touched the greasy peak of his cap with two fingers.

"Orright, Miss Mortimer? The work suit you, do ut?"

She waved the remainder of the strawberry at him: a gesture that might have meant anything. The coral-pink flesh of the fruit was neatly grooved by her teeth.

The two boys walked down their rows to where they'd left their marker, three lines of brown earth scraped in the straw. They bent and rummaged, saying nothing to each other. A quarter of an hour later, Goz was a good five yards ahead of Clem. He straightened and carried his full basket back down the row. It was his second; Clem was still on his first.

"Yer mind's not on the job, comrade. I'm not gorn halvsies if you don't pull yer finger out."

Clem looked up. With his back to the sun, Goz was a glowing silhouette.

"Christ, Goz. What a bit of stuff! You see the chest on her?"

Goz leaned down. Blinding light streamed over his shoulder.

"She Mortimer, you Ackroyd. She Montague, you Capulet. Or is it the other way round? I never can remember."

"What the hell're you on about?"

Goz punted Clem's half-empty punnet with his toe. "Do the work, comrade. Me mum's gonna have the tea on the table in an hour whether I'm there or not. And I'm bleddy starving."

When they joined the line for the cashing up, the girl had gone.

The next day, Friday, she wasn't there. Clem and Goz made five shillings in an hour and a half.

20.
THE GIRL WHO ATE HIS
HEART BUMS A SMOKE

SATURDAYS AND SUNDAYS were the busiest days for picking. Whole families went: mothers with toddlers perched in wickerwork child seats behind the saddles of their bikes, men with boys on their crossbars and lunch bags over their shoulders. Clem and Goz stood up on their pedals, overtaking at high speed.

The picking had moved to an adjacent, much larger, field. There were two weighing stations. Mortimer's men were stretching a tarpaulin over a three-sided shelter made of hay bales. Even at this early hour, the day was very hot, and the filled punnets of strawberries would need shade. The two boys pushed their bikes over the baking ground to the far side of the field, where a line of ash trees separated it from a shimmering expanse of ripening wheat.

"There," Goz said, gesturing with his head.

One ash had lost its grip on the earth and slumped against its neighbor. In their conjoined shadows, a few of last season's bales had been overlooked. The boys parked their bikes there and stuffed their rucksacks into the spilled hay.

At dinnertime they returned to this den, away from the noisy mob, shuffling themselves into the narrowing shade. They unwrapped their sandwiches with reddened fingers.

"Wanna swap one?"

"Dunno," Goz said. "Wotcher got?"

"Cheese and piccalilli."

"Cawd, no. Dunno how you eat that stuff. It's like yellow sick."

"Thank you very much, Gosling. I'll enjoy them all the more for that."

"My pleasure."

They drank over-sweet orange squash from a flip-top Corona bottle. It was as warm as blood, despite their precautions. Goz had a packet of ten Bristol cigarettes. They smoked, sighing pleasure. A segment of time passed.

A voice that was neither of their own said, "Give us a drag on that."

They squinted up. She was wearing the same knotted shirt and short blue jeans as before, stained now, and a misshapen, big-brimmed straw hat that webbed her face with shadow.

Goz reacted first. He held up his ciggie, and she reached down and took it from his fingers. She took a theatrical pull on it, then stepped forward, pushed the boys' legs apart with one of her own, and flopped onto the ground between them, her back against the broken bale. She took another drag, with her eyes closed.

"I hope you don't mind," she said. "Daddy doesn't know I smoke."

Clem and Goz leaned forward and goggled at each other *(Daddy?)* and then, as one, took a peek down her shirt.

Goz found his voice. "Your dad? That'd be the Lord High Mortimer, would it?"

She laughed, snortling smoke. "God, is that really what they call him?"

She opened her eyes and looked at them in turn. There was a little slick of perspiration in the hollow where her throat met her chest. She smelled of sweat and strawberries and something like vanilla ice cream.

"Some do," Goz said. "We don't. We're Communists. We're making plans for the revolution."

"Are you? Are you really? Is that why you're down here away from all the other workers?"

"Yeah. People talk. You can't trust anybody. There are informers everywhere. Walls have ears."

"So do corn," Clem said, and instantly regretted it.

"That was feeble, Ackroyd," Goz said.

She turned to Clem.

God, her eyes.

"Ackroyd? Any relation to George Ackroyd?"

"Yeah," he admitted. "He's my old man."

She studied him. He trembled with the effort of holding her gaze.

"Yes," she said. "You look like him, come to think of it. I like George. He's nice. Daddy thinks the world of him."

"Yeah, well," Clem said, thinking, She knows my dad? He knew she *existed*?

"So what's your first name, son of George?"

"Clem. My ugly mate is Goz."

The girl stubbed the cigarette out, carefully, on a patch of bare soil and pushed herself forward onto her knees. She looked around the field, then stood up.

"Okay," she said. "Thanks for the smoke. I'll see you later, alligator."

"Hang on," Clem said. "What's your name, then?"

"Frankie."

"Frankie?"

"Short for Françoise." She pronounced it ironically, with an exaggerated Norfolk accent: *Fraarnswaars*.

"Cawd strewth," Clem murmured, watching her walk away.

"Dear, oh, bleddy dear," Goz said sorrowfully.

At three o'clock, Clem straightened up and faked a groan.

"'S no good. I gotta find somewhere for a leak."

Goz didn't lift his head. "Don't let me stand in your way."

Clem hurried for the hedge, stepping over rows, then glanced back, turned right, and walked casually up the field.

She was not among the throng at either of the weighing stations. A tractor was pulling a laden trailer out of the field. Was that her riding on the back of it? No, just a boy in a blue shirt. Clem stood, indecisive and achingly disappointed. She'd gone. Like a drunk surfacing from a stupor, he realized that he was being looked at and that he knew most of the faces around him. Half the Millfields estate was here today. God, what was he thinking of?

"Orright, young Clem? Lost someone, hev yer?"

That nosy cow Mrs. Parsons from Chaucer.

"No, I . . . No. I was just . . ."

He retreated hastily.

Halfway back, he looked over to where their camp was and saw—could it be?—a soft flash of blue. Just beyond the trees. Two brushstrokes of blue and one of black where the leaf shadow edged into the green-gold haze of wheat. Yes. His breath failed briefly. He made his legs move, made himself take care where he set his feet, crossing the rows. When he next looked up, the vision had gone. Dismay made him gasp and swear. And hurry. He stumbled up and through the gap between two of the ash trees. Their dense shade was like a moment of night, and his eyes were baffled for an instant. But then, there she was, sitting cross-legged but leaning back on her hands, on the narrow berm of dandelion-freckled and daisy-splashed grass beyond the tree line. The straw hat was on the ground beside her left knee. Her head was lifted away from him, and her eyes were closed. She was smiling. She seemed to be listening to the frantic debate being conducted by a parliament of greenfinches in the branches overhead.

He would remember all these things long after they'd been blown away. Scraps of talk, sound, would drift back like flakes of burned paper on a spiraling wind:

"You took your time."

"I thought you'd gone. . . ."

The chirrupy hissing of grasshoppers.

"Yeah. A levels. Art, English, history. . . ."

Her comical grimace. "Brainy with it, then?"

A noisy exodus of skirling birds.

". . . I dunno. Art school, probably."

"Dirty devil. So you can look at girls sitting there in the nude? I don't know how they can do it. . . ."

A whisper through the grain.

"No, not that. I want . . ."

"Are you any good at kissing?"

An intense silence, everything stilled, at the moment she took hold of his collar and pulled his face down.

The panicky thrill throughout his body with her mouth on his. Not knowing what to do with his hands, so keeping them pressed into the grass. Something, an ant perhaps, crawling on the stretched skin between his thumb and forefinger. Awkward twisting of his shoulders. Tongue? Hers doing it. Slithering into his mouth. Hot breath tasting of cigarette and strawberry juice and something else. Coarse distant laughter, like a pheasant's call, coming from somewhere. Squirming to keep the hard thing in his jeans from touching her leg. Wanting the aching moment to go on and on and on, because he had no idea what she might expect him to do next.

And then a snappy rasp from behind them: Goz, with his back against a tree, lighting a ciggie.

"Funny sort of a widdle, comrade," he said.

Clem pulled away from her, gasping, lost.

21.

THINGS CLEM DIDN'T KNOW
ABOUT FRANKIE AT THE TIME

SHE WAS YOUNGER than he was, which would surprise him. He'd thought she was at least his age. She seemed it. But she was only just sixteen. She'd been born in Montreal, Quebec, in 1946, on an April night during which an unseasonably late snowfall muffled the city. Hers was a difficult birth. Afterward the senior obstetrician took her father aside and told him that it would be extremely unwise for his wife to have another child. Gerard took it badly. The Mortimer estates in England had been inherited by sons for countless generations. That he—or Nicole, rather—would break that continuous line troubled him enormously. He stood over his daughter's hospital cot, gazing at her yellowish and clenched little face, and understood that he would have to be very careful about whom she would marry.

One of her earliest memories was of her father and mother pulling her bumpily to the crèche on a sled. The cars parked on the silent suburban streets had fat white pillows on their roofs. She wore a coat with a fur-lined hood that teased her face.

Almost effortlessly, she became bilingual, like her mother. Her schooling and her friendships were in French. Her home life, when her father was there, was in English. (Gerard spoke French like a man translating a dead language. Nicole couldn't bear to listen to him; she'd cover her ears and sing loud nonsense when he tried.) Françoise flip-flopped between the two languages almost without thinking, as you might turn the pages of a book. Just now and again she'd forget and speak to her mother in French at dinner. Then Gerard would slap the tabletop, making the wineglasses and the maid jump, and bark, "In English, please, Françoise!"

Her father loved her in a prowling, anxious sort of a way. He called her Treasure but often seemed disappointed in her, like a miser with too small a hoard.

Nicole Mortimer was a famous beauty from a rich family. Françoise liked to kneel on a chair beside her while she applied her makeup before going out for the evening. The fastidious ritual and its materials—the lotions, the powders, the brushes in their shiny little scabbards—hypnotized the child. She would stare into the boudoir mirror, not breathing, during the tricky processes that transformed her mother's eyes.

"Voilà!" Nicole would say, at last. "Qu'en penses-tu, Françoise?"

And Françoise would say, "*Tu es belle, Maman,*" and lean to kiss her.

But always her mother turned her face away.

"*Pas de bisous, ma chérie. Tu vas gâcher mon lipstick.*"

The slow calamity, England, began when Françoise was ten years old.

She came home from school to find Agnes, the maid (who was also Françoise's nanny and best friend), in tears. From the hallway Françoise could hear her father talking loudly, in his terrible French, on the telephone. She found her mother in her dressing room, tapping cigarette ash into a tray already half full of butts.

Grandpa Edmund, her English grandfather, had had something called a heart attack: *une crise cardiaque.* He might die. They were all going to England soon. They might have to stay for quite a long time.

The train journey from Quebec to New York was boring and thrilling in equal doses. A black man with a shining face and a beautiful uniform served them dinner while Vermont blurred into darkness outside the window. He risked a wink at her when he poured her Coke from a frosted bottle. In the sleeping car, she insisted on having the curtain of her bunk open so that she could see where her parents were, across the aisle. Eventually she was jiggled, juggled, into sleep by the regular racketing of the wheels on the rails beneath her.

Of New York she had only two abiding memories: a huge ice-cream sundae in the cafeteria of a huge store (Bloomingdale's?) and the vast black wall of the ship.

During the whole long Atlantic crossing, she felt slushy in her guts. One night, wearing a bib-fronted silk dress, she sat on a velvet-upholstered chair at the edge of the ballroom, watching the adults dance. The window behind her right shoulder framed an infinite moon track, shifting on the soft swell of the sea. The little orchestra was playing a waltz. Her eyes were locked on her parents. Partway through the dance, she saw her mother break away from her father and raise her hands and shake her head. She saw him say something angrily. Her mother hurried away toward the arched doorway into the salon, with one hand over her mouth. For a moment, her father stood islanded on the dance floor with his hands in his pockets, then set off after her. At the doorway, he remembered and came back. He stooped down to her.

"Bedtime, Françoise. Your mother is not feeling well."

England was dismal. Sooty rain streaked the windows of the train that took them from Southampton to London. Cattle stood, like unfinished black-and-white jigsaw puzzles, in sodden fields, watching them pass. The compartment smelled of fart and smoke.

London was full of wet gray air, and Françoise was amazed that it was still so bomb-damaged. Long lines of black brick houses were punctuated by areas of rubble, in which grubby children swarmed. Colorless and poor-looking people stood in queues outside dimly lit shops.

Her father tapped her arm and pointed.

"There, Françoise, look: Saint Paul's Cathedral!"

But she was still looking back from the taxi window at a pair of houses propped up by great balks of wood. Their faces had been ripped off, exposing peeled wallpaper, bedroom fireplaces, the splayed blackened rib cages of floors under torn linoleum skins.

She was astonished, alarmed, by how foreign England was. The fact that she spoke its language was—it seemed to her—no more than a weird coincidence.

Grandpa Edmund had sent a car to collect them from the railway station in Norwich. The driver was a red-faced young man with receding hair. Neither Françoise nor her mother could understand a word he said.

When the car emerged from the city, Norfolk was in its autumn beauty. Fields rolled away toward woods and hedges the colors of spices: cinnamon, ginger, paprika. A tractor towed a plow and a snow flurry of seagulls. The sky was immense.

Her father pointed out items of interest: "A windmill, Françoise; see?" A black-and-white wooden building, like a giant cuckoo clock with four overgrown hands.

They passed through a village where a humpbacked bridge gave them a view of sailing boats and a tract of glittering water.

"The Norfolk Broads," her father announced.

Her mother laughed incredulously. *"Broads,* Gerard? Did you say *broads?"*

"I did," he said, turning in his seat to look at her, grinning. In American parlance it was a vulgar term for women.

A little later, he pointed again, his finger just under the driver's nose. "You see that church, Nicole? That's where I was christened."

Its great gargoyled tower dwarfed the brick and flint cottages clustered around it.

Françoise had been to Norfolk once before, as an infant. She had no memory of it. Now she was baffled that things that were small by Montreal standards should look so big. It was hard to make sense of scale. Of anything. She was Alice in Wonderland. She had been removed from the story of her life and plopped into a different story altogether, a story in which words wandered around the dictionary, and everything was old-fashioned. No, *ancient.* Like in a book where witchcraft and stuff like that was real. The huge chestnut trees that lined the avenue to the manor, for instance, with their swirled crusty bark and their branches that were all gnarled elbows and knuckles. What might they do in the night? What might emerge from their darkness?

What emerged now was the house, and when Françoise saw it, she leaned forward between the front seats of the car and said, *"Wow!"*

* * *

Grandpa Edmund was not (as she had feared) a croaking yellowing thing on a shadowed deathbed, with a heart fumbling for its next beat. He was, first, a voice calling greetings from the terrace above them. Then he was a white-haired, leathery-faced, black-waistcoated man who wrapped his left arm around her while leaning on a walking stick. He smelled of horse and old apples, and the only thing really wrong with him was that he was laughing and crying at the same time.

She grew to love the place, despite the scowling furniture in her bedroom, the peculiar food served in heaps, the sad painting of her dead grandmother that hung over the parlor fireplace. When it finally dawned on her that she was not going home, she was not unhappy.

She learned to ride the bicycle that Edmund had bought her, even though Nicole lamented the scabs on her daughter's knees. And on a glittering morning in late October, her grandfather led her out into the courtyard to where Magnus, one of his great shire horses, stood waiting, its dappled coat like the shadows on the moon.

Peter, the groom, was the man who had driven them from Norwich; he looked more self-assured holding Magnus's bridle than he had with his hands on the steering wheel of the car.

Edmund produced a carrot from his jacket pocket.

"Hold it like this, with your hand out flat," he said. "He'd hate to bite your fingers off. Nasty taste to a horse, young girls' fingers."

She did it, daring herself not to close her eyes. The massive head loomed down. The soft clever lips explored her hand. She shuddered. The upper lip lifted; a scoop of monstrous yellow teeth, and the carrot was gone. Edmund applauded her by banging his stick on the cobbles.

"Well done, my lovely! Well done. He knows you now. Very well, then. Peter?"

"Sir," Peter said. "Here we go, then, Miss."

And he put his hands under her arms and hoisted her onto the horse's broad back. Her legs stuck out sideways, like a dropped puppet's. Peter passed the reins up to her.

"You won't need 'em," Edmund said. "Magnus knows where to go. Just you hold on. How's the world look from up there, young lady?"

It all came to end just before Christmas. Gerard Mortimer had been making inquiries about the local schools. None of them met his standards (which were more disciplinary than academic), so he sought farther afield. Over breakfast on a bitingly cold December morning, he announced that in the New Year Françoise would enroll at a Roman Catholic girls' boarding school near Cambridge. He extolled its virtues and emphasized the cost. His words meant almost nothing to Françoise. She turned to her mother for help.

"*Maman?*"

But Nicole didn't look at her. She punted bits of fried egg around her plate, as though fascinated by the yellow smears they made. Her grandfather would not meet her eyes, either.

He bit his lower lip and retreated deeper into the woolen blanket that he was wrapped in. (Françoise had no way of knowing that her education had been one of the many things that her father and grandfather had argued over, bitterly.)

Her banishment changed her utterly. Saint Ethelburger's was the bleak obverse of the fairy tale: the orphaned, lost-in-the-woods, lonely, and menacing side of the story. The dark stepmothers of the castle were nuns, and they hated her beauty the instant she arrived. Her dark liquid eyes cut no ice with the sisters. Françoise responded to their animosity in kind. She became difficult, truculent, sullen, willfully stupid. Her attractiveness and foreignness made her a victim of the other girls. In less than a term, she shucked off her accent. Still she failed to belong. When she returned to school after her grandfather's funeral, Gerard had to drag her, howling, from the car.

He made generous donations on top of the fees to keep her there; nevertheless, she was suspended twice, for a fortnight each time. Since this was exactly what Françoise earnestly desired, it was not exactly a smart tactic on the school's part.

Against the odds, and under protest, she enrolled in the fifth form at the beginning of September 1961. She found herself sharing a dormitory with three older girls. One was an upper sixth-former called Madeleine Travish, and Françoise fell under her spell.

It was Maddie who renamed her Frankie: "It's rather sweet, don't you think?"

*　*　*

In the evenings, after prep and prayers, the talk in the dormitories turned, frequently and inevitably, to sex. Inevitably because the sisters hunted down any word or whiff of sex like terriers after a rat, thus guaranteeing it a welcome refuge in the girls' imaginations, where it bred a host of impure and wildly inaccurate thoughts. Maddie knew a thing or three, though, and had scant respect for the Dire Warnings regularly issued by Sister Benedicta.

"Listening to what *she* has to say about sex is like, well, I don't know. Like taking music lessons from someone who's been deaf from birth. *God!* Did I ever tell you what she said to me about patent-leather shoes? No? Well, this is true, as I live and breathe. *'Madeleine,'* she says, *'you must never go into town wearing patent-leather shoes.'* '*Why not, Sister?*' says I. *'Because,'* says she, *'boys might see your knickers reflected in them.'*"

"Golly," said sweet, plump Veronica Drewe. "I'd never have thought of that."

Which caused Maddie to roll her eyes.

Maddie had a boyfriend back home in London. He was called Giles. They hadn't done It yet, hadn't Gone All the Way, but they'd gone a good part of the distance. Maddie's detailed accounts of their swoony gropings and fumblings enthralled and horrified her roommates in equal measure.

"Gosh, Maddie, you never!"

"Urgh! Doesn't that feel horrid?"

"No, actually. It's rather delicious."

* * *

One late afternoon, Frankie and Maddie found themselves alone, walking back to school along the short and shadowy avenue from the playing fields. They were in sports kit. The wind off the Fens goosepimpled their skin.

Apropos of nothing, Maddie said, "God, I love snogging. I miss it like mad. I can't wait for Christmas."

Frankie nodded sympathetically. "Yes, it must be awful. Giles sounds like a brilliant snogger."

"He is, actually."

Frankie considered this for a few paces. Then she said, "I . . . When you and Giles. I mean, when you're snogging . . ."

"Come along, Mortimer. Out with it."

"Yes. Sorry. What I mean is, Maddie, you seem to do it for hours and hours. What's actually so good about it?"

Maddie stopped walking, so Frankie stopped, too.

"It gives you the most wonderful sort of a flutter. Down There. Do you know what I mean?"

Frankie shook her head. Maddie sighed. Then she grabbed hold of Frankie's hair (which was tied back in a ponytail, for hockey) and tugged her face to her own and pressed her mouth against Frankie's, which had opened in surprise, or possibly protest. And then Maddie's tongue was wriggling about in it, as if urgently searching for something valuable it had lost among Frankie's teeth. Maddie's other hand slid down Frankie's back, pressing her belly into hers.

"Mnnn . . ."

Frankie tried to push Maddie's tongue away with her own,

which only encouraged it. After this wet battle had gone on for some time, Maddie's teeth fastened on to Frankie's lower lip and nibbled at it.

Eventually Frankie fought free, and the two girls came apart and stood looking at each other, breathing hard.

Frankie wiped her mouth on her wrist and said, "*Bon Dieu.*"

"*Exactement,*" Maddie said. "Don't tell me you didn't feel a bit of a flutter downstairs, darling." She adjusted her sports bag on her shoulder. "That's called French kissing, by the way. Did you know that?"

On the first day of the summer term, Maddie walked into the dormitory and tossed her blazer and her beret onto the floor. Somehow the other girls knew and were agog.

"Maddie?"

"Tell us, Maddie."

She fell cruciform onto her bed.

"I am no longer a virgin," she declared to the ceiling. "In fact, Giles and I have been at it like billy-o the entire hols. I can't imagine how I'm going to get through a whole term without it. I expect I shall get Frustration Migraine. Which is an actual medical condition, incidentally. The Victorians suffered terribly from it."

The girls considered this in silence.

Then serious bespectacled Teresa Candless said, "Aren't you worried about, you know, getting pr — in the family way?"

Maddie waved a hand languidly. "We take precautions, naturally."

Veronica gasped. "Maddie! You don't mean *birth control,* do you?"

Maddie laughed and sat up. *"Birth control!* God, what an expression, Drewe. Sounds like something on a spaceship or something. *Switch on the birth control, copilot. We're going in!'* Ha!"

She regarded poor Veronica with benign contempt.

"If what you mean is, do we use contraceptives," Maddie said, "the answer is yes. Of course we damn well do."

This was awesome. Venial sin compounded by defiance of the Holy Father's sternest prohibition! The girls' shock was sharpened by incomprehension. It was Frankie who asked the question.

"How, exactly?"

After a long moment, Maddie got off the bed and went to the door, opened it a crack, and peered up and down the corridor. Then she went to her suitcase, unbuckled its straps, and rummaged. She brought out her toilet bag, opened it, and sat back down on the bed. She opened the bag and produced a little yellow package, displaying it on the palm of her hand.

"Behold," she said, looking at Frankie, "a French letter."

"A *what?*"

"Giles calls them rubber johnnies, actually, which is rather vulgar, but never mind. The proper term is a *sheath.* Like what you keep a knife in."

She peeled the packet open and plucked out a brownish, flaccid, circular object the size of a large coin. The girls goggled at it. Its very presence in Saint Ethelburger's was like one of

Satan's horny toenails appearing on the chapel altar during Mass. Just to be on the safe side, Teresa crossed herself, twice, rapidly.

To Frankie, it looked like a thin, greasy toffee.

After a pause she said, "How does it work, Maddie?"

"How does it *work*?"

"Yes."

"Dear God, *ma chérie*. Giles puts it on his thingy, of course."

"His willy?"

"Of course his willy, you goose. What did you think? His *foot*?"

Frankie studied the limp object. By now she knew a good deal about Giles's fabled willy, but she couldn't imagine how the two things might fit together. Maddie read the blankness in her gaze and sighed theatrically.

"Lord love us and save us," she said, and cast her eyes around the room. They came to rest on the hair brush on Frankie's bedside cabinet.

"Pass us that."

Frankie did so. Maddie eased the French letter onto the end of the brush's handle, where it hung, drooping. She circled its thick rim with her thumb and forefinger and slid it, unfurling it, up to where the handle widened.

The three other girls stared at the result. The oily johnny hung slackly from the brush, with its little nose aimed at the floor.

Maddie sensed their disappointment.

"It's not like that on an actual willy, of course," she said.

161

A couple of months later, Frankie sulked through her O-level exams. The last one was Latin, and as soon as it was over, she went back to the dorm, where she tore off the hateful uniform and cut it to shreds with a pair of scissors she'd pinched from the sewing room for the purpose. Then she dressed in proper clothes. There was no way she was going to lug her heavy suitcase, so she packed a few things into her sports bag. She walked unhurriedly past the chapel, whence came the reedy uncertain sound of Junior hymn practice, and down the drive. To her surprise—and slight disappointment—no one tried to stop her. She shinnied over the locked gates and marched through light drizzle up to the main road, where she hitched a lift in a butcher's van. She cadged a cigarette from the driver and without much difficulty charmed him into taking her to Cambridge station. At Norwich she phoned her mother from a call box. Nicole was dismayed, though not surprised; she'd already had a call from Saint Ethelburger's. Sister Benedicta had made it plain that Françoise's return would be neither expected nor welcome.

Her father ranted at her, of course. She endured it more or less silently. He sentenced her to hard labor, which is how she came to be working in the strawberry fields. And how she came to test Maddie's snogging technique on awkward but absolutely gorgeous Clem Ackroyd.

22.
NERVY PASTORAL

FOR WEEKS, SOFT fruits gave them cover. After strawberries, there were gooseberries, black currants, raspberries. Frankie worked her sentence, weighing and loading, stacking the stained empty punnets. And at every opportunity, at increasingly risky opportunities, she would excuse herself through a gap in a hedge, slip into the shade of a tree, amble behind a trailer, to be with Clem. They kissed avidly, clumsily, not knowing what to do with their sticky, juice-stained hands. They did not talk much; they were short of time, and breath. When they did speak, death often cropped up.

"I was dying for that."

"God, my father would kill me if he knew I was . . ."

"My dad'd skin me alive . . ."

"Wouldn't it be delicious to die like this?"

At first it was a game; it was a hazardous mischief. But not for long. They each soon found the hot days shrinking into the stolen minutes — ten, fifteen at most — when they were together. Other time became numb.

Clem trembled, waiting in hiding for her. Shook physically. He found these moments hard to bear because it was like being too much alive. His own blood seemed to torment him.

"Yer got it bad, comrade," Goz said, riding home.

The boys still went to the fields together but worked separately now. Clem's distraction was proving uneconomic.

"Have I?"

"Yeah. And yer playing with fire. It's a good job yer so bleddy wet."

He couldn't stop thinking about her. It was ridiculous. It was like a mental illness or something. A continuous rerunning of little films in his head. Her eyes slowly opening after a long snog. Tipping her head back to swing the hair away from her face. Pulling a damp strand of it from her lips. The movement of her bum as she walked away. At home, he sat in the living room trying to stop the projector, black out the images. Silently reciting the names of the kings and queens of England until the shameful bulge in his jeans subsided and he could stand up.

Ruth turned away from the telly.

"Wassup with you, Clem?"

"Nuthun. I'm orright."

"You look like someone who're lost a fiver and found a shillun."

"I'm orright, Mum. Bit bored, is all."

"You usually like this program."

"Yeah. Not very good tonight, though, is it?"

George said, "Do you mind? I'm trying to watch this."

Clem checked the state of his lap. He stood up. "I might go out for a bit."

He spent the nights praying that his bed wasn't creaking too audibly. Luckily, his grandmother was often loudly murmurous in the nights, praying for something else altogether. Clem synchronized his devotions with hers.

Hiding, waiting for him, Frankie felt angry. Angry that she hungrily fancied a badly dressed working-class boy like Clem Ackroyd. Angry that she couldn't be with him whenever she wanted to. Angry that she should have to conceal herself from people who worked for her father. Then Clem would step through a gap in the hedge or brush aside a veil of leaves, and her breath would catch in her throat and her whole body would come alight.

Over dinner, her mother looked at her. "What's the matter, darling?"

"Pardon, Mummy?"

"You've hardly eaten anything. Don't you like it?"

"It's good. I'm just a bit tired."

Nicole turned to her husband. "Gerard, how much longer are you going to continue this farce, treating your daughter like a laborer? She is exhausted. She can hardly lift the food to her mouth."

"Nonsense, Nicole. It's doing her the world of good. Look at her. She's the picture of health."

"She is too much in the sun, Gerard. She looks like a Gypsy. Her nose is peeling."

Mortimer dabbed his lips with his napkin, then grinned.

"Very well," he said. "Françoise, I'm putting you on parole. Time off for good behavior."

She looked across at him, frowning, not understanding. *Parole* was French for "word" or "speech."

"You don't have to work anymore," her father said.

Frankie tried to keep her hand steady, lowering the heavy silver fork onto the tablecloth.

"It's okay, Daddy. I like it, actually. The people are nice. Funny."

"Françoise," Nicole said. "What has that to do with anything?"

Frankie forced a shrug. "Nothing, I guess. I just like being in the fresh air. And it's something to do. I'll work until the end of the season."

Gerard Mortimer leaned back in his chair. "Well said. Spoken like a farmer's daughter, eh, Nicole?"

His wife pulled the corners of her mouth down and cut a neat slice from her veal for the spaniel who sat by her chair.

On the day following this conversation, Frankie did not plant her mouth on Clem's as soon as they were alone. She did not even look at his face. Instead, she unbuttoned his shirt, silently concentrating, as if it were a strange and difficult task.

"Frankie?"

They were kneeling in the lee of a low brambly hedge where the long lines of raspberry canes petered out. The sky was paper white and the air was heavy and thick.

A vortex of midges coned above their heads.

She opened his shirt and put her arms inside it, holding him, her palms against his shoulder blades. She rested her head on his shoulder. After a moment or two, he put his arms around her, his fingers meeting on the hard nubble where her bra fastened.

"Frankie?"

Still she wouldn't speak. He lifted his right hand and buried it in her hair. Cautiously, he caressed the place where her neck met the base of her skull, marveling at how fragile it felt. He was certain that this silent embrace was her way of telling him it was over. That she was finishing with him. It made him gasp, as if he had been slapped by a gust of sleet out of the hot summer sky. He pulled her head away. She lifted her face. He was baffled to see that her eyes were wet, yet she was smiling.

"What?" He failed to keep the anger, the vast disappointment, from his voice.

"You smell nice," she said. "For a boy."

Then at last she kissed him, more urgently than ever before. She lifted herself up on her knees, and her hands rose up to the nape of his neck. Her nails pressed into his skin, hurting.

He was convinced that this was their good-bye kiss, the parting embrace.

So when they broke apart, he blurted, "I love you, Frankie."

It was a shameful and desperate declaration. They were like foreign words. He had never heard real people use them. He'd shocked himself. He needed her to say that she loved him, too. To cancel out, to pardon, what he'd said.

She didn't.

Instead, she said, "We can't go on like this."

It was like something you heard on the telly. He lowered his head like King Charles I inviting the executioner's ax.

Frankie leaned away from him, pushing stray hairs from her face.

She said, "D'you know the little lane between Borstead and Bratton Morley?"

He looked up at her gormlessly. "What?"

"Do you?"

"Yeah."

"There's a place where it goes through some woods. Skeyton Woods, they're called. There's a bridleway that goes off the lane. It's got an old gate across it. Know where I mean?"

"Yeah. Frankie—"

A man's voice called from dangerously close by, startling them. Frankie got to her feet, stooping to stay below the level of the raspberry canes.

"Meet me there tonight. Seven thirty. Okay?"

He nodded. Then she was gone.

Clem shoved his bike through the gateway and concealed it in a shallow ditch screened by bracken. He knew the place well, had known it all his life. He had a faint memory trace of walking in these woods with his mother when he was little. Before they'd moved to Borstead. For some reason the memory had a sad coloring to it.

A quarter of a mile or so from where he now stood, waiting, was the Dip, an old gravel pit overhung with trees. In the days before he'd become an outcast Grammargog, he'd been one of the Millfields Gang, who'd bike to the woods to play hectic day-long games of stalking and warfare there. Beyond the Dip, the bridleway forked. The left branch emerged, eventually, onto a farm track behind Bratton Manor. He assumed that Frankie would come from that direction. After an eternity of ten min-utes, he could hardly resist the urge to set off to meet her, to get to her sooner. But she'd said the gateway. It seemed to him that his insides were actually vibrating with indecision. And the swelling fear that she would not come.

She wouldn't, he realized; she'd never intended to. She'd planned this cruelty as a way of ending things between them, knowing that he'd be too hurt, too humiliated, ever to go near her again. This sudden, terrible certainty untethered his heart. He groaned aloud, and although he was alone, he felt shamed by the hot tears that blurred his vision. He took refuge in anger. At himself, for spoiling everything by saying he loved her. By getting serious. How *could* it get serious, seeing who he was and who she was? He'd scared her off. He cursed himself: *You effing idiot, Ackroyd.* He made himself curse her: *Stuck-up bitch.*

He'd go home. Sod it. In a minute. Definitely.

After a while, he heard a soft thudding and looked down the track. Christ, someone on a horse. He was about to duck back out of sight when he realized it was her. Bucking up and down in the saddle to the easy rhythm of the horse's trot. A brown horse dappling bright then dark in the light slanting through the trees. Seeing Clem, it slowed, hesitated. He saw her urge it forward by tightening her knees and heels against its body. It came on cautiously, tossing its head a little, whiffling. She was wearing clean jeans and a beige tweed jacket over a white T-shirt. Her hair was partly tied back, leaving long tresses hanging on either side of her face. Clem stuck his hands into his pockets, trying not to look like someone about to faint from relief. Or joy. Or fear of horses.

"Easy, boy," Frankie said, bringing the uneasy horse to a halt. She swung herself out of the saddle.

She said, "Hello," as if to someone she'd met by chance, and walked to the horse's head. She put her hands on its hard flat cheeks.

"This is Clem. Clem, this is Marron. Isn't he gorgeous? This is one of our favorite rides."

She looked at Clem at last. "Say hello. Wait, give him these." She took three sugar cubes from her jacket pocket.

"Sit them on your hand, like this."

He let the horse slobber them up, then wiped his hand on his jeans.

"Have you been waiting ages? I'm sorry. But listen, I had this terrific idea. I told Mummy that I was feeling guilty for neglecting Marron while I was working in the fields. I said that I'd try to find the time to take him out once or twice a week when I got home. And she bought it! She said that it was a *très bonne idée*.

It means we can meet in the evenings! Don't you think that was clever of me?"

He did, yes, and was dizzied by these new possibilities. But her brittle-sounding chatter was like a barrier between them. He was keenly aware of Marron's rolling eye. And, yet again, of how achingly beautiful this girl was, how impossible all this was.

"Clem? Don't you?"

"Yeah. Brilliant."

"What's the matter?"

"Nothing. I . . ."

He moved toward her. She turned her head to glance back down the track, and he understood.

"This way," he said, and walked to where a narrower path led away into the bracken. The horse was reluctant to turn and was nervy on the path. Frankie led him by the bridle, making encouraging *chut-chut-chut* noises. After five minutes, they came to a little dell inside a group of ancient beech trees, their trunks like huge clenchings of gray-green muscle. Light came in shifting dazzles through fans of leaves that descended almost to the ground.

"Will this do?"

Frankie surveyed the scene. "Hmm. Is this where you bring all your girls, Master Ackroyd?"

"Only the special ones."

She looped and knotted Marron's reins onto a low branch, then regarded Clem mock seriously.

"How many special ones have there been?"

But he was too impatient for games. "None. You're the first, Frankie. Honest."

"I'm glad to hear it."

"Come here, then."

They stooped under the fringe of the leaf mantle. Their feet rustled the rust-colored leaf litter. Frankie took her jacket off, spread it on the ground, and sat on it. He knelt in front of her and slid his hand into her hair, finding that delicate place at the top of her neck. He leaned toward her.

"No," she said, "like this," and lay on her side, resting her head on her hand.

They had never lain down together, and Clem hesitated, fearing he would not be able to hide his uncontrollable stiffening from her.

"Come on," she said. "We haven't got *all* night, you know."

"You mustn't go too fast," Maddie Travish had told her. *"Because if you do, the boy will think you're a tart. So no touching anywhere on the first three dates, okay? After that, a hand on the bum is perfectly acceptable. If you like him, if his breath doesn't stink or anything like that, you can let him touch you up here. But only outside the bra. Definitely not inside the bra until at least the fifth date."*

"Why, Maddie?"

"Because boys like to think they're making progress. They'd absolutely loathe to think that you are in control of things. They want to believe that you're absolutely dying for it, but terribly afraid of giving in. So when you do give in, they think it's because

they're irresistible. Besides, it's the most wonderful fun, making them wait. They get into the most extraordinary states. You can do almost anything with them, darling."

Frankie wasn't sure if countless stolen snogs in the hedges of fruit fields counted as dates. Perhaps parts, or fractions, of dates. If they did, the arithmetic was complicated. But the answer probably came to five, at least. So she shifted onto her back and took Clem's right hand and guided it up inside her T-shirt and pressed it onto the slithery nylon that cupped her left breast. This had a startling effect: Clem sucked all the breath out of her mouth and moaned at the same time. She opened her eyes and found herself looking into his. They were sort of glazed.

He said, "God, Frankie. God."

She could feel his hard thingy against her leg. Little electrical currents ran through her.

"Do you really love me?"

"Yeah. Christ, Frankie."

She pressed her fingers on his and showed them what to do.

"I love you, too."

She was both relieved and surprised that she meant it.

23.

A LATIN-AMERICAN INTERLUDE

AT THIS POINT I need to take you on a short detour. I'm very much a cause-and-effect sort of a fellow. I'm fascinated by the way things fit together (and come to pieces). And if we were to take what eventually happened to Frankie and me and drew something like a flowchart of how it came about, one of its arrows would lead us into the darkness of a Caribbean night: the night of February 15, 1898, in fact. Just off the north coast of Cuba, in Havana Bay.

The half-moon appears only fitfully among slow-moving clouds, and stars are few and far between. It is very quiet. The only scraps of sound are the clop and trundle of the horse-drawn carriages along the Malecón, Havana's seafront boulevard, and snatches of brassy music. Apart from where the city's lights spill into the harbor, the sea is black. In its vastness, tiny spangles bob, the lamps of fishing boats. But there is one larger concentration of lights, those of an American warship, the USS *Maine*.

It is nine forty p.m. There are few strollers or lingerers along

Havana's shoreline; the authorities, having recently crushed another revolution, do not encourage the populace to gather after dark. But for those who witness it, who stagger and scream or are momentarily paralyzed by it, who are physically rocked by it, the explosion will be unforgettable. A vast plume of fire erupts from the sea, then forms itself into a boiling globe of red and orange that recolors the city. The sound comes an instant later, a lumbering thunderclap that seems to last an impossibly long time, echoing, even though there is nothing for it to echo from. The *Maine* has blown up. The front third of the ship, where most of its crew were sleeping or playing cards or writing letters, has been transformed into fiery vapor. The sleepers, the gamblers, the writers, have disintegrated. Their bits, their atoms, are hurled into the sky, then rain down onto the surface of the sea, like the grains of an exhausted firework. Within minutes the remaining hulk of the ship has gone, gulped onto the floor of the bay. Two hundred and sixty-six men are dead.

(By one of those coincidences that make you wonder if there is in fact a Scriptwriter Beyond the Stars, my grandmother Winifred entered the world, red, slippery, and resentful, just a few minutes later. Perhaps even before the waters had regathered themselves above the wreck of the *Maine*.)

Pretty much as soon as they were united, the United States of America started hankering after Cuba. (And still do.) How could they not? It was the biggest island in the Caribbean. Tropical and lush, blessed with lovely beaches, it was so temptingly close: only ninety miles from the southern tip of Florida. Its capital, Havana, is the same distance from Miami as Washington, D.C., is from New York City. The island grew lots of sugarcane, and America had a very sweet tooth. Unfortunately, Cuba was part of the Spanish Empire. (Spain's hired Italian explorer, Christopher Columbus, had discovered it, much to the surprise of the people who already lived there.) In 1848 President James Polk offered to buy it. The Spanish declined, in no uncertain terms, and continued to treat the Cubans very harshly, which greatly distressed the freedom-loving and slave-owning Americans.

In 1895, after another failed uprising, the Spanish sent a general (fondly nicknamed *El Carnicero,* the Butcher) to get Cuba more firmly under control. One of his tactics was to herd huge numbers of people into concentration camps, where the military could more conveniently keep an eye on them. And while the military watched, the internees died, hundreds of thousands of them, from disease and starvation.

There was widespread outrage in the United States, and the newspapers clamored for President McKinley to *do something:* ideally, turf the goddamn Spaniards out of Cuba and take over the place. McKinley didn't do that. He issued dire warnings to the Spanish, who ignored them and continued on their brutally merry way. Then, toward the end of January 1898, the president sent the USS *Maine* to Havana, thinking, I suppose, that the sight of American sea power might persuade them that he was serious. The Cuban authorities treated the crew—the officers, at least—with careful courtesy. (The ordinary sailors were not allowed ashore, in case trouble broke out. Which must have been deeply frustrating, so close to a tropical island reputedly full of beautiful dusky women and awash with rum.)

And then — *WHUMPH!* — the *Maine* was gone.

The U.S. Navy conducted an inquiry and concluded that the ship's magazine — its ammunition store, containing several tons of explosive charges for its guns — had blown up. That was pretty much a no-brainer, given the violence of the cataclysm. But the navy also decided that the explosion had been triggered by a mine. And, of course, the only people who could have planted the mine were the Spanish. This conclusion was almost certainly wrong, but that didn't matter. It gave the Americans a reason to go in.

On April 22, 1898, McKinley ordered a sea blockade of Cuba to strangle the trade in and out of the place. Two days later, Spain declared war on America. It was one of the dumbest moves in all history. The U.S. trounced them. The war was over in less than three months, and the Americans took possession of the Spanish Empire, which, in addition to Cuba, included the Philippine Islands on the other side of the world altogether.

Surprisingly, the U.S. did not declare Cuba to be part of its territory; it didn't make it one of the United States. Officially, it occupied the country for only four years. In fact, it controlled the country for the next sixty, until, in my lifetime, the nightmare figure of Fidel Castro loomed over the horizon.

But I'm getting ahead of myself again.

* * *

In the 1930s, '40s, and '50s, Cuba became the holiday destination for rich Americans. And where you find rich Americans, you will find the Mafia. The Mob moved in pretty early. Meyer Lansky, probably the cleverest gangster ever, saw the possibilities quicker than most. If Americans with plenty of money were sailing or flying south for a suntan, what else might they want while they were there? Class hotels? Certainly. Casinos, bars, brothels, drugs, racetracks, nightclubs? Definitely. Lansky went to Cuba and got himself appointed "adviser on gambling reform" to the U.S.-sponsored dictator, Fulgencio Batista. You can imagine what kind of gambling reform advice a casino-owning mobster would offer a tyrant: "Like, just keep the cops away, Fulgencio, unless we need a bad loser beaten up, okay? And let's not talk about taxes. Here, put this fat envelope in your pocket."

Lansky built himself a twenty-one-story hotel on the Havana seafront. His brother built one just down the way. Cuba became America's marijuana-smoking, coke-snorting, sex-drenched, rum-addled tropical playground. One of the privileged young Americans who went there, as an official guest, was John Fitzgerald Kennedy. Years later he would be one of the men who played a game of political poker, with the survival of the world at stake, and hurried me and Frankie toward our fate.

Yet again, I'm getting ahead of myself. It's not easy, keeping history in line. Herding cats in fog is easy by comparison.

* * *

America's party in paradise came to a sudden and shocking end. Castro's boatload of revolutionaries landed in Cuba late in 1956. They were betrayed almost immediately and ambushed by government forces. Fidel, his brother Raúl, and Che Guevara survived and hightailed it into the mountains. From there, the *Barbudos* (Bearded Ones) gathered new recruits and conducted a guerrilla war that lasted two years. Amazingly, the *Barbudos* won it. In December 1958, Batista fled and Fidel assumed power. He turfed the Yankees out and took their mining companies, sugar plantations, and fruit farms under state control. The music died and the lights went out in the hotels, casinos, and brothels.

For the U.S., it was a humiliating trauma. It was like losing your elegant, beautiful, easygoing mistress to a sweaty, hairy lout. The Americans were very sore about it. When John F. Kennedy was elected president in 1960, Castro was high up on his list of Things to Take Care Of. The Central Intelligence Agency created Operation Mongoose, dedicated to getting rid of Fidel. It planned acts of sabotage inside Cuba: propaganda, subversion, assassination attempts. Kennedy's younger brother Robert was given the task of overseeing the operation. The truth is, though, that Mongoose was a crackpot, cowboy organization. It came up with some highly imaginative plans to unseat Castro. They would put explosives into his cigars. They'd spray LSD into the radio studio from which Fidel broadcast his endless speeches to the nation; the tripped-out leader would start burbling about turning into a flying peacock or some such, and the Cubans would think he'd gone insane. They'd doctor Fidel's clothes with a chemical that caused total hair loss; without a beard, the leader of the Bearded Ones would also lose his credibility. Maybe those gullible Cubans would see his denuded chin as a sign from God.

The CIA also tried a more direct approach. Thousands of anti-Castro Cubans had gone into exile in the U.S. The CIA recruited fifteen hundred of them, armed them, and trained them (in secret, and not very well) to reinvade Cuba. The adventure turned into a disaster. When, in 1961, this amateur army landed on the island, Castro's forces overwhelmed them at a place called, rather unfortunately, the Bay of Pigs. The Americans had ships offshore and warplanes on standby. But President Kennedy, wanting to conceal his government's involvement in the plot, refused to send them to the rescue. The survivors of the invading force ended up in Castro's jails.

Two things that are important to our story came out of this sorry episode. The first is that among the high command of America's military, Kennedy instantly acquired a reputation for being "gutless." The word haunted him. When, a year later, he found himself in a showdown with the world's other superpower, the Soviet Union, he needed to show that he did have guts actually. And since nuclear missiles were involved, that was dangerous. The second thing is that after the Bay of Pigs fiasco, Castro announced that he was not just a nationalist but also a Communist and that Cuba would be governed much like the Soviet Union and would consider itself an ally of the Russians.

This was too much. This was a major upping of the temperature of the "cold war" between the West and the Soviet Union. America yelled, *"What? A Communist state just off Florida? A Russian outpost in the goddamn Caribbean? No way!"*

The U.S. military and the CIA got busy working on plans for the conquest of Cuba. And it would be no Mickey Mouse boat operation this time. This time, Fidel Castro and his hairy henchmen would find out what it felt like to have American fighter-bombers drop the fires of hell on their heads three hundred times a day.

As it turned out, things were not going to be that simple.

The leader of the Soviet Union, Kennedy's counterpart in that divided world back then, was Nikita Khrushchev. He'd been delighted, of course, when the crazy guy Castro had chucked out Batista and given America a bloody nose. Seeing as how the Soviets and the Americans were locked into a battle for world domination, any American loss was Russia's gain. My enemy's enemy is my friend, and all that. Besides, Khrushchev secretly harbored a romantic view of revolution. He'd spent most of his life struggling to survive the quiet treachery of Russian politics and was tired of it. The nice, clean idea of running from rock to rock shooting at Yankee capitalists, actually killing enemies rather than making deals with them, appealed to him very deeply. The trouble was that although he admired Fidel Castro, Khrushchev didn't know what to make of him. Castro hated America, which was good. But he talked about freedom all the time, and that was worrying. Freedom had no place in the Soviet system. Freedom was another word for anarchy, and that wouldn't do at all. And Comrade Khrushchev had a deep-seated distrust of men who wore beards. All the same, when Fidel announced that Cuba was an ally of the Soviet Union, Khrushchev was pleasantly surprised. For years now, the damned Americans had positioned their nuclear missiles on the Soviet Union's borders, in Turkey, Iran, South Korea. But now there was a pro-Soviet Cuba, deliciously close to the U.S. It offered some very tempting opportunities.

In April 1962 Khrushchev was entertaining his defense minister, Malinovsky, at his holiday home on the Black Sea coast. Standing on the balcony, looking south toward Turkey, Khrushchev said, "How about we stick a hedgehog down Kennedy's shorts?"

In May 1962, when, in England, Frankie should have been working for her O levels, when she was still beyond my wildest and most fevered dreams, a delegation of Russians arrived in Havana. They wore civilian clothes. They were, officially, "agricultural advisers" led by "Engineer Petrov." Petrov was, in fact, Marshal S. S. Biryuzov, head of the Soviet Strategic Rocket Services. His men didn't know anything much about agriculture, but they knew an awful lot about building bases from which ballistic missiles could be launched at the United States. By the time Frankie first slid her sweet and smoky tongue between my lips, the Russians were busy clearing patches of jungle and laying concrete pads for rocket launchers. And all through that summer, while Frankie and I sought secret places to explore each other, Soviet men and armaments were being smuggled into Cuba. They made the immense voyage from the Black Sea to the Caribbean in innocent-looking freighters or passenger ships. On the day in September that I returned to school, reluctantly and dazed by love, a ship called the *Omsk* arrived in Havana. Its cargo was sixty R-12 missiles, each capable of carrying a nuclear warhead equal to a million tons of high explosive.

Astonishingly, the Russians managed to do all this without the Americans catching on. It was an incredible feat. In all, eighty-five ships carried two hundred and thirty thousand tons of stuff from the Soviet Union to Cuba: trucks, bulldozers, prefabricated missile shelters, cranes, planes, food, petrol—the raw materials of war. American high-altitude reconnaissance aircraft—known as U-2s—regularly took photographs of Cuba, but it took months for the CIA to realize the significance of those funny little clearings and the barnlike structures taking shape around them. American naval patrols and American aircraft monitored the sea traffic in and out of Havana but could not see the thousands of men packed, like African slaves, in the unbearably hot and fetid spaces belowdecks. Relying on intercepted Soviet messages, U.S. intelligence agencies concluded that the *Omsk* was carrying barrels of oil. (Understandable, really, since the Russians didn't transmit useful messages such as: "Greetings, comrade. I hope the ballistic missiles aren't rolling around too much in that rough weather.") CIA agents in Cuba reported the swelling numbers of "agricultural advisers."

Kennedy and his military chiefs strongly suspected that these agronomists were Russian troops, but they hugely underestimated their numbers. The awesome truth was that by the third week of October 1962, there were forty thousand Soviet personnel in Cuba. And they had enough nuclear-capable missiles and planes to obliterate a good half of the United States.

The stage was set for what would become known as the Cuban Missile Crisis.

Frankie and I had no idea, of course, that all this was going on. And if we had known, we probably wouldn't have cared. We had other things on our minds.

24.
SEEING THE FOREST FROM THE TREES

THEY HAD RELUCTANTLY concluded their second assignation beneath the beeches. Frankie was tingling all over from what they had done: she'd let him put his hand *inside* the bra! Clem had been positively beside himself. The fluttering low inside her had been almost unbearably delicious.

Clem, followed by Frankie leading Marron, was about to step out onto the bridleway when he heard voices, laughter, from the direction of the lane. He held his hand up, signaling halt, and peered through the trees. Oh, God. Cushie Luckett and a girl. Susan Parsons! Oh, double God. Behind him, Frankie was calming the fretful horse. She looked over her shoulder.

"What?"

"People I know. They'll see us."

She bit her lower lip. It was what she did when she was thinking.

"Okay," she said. "You go back. I'll wait until they're gone."

Crouching in the undergrowth, he heard her *chut-chutting* Marron onto the track. Then silence, apart from late and busy birdsong.

She reassured Marron and pretended to busy herself with the buckle of his girth strap. The couple drew level with her. The boy had fair hair and a smirk. The girl was plump and had put on a sullen face.

"Orright, then, Miss Mortimer?" the boy said.

It was a horrible surprise that he knew who she was. She tried not to show it.

"Yes, thanks. Lovely evening, isn't it?"

"Yeah."

His gaze slid down Frankie's body, then back up again, unhurriedly.

"Nice 'orse," he said, not looking at it.

"Thank you."

"I daresay you'd sooner be ridun aroun on him than workun in them ole strorbry fields an that."

The plump girl pushed his arm.

"Leave orf, Cushie. Come on."

He gave Frankie a sort of salute.

"Nice meetun yer, Miss Mortimer. Mind how you go."

They walked away. The boy said something. The girl pushed him again and looked back, laughing.

Frankie leaned her head against Marron's flank. After a while she said, "They've gone."

Clem emerged from cover. Frankie made a gesture that included everything. The huge countryside her father owned.

"You'd think," she said, "that in a place like this a person could get a little privacy."

She made the remark lightly, but it acknowledged the heavy thing, the need, that was like a third presence when they should have been alone. *Privacy* wasn't the word, though. All young couples sought that and usually found it hard to come by. What Clem and Frankie needed, what was absolutely necessary, was *secrecy*. They knew that for them discovery would not be an embarrassment; it would be a calamity. During brief respites between kisses and caresses, they had whispered of it, giggling at the awfulness of the thought. Reducing peril to a thrilling riskiness. In truth, they were very afraid, particularly when they were apart.

What would her father do, Frankie wondered, when his rage (which she feared less than her mother's frigid disdain) had subsided? Put her under permanent guard, maybe? Lock her up? No, he'd send her away—that's what he'd do. To her ghastly grandparents in Quebec. She'd never see Clem again, that was for sure. She would almost certainly die of misery. She pictured it. Her deathbed in the gloomy old house in Montreal. The life draining from her wasted body. His murmured name on her dying breath.

Clem brooded homeward on his bike. Try as he might, he could not restrict his thoughts to her and what they had done, what she had let him do. His hands remembered it; his head was full of disaster. If his parents—let alone his gran, for God's sake—found out that he'd been doing dirty things in the woods

187

with *any* girl, there'd be hell to pay. His family had a fantastic capacity for disgust. But with *Gerard Mortimer's daughter?* It would be like . . . He couldn't think of an analogy. A bomb going off or something. The real horror, though, was what might happen if Mortimer found out. He'd come around to the house with a horsewhip or a shotgun. Or both. And he'd give his dad the sack. Definitely. And then . . . well, there was no "then" after that. Clem could not picture a life after that. He'd have to run away, though he had no idea what running away involved, where you might run away to. He imagined himself dying in a ditch, wearing rags, halfway to Moscow.

He gripped the handlebars more tightly and swung the bike left at Black Cat corner.

The sky was as pink as melon flesh. The shadow of the old air-raid siren fell across the road, and he passed through it. His family, sitting in the false moonlight of the television, would be silently asking themselves where he was.

25.

YOU LEARN NOTHING ABOUT SEX
FROM BOOKS, ESPECIALLY IF THEY'RE
BY D. H. LAWRENCE

BEFORE HE MET Frankie, Clem's ideas about sex were a greasy tangle woven from very unreliable materials: dirty rhymes and bawdy songs, smutty jokes, anatomically inaccurate drawings on lavatory walls, the lies of boastful older boys, the reported activities of someone's sister. No adult, no one who'd actually had sex, had ever told him anything about it, except to expressly forbid masturbation and warn of its crippling consequences. He had joined sniggering huddles with other boys, talking dirty, but their imaginings, like his, lived in fingery darkness, like wood lice under a brick. (Goz usually excluded himself from these lubricious debates. If he spoke of sexual matters at all, he did so with a casual dismissiveness, as if he knew all about them but they were beyond the horizon of his interest.)

Naturally, Clem had spent countless hours trying to imagine what a naked girl might look like, but he lacked certain key items of information. In his fourth year at Newgate, a boy called Taplock had circulated (for sixpence a loan) a nudist magazine with the strangely irrelevant title *Health and Efficiency*. It featured black-and-white photographs of robust and plain young women engaged in wholesome outdoor activities, such as netball and gardening. None of them wore any clothes, but when Clem's eyes zeroed in on the really important part of their anatomies, there was nothing there; their lower bellies tapered into a blur, a cloudy vacancy. He found this puzzling. Surely something so talked about, something for which there were so many forbidden names, must have some sort of substance.

(He had never heard, then, of doctoring photos with an airbrush. Later in life he would become an expert at it.)

Very occasionally, and with a warning glare, Jiffy would project painted nudes onto the art-room wall. During the Renaissance, it seemed, naked ladies were often to be found in the Italian countryside, sometimes in large numbers. Invariably, though, their Important Parts were obscured by wisps of gauzy stuff or annoying bits of foliage. Besides, Clem was not stirred by these women; they were a bit on the old side, and hefty-bottomed. Later, the class had looked at nudes by Picasso, but these were of no help at all.

Clem had, of course, studied the anatomical atlas kept on the top shelf of the art-room bookcase, paying particular attention to the chapter "The Reproductive Organs of the Female." The cross-sectional drawing, all interfolding tubes and hollows, labeled in vaguely religious-sounding Latin, revealed nothing to him about the dark magic of sex. In fact, it made him think, queasily, of a slice through a crustacean or some other form of marine life. He wondered and worried about how his own increasingly restless reproductive organ could possibly get involved in this complex and messy-looking arrangement.

Then, in October 1960, when Clem was in his first term in the fifth form, Penguin Books was taken to court for publishing an "obscene" novel that was "likely to deprave and corrupt" anyone unfortunate enough to read it. It was a modest paperback, costing three shillings and sixpence, entitled *Lady Chatterley's Lover*. The author was D. H. Lawrence, who had been dead for thirty years. It told the story of a supercharged love affair between Connie, the wife of a paralyzed aristocrat, and her husband's gamekeeper, Mellors. The trial (which was very comical and in all the papers) ensured that thousands of people who normally took little interest in books were very keen to read it. A copy was passed from hand to eager hand in the fifth-form locker room at Newgate. By the time it reached Clem, it was close to exhaustion. Its spine was done in. It fell open brokenly at the really dirty bits.

Even though Clem was astonished and thrilled to see the two rudest words in the English language printed in a proper book, he found the story heavy going. A lot of it was posh people conversing about life and the "spirit": the kind of talk his mum would dismiss as "squit." He couldn't relate in any way to the characters. (Although Mellors reminded him slightly of his dad, which was disturbing.) The sex didn't really get going until about halfway through. After that, Clem skipped the narrative and read the dog-eared juicy sequences, avidly and with mounting bafflement. Mellors didn't have a penis; he had a *"phallos,"* which he called John Thomas. It seemed to have mesmeric and magical powers that, as far as he knew, Clem's own unruly member sadly lacked. Lady Chatterley didn't like sex very much at first, as far as he could tell, but then she liked it a lot. As far as he could tell. Clem was keenly interested, suddenly, in why. In what girls felt, doing it. What, exactly, they liked about it. If, as he had been led to believe, sex was the hostile pronging of female flesh, why would they encourage it? How could they possibly enjoy it? But D. H. Lawrence's excited, turgid prose failed to enlighten him. Rather, it confused him. All sorts of things went on in Lady Chatterley's insides when she and the gamekeeper were at it. Bells rang, soft flames were ignited, feathers melted (there was a great deal of melting, generally), whirlpools swirled, waves swelled and billowed onto a distant shore, sea anemones clamored with their tendrils.

Clem couldn't quite believe it. He was fairly certain that he wouldn't like to be the cause of such a hubbub. What's more, it seemed to go on not only in Lady C's womb, which was fair enough, Clem supposed, but also in her bowels. This was surprising and deeply worrying. He hadn't imagined that *they* were involved.

He handed the book on to Clive Lines, who'd been pestering him for a week, and eventually succeeded in forgetting about it. But he would recall its troubling imagery—and the questions it left unanswered—when he rustled and wrestled with Frankie beneath the beech trees.

Clem's yearning curiosity was more encoiled by fear than it was for most other boys. This was because he belonged to a family that lived in dread of the very mention of sex, or anything remotely associated with it.

Win, of course, was long past thinking about you-know-what in personal terms. But it was out there. Everywhere. The young women in the laundry canteen, smoking cigarettes, sniggering about it. The young strumpets on the estate giving boys the come-on. That rock 'n' roll music all about what they called love. Now that Win was a member of the Brethren, the Saved, it was vital that she not be tainted by any of it. That its filthiness not come near her, lest she be infected and denied her place by the throne; that it cost her the cleansing bath in the blood of the Lamb. It was essential that the house she lived in was not sinful. And it wasn't. It was solace to her that the only nocturnal sound that came from the bedroom her daughter shared with George Ackroyd was snoring. Clem was a danger, being a young male and good-looking with it. He reminded Win of Percy. But he was a good boy. Hardworking. With any luck, he'd escape the snares of carnal sin until the Apocalypse. Nightly she prayed for him on the floor beside her bed, the rim of the chamber pot cold against her knees.

Ruth and George knew that the sexlessness of their marriage was unnatural. They were quietly ashamed of it, as other couples might be ashamed of a perversion. It was their closely guarded secret, and shared secrets are, of course, what keep people together. All the same, they were embarrassed by it. Hurt by it.

They coped by pretending that sex simply didn't exist. They wouldn't hear of it. Which was as difficult as Eskimos refusing to admit there is such a thing as snow.

Most evenings they would watch the television. Clem sat at the table, paying intermittent attention to the homework spread in front of him. Ruth and George sat on the new mock-leather sofa, George's ashtray between them. Win sat on an uncomfortable wooden stool because it was small punishment of her flesh.

Sometimes (with increasing frequency, it seemed to them) there would be a program in which love raised its ugly head. A couple would confess it, and then their faces would come close together, a slow, ghastly prelude to the inevitable kiss and the fade-out that suggested they were Doing It. At these awful moments, the dread entered the living room of 11 Lovelace Road like a chilling fog. In response to it, Win would look down, muttering, and accelerate her knitting. George would frown and light another Player. Ruth's plump neck would redden, and she would get to her feet.

"I can't put up with this soppy old squit," she'd say. "I'll go an put the kettle on."

And Clem returned to his homework until the embarrassing scene was over. Before, that is, Frankie happened to him. After, he gazed furtively at the screen from the shelter of his hand, afraid of the fear in the room, his poor heart tumbling to the memory of her parted lips and busy tongue.

26.
MAN IS NOT AN ISLAND; HE'S A PENINSULA

TIME, LIKE EVERYTHING else, was against them. By mid-August, the fruit-picking season, and Frankie's delicious penance, was at an end. Soon, very soon, there would be no more casual, urgent encounters with Clem in the nooks and fringes of her father's fields. The inevitability of this disaster made them frantic and despairing by turns. How would they be able to speak to each other? How could they arrange to meet?

The telephone offered tantalizing possibilities that were fraught with risk. There were three phones at Bratton Manor: one in the morning room, Gerard Mortimer's "center of operations"; another in the master bedroom, on Frankie's parents' bedside table; the third in the front hall. The morning room and her parents' bedroom were more or less out of bounds. If Frankie were discovered using either of those phones, it would be immensely suspicious. If she used the hall phone, there was always the chance that she would be overheard by Mrs. Cutting, the housekeeper, or one of the two live-in maids, or one of the part-time staff. All this was complicated by the fact that the phones were all on the same line, which meant that a conversation on one phone could be overheard by anyone who picked up either of the others. Clem could not call her, of course. It was not proper for the youngest member of the household to answer the telephone. And if she did, thus arousing suspicion, her parents could simply ring the local operator and ask who had just called, and then the game would be up.

Despite all this, they settled on a desperate stratagem. Clem would be at home between three thirty and four thirty every weekday. Frankie would call him from the front hall phone sometime during this hour, it being a relatively unbusy part of the day at the manor, and say, "Tonight, quarter to eight," or "Tomorrow, two o'clock." (But she could not call on a Wednesday, because it was Ruth's half day off from the chemist's.) Clem would name the place. They'd hang up. Five seconds, at most. Even so, there were days when she dared not or could not make the call. Then Clem would spend the hour in an agony of waiting and the remainder of the day in numb despair. Naming the place was increasingly problematic. They'd abandoned their hiding place in Skeyton Woods. Twice they'd been almost discovered: once by warring young boys, then by a man with a dog. So, after his parents and Win had gone to work, he'd set off on his bike to reconnoiter places that were roughly equidistant from Millfields and the manor. He'd found one or two that might be suitable. The trouble was that he knew the surrounding countryside far more intimately than Frankie did, and their furtive calls were not long enough for him to give her foolproof directions. One afternoon he waited in a snug little copse for two hours, not knowing that she was urging Marron up and down a lane half a mile away, looking for the way to it. They had their first argument the following day.

"It's simply ridiculous," Frankie said, refusing to lie down on the thick bed of tea-brown pine needles.

"Frankie, I said just look for—"

"I *know* what you said. That's not really the *point*, is it? The whole thing is ridiculous. I must be mad."

She was still angry, or pretending to be, when she unbuttoned her blouse.

Then he found the perfect place.

He was in misery at the time. Three whole days had passed without a call. He'd spent them getting nowhere with his holiday homework.

Is Keats "half in love with easeful Death"? Cite evidence from two of the poems.

Explain the consequences of the Treaty of Utrecht, 1713, in terms of subsequent European history. Quote your sources.

Produce a piece of work entitled The Intensification of Red. *It can be either representational or abstract.*

When Frankie lets you put your hand Down There, which soon she will surely do, what will you do with it? Show your work.

On the morning of the fourth day, he rode to a telephone box on the far side of Borstead and dialed Bratton Manor. His finger in the dial shook, then slipped. He had to start again. A woman answered.

"Bratton Morley 239."

As if it were a question. A Norfolk accent, the *t*'s of "Bratton" gone missing. He hung up and pressed the button to get his coins back.

He mounted his bike and rode nowhere in particular. He found himself on the Gunston road and regretted it: it was a long, slow, undulating climb. He thumbed the gearchange and leaned down on the pedals, lifting himself from the saddle. The effort of it, if he focused on it, almost drove the hurt away. It was not a road Clem knew well. There were no fruit fields in this direction, and Gunston was nothing. Borstead was Las Vegas compared to Gunston. At the top of the rise, he stopped to rest for a minute, intending to turn back. There were no hedges alongside this stretch of road, just low banks of fading grass punctuated by stunted hawthorns.

He was surprised how vast the view was from this modest elevation: almost three hundred and sixty degrees, although the horizon was blurred by heat haze. Ahead and off to the left, he could make out the stumpy tower of Gunston church. On either side of the road, fields of wheat stubble stretched into the distance. Huge fields, bigger than any he had ever seen, uninterrupted by hedgerows. Alien, somehow. Had it always been like this? It had been a couple of years, maybe, since he'd been out this way, but Clem was fairly sure it hadn't been possible to see such distances back then. What had happened? Where had all the trees gone?

He became aware of a faint, uneven rumbling. Shading his eyes, he could just make out the lumbering bulk of a combine harvester. No, *three* combine harvesters, working side by side in a wide cloud of dust. He'd never seen that before, either.

The openness of this landscape, its bareness, confused him. Spooked him slightly. It was as if he'd accidentally cycled into another country. He climbed onto the bank to his right and gazed around, trying to get his bearings. He'd been riding south, so he was facing westward. He'd come about three miles, so he was looking toward Bratton Manor. And Frankie, perhaps. About two miles away? He could just make out the gray-green hump of Skeyton Woods, but the house was hidden by a fold in the brown and naked land.

Clem remounted the bike and turned toward home. He reckoned that after a few shoves on the pedals, he'd be able to freewheel downhill for the best part of a mile. It was the first pleasant thought of the day. Then in the afternoon there'd be the hour of waiting for the phone to ring. The hour willing it to ring.

He coasted down the dipping road for five minutes, and then, where it leveled again, braked. He hadn't noticed the knot of trees and the tangled hedge on his way up the hill. He'd been concentrating on the climb, and besides, he hadn't known at the time that something so ordinary was about to become an unusual feature of the landscape. Now he saw that the disorderly hedge had overgrown a line of bent and rusty railing and that the gap in it contained a wrought-iron gate hanging aslant from a single hinge. Something—curiosity, luck, instinct—made him wheel the bike over to it. A rectangular slat of wood lay in the grass under the drunken gate. He picked it up and turned it over. A word had been carved into it, long ago. Clem cleaned the dirt away with the edge of his palm. The first five letters jolted him: *Frank*. Then: *lins*. *Franklins*. He heard the sound of a car and dropped the sign and shoved the bike through the gateway. He crouched behind the hedge. The car passed. He stood up, wondering why he had needed not to be seen.

The trees nearest him were youngish sycamores. Trees that grew like weeds if you let them. They'd colonized what might once upon a time have been a lawn. He was standing on what might once upon a time have been a path or drive. He left the bike where it was and followed the path, here and there turning sideways to shoulder through branch and bracken.

He almost stumbled into the pit where the house had once stood: its cellar, he supposed. Three sides of it marked by the low remains of walls, a gable wall higher than the others, all now gripped and pierced by tree roots and sprouting fern. The overgrown path continued past the ruin, and Clem pushed along it, arriving at last at the rear of a mossy redbrick building that looked pretty much intact. He walked around its corner and stopped dead, confounded.

He found himself standing on a low peninsula of wilderness that protruded into the vast ocean of stubble. Its edge was defined by a stand of tall and ancient Scots pines, their trunks all reddish, peeling scales. He stood in the mottled shadow of the trees and gazed out. Everything ahead of him and around him looked scalped and baked, but now this did not dismay him. Because he was looking down on Bratton Manor. It was closer than he'd thought it would be. He could make out the stubs of its chimneys, part of its walled courtyard, the drive curving away between the chestnuts. He couldn't resist the desire to cup his hands around his mouth and call her name. The word disappeared, echoless, into the enormous sky.

Clem turned away and looked at the brick barn behind him. It was quite large, about forty feet long and twelve high. It had no doors, just a wide opening with a weathered timber frame. Above that, a slumping oak lintel under a roof of skewed slates. The only window, a small shuttered aperture, high up, to the right of the door.

Inside, it took several moments for his eyes to adjust to the dimness. It was not entirely dark; sharply defined shafts of light tilted down from where slates were missing. He stood still until he could make out the obstacles on the leaf-strewn floor: a bundle of fence stakes wrapped in barbed wire, a heap of moldering sacks, an upended wooden thing like a child's crudely carpentered bed. Close to the back wall, a rough narrow board rose up. A banister, of sorts, beside a flight of steps. He looked up. The building had a second floor. Or rather half of a second floor: a hayloft supported by heavy wooden beams that spanned the building. The steps were narrow, no wider than the rungs of a ladder. He tested each tread with his foot before trusting it with his weight. They all gave and groaned, but did not break.

At the top, the darkness was more intense. On the far side of the loft, there were four thin lines of light, forming a square. It took Clem several moments to work out that this was the shuttered window he'd seen from outside. He made his way toward it on his hands and knees, slowly, horribly afraid of the floor giving way, of falling into darkness among its wreckage. His hands encountered dry leaves, straw, splintery planks. When he reached the window, he steadied his breathing. His fingers found a wooden latch but could not turn it. He clubbed at it with his fist, scraping his knuckles, until he felt it give way. He thumped the shutters, but they wouldn't open. He thought about it, then pulled instead and fell backwards in a blaze of light.

Kneeling—the roof was close to his head now—he peered out. For an absurd moment he felt like a character from an adventure story. The powder boy looking out through the gun port of a man-o'-war. The young hero finding his way out of a dark labyrinth of caves. Then far more thrilling possibilities occurred to him.

He was looking between two pines at the bare undulating fields. There were the roofs of Bratton Manor again. The combine harvesters were out of sight beyond a swell of the land, but he could tell where they were from their dust cloud. So how did they get there? Bratton Manor Farm was farther over to the right, invisible from where he was. But the machines must have come to the fields from there.

And if they could, so could Frankie.

* * *

The phone rang at three forty, almost stopping his heart.

"Seven this evening," she said, very quietly.

He was so sickened by relief that he almost forgot the short speech he'd practiced.

"Go to the farm, Frankie, then up into the fields where your dad's combines are working. Thas eastwuds, toward the Gunston road, okay? Look for a group of big pine trees and a barn. You can't miss it. About a mile and half. It's called Franklins."

He waited.

She said, "I don't . . ."

Then she was speaking more loudly. "I don't know, I'm afraid. Yes, I'll tell him you called. Thank you. Good-bye."

Click.

His hand was shaking as he put the receiver down.

It had been the longest phone conversation they'd ever had. He prayed they hadn't blown it.

Frankie loitered in the hallway until she was fairly sure that the coast was clear. Then she slipped into the morning room. The big collage of aerial photographs was now liberally marked with blue rectangles, arrows, and dates. She tracked her finger from the manor toward the Gunston road. Her nail passed through several groups of trees and meandering hedges, but she knew that the landscape didn't look like that anymore. She tried to repicture it, to wipe those details out. She reached the road and tracked south a little way until she came to a clump of trees shaped a bit like an arrowhead aimed at the manor, at her. She studied it closely, biting her lip. Yes, those might well be pines. And was that a roof?

It seemed to her that the thump of her heart might be audible.

Her parents were going out tonight.

She would have time.

Okay.

She went to the door, then glanced back. There was a pack of Three Castles cigarettes on her father's desk. She hesitated, then went and picked it up and shook it. It sounded sort of half empty. She stuffed it into her skirt pocket.

Clem and Frankie leaned on their elbows, their shoulders touching. Outside the small window, the sky above the horizon was a deep amber. Thin streamers of cloud the same color as their cigarette smoke.

"I'm really sorry. Daddy suddenly announced that he was going to London for a business meeting. I thought, Great. Then Mummy decided that we would go, too, and do some shopping. I tried to get out of it, honestly. I couldn't call you before we left. You must have been worried sick."

Below them, Marron snuffled and stamped his feet.

"Yeah, I was. I thought you'd . . . You know."

She turned her face to his.

"What? Gone off you?"

They kissed, tongue slithering over tongue, cigarettes held away.

"So what did you do? In London."

"I told you. Shopping."

"What, for three days? What did you buy?"

She shrugged.

"You know. Clothes and so forth."

He felt there was something she wasn't telling him. He didn't want to know what it was. But he couldn't keep the sulk from his face. She saw it and plucked the cigarette from his fingers and stubbed it out on the floor, then did the same with her own. She rolled on top of him, pressing down on him, kissing him.

When she had breath enough, she said, "Put your hands lower down. Please."

A lifetime later she lifted herself off him, tossed her hair aside, and looked at her watch, a small silver-framed square on a black leather strap.

"I don't want to stop," she said, "but I have to go now."

"I thought you said your mum and dad were out."

"It's not just them."

She was kneeling astride him. With the last light behind her, all he could see of her face was the glimmer in her eyes. He took her breasts in his hands.

"Oh, Lordy," she said.

"Frankie."

"No. Clem."

"Please."

"No. I have to go."

She stood, stooping under the roof. He thought she was angry.

He said, "What d'you think of this place, then? Will it do?"

She looked over her bare shoulder into the gloom.

"It needs tidying up a bit. But, yes, it'll do."

27.
A BIT OF CHIAROSCURO

THEY FURNISHED THE loft modestly. An inventory of its contents would be brief: a horse blanket (clean) from the manor's tack room; a sleeping bag (only slightly less so), last used three years ago on Clem's one and only (and miserable) school cadet camp; a few candles and a box of matches (sometimes, when dusty rain flurried at them over the naked fields, they found it necessary to close the shutters); a shallow wooden box, found beneath the loft, kept supplied with carrots and apples (to placate Marron when he grew restless); fear (often); delirium (frequently).

They embarked upon their halcyon days. Their brief golden age.

Over breakfast, Frankie would tell her parents that she thought she might take Marron on a nice long hack, then go to the kitchen and ask Cook, sweetly, if she would prepare a packed lunch.

Nicole found it vaguely worrying.

"Don't you think it strange, this sudden enthusiasm for riding, Gerard?"

Mortimer replied from behind the *Daily Telegraph*.

"Is it? She's always been rather keen, hasn't she? It's good for her, anyway—keeps her out of mischief."

He lowered the newspaper. "Besides, what else would she be doing?"

Nicole pursed her lips and tilted her head: a Gallic gesture Gerard had once found charming, but which now irritated him.

Frankie was careful to vary her route away from the manor, and this might add a mile or more to the ride. No matter; the thought of Clem's impatience, and the ways he would show it, excited her. She smiled, remembering Maddie: *They get into the most extraordinary states.*

"Where're you been all day, Clem? You weren't here when I come home for dinner."

He'd been waiting for the question.

"Homework, Mum."

"Homework? What homework?"

"Art. We're doing landscape next term. I'm supposed to do loads of sketches over the holidays."

Ruth filled the teapot from the electric kettle and looked at him.

"And hev you?"

"Yeah."

"Can I see 'em?"

Clem shrugged. "If you want to."

He was almost always at Franklins long before Frankie got there. He felt, though he'd never acknowledged the feeling, that he should be. Because he'd found the place and therefore had a kind of ownership of it. Because it was important that *she* come to *him*. A kind of power. Besides, the waiting excited him. He was becoming addicted to the anticipation of her arrival, the long bodily thrill of expecting her. Then she would lead the horse into the barn and throw herself upon him, having worked herself up into a state, hoping he'd be there.

It was like dreaming and waking into the dream.

Instinct, rather than the need for an alibi, made him bring his sketchbook and his pencils to the barn. Waiting for her, he drew the coarse, complex bark of the pines. The way the trees looked from twenty daring paces into the field. Or the ferns bursting through the walls of the ruined house. The overhanging shadows on the path. Drawing was like putting the lid on a pan coming to the boil. The pictures had a jittery spontaneity and quickness that he'd never previously found within himself.

Ruth said, "Where's this, then?"

"Them trees? Out Swafield way."

"I like this one, that ole building. Where's that?"

Clem tried to look ashamed of himself.

"Nowhere. I made that up. Jiffy'll never know."

There were other drawings, hidden drawings, that he would slit his own throat rather than show her.

On Saturdays he'd tell Ruth that he was going to the matinee at the Regal and afterward he was going to muck about with Goz. On his way home, fizzing from his day with Frankie, he'd stop at a phone box and call Goz, who'd tell him what to say. There'd been a cartoon, an episode of *Flash Gordon,* another cartoon, then the main feature: a Western starring Alan Ladd. Goz always went to the matinee. It was the nearest he got to religious observance. The petty vendettas in the stalls, the ostentatious flirting behind him, the lobbing of chewed sweets out of the dark, never distracted him. His recall of films was perfect.

Clem got bored, listening to the recitation.

"Orright, comrade. Got that. Ta."

He and Frankie discovered each other because now they could spare the time to talk. They found each other equally astonishing, their ways of life equally unimaginable, exotic. School was common ground, though; the horrors of Newgate and Saint Ethelburger's were interchangeable. They worked themselves into ecstasies of giggling, fantasizing about the sexual predilections of nuns and schoolmasters.

"You're clever, though, Clem. I could never do A levels."

"'Course you could."

"No, honestly. What would be the point, anyway?"

This troubled him. It had never occurred to him to question

the purpose of education. It was, obviously, a means of escape. A way into a different life. He chewed on one of Frankie's sandwiches while it dawned on him that she probably wasn't looking for, didn't need, a flight from whom and what she was.

"What's in this?" he asked her.

"Smoked salmon. Do you like it?"

"It's orright."

She'd filched a flagon of cider from the pantry on her way out to the stables. They'd drunk half of it. They were both a little high. She took another swig.

"What'll you do after art school? Will you starve in a garret, painting things too brilliant for anyone to appreciate until after you're dead?"

He laughed, although he didn't know what a *garret* was.

"Shouldn't think so."

She looked at him very seriously, resting her head on her hand.

"We'll run away," she said. "We'll live in Paris. It'll be okay because I speak French, but we'll be terribly poor and have to live on bread and wine and tangerines. I'll be your model. You'll paint me over and over again. Then a rich gallery owner will discover you, and you'll be fabulously successful and famous."

(Frankie had once read a slightly racy novel in which these things happened. She left out the last bit, when the model ran off with the rich man, leaving the artist to paint her, obsessively, from memory, until he died of heartbreak.)

"Isn't that a simply gorgeous idea? Let's do it, Clem."

"Yeah. Okay, that's what we'll do."

"I mean it. Promise me that's what we'll do."

"Frankie . . ."

"Apart from anything else, it means you could spend all day looking at me in the nude. You'd like that, wouldn't you?"

His throat tightened. They'd reached the underwear stage of their courtship. Feeling each other in the gloom was one thing, though. Gazing frankly at each other was another. They'd tacitly avoided it. He'd turn away from her to pull his jeans up while she rebuttoned her blouse.

"I want you to draw me," she said now.

"No."

"Why not?"

He turned away from her. "I can't."

"Why not?"

He shrugged. The way the muscles worked in his narrow back delighted her.

"I want you to. Clem. *Please*."

"I ent . . . I'm not much good at that sort of thing."

She put her arm around him and pressed the side of her face against his skin, but he remained tense, withdrawn from her.

"Clem? Clem, what?"

"You're too beautiful. I draw you all the time, but it never really look, looks, like you. I'm not good enough."

"Yes, you are. It's because you've been doing it from memory."

It had been a silly dare, a whim, but now she found herself wanting, needing, him to do it. To gaze at her, to study her.

And in the end he yielded, as she'd known he would.

He crawled over to his bag and took out the cartridge-paper pad, the drawing board, the old slide-top wooden pencil box. When he turned back to her, the breath snagged in his gullet. She had removed her brassiere and was lying on the sleeping bag in what she imagined to be an artistic pose. On her side, her head supported on her right hand, her legs drawn slightly up, the left hand resting on her thigh.

"Like this?"

He could only nod.

He sat with his back against the wall, the bricks cool and coarse against his skin, and propped the drawing board against his knees.

His first lines were weak, uncertain. How could they not be? His hand and breathing were unsteady, and he could only bear to look at her in quick, furtive glances.

He erased the effort.

"I can't do it."

"Oh, Clem. *Please*." She drew the word out childishly. "You can't give up already. Try again."

He stared down at the paper.

She said, "It's because you're not looking at me."

"'Course I am."

"No, you're not. Not properly."

So he raised his head. His imagination was so hectic with goatish schoolboy lust that he could not see her. Her serious- ness, her concentrated stillness, both aroused and frightened him. Eventually, it was only the fear of disappointing her that forced him to see her as what she was, rather than as something he urgently wanted.

In the strong low light from the little window, she was an almost abstract arrangement of pallor and shade. One half of her hair shone above the pale descending curve of her arm. A bright cheekbone, one bright eye. An unutterably beautiful track of light that was her left shoulder, arm, thigh. Her breasts, two soft, almost luminous, crescents.

"*Draw the shadows,*" Jiffy always said. "*Start from the dark and work inward.*" Clem found a 4B pencil and, using it at an angle to the paper, blocked in the darknesses of Frankie's body, smudging and shaping the lines with his forefinger, cleaning their edges with the eraser. She emerged, ghostly at first, then solidified. Every time he looked up, the light had reduced her. He worked faster, brightening her with chalk.

"My arm's going to sleep," Frankie said, not moving her head.

"Hang on. Nearly finished."

He bluffed the folds of the sleeping bag and leaned back from the drawing, slumping against the brickwork.

No; it hadn't worked. It was weak. It contained nothing of what he really felt about her.

He scrabbled in the pencil box for the fat 6B pencil and used it to obliterate the tentative lines he'd used to suggest the background. Working quickly, he used his fingertips to press the graphite into the surface of the paper, forming dark clouds that became intensely black where they met the luster of her body. He did the same with the foreground, casting heavy shadows over the nervous cross-hatching meant to suggest straw. He deepened the shading of her lower leg, belly, and left breast.

Yes; he had her now. Or something like her. The old sleeping bag was like an opening in a night sky. She floated in it, burnished by moonlight, not daylight. Dressed in shadows, she seemed utterly naked, confident, expectant.

He had drawn his dream of a night with her.

"Okay," he said, "you can move now. If you like."

She sat up, cross-legged, tossed her hair back, massaged her right arm with her left hand. She saw his gaze shift to her bosom. It was a different kind of looking now. She shivered, pretending it was because she was cold, and pulled the sleeping bag around her.

"Well? Are you going to show me or not, Picasso?"

He set the pad down in front of her and rummaged in the pockets of his discarded jeans for the cigarettes and matches. He lit up a Woodbine and went to stare out of the window, not willing to watch her face.

"Gosh."

He waited.

"It's nothing like your other drawings. It's sort of . . . spooky."

"I told you I wasn't any good at—"

"Shut up, you idiot. It's absolutely fabulous. I had no idea."

"You don't hev to be nice about it. It don't even look like you."

"It doesn't have to look like me. It *is* me. It's beautiful, actually."

She said it so coolly, so matter-of-factly, that he could not

215

believe her, although he desperately wanted to. He heard her move, then felt the naked press of her body and the tickle of her hair against his bare back, her arms coming around him. He gasped smokily.

"It *is* beautiful, my own boy genius," she said.

He tried to turn to face her, but she clasped her fingers together on his chest and held him still.

"Don't move yet," she whispered.

She didn't want him to see that her eyes were wet.

He had captured her. He had taken from her the safety of believing that he was less than her. That penultimate barrier was down.

She said, "Can I keep it?"

Later, when she undressed for her bath, she saw the prints and smears his blackened fingers had left upon her.

28.
THE NIGHTS DRAW IN

IN ALL, HE made five drawings of her. The best one, in his opinion, was of her naked back.

He asked her to sit facing the window, cross-legged, with her hands in her lap.

She said, "I'm cold."

"Wait," Clem said. He lit the remains of three candles glued by their own wax on to a short plank of wood, then closed the shutters.

"Is that all right?"

"As long as you're quick."

He'd added five sticks of pastel to his kit. He used one to yellow the central area of the paper into candlelight. Her right side was slightly uplit from the open doorway, and he chalked the curve of it, highlighting the shoulder blade, marveling at the swell of her hips. As always, he blacked out everything surrounding her, then, with a soft pencil, devoted himself to the delicacy of her flesh. Again, he made her a glowing abstraction. He could hardly see what he was doing, but that didn't matter. Drawing her had become an act of love, of seduction. A ritual.

He showed her his work, disowning it.

Still studying it, she sighed and dragged him down onto her. Parting for him. Letting him do almost everything.

Pulling away at the last fevered moment because—

"We mustn't. I can't. . . . You know I . . ."

He rolled onto his back. She watched his chest rise and fall to his quickened breathing.

"Clem?"

"Yeah. I know. Sorry."

"You're not angry, are you?"

"No."

"You are."

He turned his face to hers, touched it with the backs of his fingers.

"I'm not. I love you, Frankie. It don't matter."

"It does, actually." She bit her lip. "It's not that I . . ."

"I know. It's all right."

Then everything diminished. Clem went back to school. The autumn evenings dwindled and chilled. Now they had only weekends and could not rely on those.

They lost the second to savage rain.

He sat through classes a lummox.

"Ackroyd? *Ackroyd!*"

"Sir?"

Tash Harmsworth was glaring at him.

"You are, I believe, reading the part of the Fool?"

"Sir."

"King Lear's Fool is a *jester,* a *wit,* not an idiot. Therefore it is not necessary for you to adopt the facial expression of a demented sheep. It is, however, necessary that you read the lines aloud."

"Yes, sir. Sorry, sir."

Goz slid a helpful finger onto the page.

Clem cleared his throat, if not his mind.

"'Dost thou know the difference, my boy, between a bitter fool and a sweet fool?'"

On the morning of the third Friday of term, he knew that he couldn't get through the day. It had been eleven days since he'd been with her. The effort of hiding his dejection, let alone his anguished tumescence, from his parents was exhausting him. He was terribly afraid that if he did not regularly tend the fire of Frankie's love, it would go out. Eleven days! Ashes, ashes. He wanted to be alone to grieve.

At the corner of Norwich Road, he said, "Goz, wait a minute."

Goz braked and came back.

"What?"

"I'm gorna skive off for the day."

"And why is that, comrade?"

"I just am."

Goz cocked his head.

"Art thou meeting thine own true love, where a 'willow grows aslant a brook'?"

It was a morning of shifting drizzle. They both wore the awful and compulsory school raincoats.

"There's no need to take the piss. Anyway, no."

"Anything you want me to say, if they ask?"

Clem shrugged. "I dunno. I don't care. Whatever you like."

"Right. Please, sir, when I called for Ackroyd, there was a cross crudely painted on the front door. I assumed the Plague had spread to Lovelace Road, so I hastened by with a bunch of medicinal herbs pressed to my nose. I expect they're shoveling quicklime onto his bloated corpse as we speak."

"Yeah. Ideal."

"I'll drop the homework round later, then, shall I? Fiveish?"

The weather was in two minds. Behind the veils of mizzle, the sky was a white glare. Half a mile along the Gunston road, Clem, sweating, stopped and took off the raincoat. He rolled it up and belted it to his handlebars, then stood gazing into the blurred ocher distance. His moment of liberation had passed; now the thought of the lonely and silent day ahead was dreadful. Instantly, he was overwhelmed by self-pity, dizzied by it. He leaned his forearms on the bundled raincoat and lowered his head, gasping in air, fighting back tears.

He couldn't go home. The house would be empty, but some nosy bleddy neighbor would see him and be around as soon as his mother came home, pretending concern for his health.

Onward to Franklins, then. There was nowhere else.

The approach to the remains of the house was carpeted with big five-pointed sycamore leaves: stars cut out of yellow paper by inexpert children. They attached themselves to his wet shoes. He trudged around the corner of the barn, then, at the doorway, recoiled in shock when he found himself face-to-face with Marron. The horse was alarmed, too, throwing its head up and backing away.

"Frankie?"

A small frightened cry from above. A scuffling.

He thought, She's here with somebody else.

Her face, all eyes, appeared below the rail of the loft.

"Clem?" It was not much more than a whisper.

He eased past Marron and stumbled up the stairs. The shutters were only slightly ajar, and he stood unsighted for several seconds, holding on to the stair post. Neither of them spoke; they stared at each other almost as if each had trespassed onto the other's private space. Caught each other out.

She was alone. Thank God, thank God. Kneeling. Wearing a black turtleneck sweater and brown cord trousers. A heavy-looking waterproof jacket was spread over the sleeping bag.

At last she said, "I've never seen you in your school uniform. It's terribly smart."

"Frankie."

"How did you know I was here?"

"I didn't. I just . . ."

"You just knew."

She lifted her arms toward him, and he stumbled over to her and knelt and held her.

After a while he sensed that she was hiding from him. He lifted his hands to her shoulders and pushed her gently back.

"You've been crying."

She snuffled.

"Haven't."

"Have."

She unbuttoned his blazer and slid her hands inside it. She pressed the side of her face against his shirt.

"Yes, all right, I have. I've been here a couple of times for a jolly good cry."

"Hev you? Why?"

"Because, you idiot, it's not exactly possible to do it at home. It might just arouse suspicion if I traipsed about the house in tears, wailing your name."

Shamefully, he exulted in the thought, the image, of her doing it.

"And," she said, "when I come here and wrap the bag around me, it's almost like you're here, too. I can smell you. I mean that in the nicest possible way, actually."

"I think about you all the time, Frankie. All the time. I've been going nuts."

For some reason this made her giggle.

"What?"

She didn't explain. She lifted her face to his.

Halfway through the long kiss, they let themselves fall sideways onto the floor.

"How long've we got?"

She propped her head on her hand and looked down at him.

"I have to be home for lunch at one o'clock."

"What about this afternoon? I'll wait here for you."

"No. Tomorrow afternoon should be all right, though. Unless the weather is beastly."

She lifted herself up and knelt over him. She pulled the turtleneck off over her head and threw it away. Loosened his green-and-gold tie, pulled it off him, and draped it around her own neck. Looked down at him coquettishly.

And for him it was as though everything had fallen apart, rearranged itself according to some pattern beyond his imagining or courage. The dark tumble of her hair, her teasing eyes, the stupid school tie with its pseudo-mythic crest hanging between her lace-cupped breasts, the fact that he should not be there, the fact that he was there, lost, that this rich, beautiful girl would take off most or all of her clothes for him, that a dirty dream was real, his dreadful uniform hurled off and strewn in a dim and trespassed space, that it was all incredibly dangerous, that they could get killed for love, that his gropy imaginings had resolved into adoration, that her nipples were discernable through the skinny fabric, that her groin was lowering onto his, that his parents and his gran would go gaping into death not knowing what they'd missed, that there was an impatient horse downstairs, that instead of being in history he was in love, that all shyness was gone, that cold was irrelevant, that everything was against them, that she was against him, pressing herself against him, that it was all, like art, outrageously delicate and exultantly poised in the void, her wonderful flesh in the dimness, his breath her breath, her hands taking his hands wherever they wanted.

Like this, forever. Please, forever and ever. A prayer. A jointing of their bodies in and against the dark. Amen.

"No. Clem. No. Please."

"You want us to."

"Yes. I do. You know I do."

"Frankie."

She rolled onto her side, her back to him.

After a long silence she said, "I know it must be awful for you."

"It's not that. It's just . . ."

"What?"

"You and me, the way we feel . . . it just seems wrong not to."

Again she was silent for a long moment. Rooks croaked at one another. He shivered as the sweat cooled on his skin.

Then she said, "Yes. It does. It *is* wrong."

She turned onto him and teased the tip of his nose with hers.

"Do you think you could get a sheath from somewhere?"

"A what?"

She bit her lip.

"A rubber johnny."

29.

THE LIMITED OPPORTUNITIES FOR OBTAINING CONTRACEPTIVES IN NORTH NORFOLK IN 1962 . . .

O R, TO BE more precise, in Borstead.
There were two options:
1. Scott's, the barber's
2. Griffin's, the chemist's

The small window of Albert Scott's shop on Church Street featured four photographs of handsome, smiling men sporting oiled but different hairstyles, none of which was available to clients on the premises. Scott did only one kind of haircut, the kind that he had been inflicting on the men and boys of Borstead since 1936. It involved ten minutes' smart work with comb and scissors, followed by several runs up the back of the neck with manual clippers that clacked like a mad dog's teeth. The window also displayed a dusty collection of combs, brushes, and gentlemen's shaving requisites, and, down in one corner, a little yellow plastic sign shaped like a tent. On it, the almost-word ONA above the word LUBRICATED. ONA was also printed on the small packages that Scott would supply to men who nodded when he murmured, brushing the hair from their lapels, "Something for the weekend, sir?"

Scott had been murdering Clem's hair, and his father's, since Clem was five. So it would be perfectly fine if he marched in there and requested, "A packet of three Ona, Mr. Scott, please. No, on second thoughts, make that two packets. I've got a lively weekend coming up."

No, it wouldn't.

And his mum worked in Griffin's.

So that was that.

MRBM LAUNCH SITE 1
SAN CRISTOBAL, CUBA
23 OCTOBER 1962

MISSILE SHELTER

FUEL TANK TRAILERS

SILE ERECTOR

CABLE

PART TWO

BLOWING THINGS APART

TRACKED PRIME MOVERS

30.
WASHINGTON, D.C., TUESDAY, OCTOBER 16, 1962: "THOSE SONS A BITCHES RUSSIANS!"

IN THE CABINET Room of the White House, President John F. Kennedy sat, as usual, halfway down the long table, with his back to the tall windows that looked out onto the Rose Garden. On the mantelpiece of the unused fireplace to his right sat a model of the *Mayflower*. Above that, a portrait of George Washington. Hidden in the light fixtures, microphones that fed tape recorders in the White House basement. Of the sixteen men in the room, only JFK and his brother Robert — Bobby — knew the microphones were there.

Two CIA men were in the room: Lundahl was the expert on aerial photography; Graybeal was the expert on Soviet missiles. On the table, mounted on boards, were three large black-and-white aerial photographs of parts of Cuba. They'd been taken, through a powerful zoom lens, from a U-2 spy plane. Lundahl used a wooden pointer to indicate items of interest.

"These are missile trailers, Mr. President. Tent areas over here. This is equipment for erecting launchers."

The men around the table leaned forward to the pictures.

"Are you sure? To me, uh, I dunno. Looks like it might be just the basement for a farm or something."

"No, sir," Lundahl said. "These rectangular objects here? These are medium-range ballistic missile trailers."

"How do you know that? That these are for medium-range missiles?"

"From their length, Mr. President," Graybeal said. "They are sixty-seven feet long, precisely the length of the Soviet MRBMs paraded through Moscow last May Day."

"I see. And the range of these missiles?"

Graybeal said, "Launched from this site in Cuba, they'd come through the roof of this building thirteen minutes later."

Bobby Kennedy whacked his bunched fist onto the table.

"Shit! Those sons a bitches Russians!"

"Are they ready to be fired?" JFK wanted to know.

"No, sir."

Robert McNamara, the defense secretary, interrupted. "We have *some* reason to believe that the nuclear warheads are not yet present. And hence that they are not ready to fire."

JFK looked to the CIA missile man. "Mr. Graybeal?"

"That is correct, Mr. President. Nuclear warheads require specialized storage facilities. We have no photographic evidence that these are in place."

"So how long have we got? We can't tell, can we, how long before they could be fired? Before they're, uh, mated with the warheads?"

McNamara, a man with rimless spectacles and hair like

231

thick black varnish, said, "No. But clearly we do have some time before these missiles are ready."

General Maxwell Taylor growled, clearing his throat. Taylor was the chairman of the Joint Chiefs of Staff—in other words, the supremo of the armed forces. He'd parachuted into Normandy during World War II and had fought in Korea. He wasn't particularly fond of McNamara, whose previous job had been head of the Ford Motor Company. He wasn't particularly fond of the Kennedys, either.

"I have to disagree, Mr. President. Time is what we do not have. The Soviets clearly have a lot in place. It's not a question of waiting for extensive concrete launching pads or that sort of thing. They could hit us in days. Weeks, at most. We have to take these bases out *now*."

"Can we do that with air strikes?"

"Not with one hundred percent certainty, sir, no."

"I see. So, uh, let's say we miss a couple of sites. Or leave them functional. Say, two or three Russian MRBMs still ready to fire. What, we lose Miami? Atlanta? Washington?"

Taylor, a soldier, was unhappy about discussing casualties. Especially civilian ones.

He said, "All this would be a preamble to the invasion of Cuba, obviously. We'd have to neutralize . . ."

"Yes," JFK said. "And are we ready to invade Cuba, General?"

"Our plans are at an advanced stage, Mr. President."

"That means no, I take it?"

"Yes, sir."

A pause, then McNamara said, "I don't know what kind of world we live in after we've struck Cuba."

I'd like to think that the image of a globe of radioactive ash circling the sun might have flashed into the minds of those men at that moment. Maybe it did.

"Okay," the president said, "we meet again at six thirty. In the meantime, we keep the lid on this thing. No one talks; everyone thinks. That clear?"

"Sir."

"Yes, sir."

"I will fulfill my scheduled engagements. I don't want the press thinking that anything unusual is going on. General Taylor? Please confer with your Chiefs of Staff. By this evening, I want a realistic assessment of all military options, so far as that's possible."

The Kennedy brothers met outside the West Wing of the White House. Two men in sober suits among the white columns. The maples and birches dressed in rich autumnal colors. The sky impossibly blue. Elegant and beautiful things you could not dare risk or surrender. Lovely things suspended against the impending dark.

The Kennedys were young to be burdened with the fate of the world. Elected two years earlier at the age of forty-three, JFK was the youngest-ever president of the United States. Bobby, officially attorney general but in effect deputy president, was thirty-six. Both men would be assassinated by gunmen:

JFK in Texas, thirteen months after this conversation; Bobby six years later in California. A shimmery golden haze of martyrdom, of sainthood, almost, has settled upon them.

"The hell is Khrushchev up to, Jack?"

"I dunno, Bobby. He told me they weren't interested in Cuba. He said that Castro was a kinda wild card."

"Yeah. The bastard lied to you."

Kennedy and Khrushchev had met, for the first and only time, at a summit conference in Vienna in June 1961. No two men could be less alike, yet they had one thing in common: neither was quite what he seemed.

Nikita Sergeyevich Khrushchev was pudgy, porky, bald, and sixty-seven years old. He had been born a peasant, had been a shepherd boy. He liked to boast that he hadn't learned to read until he was twenty-five. He had extra chins where his neck should have been. When he scowled, he looked like an angry butcher. When he smiled, all chins and gappy teeth, he looked clownish, like the kind of bit-part actor who plays the Cheerful Village Idiot in film comedies. His moods were volatile, unpredictable: the chubby, playful uncle one minute; a ranting, bulge-eyed, desk-banging horror the next. In the Western media, he was often a figure of fun and was a joy to cartoonists.

John Fitzgerald Kennedy, by almost ridiculous contrast, was the youthful-faced, smoothly barbered, sharply suited son of a self-made millionaire. He'd studied at Harvard and in London, then won medals for his exploits as a torpedo boat commander in World War II. He'd been awarded the Pulitzer Prize for a book called *Profiles in Courage*. He was also the first (and so far the only) Roman Catholic U.S. president. His predecessor, Dwight D. Eisenhower, was an aging, uncontroversial, golf-playing ex-general; Kennedy was all about newness and dynamism and bringing America out of the shadows of war into the bright sunlight of . . . well, something different. He was glamorous. His wife, Jacqueline, was also very glamorous. (Jack and Jackie; how could you resist that lovely alliterative coupling, or the golden children it produced?)

From another angle, through a different lens, each of these men becomes something else.

Beneath the fat and the bad suits, behind the histrionics, Khrushchev was as hard as a drill bit and as cunning as a lavatory rat. During World War II, he'd led guerrilla resistance to the German invasion of the Ukraine. He'd clawed his way to the top of the Soviet leadership, a climb with treachery and murder perched on every step. He knew when to lie low, to get forgotten, and when to make his move. He'd survived—and no mean feat, this, because many hadn't—the dictatorship of Joseph Stalin. No one had given him a leg up, a helping hand. In his homely peasant fashion, he'd put his short arm around the shoulders of rivals, who then suddenly disappeared. When Stalin died, there Khrushchev was, somehow first secretary of the Communist Party. The gleeful mourners around Stalin's coffin looked up and found Nikita in charge. *How'd that happen?* they asked themselves, in Russian.

Kennedy had the style and bearing of a New England aristocrat, but his father, Joe Kennedy, had amassed the family fortune by ruthless swindling and smuggling whiskey. Underneath the cool and the tailored suits, and beyond the photo shoots, JFK was, physically, a mess. He was — forgive the cliché; I like the word *riddled* — riddled by disease. He suffered from bone complaints — osteoporosis and osteoarthritis — which forced him to wear a back brace; he could walk only short distances without experiencing pain. He had a sexually transmitted venereal disease. (I'd like to think that he caught it in Cuba, but that's maybe too neat.) He suffered from Addison's disease, which is a rare dysfunction of the adrenal glands. It lent his face a permanent yellowish tan. Colitis affected his bowels, noisily. He had high cholesterol and asthma. And several allergies. For these reasons he was pumped full of drugs much of the time. His weight and the shape of his face varied according to how and when the drugs kicked in. (He doesn't look quite the same in any two photographs.) It seems that there was no expert medical overview of his medication. The president woke up, gobbled down thirty pills, and then went downstairs in a haze of brain chemistry to take charge of one of the world's two superpowers and its nuclear arsenal.

JFK was also lecherous. Very lecherous. He once told Harold Macmillan, the courtly prime minister of Great Britain, that he would get migraine headaches if he went three days without a woman. And we're not talking about the lovely Jackie here, not exclusively. It seems improbable that such a wreck of a man, a man who couldn't take his shoes and socks off without help, had a string of lovers. But he did.

Somehow the truth about Kennedy stayed out of the public domain. The press was more respectful toward politicians in those days, I guess. Or more afraid of them. Or, possibly, America really needed the fragile glass bubble of Jack and Jackie, that aura of youthful glamour, to remain intact, believable. I don't know. I wasn't there. I was too busy getting Above Myself, falling in love with a posh girl, ineptly capturing her lovely body in a shadowy barn, to take much notice of what was going on in the real world.

I had, as it happened, only a few more days of ignorance, innocence, left to me.

I digress. I've gone off on a tangent again.

Anyway, the fact is—was—that JFK was a very sick man within kissing distance of a career-exploding scandal. It's likely—no, it's highly probable—that Nikita Khrushchev knew all of this; the Russians were good at espionage. That may be why, in Vienna, the Russian steamrollered the American. Why Khrushchev lectured, hectored, Kennedy like a bullying schoolmaster humiliating a new boy with a wet patch on his pants.

Later Kennedy would admit that the meeting with Khrushchev was "the roughest thing in my life. He just beat the hell out of me."

What frightened JFK more than anything was that the Russian leader seemed not to share his dread of nuclear catastrophe. Kennedy had gone to Vienna in the hope that he could persuade the Soviet Union to agree to a ban on the testing of new nuclear weapons. To sign a nuclear nonproliferation treaty. Khrushchev was having none of it. In fact, he told Kennedy in no uncertain terms that Russia intended to continue to build its arsenal and that, in the event of a military conflict with the United States, Russia would not hesitate to fire its missiles. Kennedy came back from Vienna badly rattled, convinced that Khrushchev was "a ruthless barbarian." Not the kind of guy to put nukes into Cuba as a mere bluff.

In America the story of the Cuban Missile Crisis, the narrative of our brush with extinction, has been mythicized. Retold as a showdown between Freedom and Tyranny, Light and Dark, Good and Evil.

Kennedy's generation was the first to have had its imagination shaped by movies. It grew up, experienced its major thrills, in cinemas. And the cinemas showed Westerns. It's *High Noon,* and the Bad Guy in the black hat stands in the middle of the street of the frontier town with a gloved hand poised over his holster and calls out the sheriff, who is the Good Guy and wears a white hat. The sheriff is afraid because he is not as quick on the draw as the Bad Guy, but he does not show his fear because he is the chosen representative of the people, their champion. He is the one who stands between them, their desires for peace and prosperity, and the dark anarchy of the Bad Guy, who will abuse their homes and their wives and daughters. And the Good Guy wins, of course. Even though, sometimes, he is mortally wounded in the process.

Kennedy, in the white hat, won the showdown with Khrushchev, in the black hat. (Or maybe that should be red hat.)

At the time, the version of this myth that established itself was the "eyeball-to-eyeball" variant. The man who put this about was Kennedy's secretary of state, Dean Rusk. He saw the world's glimpse into the burning precipice in terms of the game he'd played as a boy in Georgia, where two kids would stand staring into each other's face, and the loser was the one who blinked first.

"We went eyeball to eyeball with the Russians," Rusk would say when it was all over, "and the other guy blinked."

Well, maybe, Dean. Or maybe this: you and the Russians were like two guys in a cellar, up to their waists in petrol, arguing about who's got the bigger box of matches.

And besides, the truth is that the face-off, with my life and Frankie's and the planet's at stake, wasn't between Kennedy and Khrushchev. It was between Kennedy and his bomb-happy generals, in particular, a cigar-chomping maniac called Curtis LeMay. I, we, owe our continuing existence to the fact that JFK held his nerve against his own armed forces. Or, to put it another way, that he had the courage to show fear when his generals hadn't.

I'll get to that, and LeMay, in a minute. First, we need to have a stab at the mental arithmetic of annihilation.

31.
MAD

YOU'LL HAVE SEEN the photos of the Japanese cities of Hiroshima and Nagasaki after the American atomic bombs hit them in August 1945. Those black-and-white pictures of what looks like an archaeological dig: the husks and shadowy traces of an ancient civilization revealed by scraping the surface of the earth away. The grid of streets traced in pale ash. Here and there, rectangular shadows that might have been houses, office blocks. Black holes, pits, that once had a purpose, once had been part of something. Scorched wisps of what look like hair but are congealed tangles of steel. Of human beings, those frail things, there is no sign or remnant.

Strangely, Hiroshima and Nagasaki look gray and frozen, as though they'd been scoured by some awful polar wind. Actually, they were purged by a fire so intense that their inhabitants were vaporized by it. Their last breaths set fire to their lungs as their eyeballs melted.

A mother takes her baby to suckle her breast; the world roars, explodes; for a microsecond, they are linked joints of cooked meat; for another, white-hot bones; then they are gone, particles of dust whirled away in the exhale of the holocaust.

At the square-mile epicenter of the blast, the heat would have melted granite. Most of the buildings in Hiroshima were made of wood.

Twenty minutes after the initial explosion, while the mushroom cloud towered and boiled above the city, while the fires raged, rain began to fall on the remains of western Hiroshima. It was black rain, and radioactive, and it continued for two hours.

One hundred and forty thousand or so people were killed by the bomb. Most died either during the impact or within the following two weeks, of burns or other radiation injuries. For several days, a southerly wind blowing across Hiroshima carried with it a smell like burning fish.

There were survivors, of course. Some were unwise enough to flee southwestward to the city of Nagasaki, upon which, three days after Hiroshima, the Americans dropped an even bigger bomb.

Nuclear weapons go on killing long after the fires have gone out and the toxic fallout has settled. Within weeks of the bombings, people in the environs of Hiroshima and Nagasaki began to sprout keloids, grotesque rubbery scars that claw and spread across the surface of the body and face. The incidence of these disfiguring growths peaked in the years 1946 and 1947, after the war was over. Babies of mothers exposed to radiation were born deformed or were condemned to early death from diseases of the nerve and brain tissue. Eye disorders, especially cataracts, became increasingly commonplace. The long legacy of nuclear bombing is, of course, cancer. By the mid-1950s, Japan had more people dying from leukemia than anywhere else in the world. And for a very long time, the fields around the two cities produced poisonous harvests.

For all this, the Hiroshima and Nagasaki bombs were feeble squibs compared to the infernal firecrackers that Kennedy and Khrushchev had at their disposal in 1962. Nuclear warheads are measured in tons, kilotons, and megatons. A ton, here, is not a measurement of weight; it's a measurement of blast power. It's the equivalent to the bang you'd get from a ton of high explosive. A ton of trinitrotoluene, or TNT, which was the stuff in the bombs used during the Second World War. A ton of TNT will make a very big hole in the ground, or demolish a large factory, or erase a neighborhood. A kiloton produces an explosion equivalent to a *thousand* tons of TNT. The Hiroshima bomb was about thirteen kilotons. More than enough to convert a city into a furnace. But, as I say, it was a baby compared to what came later. A big, ugly baby. And quite primitive, really. It was ten feet long and weighed nine thousand pounds. It looked like a small whale with only tail fins. The humorous Americans called it Little Boy. (And the Nagasaki bomb Fat Man.) It took two dozen technicians three days to complete the nerve-racking task of assembling its various parts, arming it, locking in its safety devices, and loading it into the belly of a B-29 bomber.

(The plane was called *Enola Gay*, after the pilot's mum. Cute.) Then it took six and a half hours to fly it to its target from the Pacific island of Tinian. All very laborious and troublesome.

But such is the furious inventiveness of man when it comes to weapons of mass destruction that just twelve years later, the U.S. had built enormous rockets — one type called Thor, the other Jupiter — capable of carrying nuclear warheads of one and a half megatons. A megaton, as you will have worked out, explodes with the force of a *million* tons of TNT. So a single Thor or Jupiter could do as much damage as 115 Hiroshimas, or thereabouts. (You might want to check my figures. I enjoy math, but I'm not terribly good at it. Calculation would be easier for me if I had ten fingers, and I don't.) If I'm right, that works out to 115 times as many deaths, grotesque disfigurements, deformed babies, cancers, etc., as Hiroshima.

All the same, it wasn't good enough. Thors and Jupiters couldn't *quite* reach America's enemy, which was the Soviet Union. They certainly couldn't reach *all* of the Soviet Union, which consisted of most of the far side of the world, from Germany in the west to Manchuria in the east. And then there was China, which was Communist, too. So, quietly, the Americans placed their huge missiles in friendly countries closer to Russia: England, Italy, Turkey. Places that put Moscow within half an hour of a rocket's launch.

Even that was unsatisfactory. By the time I was delighted by the belated arrival of my pubic hair, the United States had developed rockets—called Atlases and Titans—that could travel seven thousand miles to dump four megatons of explosive onto Russia. Given the aftereffects of these multiple Hiroshimas—let alone the Soviet response—America had acquired the power to destroy the world several times over.

The Russians were not, of course, sitting idly by while all this was going on. They'd built and exploded an atomic bomb of their own by 1949. The Americans were shocked by how quickly the Communists had caught up. (They didn't know, then, that Soviet spies were embedded in their weapons research projects.) By the 1950s, it seemed that, as far as rockets were concerned, the Soviet Union had pulled ahead in the arms race. Or at least in the space race, which, in the eyes of many Americans, was the same thing.

In early October 1957, the Russians fired the first man-made object to orbit Earth. It was a small satellite called *Sputnik 1*.

A month later they launched *Sputnik 2*. On board was the first living mammal to journey into space. She was a small, bright-eyed, black-and-white dog called Laika.

She didn't make it back. She was already dead when *Sputnik 2* burned up on reentering Earth's atmosphere. The first *man* in space did make it back, however. He was a Russian called Yuri Gagarin. On April 12, 1961, his spacecraft made a single orbit of the planet in 108 minutes. He was the first human being to see Earth suspended in its dark and awful solitude. Afterward he said, "Earth was blue. There was no God."

* * *

I think I was less impressed by these feats than I should have been. By the time I was twelve, I'd already traveled to various parts of the universe in the company of Dan Dare, Captain Condor, and other heroes of my comics. Compared to battles with the Mekon's evil empire or the vast mechanical centipedes of Zardos, a satellite the size of a beach ball and an incinerated dog seemed pretty unimpressive. But I was sixteen when Gagarin circled the earth, and his words gratified the narky little atheist I'd then become. I read them aloud to my grandmother, sadly announcing the nonexistence of God. Her reaction disappointed me.

"I shunt be surprised," Win said placidly, "if that Rushun wunt lookun the wrong way."

While Win and I took the Soviet conquest of space calmly, America and the rest of the so-called Free World didn't. Russian satellites! Russians in space! It was just a tiny step of the imagination to get to Russian satellite *missiles* in space! My God!

When Gagarin's spacecraft passed over the U.S., it was less than two hundred miles up. No distance at all! Commuting distance. From that height, a tiny puff of rocket fuel could send all hell down on America's head. The U.S. Paranoia Meter swung into its red zone.

Then the Russians created the biggest man-made explosion in the history of humanity (so far).

A few months after Yuri Gagarin had landed and confirmed the nonexistence of God, a Soviet Tupolev took off and flew north into the Arctic Circle. It carried, like a gross and ugly pregnancy—so big that the doors of its underbelly had been removed to accommodate it—a huge nuclear bomb. Five miles above the frozen wastes, the crew released it, suspended from a vast parachute. Two and a half miles from the surface of the earth, it exploded with a force of *fifty* megatons. Fifty million tons of TNT. Ten times the total power of all the explosives used by all sides in the six years of the Second World War. When it was detonated, it created a fireball five miles in diameter. Its base touched the ground and melted it. Its crown reached the altitude of the plane that had dropped it. It was like the invasion of a furious planet. It was like the ferocious roar of God (had He existed). Dropped onto the inhabited parts of the world, it would have stopped civilization in its tracks.

Which was all to the good. It meant that the U.S. and the Soviet Union each had the ability to annihilate the other. Therefore—in theory, at least—neither of these growling superpowers would dare attack the other, because to do so would result in its own immolation.

That was the basis of peace while I was growing up.

It was called Mutually Assured Destruction, or MAD.

MAD has worked fairly well, I guess. I mean, here we both are, me writing, you reading, both of us breathing. It was delicate, though. The thing about MAD is that it depends upon powerful people being sane. That nobody sensible would actually want to convert to lifeless ash the hand that traced the lovely curve of Frankie's breasts and belly in the gathering darkness of a Norfolk barn. Or turn to radioactive vapor a mother and child in Minsk or Memphis. Unfortunately, however, weapons of mass destruction tend to attract maniacs: men — it's almost always men — who want to jab the red button and yell, "Take that, you heathen infidel bastards!" and sit in their revolving leather chairs in their underground lead-lined bunkers or caves, watching World War Three or the Final Jihad or whatever on their monitors. Watching Anchorage and Islamabad, Istanbul and Aberdeen flicker and vanish.

Unluckily, in 1962, America's nuclear arsenal was under the command of just such a man.

32.

HAWKS, DOVES, DOGS

DURING THE DAYS that followed the discovery of missiles on Cuba, the White House—and the Pentagon and the State Department—rapidly came to the boil. Further U-2 photographs revealed that as well as MRBM sites, the Russians and Cubans were building launchpads for IRBMs—intermediate-range ballistic missiles. These had twice the range of MRBMs; launched from Cuba, they could reach all of the U.S. apart from the far Northwest. The CIA wanted to send low-level flights over Cuba, to get a much closer look at the Devil's handiwork. JFK was hesitant. Sending warplanes into Cuban airspace, even on photographic missions, would clearly be an act of aggression. If the Cubans had got their hands on Russian surface-to-air missiles, they might just be crazy enough to shoot down an American plane, and that would force Kennedy's hand; an all-out war would be almost inevitable. Besides, U.S. planes scooting over Cuba would give the clear message to the

Beardies and the Russkies that America had found out what was going on. And Kennedy didn't want that. Not yet.

The president had formed an executive committee — ExComm, for short — to deal with the crisis. It consisted of people he liked and trusted, people he didn't like but trusted, people he didn't trust but who were good at what they did, and people he neither liked nor trusted but who had to be there. Among that last group were a number of people in military uniform whose usual habitat was the Pentagon.

After a week of fearful debate and fierce wrangling, two rough options emerged. And ExComm had divided, although not cleanly, into two groups that JFK would later refer to as the Hawks and the Doves.

Option One was the Hit the Bastards Right Now option. Bomb the missiles sites, bomb the Cuban air defenses, their military bases, without warning. Then send troops in to whack Castro and take over the damn island, the way we should have done years ago. This was the Hawks' preference.

The Doves pointed out the obvious problem: we'd kill lots of Russians. Moscow would then have an excuse to nuke Berlin, or Turkey, or Iran, or anywhere else that America had parked missiles. They might even launch a nuclear attack on the U.S. itself. Then we'd do the same to them. So good-bye, world.

Nah, the Hawks said. Khrushchev isn't gonna do that. He's not going to bet his whole empire on Cuba. No way. Cuba doesn't mean that much to him. What he's doing in Cuba is like an adventure, a game. He's not going to bet his personal ass, let alone the entire Soviet Union, on it. He'll bluster and bang his shoe on the desk and rant. But he's not crazy enough to start World War Three over this thing. Besides, he knows that we've got more firepower than they do. So let's do it.

But Kennedy was not perfectly sure that Khrushchev was an entirely rational being. He was not absolutely certain that the Soviet Union wouldn't be happy to rule a world that was half toxic ash.

Option Two was a sea blockade of Cuba. Send ships and submarines and planes to stop any ships that might be bringing war materials to Cuba. Draw a circle two hundred miles out from Havana, say. Stop anything we don't like the look of from going any farther. This was the Doves' preference. Actually, no, they said, let's not call it a blockade. That sounds warlike. Let's call it a *quarantine*. As if Cuba has got a disease we need to stop from spreading. Then we talk to Khrushchev. Tell him that enough is enough. He has to remove his missiles from Cuba, and we're not going to let him send any more material in. Especially not nuclear warheads. If we're right, and those warheads aren't in Cuba yet, the priority is to stop them from getting there.

(The Doves had a point. They didn't know it, but while ExComm was arguing back and forth, a Russian freighter called the *Aleksandrovsk*, stuffed with warheads, was steaming across the Atlantic en route to Havana. Another thing the Americans didn't know — and it's just as well they didn't, really — was that there were already ninety warheads on the Cuban mainland. They'd arrived at the port of Mariel on the fourth of October, in a ship designed to carry frozen fish.)

This talk of quarantine and diplomacy caused the Hawks to huff their feathers and narrow their raptor eyes.

What if, they wanted to know, one of those Commie ships refuses to stop?

Well, the Doves said, guess we'd have to board it. Or disable it. Shoot its rudder off, or something.

Well, that would be an act of war, wouldn't it? And where do you think that will lead?

Hmmm, the Doves murmured.

And what if we shoot up some ship that turns out to be carrying baby food? How's that gonna look? We end up with a goddamn public-relations disaster on our hands.

Hmmm.

And what if, the Hawks further demanded, Khrushchev turns around and tells us to go screw ourselves? That he's gonna keep his nukes in Cuba, blockade or no blockade. Excuse us, *quarantine*. What then?

Well, the Doves flustered, we suppose we'd have no choice but to go for the bombing and the air strikes and so forth.

Right, the Hawks glittered, so why wait? Why give them any warning? Let's hit the mothers now, when they're not expecting it.

* * *

Leading the Hawks were the military men, the Joint Chiefs of Staff, and fiercest of them was the aforementioned nightmare and chief of the air force, General Curtis LeMay. During the final stages of World War II, LeMay had initiated the strategy of firebombing Japanese cities. Flying at night, his planes dropped thousands of tons of explosives, incendiaries, and napalm (that's the stuff that glues itself to people when it's burning) onto military and civilian targets alike. LeMay proudly boasted, "Our B-29s scorched, boiled, and baked to death three hundred thousand people." He cheerfully admitted that if he'd been on the losing side, he'd have been executed as a war criminal. Postwar, LeMay was the architect of SAC, Strategic Air Command, a huge fleet of nuclear-capable aircraft and an arsenal of missiles that tipped the MAD balance in America's favor. His attitude toward Russia, as toward any enemy of the U.S., was uncomplicated: "We should just bomb them back to the Stone Age."

JFK was repelled by and frightened of LeMay. "I don't like that man," he told Bobby. "I don't want him near me."

When LeMay was promoted to head of the air force, he was replaced as head of SAC by General Thomas Power. Power, believe it or not, was worse than LeMay. His own deputy was profoundly worried that such a "mean and cruel" and "psychologically unstable" man had control over so many weapons and weapon systems and could, under certain conditions, "launch the force." Even LeMay considered Power "mad."

It still, after all these years, puts frost into my blood to remember that men like LeMay and Power had their fingers so close to the button.

On the morning of Friday, October 19, 1962, President Kennedy braced himself for a meeting in the Cabinet Room. Among the men waiting for him were LeMay, Maxwell Taylor, and the heads of the navy, the army, and the marines. The navy guy was Admiral George Anderson. He looked like a Hollywood actor cast in the role of Head of the Navy. His sermons on clean living had earned him the nickname Straight Arrow. The army guy was General Earle Wheeler, a clever man and politically connected to Kennedy's opposition, the Republicans. The marines guy was Commandant David Shoup. Shoup was a warrior who'd been involved in lots of bloody business, fighting the Japanese during World War II. His way of speaking involved biting off bits of the English language and randomly spitting them out in lumps of profanity.

All in all, they were not JFK's ideal audience.

The meeting did not go well.

When it became clear that JFK was leaning toward the Doves' quarantine option, with military action kept on hold, LeMay could barely conceal his contempt.

"We made pretty strong statements about Cuba, that we would take action against offensive weapons. I think that a blockade and political talk would be considered by our friends, and neutrals, as being a pretty weak response to this. And I'm sure a lot of your own citizens would feel that way, too."

There it was again, that word: *weak*. Kennedy bridled.

"You're in a pretty bad fix, Mr. President," LeMay added.

"What did you say?"

"You're in a pretty bad fix," LeMay repeated flatly. The indifference in his tone was worse than a sneer.

Kennedy's face wore an expression of restrained disgust, like a man watching his wife throw up into the toilet.

He said, "Well, you're right in there with me. Personally."

A flutter of nervous laughter from around the table. Taylor shuffled papers. The discussion turned to military preparedness.

LeMay announced that the air force would be ready for attack at dawn on Sunday, although Tuesday would be better. The implication was clear: we professionals are getting ready; you politicians are sitting on your thumbs.

When the meeting adjourned, the men in uniform lingered in the Cabinet Room. Blissfully unaware that it was bugged, they waxed candid.

"You really pulled the rug right out from under him," Shoup told LeMay admiringly.

"Yeah," Wheeler agreed, chuckling.

LeMay soaked it up.

Then Shoup made what was, by his standards, a speech.

"Somebody's got to keep him from doing the goddamn thing piecemeal. That's our problem. Go in there and friggin' around with the missiles. Go in there and friggin' around with the airlift. You're screwed, screwed, screwed. Some goddamn thing . . .

some way, that they either do the son of a bitch and do it right and quit friggin' around."

The others nodded in solemn agreement.

Such was the level of debate among the American military on the subject of human annihilation.

Listening to the tapes later, JFK could have been left in no doubt that his dogs of war were eyeing their master's crotch. As he said to his personal assistant, Dave Powers, "These bastards have one great advantage in their favor. If we listen to them and do what they want us to do, none of us will be alive later to tell them they were wrong."

33.
GEORGE DOES A BIT OF TIDYING UP

JUST BEFORE TEN o'clock on the morning of Saturday, October 20, Clem stashed his bike inside Franklins' unruly hedge, then froze. The sound was harsh, grating. And loud; it had come from close by. Then another, the coarse roar of some sort of machine. And above him, rooks in tumultuous outrage. The wind was light but bitter. His imitation-suede jacket was little defense against it. He stood, indecisive, shivering, then moved cautiously through the undergrowth toward the ruins of the house. When he got to the stump of its gable wall, he stopped. He stopped totally—breathing, heartbeat, brain function all at a standstill. He heard laughter, and because nothing made sense, he thought it might be his own.

It had all gone. All of it. The barn, the pines, the bramble and bracken. The low table of land that they had occupied was a smear of raw brown soil and torn roots. Beyond it, fifty feet into the vast field, a bonfire plumed smoke into the wind. As he watched, half a flight of stairs collapsed in it, like a blackened accordion. Then a huge caterpillar-tracked bulldozer reversed into his line of sight. The man perched at its controls, looking backwards, with a cigarette in his mouth, was his father. Clem dropped to the ground as if he'd been shot.

They'd found out. Him and Mortimer, they'd found out. And this was what they'd done about it. Smashed them. Erased them.

He sat with his back against the wall, numb at first, then slowly filling with fierce grief. The sound of the dozer settled into a heavy chug, then died. Voices. A second engine fired up, somewhere off to his left. Clem got to his knees and peered over the wall. His father was sitting atop the machine, speaking to someone hidden from view by the remaining walls of the house and a surviving clump of hawthorn and gorse. Clem crawled to the corner of the ruin and out behind a low, overrun bank, perhaps once the edge of a kitchen garden. He raised his head again.

Three other men, one maneuvering a tractor fitted with a toothed digging bucket. The trunks of the felled pines, decapitated, their limbs amputated. A big trailer, half full of rubble. A huge mound of brick and slate and jutting broken timbers that had been the barn.

A stocky man in dirty blue overalls and Wellington boots was poking around in the wreckage. He lifted something on the end of a stick: the sleeping bag—their sleeping bag—barely recognizable, the filthy ragged skin of an ancient roadkill.

"That look like some ole tramp're being sleepun rough up here, George."

Grinning.

His father laughed from on high.

"Aye. The bugger'll get a right shock if he comes back tonight."

The third man, rolling a cigarette, said, "'Specially if he're got your sister with him, Will."

Clem fell onto his back among the damp leaf fall, stunned by loss.

Frankie.

He knelt again, and there she was, appearing and disappearing beyond the swirling smoke, she and Marron silhouetted motionless on the low swell of the land.

He went home. A few minutes after twelve thirty, the phone rang.

"Clem?"

"Frankie?"

"Clem. Oh, Clem."

"Can you talk?"

"Only for a second. I had no idea, honestly. I couldn't believe my eyes."

"The *bastards.*"

"Yes. Can you come to the woods later? Where we used to meet?"

"When?"

"Three."

"Okay."

Ruth came in the back door.

"Who're you talking to, Clem?"

"Goz."

"Clem?"

"I'll see you there, then. Cheers, Goz."

He put the phone down.

"What was that all about, then?"

"Oh, nothun. Said I'd go round his later. Bloody English prep."

Ruth hung her coat on the pegs under the stairs.

"Takun up swearun now, hev you?"

Frankie came on a bicycle. He hadn't known she could ride one, or had one.

34.
GOOD EVENING, MY FELLOW CITIZENS

I T'S VERY DIFFICULT for a world superpower to prepare for war discreetly. When huge military convoys lumber south into Florida, when sports fields suddenly become army camps, when fleets steam out of ports, when squadrons of fighter-bombers suddenly get dispersed to obscure civilian airfields, when thousands of servicemen are told to kiss their girlfriends and wives and children good-bye, when the lights burn all night in the Pentagon, well, these things tend to get noticed.

The story of a "defensive buildup" in Cuba had been simmering in the American press for several weeks. Kennedy's political opponents had been making a fuss about it. He'd been stung when ex-president Eisenhower, in a piece in the *New York Times,* had accused him of being "weak on foreign policy." Code for "fluffy with the Russians."

By the end of the first week of the crisis, JFK knew that he was going to have to go public. His speechwriter, Theodore Sorensen, had written two versions of a broadcast to the nation.

Version One said, in essence, "Good evening, my fellow citizens. It is my sad duty to inform you that, as I speak, U.S. forces are bombing Cuba in advance of an all-out invasion. You might like to get yourselves ready for World War III."

Version Two said, in essence, "Good evening, my fellow citizens. I have to tell you that the wicked Russians have put nuclear missiles in Cuba, and we won't stand for it. So we've put a sea blockade around Cuba, and I've sent a stiff note to Chairman Khrushchev."

Right up to the wire, it was odds-on which of these two speeches would go out.

On Monday, October 22, the White House sent a request to all TV and radio networks that they make airtime available for a presidential address at seven p.m. Its subject would be "a matter of the highest national urgency." Hearing of this, Cuban and Russian intelligence—who had already reported the unusual levels of activity at the White House and the Pentagon—immediately informed Havana and Moscow. Reactions in these cities were very different.

It was late evening in Moscow when Khrushchev got the word and summoned his ministers to the Kremlin. He was gloomy and fretful. And deeply disappointed. His plan had been splendidly cunning. Once all the nuclear weapons systems were installed in Cuba, he would fly to Havana, where and he and Castro would sign a formal agreement on mutual defense. (The Americans would make a fuss, but since they'd done much the same thing with countries like Britain and Turkey, they'd not have a leg to stand on.) Then, and only then, he and Fidel, brother revolutionaries, would take the salute as Russian troops marched past, side by side with their Cuban comrades. And with their smart new missiles. It would present the Yankees with a shocking fait accompli.

Now it seemed to Khrushchev that this delightful scenario would be denied him.

"They've rumbled us," he said. "I'm almost sure of it. Kennedy will announce an invasion. The son of a bitch may already have ordered it. *Shit!* We should have announced a defense treaty with Cuba *before* we sent the stuff in."

No one said anything for a minute. No one was especially keen to agree with Khrushchev that he'd made a mistake.

"Comrade Chairman," Defense Minister Rodion Malinovsky said eventually, "our best information is that the Americans would not be ready to mount an invasion for several days. For a start, they do not have enough ships in the Caribbean to support such an action."

"So they'll send in their planes," Khrushchev said. "And we're not ready for air strikes. They'll take us out in a single swipe. Then invade."

"Will they? Will they kill hundreds, perhaps thousands, of our people, knowing that we would then have to retaliate?"

Khrushchev was silent for a moment. I'd like to imagine that the shadows inside the Kremlin deepened.

"Tragic," he said eventually, quietly. "They hit us; we respond; it all ends up in a big war. Are we ready for that?"

Malinovsky shrugged: an articulate gesture.

Silence fell. Khrushchev broke it.

"So, how about this: we announce a defense treaty with Cuba immediately. Over the radio, so that the CIA hears it, loud and clear. We transfer control of all Soviet nuclear weapons to the Cubans. We can't *really* do that, of course, because only Biryuzov and his people know how to use the damned things. No matter. Fidel will then announce that he will use them to defend his country from imperialist attack. The Americans believe that he's crazy enough to do just that. So do I, as a matter of fact. They'll mess their pants. They'll hold off. What do you think?"

Malinovsky said, "With respect, Nikita Sergeyevich, I think we should do nothing until we hear what Kennedy says. The gutless playboy might well be bluffing."

By contrast, in Havana, on Monday afternoon, Fidel Castro put his defensive forces on red alert and ordered his reserve forces to report to their regional headquarters. Then, energized by crisis, he went to the offices of the newspaper *Revolución* and dictated the next day's headline: *"¡Patria o Muerte! ¡Venceremos!"* (The Motherland or Death! We Shall Overcome!)

As it turned out, the Kremlin did not have to wait for JFK's speech.

At six o'clock Washington time, the Soviet ambassador to the United States, Anatoly Dobrynin, arrived, as requested, at the State Department. There, he was handed the text of the speech that Kennedy would make in less than an hour's time, along with a private message to Khrushchev, which warned the Soviet leader that he should not underestimate America's will and determination to unleash all manner of hell in order to maintain peace.

Poor Dobrynin went as white as a graveyard lily. For security reasons, the Kremlin had told him nothing about what was going on in Cuba. He went shakily back to his embassy and wired JFK's speech and letter to Moscow.

When Nikita Khrushchev read them, his mood climbed back up the graph. He returned to the meeting, waving a triumphant fist in the air.

"We've saved Cuba," he announced. "Kennedy, the coward, has announced a sea blockade. Which he has no right to do. No matter what they might think, the Yankees do not own the high seas. They are pirates now. Aggressors. We have them by the balls."

There was applause.

Then Admiral Sergey Gorshkov, head of the Soviet Navy, spoke up.

"This is very good news, Comrade Chairman. The brave captains of our merchant fleet will be resolute in the face of this illegal act by the Americans. However, there is the problem of our submarines."

"What about them?"

"We don't know exactly where they are," Gorshkov admitted. "They might be outside or inside the American blockade."

"So radio them," Khrushchev said. "Tell them what's happening."

"Unfortunately, Comrade Chairman," Gorshkov said, "communications with our submarines are unreliable. We can only be sure of clear signals when they surface."

"And if they surface," Malinovsky said, "they might find themselves face-to-face with an American warship."

"Shit," Khrushchev said.

The Oval Office of the White House had been improvised into a television studio. At seven p.m., JFK sat at his desk, which had been draped in black cloth to cut out light flare, and addressed the cameras.

"Good evening, my fellow citizens," he began.

A hundred million of them were listening or watching. He told them about the missiles on Cuba and how they could fly mass death as far north as Canada and as far south as Peru. He told them how the Russians had lied through their teeth about what they were doing, how they'd insisted they were merely aiding the Cubans with defensive systems. He told them that if World War II had taught us anything, it was that letting military aggression go unchallenged would lead inevitably to war. Even so, Kennedy said, the U.S. would not "prematurely or unnecessarily risk the costs of a worldwide nuclear war in which even the fruits of victory would be ashes in our mouth." Then he announced the "quarantine" and close surveillance of the military buildup in Cuba. He declared (in politer language than mine) that if any missile of any sort were launched from Cuba, America would blow the Soviet Union to kingdom come. He addressed Khrushchev personally, urging him to move the world back from the abyss of destruction. He spoke to the people of Cuba, that "imprisoned island." He was their friend, but their leaders were Soviet puppets. He assured them that one day soon they would be free. Then he mentioned God and said good night. And all around the world, newsrooms went crazy.

35.
THE LAMBS OF GOD ARE SHORN

BUSINESS WAS SLACK, so Albert Scott had got himself comfortable in his barber's chair with a cup of tea and the *Daily Sketch*. When his door pinged, he sighed and folded the paper; getting to his feet, he was most surprised to discover that his customers were Enoch and Amos Hoseason.

Enoch took the chair first, filling it with his bulk. Albert bibbed him and cranked the chair up a little. Amos sat stiffly against the back wall, flaring his nostrils slightly at the Babylonian aromas of Brylcreem and cheap cologne.

Albert, without pleasure, regarded his client's hair, which was long and thick and none too clean. It gave off a whiff of old fireplaces and something rodenty.

"So, how would you like it, Enoch?"

"Off."

"Pardon?"

Hoseason took a last look at himself in the mirror, then closed his eyes.

"All off. Hair and beard. Clean shaved all over. Make me like unto a newborn babe."

Albert laughed uncertainly. "You want me to shave yer *head*, Enoch?"

"Thas what I said."

"Well, I . . . Bleddy wars, Enoch. Newborn babies hev *some* hair. Most of 'em."

Hoseason said nothing further. In the mirror he looked peaceful, like the severed head of John the Baptist resting on a napkin. Albert turned and looked at Amos.

"And will you be wantun the same?"

"I will, indeed."

Albert puffed out his cheeks and rubbed his bald spot. Then he went through the shop and locked the front door. He turned the OPEN sign the other way around. When he returned, Amos asked him a question with his eyes.

"This'll take some time," Albert said. "Ent no point other customers sittun here waitun."

This was not his reason. What he'd been asked to do was not barbering; it was barbarism. Albert didn't want anyone coming in and catching him at it.

When he'd scissored Hoseason's head to a stubbled knob and covered it with a hot towel, and while he was stropping the cutthroat razor, Albert said, "So, Enoch, what d'yer make of this here Cuba business, then?"

Hoseason possessed neither radio nor television, considering both to be mouthpieces of Satan. And many months had passed since he'd read anything other than the Holy Scriptures.

Without opening his eyes, he said, "What Cuba business?"

Janice Pitcher was minding the newsagent's shop while Arnold, her father, took his afternoon nap. Like him, she was myopic and wore thick circular spectacles that gave her the appearance of a startled carp. So when the two dark-suited strangers came in, she thought at first that they were both wearing tight-fitting white bathing caps. It occurred to her (she was partial to crime novels) that armed robbers might adopt such a disguise. Her hand moved slightly nearer the button of the electric bell that would summon her father from upstairs. Only when the two men approached the counter did she realize that they were utterly shiningly bald.

Enoch Hoseason surveyed the array of newspapers and magazines. Under his hot gaze, the lewd covers of *Tit-Bits* and *Reveille* might have smoldered and flamed. He selected a newspaper at random and held it up. The jittery mix of maps, photographs, type, and headlines confused him. He opened the paper and beheld a photograph of a towering, apocalyptic explosion capped with a halo of cloud. (It was, in fact, a picture of a British nuclear test, a bomb exploded on Christmas Island, in the Pacific.) As he gazed at it, understanding rumbled through him like divine indigestion. He turned to Amos, his eyes moist.

"The prophecy, brother! Remember? 'The seed of the fire is already in the hands of men. It shall become a mighty tree that groweth up to heaven.'"

He jabbed the photograph with his forefinger.

"'And all shall be consumed in the leaves and branches of its burning.' It is upon us, Amos. It comes!"

"Amen!"

Enoch seized up another couple of newspapers and shook them in his fist, his eyes glazed by inspiration.

"What price now, ye sneerers and jeerers?" he crowed. "What price your proud vanities?"

"That come to a shillun and five pence all tergether," Janice said cautiously.

36.
RUTH GETS THE CHOP

A T 11 LOVELACE Road that evening, George sat with a fork-ful of fatty pork halfway to his mouth. The chap on the telly was using a pointer to indicate a series of circles on a map with Cuba at its center. Little things like pointy footprints represented Russian ships. Some of them were very close to the part of the circle that seemed to matter most.

"Ruddy hell," George said.

"Eat that up before that get cold, George," Ruth said. "That was the best chop in Dewhurst's."

Soviet missiles being trundled through Red Square. Khrushchev watching from a balcony, flanked by slab-faced men in gangster hats. A clip of a nuclear explosion unfurling its monstrous corona.

"George?"

"For Christ's sake, Ruth. Aren't you listening to this?"

"No, I ent. Thas all a load of old squit. Wha's Cuba got to do with us? Up till now, I dint have any idea where it even was. And don't tell me you did, neither."

"As a matter of fact, I did," George said fiercely. "Some of us takes a bloody interest."

A man had appeared on the screen who looked a bit like a policeman. He spoke calmly as he held up a booklet with an illustration of a smiling family on the cover.

"This little publication will show you how to defend your home and your loved ones against nuclear attack. It's not as difficult as you might think. Most of the materials you will need are easily available. At the present time there is no need to be alarmed. But we ask you to read this book, which you can get free from your local post office or library."

The camera angle shifted. The sort-of policeman turned his head and put on a sort-of smile.

"This country of ours has come under attack before. But our courage, our resolve, and our absolute commitment to freedom have sustained us and will do so again."

Another voice said, "That was a public service announcement on behalf of . . ."

George swallowed his pork and turned to his son.

"What you think of that, then, Clem?" He grinned sickly. "You reckon we ought to build a shelter, or what?"

Clem had left his chop untouched, a small gesture of protest at having to share a table with the wrecker of his love nest. Since Saturday, he had observed a vow of angry silence toward his father, but now he gave voice to his bitterness.

"Makes no difference either way."

"What d'you mean by that?"

As though speaking to a wearisome pupil, Clem said, "If there *is* a nuclear war, that's it. We're all dead, one way or the other."

"Not necessarily," George said, pointing at the telly with his fork. "Not if we take precautions."

Ruth said, "Me and Mum spent night after night under the stairs, during the war. Oh, that was horrible, wunt it, Mum?"

Win said nothing, concentrating on her piece of fish. Along with the rest of the Brethren, she had renounced meat for the advent of the Apocalypse. Win disliked fish, but it gave her the opportunity to rail at the fishmonger, against whom she held an ancient grudge. ("You'll answer to your Maker for the price of that haddock, James Wisby, and sooner than you think.")

"There'd be no *point* in surviving," Clem said. "Okay, so you live in your shelter for a fortnight—"

Ruth said, "George, whatever would we do for a toilet?"

George ignored her. "Aye?"

"And then," Clem said, "you come out. And there's nothing left. No houses, no trees, nothing. It'd be a desert of radioactive dust."

"You know that for a fact, do you?"

"Yes, actually."

"Oooh. *Actually*," George mimicked. "Well, thank you, Einstein. I'll get on the phone and tell the government that. I'm sure they'll appreciate it. Probably revise their plans accordingly."

Clem pushed his chair back and stood up.

Ruth looked up from her plate. "Where're you gorn to, Clem?"

"Out."

"Out where?"

"Just out."

"You won't be wantun that chop, then?"

From the hallway Clem said, "No. You can eat the bloody thing."

"Hoy!" George yelled as the back door slammed.

Later, after the rice pudding, when George and Ruth were watching some rubbish or other, Win went quietly upstairs and closed her door. She clicked on her bedside light, got stiffly down onto her knees, and groped under the bed for her Robe of Deliverance. She'd cut it out of her bottom bedsheet. It shouldn't have mattered, but she was unhappy with its roughly cut hem. It didn't seem right to her that she would go Home looking all raggedy. She straightened up and got her sewing things out of the cupboard drawer. She perched her old bum on the side of the bed and started to stitch, humming the words of the twenty-third psalm.

37.
THE BOGS

"O God, our help in ages past,
Our hope for years to come,
Our shelter from the stormy blast,
And our eternal home."

CLEM AND GOZ mimed the words from the sixth-form pews in the organ loft. At the close of the hymn, while the boys shuffled and clonked onto their seats, Stinker Bloxham stood at the lectern wearing his fur-trimmed bat robe and an ironically patient expression. When something close to silence had been achieved, he turned to the man who sat onstage among the school staff.

"Over to you, Mr. Wagstaff."

Wagstaff was a trim little man in a dark-blue uniform with an armband embroidered with the words CIVIL DEFENSE.

"Thank you, Headmaster, and good morning, young gentlemen. Yesterday, as I'm sure you'll remember, I spoke to you about the ways you can help your parents prepare their homes against the possibility of nuclear attack."

Clem grinned, noting Tash Harmsworth's scowl. Tash was a bugger for an incorrect preposition.

"The very *unlikely* possibility of nuclear attack. However, preparedness is everything, as I'm sure you'll agree."

Wagstaff waited for a response, but none came. So he soldiered on.

"Today I'm going to tell you what to do if you *are* caught in the open when the four-minute warning sounds. Let me remind you what the four-minute warning will — might — sound like."

Wagstaff closed his eyes and emitted a doglike wail. As it rose in pitch, he slowly lifted his arms. As it faded, he lowered them. As it rose again, he lifted them. Some of the younger boys tittered and sniggered. Stinker got to his feet and glared. From their stations at the ends of the pews, the Gestapo, like hunting dogs, aimed their fierce gazes at offenders.

"It's not funny," Wagstaff said, opening his eyes. "It really isn't. Anyway. When you hear that, gentlemen, you must take cover in any available building and adopt the blast position that I demonstrated yesterday. It is exceedingly unlikely that you will be unable to reach a protective building. After all, these days an Englishman can run a mile in less than four minutes."

Again, he waited vainly for appreciation.

"However, if you are caught in the open some considerable distance from cover, here is what you must do. First, look for a depression in the ground. A trench or ditch, for example. Lie in it with your face to the ground. And make sure that exposed parts of your body, such as your head and hands, are protected. If you happen to be carrying a newspaper or something similar, place it over your head. If you are not, use your clothing to cover yourself completely. I shall demonstrate."

Wagstaff unbuttoned his tunic and prostrated himself on the stage. He pulled the back of his tunic up over his head, then tucked his hands between his thighs.

"Like so," he said, muffled.

A man lying on the stage of Newgate's school hall with his head covered by his jacket, his braces showing, and his hands on his nadgers. The silence that ensued was like the insuck of the sea before a tidal wave, or the ponderous gap between lightning and thunder.

Clem nudged Goz, then looked at him, expecting his face to be taut with suppressed laughter. It wasn't. It was pale with rage. Grim.

"Goz?" (Whispered.)

Nothing.

Wagstaff got to his feet and adjusted his clothing.

"Now," he said, "a word about fallout. Fallout is the radioactive material that falls from the sky after a nuclear explosion. It might fall in the form of rain or, more likely, ash or dust. If you do find yourselves in an exposed space, and you are in a fallout area, you should remain in the covered position, which I have just demonstrated, for two hours, which is the maximum time in which fallout will occur. After that time, you should seek shelter within the nearest building. However, before you do so, you must remove the fallout from your clothes, thus."

He removed the tunic and shook it vigorously with his face averted. Then he used the tunic to slap at his trousers, fore and aft. Finally he flapped a handkerchief at his shoes.

"Fallout is a form of contamination, and it is vital that you free yourself of it before you rejoin your families or other groups. I cannot stress enough the importance of this, gentlemen."

He regarded his audience somberly. Then he smiled.

"So pick yourselves up, dust yourselves off, and start all over again, as the song has it. Thank you for your attention."

He returned to his seat.

There came a light scattering of uncertain applause from the Worms and Maggots in the front pews, which the Gestapo quickly suppressed.

Goz walked slightly ahead of Clem toward the sixth-form common room. He went past the doors, saying over his shoulder, "Fag. Bogs."

The Newgate lavatories had been built a hundred years earlier, less as a convenience than a warning, their squalor and discomfort a stern reminder of the vileness of human bodily functions and their attendant temptations. The building was roofless, the urinal a black-painted wall with a low gutter at its foot. The cubicles lacked doors, doors being an encouragement of the Solitary Vice. Now and again Hake, the school caretaker, sluiced the place out with a bucket of diluted Jeyes Fluid, which added an acrid sweetness to the bogs' ancient aroma.

Goz went to the far corner and leaned against the stained trough that served as a washbasin. He took a packet of ten Anchor from his inside pocket and lit one up. Clem waited silently. After three drags, Goz passed him the ciggie and let forth a stream of elaborate obscenities.

Clem laughed smoke.

"What're you laughing at, Ackroyd? You think it's funny, sitting there and being idiotized?"

"Is that a word?"

"Yeah. I just used it. Give us that fag back."

Goz emitted a mean stream of smoke and said, "One: nuclear missiles do not explode when they hit the ground. They explode *above* it. So lying in a ditch with a bloody newspaper over your head is . . . is about as stupid as you can get. Two: fallout is effing radioactive. What did that moron mean, *brush it off*? Like it was *dandruff*, or somethun? Lie in a ditch with that shit dropping on you for two hours, then just tidy up and go home?"

"Goz, I know all that. Why're you —?"

"Three: RAF Beckford is five miles away. It's a base for V-bombers, if I remember correctly. Planes that're got nuclear bombs on them. Plus, there are two Yank air force bases within fifty miles of here. They're got nuclear bombers there as well. And what that means, comrade, is that we are slap in the middle of a Russian target. If Kennedy presses the button,

Khrushchev'll press his bloody button, and we get wiped out five minutes later. And to have to sit there listening to that gormless, lying little twot . . ."

"Goz, Goz. Orright. But look, it's not really gonna happen, is it? It's too . . ."

"You not been watching the box? Reading the papers?"

"Yeah, but . . ."

Goz opened the tap behind him and drowned the cigarette end and flicked it backward over the wall into the butcher's yard that bordered the school.

"Listen," Goz said, "and no offense, comrade, but I know for a fact that the be-all and end-all of existence for you is getting your end away with the lovely doe-eyed Miss Mortimer. Fair enough. But I've got *plans,* comrade. I've got ideas about what I want to do with my life. And it dunt include getting fried alive because some pillock wants missiles on Cuba and some other pillock don't. And you know what? It *seriously* cheeses me off when some bloke called Wankstaff stands there and tells me that all I have to do is lie down and pull my jacket over my head and then carry on as normal. 'Cos we are *gone,* comrade, when the Bomb goes off. *Gone.*"

Tash Harmsworth appeared around the far end of the urinals and said, "Ah. My Fool and my Bastard. I was wondering where you were."

(Harmsworth was not being gratuitously offensive. Goz was reading the part of Edmund, the illegitimate son of the Earl of Gloucester.)

"Sir," Goz said, straightening up but keeping his eyes on the stained concrete floor.

Tash pushed his vampire robe aside and took a metal cigarette case out of his pocket. He lit an untipped Capstan with a gold Dunhill lighter.

"The rest of the cast is disturbed by your absence. Cordelia is particularly distressed; it's her big scene this morning."

"Sorry, sir," Clem said.

"I'm sure you are. I assume you had something of significance to discuss?"

"Only the end of the world, sir," Goz said.

"Ah," Tash said. "*That.* And here was I thinking you'd merely sloped off for a smoke. May I inquire as to what conclusions you have come to, regarding the Apocalypse? Ackroyd?"

"We're against it, sir."

"Are you, indeed? I shall write notes to President Kennedy and Chairman Khrushchev immediately. I'm sure that when they learn that two scholars as eminent as yourselves disapprove of their actions, they will come promptly to their senses."

Tash took a deep pull on his Capstan, studying the bitterness on Goz's unresponsive face.

"Nothing to say, Gosling?"

"No, sir."

"Very well." Tash tossed his half-smoked cigarette into the urinal. "Shall we go, then? Because 'at my back I hear Time's wingèd chariot hurrying near.' Who wrote that, Ackroyd?"

"Don't know, sir. Sorry, sir."

"Andrew Marvell," Goz muttered as if he didn't want to but couldn't help it.

"Correct, Gosling. Give that man a cigar. 'To His Coy Mistress.' You've not read it, Ackroyd?"

"No, sir."

"You should. A rare example of a poem with a practical purpose. Even you, Ackroyd, might find it handy one of these days."

The boys followed him out of the bogs.

"Essentially," Tash said as if resuming an interrupted lecture, "each of us is a single consciousness. Therefore, when we die, all else dies. The light goes out, and all is darkness. Some find that concept bleak. I find it comforting."

Goz said, "What about envying the people that go on living, sir?"

"I bloody well don't," Tash said.

38.
STUMBLING TOWARD THE BRINK

O N **WEDNESDAY,** October 24, the Americans made their first low-level reconnaissance flights over Cuba. Six U.S. Navy Crusader jets took off from Key West, Florida, and headed south, flying so low that they wet their bellies with sea spray. Having slipped under Cuban radar defenses, they climbed and started taking photographs. Their pictures would show, in clear detail, the construction in progress of a nuclear warhead storage bunker near San Cristóbal. Close by stood lines of fuel tankers, warhead transporters, and tents for MRBMs.

That morning's ExComm meeting began, as usual, with a briefing by the CIA director, John McCone. It seemed that there were twenty-two Soviet ships steaming toward Cuba. There'd been a heck of a lot of radio traffic, in code, between them and Moscow during the night. Two of the ships, the *Yuri Gagarin* and the *Kimovsk,* could well be carrying armaments. The *Kimovsk* had a very long hold, designed for carrying timber but also suitable for missiles. Both vessels were close to the quarantine line, and there was a Russian Foxtrot-class submarine keeping an eye on them. It looked like showdown time was close at hand.

Kennedy wanted to know what the U.S. navy intended to do if the ships refused to observe the quarantine.

McNamara told him: a U.S. destroyer would intercept the *Kimovsk* while helicopters from the aircraft carrier USS *Essex* would "attempt to divert the sub, or subs."

"What does that mean, exactly?"

"Well, Mr. President, the helicopters would drop practice depth charges, nonlethal depth charges, to persuade the sub to surface."

Kennedy did not look well. He had that puffiness around his eyes that made him look slightly Asian, and his posture suggested that he was in pain.

"Jesus," he said very quietly.

"Sir?"

"Well, Bob, I guess that Russian sub wouldn't know that these were *practice* charges. I mean, is there any way . . . ? They're gonna think they're under attack, aren't they? And they might take it into their heads to retaliate. These Foxtrots, they can carry nuclear torpedoes, as I recall. If he doesn't surface, if he takes some action, some action to assist the merchant ship, are we going to attack him for real? At what point are we gonna attack him? I think we should wait on that. We don't want the first thing we attack as a Soviet submarine. I'd much rather have a merchant ship."

McNamara said, "I think it would be extremely dangerous, Mr. President, to defer attack on this sub in the situation we're in. We could easily lose an American ship by that means. . . ."

The secretary of defense clammed up. A CIA man had entered the Cabinet Room. He spooked his way over to McCone, handed his boss a note, and spooked his way out again. McCone read the note and looked up.

"We've just received information that all six Soviet ships currently identified in Cuban waters have either stopped or reversed course."

For a moment or two it seemed, and sounded, like victory. Backs were slapped, God was thanked. Then Dean Rusk spoiled it.

"Whadya mean, John, *Cuban waters?*"

McCone said, "Uh, Dean, I don't know exactly what that means at this moment."

Kennedy said, "So, are these ships that were already inside the quarantine? Were they ships going in, or going out?"

"I don't know, sir."

"Makes a helluva difference," Rusk said dryly.

Laughter, of a sort.

"I'll go and investigate," McCone said.

The commander of *B-130,* the submarine that troubled ExComm, was Captain Nikolai Shumkov, and he was a deeply unhappy man. The voyage from his Arctic base to the Caribbean was far longer than his boat had been designed for. Its batteries were faulty, and Shumkov had had to surface too frequently

285

to recharge them. In the middle of the Atlantic, he'd run into a hurricane, and the sub had tipped and slewed in the water like a drowned rocking horse. Most of his crew had fallen violently seasick, and cleansing a submarine of vomit is not the easiest thing in the world. When they reached tropical waters, the temperature and the humidity inside the sub rose to unbearable levels. They had insufficient fresh water. Shumkov and his men stripped to their underwear. A combination of noxious air, poor diet, and dehydration brought on an outbreak of a suppurating skin rash. The medical officer treated it with an ointment the color of boiled spinach. Clad in sopping singlets and sad underpants, daubed in green, the crew looked like bad actors playing Venusians in a cheap sci-fi movie. By the time *B-130* was a week from Havana, two of its three diesel engines had stopped working and the boat was struggling to keep up with the merchant ships it was meant to be protecting. Shumkov was well aware from signal intercepts that he was being tracked by Yankee antisubmarine units. The Americans were on the water and in the sky above him. But he had in his torpedo tubes a weapon with the power of the Hiroshima bomb. And he was wired enough to use it.

The Strategic Air Command had five levels of war readiness called defense conditions, or DefCons. In peacetime, with no trouble brewing, SAC ticked over at DefCon 5. The numbers dropped as things hotted up. DefCon 1 was imminent nuclear war. At ten o'clock on that Wednesday morning, General Thomas Power ordered his forces to adopt DefCon 2. An hour later, he descended into his underground command bunker near Omaha, Nebraska, and broadcast a message to SAC bases and missile stations around the world. He emphasized "the seriousness of the situation this nation faces" and assured his listeners—unnecessarily, one might think—that "we are in an advanced state of readiness to meet any emergencies." But Power wasn't speaking only to his own people. He'd chosen to broadcast on a high-frequency radio network that he knew was monitored by Soviet intelligence. He wanted to make sure that his message was heard in Moscow. He wanted the Reds to know that they were knocking at the doors of burning perdition.

Chairman Khrushchev's reply to Kennedy came through to the White House late in the evening. It had clearly been written by him personally, because it was an erratic combination of threat and persuasion, bombast and reason, indignation and pleading, all awkwardly wrapped in the language of international diplomacy. Essentially, though, it came down to this: *What you're doing is illegal; it's piracy. You don't own the seas. We and Cuba are sovereign nations, and you have no right to tell us what we can and can't do. Imagine if we had done this to you. Would you have said okay? No. Our ships will sail where they want to. Do you really want to start a nuclear war over this issue? Oh, by the way, what about those nuclear weapons you've got in Turkey?*

The American low-level flights over Cuba continued into the next day. A plane piloted by Lieutenant Gerald Coffee took photos of things the Americans hadn't previously known were there: Russian battlefield weapons, nuclear battlefield weapons known in the Pentagon as FROGs. They were mobile, quick to arm, and had a range of twenty miles. Fired from a Cuban hilltop, they could destroy anything within a thousand yards of their target. Such as a sizable chunk of an American fleet. Or an invading army heading for the beach in fragile boats.

When the glossy American planes streaked overhead, the Cubans and their Russian guests assumed that they were Cuban planes. The white stars on their fuselages were the insignia of both air forces. When it dawned on him that these aircraft were American, Fidel Castro was outraged. He called a meeting with the Russians and his own air defense people.

"There's no reason of any kind," he told them, "why we should not shoot down *Yanquis* that fly over us at three hundred feet. When those low-level planes appear, fry them."

The Russians looked edgy. They took their orders from Moscow. But those orders took a long time to arrive. Much longer than it took an American plane traveling at five hundred miles an hour to fly the length of Cuba.

With his eyes on the telly, George poured HP sauce onto his helping of Ruth's tragic cottage pie.

The same map of the Caribbean with the circles on it.

". . . conflicting reports of Soviet shipping movements . . ."

Meaningless footage of surging American warships that might have been filmed anywhere, at any time.

Harold bloody Macmillan in front of 10 Downing Street, shaking hands with somebody.

Noisy protestors in Grosvenor Square with placards. NO WAR ON CUBA! USA OUT OF CUBA! YANKS GO HOME!

"Much ruddy good that'll do," George muttered through a mouthful of gray mince.

Something about an emergency debate at the United Nations in New York. "Meanwhile, in Washington . . ."

Ruth concentrated on her food, which seemed strangely tasteless. It had happened a few times recently, this inability to taste or smell things. It was another way that things kept going out of focus somehow. Her attention would go wandering, not onto anything else but into blankness, like sleep. A waking sleep, from which she surfaced with a frightened jolt, as if she'd found herself a single step from the edge of a cliff. They lasted only moments, these driftings, but they scared her. Even worse were the hot surges that ran through her body. At least once or twice a day, these past few weeks. They reddened her face and made her sweat, and they brought a kind of panic with them that was like falling or drowning. It was awful when it happened at work. Just a few days ago, she'd had one of these turns while serving a customer. She'd frozen, staring down into the open till, unable to remember which coins were which.

Eventually, she'd summoned up the courage to visit the doctor. He was a posh chap a good deal younger than herself. He'd told her, briskly, that there was nothing wrong with her, that she was merely going through the Change. He gave her a Ministry of Health leaflet about it. On the cover there was a picture of a hale-looking middle-aged woman walking a large dog. A golden retriever, perhaps.

George would never stand for a dog in the house, Ruth had thought.

She'd lived a life of meager proportions, knew it was so and was content. She'd never been to a foreign country, never been to London, and didn't want to. The only newspaper she read regularly was the *North Norfolk News*. The wider world was vast and therefore dangerous; Ruth excluded it because it caused her only anxiety. She'd persuaded herself that politics had nothing to do with her. And anyway, when it came to politics, she had enough to cope with at home. Maintaining the Secret Treaty of Sexual Nonproliferation between herself and her husband. The bitterly cold war between George and Win. Clem's moodiness, his prickly neutrality toward his father. And now it seemed that her own body was rebelling against her.

She studied her husband, sidelong. There was gray in his receding hair and in his mustache (along with a spot of sauce). Outdoor work had weathered his lean face, but he was still, she thought, good-looking. He had not, like her, run to fat. She wondered what other women thought, looking at him. The question made a breach in her defenses. She blinked the wetness from her eyes.

"George?"

He lifted his knife hand to hush her.

"Hang on," he said.

The reedy voice coming from the television belonged to a

foxily handsome old man with a crest of white hair. He was the ninety-year-old peace campaigner and Nobel prize–winning philosopher Bertrand Russell.

"Huh," George grunted after a minute. "What would he know about anything?"

Ruth said unsteadily, "There ent really gorn to be a war, is there, George? I dunt think I could go through another one, on top of everythun else."

The news came to an end. George looked at her, frowning.

"On top of what everything else?"

She felt hot. "You know. That just dunt seem fair, after all we're been through."

"Fair?" George scoffed at the word. "Since when has *fair* got to do with anything?"

She couldn't think of any reply.

George, as if only then realizing they were alone, said, "Where's Clem?"

"He said to keep his warm. He're gone out."

"What about your mother?"

"Gone down the Brethren."

"What, again?"

Ruth managed a laugh of sorts. "Yeah. I reckon they think if they pray hard enough, that Bomb wunt drop. D'yer want any more of that pie?"

George leaned back in his chair and felt in his overall pocket for his cigarettes.

"No, I'm all right, ta. Is there anything for afters?"

39.
THE SHIFTY WORD *STANDSTILL*

BY **FRIDAY,** October 26, President Kennedy had become very twitchy, and not just because of the badly mixed cocktail of drugs he was having for breakfast. Four days into the sea blockade, and no Cuba-bound Russian ships had been intercepted or turned back. No missiles or warheads had been discovered. The "quarantine" looked like it was becoming a tactical and public-relations disaster.

JFK was used to having good press; he was skilled at media management. But now that word *weak* was showing up in the American newspapers. In Britain and elsewhere in Europe, public opinion was turning against him. The slogan *U.S. out of Cuba*, which he saw on television news broadcasts, irked him enormously. It wasn't the United States that was in Cuba, for Christ's sake; it was the goddamn Russians. They'd started it.

But the president of the United States couldn't just start yelling, "It's not fair," like an angry schoolboy.

He was under fierce pressure from the Joint Chiefs of Staff.

General Maxwell Taylor had told him, politely but bluntly, that you can't order the biggest troop mobilization since World War II and then sit on the fence whistling "Dixie."

You can't keep men tensed at High Alert for more than a few days. Something will blow.

And then, of course, there was the major question of what was going on in Cuba itself. The quarantine was doing nothing about that. Did the Russians, by now, have IRBMs ready to fire, ready to rain hottest hell down on San Francisco and Pittsburgh?

The Friday morning meeting of ExComm was a mixture of fear and farce. By then Lundahl of the CIA had taken a good look at Lieutenant Coffee's photographs.

When his boss, John McCone, told ExComm that the Cubans had battlefield nuclear weapons, it changed the complexion of things.

"These weapons are relatively small and mobile," McCone told them. "They are most likely no longer in the same positions in which we photographed them. Even if we bombed Cuba for a week before sending troops in, we could not guarantee their destruction."

There was a big blink. FROGs were the Devil's own artillery. If the Reds or Castro were crazy enough to use them, there would be thousands of marines dead on the Cuban beaches. An aircraft carrier and a destroyer or two joining the *Maine* on the seabed. Nuclear radiation spread over half the Caribbean. Not good. Not good at all.

* * *

Adlai Stevenson, America's ambassador to the United Nations, was a cultured, sensitive man. As a diplomat, he deplored confrontation and took no pleasure in humiliating an opponent. He was, in Kennedy's terminology, a Dove. His insistence that the problem be peaceably resolved by the U.N. was contemptuously dismissed by the Hawks as fatally weak. So when he returned to Washington from New York with the U.N.'s proposal for a standstill, he fully expected to get blitzed. And he did.

He spelled out the U.N.'s proposition to ExComm.

1. No ships would go to Cuba carrying arms of any sort.
2. There would be no further work on the Soviet missile bases.

Okay so far. Then.

3. The quarantine would be suspended.

The Hawks screamed down on Stevenson.

"So we do *nothing*?"

"We lift the quarantine, and the Russians do whatever the hell they like?"

"Adlai, are you crazy? This is like letting the Soviets *win!*"

"No, listen—"

"Mr. Ambassador, we are already at DefCon 2. Do you know what that means?"

Kennedy calmed things down. He asked Stevenson to explain how this "standstill" might work.

I can't resist including the following mad dialogue from the secret tapes. It could be part of a script for a TV comedy. *The End of the World Show*, or something like that.

Dean Rusk: The work on the Russian bases must include the inoperability of the missiles.

Stevenson: I think it would be quite proper to attempt to do that, but we would have to say "*keep* them inoperable." It would be a different thing to say that they should be *rendered* inoperable, because that requires —

Rusk: Okay, "*keep* them inoperable."

McNamara: Well, when did they *become* inoperable?

McGeorge Bundy: So, uh, "make sure that they are inoperable."

Stevenson: Well, that . . . You see, I'm trying to make clear to you that this is a *standstill.* No more construction, no more quarantine, no more arms shipments. Now, when you say "*make* them inoperable," that's not a standstill.

Unidentified speaker: You can *ensure* that they're inoperable. Then that leaves open the question whether it's a standstill.

Rusk: If they turn out to be *operable,* then that means something altogether different.

Wonderful, isn't it? Here are the Brightest and Best, within a gnat's whisker, as far as they know, of global catastrophe, and they're arguing about the meaning of the word *standstill.* That old pedant Tash Harmsworth would've been delighted, though not so much with the Americans' grammar.

Of course, the whole discussion was pointless. The Russians had a veto in the U.N. Security Council, and there was no way in the world they were going to vote for a "standstill" and allow U.N. inspectors to snoop around their Cuban missile sites. In the language of the Hawks, Adlai Stevenson and the other Doves were screwed. War was on its way. It was the only game in town. The only question was, who dealt?

Clem had looked up *coy* in the two-volume *Oxford Dictionary* and had been surprised to discover that it was the name for "a lobster trap." Surely not . . . No, the second definition offered "shyly undemonstrative" or "distant, disdainful." That would be it. Then he sat in one of the beaten-up leather armchairs in the Nelson Library with a copy of *The Oxford Book of English Verse* and turned its small, wispy pages until he got to *Marvell*.

He found the poem hard going, at first. Shakespearean. Until he got to the line that ended with the word *breast*. It definitely meant "tit," because Marvell was talking about taking two hundred years "to adore each breast." And "each" means there were two, therefore . . . Then came the lines that Tash had quoted in the bogs.

Clem went back to the beginning of the poem and read more slowly, and it dawned on him: the poem was about seduction; no, the poem *was* a seduction. It was pretty dirty, actually.

Marvell was saying to his tight-kneed girlfriend, "Look, we're going to die, and it might happen anytime soon. And we're going to be a long time dead. So let's have sex, right now, before it's too late."

It struck Clem as a fairly convincing argument. And urgently topical, despite having been written three hundred years ago.

He didn't understand the last two lines:

Thus, though we cannot make our sun
Stand still, yet we will make him run.

But the gist of the poem was clear enough. He went to the signing-out book on the corner table and wrote, *The Ox Book of Eng Verse,* then his name and the date.

A lower-sixther called Sullivan walked into the room and said, "The four-minute warning has just gone off. No, really. Didn't you hear it? I'm off upstairs to do Stinker's daughter before I die. Anyone coming with me? The swivel-eyed tart will never know which one of us it was."

"Go away, Slug," a prefect named Bradley said from another armchair. "Or would you prefer that in language that you understand?"

The American invasion of Cuba was code-named Operation Scabbards. It would begin with a series of massive air bombardments: three a day until missile sites and other military targets had been wiped out. Then twenty-three thousand airborne troops would seize Havana's airport — or what was left of it — south of the city. Meanwhile eight divisions, a hundred and twenty thousand men, would land on beaches to the east and west. The Americans would converge on Havana from all three directions, isolating it and cutting it off from its inland missile bases, if any had survived.

All well and good, except that the Americans still didn't

know about the forty thousand Soviet troops waiting to greet them. And until late on Friday, the officers who would be at the sharp end didn't know that the Russians had nuclear battle-field weapons. When they found out, they started demanding them, too.

Castro and his Russian allies had received a good deal of infor-mation—some of it accurate—about the American buildup. Fidel was convinced that the *Yanquis* hadn't invested so much energy, and so many of their filthy capitalist dollars, in some sort of symbolic gesture. This time they would invade, for sure. He'd been anticipating—eagerly, some thought—another invasion ever since the Bay of Pigs fiasco. He'd never really understood why Kennedy had pulled back that time. Maybe because he was a gutless playboy millionaire. But this time, he'd have to go for it. He was too weak to stand up to his generals, and besides, he was fighting a congressional election. He'd need to pretend to be a man of action, of decision.

Fidel Castro was not someone who spent much time on introspection. Had he been, he might have had to admit to him-self that he was a lousy politician. What he was good at, though, very good at, was Heroism. The crisis fueled him. Thrilled him. He'd spent the past week in incessant motion, snatching only short periods of sleep in the back of his car or in his under-ground command post across the river from the Havana zoo. To his Cuban troops, he had spoken of "patriotism" and *"dig-nidad"*—dignity. Fidel was very big on *dignity*, which is what you die with. To the Russians, he had spoken of the defense of

Communism and the revolution, and urged them to stay off the booze, of which they were very fond.

What was worrying him most, on Friday night, was Cuba's vulnerability to American air attack. His own antiaircraft defenses were weak. The Russians had SAMs, surface-to-air missiles, but he didn't have direct control over them. It seemed to him vital that the comrades not sit there twiddling their thumbs while the *Yanqui* bombs fell, waiting for instructions from Moscow. At two o'clock on Saturday morning, he sent a message to Aleksandr Alekseev, the Soviet ambassador to Cuba, telling him to expect a visit. Alekseev was a great admirer of Castro. But I bet he groaned when he was woken up. Castro could talk nonstop for hours. He could talk you to a standstill.

40.

THE BRINK

ONLY THE SPACEMAN Yuri Gagarin had flown farther from the surface of Earth than the pilots of the American U-2 spy planes.

More than twelve miles above the earth, U-2s cruised the half-dark margins of the atmosphere. They were defenseless, frail, terrifying things to fly. In order to soar to such heights, powered by a single engine, and stay there for many hours, they had to be extremely light. They had very long, fragile wings. Apart from the pilot, the plane's heaviest component was the huge camera in its belly. U-2s were, essentially, gliders: gliders designed to reach the limits of the air. The pilot, in his inflated oxygen-fed pressure suit, jammed into the tiny cockpit, needed very good bladder and bowel control. And to be crazy, in a special sort of way.

Flying at such a prodigious height, U-2s could not be shot down by conventional antiaircraft weapons or enemy aircraft.

The only thing that could reach them was a surface-to-air missile.

Early on Saturday, October 27, two U-2s took off from opposite extremities of the United States: one from Alaska, headed north, and one from Florida, headed south. Only one would return, and by the skin of its teeth.

As Ambassador Alekseev had feared, Fidel Castro kept him up for the rest of the night. Alekseev's Spanish was good, but less than perfect. Every now and again he had to raise a weary hand to stop the Cuban leader while the translator caught up. During these pauses, Castro paced up and down the room, stroking his beard in a manner that might have been comical under other circumstances. What Castro wanted was to communicate with Khrushchev personally and urgently. Less clear was what, exactly, Castro wanted to say.

It was six in the morning before the text of Castro's message was finally agreed upon. Fidel told Comrade Khrushchev that he expected the Americans to attack Cuba within the next twenty-four hours—at most, seventy-two. Massive bombing was almost certain. Full-scale invasion probable. The heroic people of Cuba would fight and die with *dignidad,* naturally. "But," Castro added, "if the Americans carry out an attack on Cuba, a barbaric, illegal, and immoral act, then that would be the time to consider liquidating, forever, such a danger through a legal right of self-defense. However harsh and terrible such a decision might be, there is no alternative, in my opinion."

In other words, Castro was asking the Russians to nuke the United States as soon as the Americans made their move.

Alekseev told his people to transmit the message to the Kremlin. Then he excused himself and went back to his bed, not at all sure that he wouldn't be incinerated in it before he woke up.

The U-2 that took off into the Alaskan night was piloted by Captain Charles Maultsby. His mission was both hazardous and routine. He would fly to the North Pole and take samples of atmospheric dust in clouds that had drifted from Soviet nuclear testing sites in the Arctic Circle. He and his colleagues did this on a regular basis. His plane was not equipped with sophisticated navigation devices. In fact, he was using the two most ancient methods known to man: the stars and a compass. Maultsby had a series of star charts tucked next to his seat. By comparing them to what he saw from his cockpit, he could figure out where he was. He had done this efficiently on previous flights, but now, nearing the Pole, these charts stopped making sense. Some kind of false dawn had dimmed the constellations; multicolored steaks of light flickered through the sky, confusing him.

A little later, he found himself adrift in a world of frightful beauty. Sky-filling curtains of light furled and unfurled around him, phasing through iridescent shades of yellow, green, turquoise, indigo. They snaked away, faded, then returned as brilliantly vibrant cliffs dropping into dark nothingness. The thin polar clouds changed color continuously, like theatrical scrims lit by a deranged lighting engineer.

Maultsby had flown into a vast music made visible. He had flown into the northern lights, the aurora borealis, and was lost.

This close to the North Pole, his compass was useless; from here, it told him, all directions were south. He could not radio his base for help; the Russians might detect his signal.

Dazed as he was, Maultsby activated the air-sampling devices, then turned his plane through what he thought was 180 degrees, to return the way he had come. He had to do this in cautious stages over a long circuit. The U-2 was so fragile that any violent maneuver, any sudden variation in speed, would tear it apart. Maultsby had a parachute and a survival kit inside his seat cushion. But this far north, no survival was possible. If he made it down onto the ice cap, the next living thing he would see would be the polar bear that fancied him for breakfast.

"The best advice I can offer," his commanding officer had said, "is that if you go down, don't bother to open the chute."

The U-2 that took off from Florida was piloted by Major Rudolf Anderson. His mission was not routine. He would fly a circuit high above eastern Cuba looking for Soviet air defenses.

After an hour, he could see from his cockpit, in elaborate miniature, the white-rimmed green chain of islands, *cays,* off the north coast of Cuba passing below him. He activated the camera and eased his course southeasterly.

* * *

The USS *Oxford* was a floating forest of radio masts and radar antennae. It coasted slowly along the edge of Cuban territorial waters, easily visible from the shore. Most of its crew wore headphones and sat listening to and interpreting the little whirrs and pings and buzzes that told them what Cuba's defense and communications systems were up to.

Anderson's camera, swinging back and forth below him, had covered the eastern end of Cuba. He turned as sharply west and north as the plane would let him and set course for home.

Two of the technicians on the *Oxford* sat up straight simultaneously. Each had picked up a repetitive, high-pitched *psip-psip-psip*. One of them said into the ship's intercom, "Chief? Chief, we've got a Big Cigar."

Big Cigar was code for Russian radar fixing a surface-to-air missile onto a target. The *Oxford*'s commander radioed this information to the Pentagon immediately. There was nothing they could do to warn Anderson; like Maultsby, he was instructed to observe strict radio silence until he was back in U.S. airspace.

It was just possible, if you spotted it in time, to dodge a SAM if you were flying a high-powered, highly maneuverable jet. You could throw your plane into a dive and turn that would leave the missile climbing blindly past you. In his ungainly aircraft, Anderson had no chance. A Soviet V-75 missile blew his U-2 to bits above the Cuban coastal town of Banes. Eerily, the tail section continued on its way, gliding out into the Caribbean Sea. Anderson was probably killed instantly; he was certainly dead before his body, in the ripped and twisted cockpit section, plunged into a field of sugarcane.

Maultsby, baffled by the outrageous magnetic beauty of the polar light display, had not turned his plane through 180 degrees. He was forty degrees out. So at eight a.m., when he should have crossed the northern coast of Alaska, he was, astonishingly, more than nine hundred miles off course. He crossed the northern coast of the Chukotka Peninsula instead. And the Chukotka Peninsula was not part of North America. It was the easternmost tip of Asia, and it was part of the Soviet Union.

Despite its cold and awful desolation, the peninsula boasted two military airfields and was ringed by radar stations. This was because the North Pole was one possible route for American bombers on their way to hit Russia. So Maultsby's plane was detected almost immediately. Six Soviet MiG jets took off to intercept it. The local air defense people sent news of the interloper to Moscow, urgently. After all, if the Americans were going to start a war over Cuba, they might also be planning a simultaneous attack from the east. These messages to Moscow from Chukotka were picked up by CIA listening stations in Alaska and northern Europe. The Americans knew that the MiGs couldn't reach Maultsby's altitude, but would they launch a SAM? The crews of American bombers over Norway and Greece were told to turn off their country-and-western stations and go on standby.

41.

POETRY DOES THE TRICK

"FRANKLINS," CLEM HAD said when Frankie had called at eleven thirty. He told himself that it was because he couldn't think of anywhere else, but he had other motives that had a good deal to do with Andrew Marvell's poem.

Marron refused to set hoof upon the newly ruined land where the lovers' barn, his stable, had stood. Frankie dismounted and walked the horse through a gap in the surviving trees and tethered him to a sycamore sapling. She and Clem kissed as though each possessed the only oxygen left in the world. Then he led her into the lee of the old gable wall. The morning rain had wandered off like a gray cat bored with a kill, but the wind had a cold edge. Frankie spread her waxed riding coat on the ground and they sat.

Her father's bare prairie now came to within twenty yards of the remains of the house. Frankie looked out at it and took

Clem's right hand in hers and tucked it up under her jumper and began to cry.

"Hey," Clem said. "Come on. It's all right."

"No, it bloody isn't," she sobbed.

And he was dismantled. He was far too young to reassure tearful girls. He had a nipple under his fingers, a partial erection in his jeans, and a copy of *The Oxford Book of English Verse* in his jacket pocket. All he could do was wait.

"It's all so *ghastly*. So *stupid*."

He thought that praising her breast with his hand might help.

"Don't," she said.

"Frankie, I . . ."

"Last Saturday," she said, with a gulp between the words, "when I rode up and saw the smoke, I didn't know what to think. Actually, I had the silly idea that you'd been there for ages and lit a cigarette and set the place alight or something. Then I saw it was your father on that machine, and the other men, and I—"

"You thought we'd been found out."

"Yes."

She looked at him and said bravely, "But we haven't. Obviously. I mean, I'd've been locked up or something."

She sniffed again. "Shall we have a smoke first?"

Reluctantly, while weighing the possible meanings of "first," he withdrew his hand. He fished a light-blue packet of Bristols out of one pocket and the dark-blue book of poetry out of the other.

"What's that?" she asked when he had lit her up.

"I, er, came across something. Something you might like. A poem."

"Really? What's it about?"

"Well, it made me think about you."

She blew out smoke, flicked ash, and turned her wet, depthless eyes upon him.

"Did it? Why?"

He had not expected her to ask.

"I . . . I dunno. It just did."

"I expect it's a love poem, is it?" She put an ironic, throaty emphasis on the two words.

"Sort of."

She said, "We didn't do much poetry at Saint Ethel's. The sisters thought it was sinful. My friend Maddie knew one called 'Eskimo Nell' by heart. Her boyfriend taught her it. It was absolutely filthy."

This was not going quite the way that Clem had planned.

He said, "There are some quite rude bits in this one, actually."

"Are there? Oh, good! Let's finish our ciggies, then you can read it to me."

His heart snagged. He'd imagined her reading it to herself, then looking up at him, aglow with revelation and impatient readiness.

"Yeah," he said. "All right."

Frankie flicked the end of her cigarette into the wet ferns and turned herself so that she was leaning against his left side.

She closed her eyes.

"Go on, then," she said. "I'm listening."

He began, his voice clogged at first by embarrassment, then with a touch more certainty.

"Had we but world enough, and time,
This coyness, Lady, were no crime
We would sit down and think which way
To walk and pass our long love's day."

When he reached the line about adoring each breast, Frankie giggled but did not open her eyes. He struggled on.

"But at my back I always hear
Time's wingèd chariot hurrying near;
And yonder all before us lie
Deserts of vast eternity."

Clem paused meaningfully. And it seemed that Frankie had understood. She opened her eyes and stared out at the desolate landscape that their fathers had created.

She said, "They're going to bulldoze this bit, too. All the way back to the road, George says."

Clem couldn't bear the way she used his father's first name. The familiarity in it, and therefore a kind of forgiveness. What was more, it was intolerable, outrageous, that his father could, and did, talk to her when he could not.

He'd gone bitter, so he hardly knew how to react when she

reached her hand up to his face and said, "We'll find somewhere else, won't we? Or we'll run away. Don't be sad, Clem. It was a nice poem, by the way."

"That's not the end. There's quite a bit more."

"Is there?"

She kissed him, then resettled herself. "Go on, then."

". . . then worms shall try
That long preserved virginity,
And your quaint honor turn to dust,
And into ashes all my lust."

"It doesn't say that," she said, laughing. "You made that up."

"No, I didn't. Read it yourself if you like."

"*Worms?*" Frankie said, doing a little shudder. "That's horrid, actually. I know it happens when you're dead and everything. But *yuck*! It's a bit sick, isn't it? Is that why you like it?"

"No. I think it's . . ."

He was miles from any appropriate adjective. *Irrefutable* might have served, but he couldn't come up with it.

"Let me read the rest of it," he said.

He mangled his way to the end of the ode. He left a pregnant pause. His underpants were charged with poetical desire. He made his move a second too late. She had stood up.

She walked away from him and folded her arms and looked out at the brown crusts of land between her and her home. Her dark hair danced sideways in the wind, baring her neck, exposing the dark little whisper in the valley of her nape.

She said, "Is there going to be a war, Clem?"

"Yeah," he said. "Probably."

"Daddy says there won't be. He says it's all a sort of bluff. He says the Russians are taking the mickey; no one's going to blow the world up over a stupid little place like Cuba."

"It's not about Cuba."

She turned back to him.

"Isn't it? What's it about, then, Clem? You're so much cleverer than I am."

He said, "It's about weapons. No one's ever had 'em and not used 'em. Like, a long time ago, someone invented the bow and arrow. Some caveman or somethun. But he didn't go up to the other cavemen and say, 'I've invented this thing that'll kill you, so do what I say.' What he did was shoot some poor bugger through the guts and then say, 'Thas what I can do, so watch it.' Same with gunpowder, and guns. Planes, everything. Same with the Bomb."

The anger in his voice made Frankie cautious.

"I suppose so," she said. "But the Bomb is different, isn't it? It would be mad . . ."

"That's what wars are, Frankie. Mad."

She came back to him and sat down. Clem reached his right arm around her, and she put her head on his shoulder.

He said, "I heard on the wireless this morning that they reckon the Yanks will invade Cuba on Monday at the latest. P'raps even tomorrow."

When she said nothing, he pulled his head back to look at her. There were tears trickling down each of her cheeks. He hadn't wanted this. But perhaps it was good.

"I don't want to die, Clem. Not yet."

Ah.

"Don't you? Why not?"

"It's . . . it's not fair."

Clem laughed, a sound like a snort. "*Fair?* Nothun's *fair,* as far as I can see. But if it did happen, you know, right now, *boomf,* it would be sort of nice, wouldn't it? Well, not nice, but . . . we'd be together, wouldn't we? It'd be a shame that we hadn't . . . you know . . ."

She sat up straight and looked at him, her eyelashes pearled with tears.

"That could happen, couldn't it? Any second. We wouldn't know. We wouldn't have time to do anything."

"Thas right," he said, sliding his hand under her sweater and onto her belly.

"Oh, God," Frankie said, or sobbed. "Poor Marron. Poor, poor Marron. It's nothing to do with him."

Sod Marron, Clem thought, but he suffered the unwelcome image of the tethered horse evaporating into fire, its meat whirled, burning from its tall bones.

Frankie got to her feet.

"I've got to go and see him," she said. "Make sure he's all right. I'll be back in a sec."

So much for effing poetry, Clem thought. When it comes to girls, it loses out to horses every time. He took the cigs from his pocket and lit one. From somewhere behind him, a pheasant croaked a complaint about its vanishing habitat. After a while, he heard Frankie making her way back, her feet slushing the leaves.

"Give me a puff on that," she said.

He looked over his shoulder. She was sitting on the stump of the wall, swinging her legs as though nothing mattered. He stood and went to her and gave her the cigarette.

"I know what the poem means," she said. "I know why you wanted to read it to me."

He said nothing, feeling suddenly and deeply ashamed and obvious.

"Do you want any more of this?"

"No." He took the cigarette butt from her and threw it away. "Come here."

He went to her. She parted her legs and hooked her heels around the back of his thighs, pulling him against her.

With her mouth close to his ear, she said, "I want to do it with you, Clem. I want to Go All the Way. It would be stupid if we . . . well, you know."

His heart and penis surged, but his mouth, for some crazy reason, said, "We don't have to. It's all right."

What?

"No. We do have to. I absolutely refuse to die a virgin. It would just be too awful."

"God, Frankie," he mumbled, and tried to press himself up to her.

"No. Not now, Clem. Not here. I don't like it here anymore."

He died slightly.

She said, "When you think about, you know, us doing it, where are we?"

"What?"

"When you're in bed. You must think about us having sex when you're in bed, don't you? I do. All the time." She hugged him tighter to hide her shame. "It's delicious, isn't it? You know what I mean."

He gaped, wide-eyed, over her shoulder at the surviving wintering trees.

"I sometimes think about doing it in the barn, which is nice. But mostly it's always by the sea. Us doing it with the tide coming in, getting closer all the time. Is that mad, do you think?"

"I dunno. No. I think that's nice."

"Where's the nearest beach from here, Clem?"

"What? Um, well, Hazeborough, I spose."

"How far is that?"

He was nibbling the lobe of her ear, something she usually liked. "What?"

"How far is Hazeborough?"

"Christ, Frankie. I dunno. Eight miles, something like that."

"So three-quarters of an hour on a bike?"

"More or less. *Frankie* . . ."

"Listen," she said. "Tomorrow, tomorrow morning, Daddy's driving Mummy to Norwich. She wants to go to the Catholic church. Just to be on the safe side, she says. They'll want me to go, too, but I won't. I'll say I've got the Curse or a headache or something. Mrs. Cutting goes to church as well, in Borstead. Clem, are you listening?"

"Yeah."

"Then stop doing that to my ear. So, as soon as they've all gone, I'll get on my bike. I could be in Hazeborough by eleven-ish. Where shall I meet you?"

"Frankie, what the hell're you on about? C'mon, let's do it now. The Bomb could drop at any minute. Please, Frankie."

She leaned away from him and took his head in her hands. She studied him with immense seriousness, as if they were about to part forever and she was memorizing his face. She bit her lip.

"*Please*, Frankie."

"No," she said. "I'm . . . I'm not ready."

"What d'yer mean? You just said—"

She silenced him with a tongue-in kiss that undid his knees. When it was over, he went for second helpings, but she stopped him.

"Where shall I meet you? In Hazeborough?"

Clem moved away from her, turned his back, sulkily. Put his hands in his pockets, adjusting himself.

"Christ, Frankie. You drive me nuts. You really do."

"I know I do. I'm sorry."

She waited.

"There's sod all in Hazeborough, really. There's two ways down onto the beach. The second one's next to a caff. Sort of like a wood shack. It'll be closed this time of year."

"I'll meet you there, then. You will wait for me, won't you? In case I'm late?"

42.
JACK AND NIKITA TALK TURKEY

L ATE ON SATURDAY night, in the White House, an exhausted but sleepless John F. Kennedy sat in his private quarters watching one of his favorite movies: *Roman Holiday,* starring that sexy little thing Audrey Hepburn and the comically wooden Gregory Peck. It was comfort food for the brain: warm, familiar, and bland. He needed it. The day had not gone well. It might actually be easier to fight a war than chair those damned ExComm meetings.

His bowel griped and he shifted in the chair, painfully, to break wind.

He was beginning to think he could see a way through this thing. Khrushchev's last letter, yesterday, was full of the usual bluster and bull, but what it came down to was that he was prepared to do a deal. Maybe the fat little bastard wasn't, after all, totally insane. Maybe he'd looked at it all and decided that fifty million, minimum, dead Russians was too high a price to pay for a propaganda stunt in the Caribbean. But Khrushchev couldn't pull his missiles out if it looked like a defeat. To save his fat face—maybe to save his life, because they played pretty rough in the Kremlin—he'd need to make it look like he'd got something out of it. Like he'd extracted a price. Won. And the price was, Kennedy thought, incredibly cheap. What Khrushchev was saying, it seemed, was that he'd disarm the Cuban missiles if the U.S. removed its Thor missiles from Turkey. And promised not to invade Cuba.

Losing the Turkish Thors was not, in Kennedy's view, a problem. They were obsolete, anyway. "A heap of junk," Bob McNamara had called them. So the thing to do was dismantle the Thors, publicly. Then station a Polaris submarine, with up-to-date nukes, off the Turkish coast and make sure the Russians knew it was there. And as for not invading Cuba, well, Jesus, even that foul-mouthed moron Shoup had to admit that at least five thousand marines would die before even one made it onto the beach. And that estimate was based on the Russians not using their nuclear battlefield weapons. Kennedy knew that public opinion would turn against him when the blood started to flow. That was the one immutable law of politics.

So it seemed to him that the Turkey trade-off might be a way out.

It brought problems with it, though. Like Khrushchev, Kennedy had to come out of it looking good. He'd have to put some smart political spin on the deal. It couldn't look like the Russians had suckered him, had used Cuba to force him to back down in Europe. He'd have to say to Khrushchev, "Okay, Nikita, you take the nukes out of Cuba; I take the nukes out of

317

Turkey. But it's a *secret* deal, all right? You can crow about it to those wall-faced comrades of yours in the Kremlin all you like, but you don't go public with it. I'm going to wait a while before I take those Thors away, so that nobody will make the connection and call me a weakling. Deal?"

So both of them would come out of the thing with something they could call *honor.*

Unless—and there was always this—the Russians had something else up their sleeves. It was no coincidence that the bastards were so good at chess.

He allowed himself to enjoy his favorite scene in the movie. He was interested in, and knowledgeable about, women's clothes. Hepburn's were terrific. She wore the kind of stuff that Jackie wore. He wondered, drowsily, whether Hollywood imitated his wife's taste or whether it was the other way around.

He dreamed a Soviet missile crunching through the floors of the White House, thrusting its awful snout through the shattered masonry, seeking him out, personally. Crushing him. Squashing him, opening its rotten metal mouth to swallow his head. Then obliterating everything for miles around, in bellying circles of fire.

"Hello, Chack."

Khrushchev in the chair on the other side of the coffee table. That awful way of sitting he has, legs apart, hands on his thick thighs. Like a man on the toilet. Dreadful shiny suit designed by a bickering committee. Smile like a bad set of dentures shoved into a steamed pudding.

"Nikita?"

"How are things with you, Mr. President?"

"Uh, okay. No, I was dreaming I was dead."

"Funny. So was I. But because of the time zones, I was dead before you was."

"How was it?"

"Oh, you know, Chack. A blinding light. A splitting headache, then nothing. I thought of my wife at the last moment, like you do. Because we were apart."

"Yes."

"There is no heaven, by the way."

"Ah. I kinda thought there might not be."

Khrushchev's sparse eyebrows lifted.

"I think your friend the pope would not be pleased to hear you say that, Chack."

"I guess not."

Khrushchev reached inside his jacket and produced something large, pinkish, and trussed.

"I brought you a gift," he said. "A turkey. For your Thanksgiving."

"Uh, that's really kind of you, Nikita. A generous thought. Thank you."

"Please. It is nothing. In the people's paradise of the Soviet Union we have more food than we know how to eat."

He put the big plucked bird down on the coffee table and patted its nude breast complacently.

"Plump," he said. "Do you have something for me, Chack?"

"Aah, lemme see."

Kennedy searched through his pockets with increasing urgency. They were all empty.

Grinning, embarrassed, he said, "Well, er, I guess nothing, right now, Nikita. But on behalf of the people of the United States of America, I thank you for the turkey."

Khrushchev's smile went out like a lamp. He reached again into his jacket and took out a large pair of scissors. He used them to cut the string that bound the bird's legs and wings. The turkey flexed its naked limbs and stood up on the knobs of bone where its feet had been. It withdrew its feathered and wattled head from inside its body cavity and looked around, stretching its raw neck. Then, with an angry gargle, it went for Kennedy's eyes with its beak.

He woke up, sweating and alone. His corset was pressing into his kidneys. He forced himself more upright in the chair. The screen was a white hiss. He drank some flat Coke from the bottle and waited for his mind to clear.

The problem wasn't Khrushchev; it was his own people: the ExComm Hawks and the military. The Hawks were deeply unhappy about trading the Turkish Thors. Shrewdly, they'd focused on how it would *look,* especially to America's allies in NATO. Mac Bundy'd had a point when he said that if the U.S. were seen to be doing unilateral deals with the Soviets, "we'd be in real trouble. If we appear to be trading the defense of Turkey for a threat to Cuba, we'll just have to face a radical decline in the effectiveness of NATO. The whole thing could fall apart."

And the military . . . well, they were at full boil. It was getting harder all the time to keep the lid on. That morning, when Kennedy had asked Maxwell Taylor for a planning update, the general had said crisply, "Aerial bombardment for seven days, followed immediately by full-scale invasion. All forces ashore in eighteen days." As if it was inevitable, a foregone conclusion. Then that poor bastard, whatshisname, Anderson, had got himself shot down. McNamara said that when the news reached the Pentagon, the desire to retaliate was so strong that you could smell it in the air, like jock sweat in a locker room. Thank God that other U-2, that'd gone walkabout over Russia, got home in one piece. If the Russians had brought down *two* on the same day, that nutcase Curtis LeMay might've climbed into a B-52 and gone off to nuke Moscow personally.

General Power (jeez, how had primitives like him and LeMay come to have control over the hardware?) had rigged the IBMs in Montana so that the double-fault fail-safe system that prevented an accidental launch of the missiles could be bypassed. Which meant, without hyphens, that two guys, maybe gone crazy or panicking in their underground bunker, could let go a nuclear missile without checking authorization.

B-52 bombers, permanently, in rotation, were cruising the perimeters of the Soviet Union. Each was loaded with four Mark 28 nuclear bombs. An Mk-28 had seventy times the power of the bomb that had obliterated Hiroshima. An encoded—or wrongly encoded—radio signal could send any one of those planes veering off to drop destruction onto Omsk or Tomsk or Gomsk, or whatever the hell those Russian places were called.

And on this night, divisions of marines had boarded ship in full expectation of swarming through tropical surf to purge the Caribbean of Commies.

And on this night, U.S. ships and planes were searching for the four, maybe more, nuclear-armed Soviet submarines within the quarantine, with orders to regard them as hostile.

And a missile ship, the *Grozny*, was going to hit the blockade line at dawn.

Kennedy had installed a situation room in the White House: screens, phones, alert young people. It occupied a space that President Eisenhower had used as a bowling alley. The SR tapped him into the information that was fed to the Pentagon. It allowed Kennedy to monitor real-time developments, allowed him to feel that he was in control. But he wasn't, and he knew it. He was not at all sure who *was* in control. Who was in control of the Cuban missiles? The Russians, who at least seemed to have some discipline? Or Castro, who might do who knew what?

It seemed to Kennedy that the whole thing was like a pyramid of eggs, or a cluster of bubbles. Unbearable delicacy. Just one component starts to roll, something pops, and *poof!* the world is gone.

The gray telephone by his elbow tempted him. He could

wake his personal assistant. Dave Powers. Tell Dave to get him a woman. Mary Meyer, perhaps. That would be nice. Mary's husband was a CIA officer, which made her a risky mistress. She was so good, though. Very understanding, very discreet, and accepting of his disabilities. And her husband, if he was doing his job, would not be at home.

Powers answered on the third ring.

43.

THE DAY THE WORLD ENDED

I**T WAS STILL** dark when Ruth heard noises from the bathroom, then the toilet flushing and Win going back to her room, singing to herself.

George was right, Ruth thought. Her mother was going a bit peculiar. And she'd be retiring from the laundry six months from now. A batty old woman in the house all day, oh, my God. Dunt even think about it. Ruth squinted at the alarm clock. Five something? George's breathing rattled in his chest. The fags. She worried herself back to sleep.

She awoke when George brought the cups of tea in, which was the Sunday arrangement.

"Did you make one for Mother?"

"No," George said. "There's no sound out of her."

"Ent there? Thas rum, ent it? She never sleep this late."

George kicked his slippers off and got back into bed.

"I better go'n see if she's all right," Ruth said, heaving her legs out from under the blankets.

"'Course she's all right. Drink your tea."

"She might be ill, George."

"Ill?" he snorted. "When's she ever been ill?"

Win hadn't opened her curtains, so it was understandable that in the dimly lit bedroom Ruth mistook what lay on the floor for a big gray cat. Understandable, therefore, that she screamed. And understandable when she realized that she was looking at her mother's chopped-off hair that she screamed again.

"*What?*" George said, from the doorway.

"Whassup, Mum?" Clem, for some reason holding his dressing gown in front of him instead of wearing it.

But Ruth couldn't say anything. With her hand over her mouth, she was staring at her mother's bed, which was empty, the blankets pulled away from the bare and lumpy mattress.

She was too distracted to manage the usual Sunday breakfast. Eventually, George ate a bowl of cornflakes, his silence worse than accusation.

When Clem wheeled his bike out of the shed, Ruth called, "Where're you gorn?"

"I said I'd help Goz with his paper round. Thas five miles on a Sunday, and them Sunday papers weigh a ton, he says."

"So you're gorn down Arnold Pitcher's?"

"Yeah."

"Nip round the corner to Angel Yard, Clem, then. See if your gran's all right. I'm that worried. I espect she're with Hoseason and that lot, but if she ent, you come back and tell me, orright?"

"Okay, Mum," Clem said.

He hid his face, making a show of checking his brakes.

It was like he flew to the coast.

Frankie.

The huge white sky smiled down on him. His legs were effortless.

Frankie.

Freewheeling the slow downhill out of Napton, he took his hands from the handlebars and put them in his pockets and fiddled with himself.

Frankie.

The sign that said HAZEBOROUGH was deceitful; there was nothing for an uphill mile. He stood on the pedals.

Frankie, Frankie!

Then the sea spread itself in front of him, like restless metal. A car, a bulbous little Austin A30, passed him with a clergyman at the wheel, who smiled and waved. Perhaps he had mistaken Clem's incandescent halo of lust for something more spiritual.

A road sign: NORWICH 21 MILES. NORWICH. People wrote it on the back of love-letter envelopes as a joke. It stood for Knickers Off Ready When I Come Home. Should be KORWICH, anyhow. The *k* is silent in *knickers*. The phrase struck him as funny, and he laughed aloud. Then something, someone, an older version of himself perhaps, told him that he was laughing because he was scared. Made him stop at the top of the low hill, the sea cliff dipping down to his right. He set his feet on either side of the bike on the tar-and-gravel road. He didn't know if he stunk when he was sweaty. Some boys did. Goz did, a bit.

The thought he had tried to smother rose up again: *It'd be better not to do it than be no good at it.*

The electrical thrill of anticipation changed polarity, became something closer to dread. He was trembling; his watch shook when he looked at it. Ten to eleven, nearly. The strident calling of herring gulls sounded like mockery.

Where, *exactly,* do you put it in?

The railway that brought holidaymakers clattering to Cromer and Sheringham did not reach Hazeborough, despite the fact that the little hamlet had a beach superior to those of its jollier neighbors. But that was not the only reason that it remained unpopular, almost, in fact, desolate.

In 1940, after the heroic disaster of Dunkirk, the Ministry of Defense made a hasty survey of England's south and east coasts to work out the likeliest places for Hitler's forces to come ashore when they invaded. It was fairly unlikely that they'd choose north Norfolk, as opposed to Kent, say, or Sussex. But if the sneaky Nazi swine *did* decide to come across the North Sea rather than the English Channel, Hazeborough was exactly the kind of place they might fancy. The cliffs there were lower than at any point for miles and miles. The sea was shallow for some considerable distance from the shore, even at low tide. So the Royal Navy tethered sea mines—big buoyant spheres of explosive with detonator spikes—a mile or so offshore. The Royal Engineers garlanded the beach, all three miles of it, with coiled barbed wire and built "pillboxes"—concrete gun emplacements—atop the cliff. When that was done, the Royal Ordnance Corps planted land mines.

The Germans never came, as we know.

After the war, a decent effort was made to clear all this stuff away. It proved more difficult, and more hazardous, than putting it there. Maps and charts had gone missing. Navy minesweepers recovered fewer sea mines than they should have done; some had broken free of their mooring chains and drifted off. Tides and wild weather had reshaped the beach. In the winter of 1944, a large chunk of cliff had toppled down onto the minefield, bringing a pillbox with it.

It was four years (during which time one ROC man was killed, and two others maimed, by land mines) before Hazeborough beach was considered safe enough to be re-opened to the public. And even then, in 1950, the farthermost reaches of the beach remained fenced off and marked with warning signs—a skull and crossbones inside a red triangle. In time, the mesh fences were slumped by windblown sand, and the signs were disfigured by boys with catapults. Even so, Hazeborough was regarded with suspicion. (Ruth was one of many who believed that you'd get blown up as soon as you set foot on the sand. She'd have had a purple fit if she'd known that Clem had gone there, even if his motives had been pure.) The place remained unprosperous and unpopular.

* * *

He leaned the bike against one of the rust-flaked uprights of the railings behind the shuttered clapboard café. He watched the sea lazily heave itself onto the shingly sand and retreat, sighing. The weather was on their side, at least. The wind up here could slice you to the bone if it wanted to, but today it was resting, or waiting. Above the horizon, a swath of sky was striped like the skin of a blue mackerel.

She wouldn't come.

No, don't think that.

The world could end now. The sky could convulse, turn sideways, become a tower of fire. He could be sucked into oblivion at any second, waiting in bloody Hazeborough to lose his virginity.

Don't think that, neither.

A man with a muzzled greyhound walked by and gave him a good looking at.

Clem lit a cigarette and smoked it, then popped a Polo mint into his mouth for his breath.

She wouldn't come. She hadn't got out of going to church. She was sitting on a pew, her tears reflecting stained glass.

A tinny chirrup of a bicycle bell, and there she was. Coming toward him, waving. She was wearing a skirt and a tight white sweater under her coat. Glimpses of stocking top and thigh flickered at him, and his heart went ballistic.

The Reverend Hugh Underwood, white-surpliced, stood at the porch of Saint Nicholas's Church, bidding farewell to his flock. It didn't take long, but even so it was tedious. The business was nearly over when two of his departed congregation returned: the spinster twins, the Misses Fiske, clearly in a state of excitement. After a good deal of mutual nudging and urging, one of them said, "If yer've got a minute, Vicar, there's somethun in the square you oughter see."

Underwood considered this unlikely.

"Really? And what might that be, pray, Miss Fiske?"

The ladies couldn't muster a reply between them. Instead, they blushed, made matching beckoning gestures, and scuttled off. Sighing, in need of a cup of tea and a cigarette, Underwood followed.

Borstead's square was, in fact, roughly rectangular. Toward its slightly wider end stood an ancient stone cross, stump armed and covered in elaborate carvings blurred by time. It was, tradition had it, more than a thousand years old, placed there on the orders of Saint Dunstan himself, when Borstead was a nameless pagan crossroads. Next to it, for reasons no one could remember, an ancient fire engine was parked. It was an eighteenth-century horse-drawn cart, a lead-lined water tank and hand pump set into a red-painted wooden frame on iron-rimmed wheels. On market days, when the square was lined with stalls, the cross and the fire engine were an irritation to traffic; at other times they were largely ignored, on account of their familiarity. On this Sunday morning, however, they were the center of attention. A good many people, and not only the Reverend Underwood's faithful, had gathered at the margins of the square to create a mocking hubbub, which hushed, gradually, as the vicar approached. Alongside Edmond's, the haberdashery, he halted, aghast.

A circle of white-robed figures surrounded the cross and the fire engine. They were so extraordinary, so utterly unfamiliar, that for a dizzy moment he thought they might have descended from space or—less likely—heaven. Clearly, some were male and some female, yet the females had hair like men, and the males had no hair at all. And they were barefoot. A single voice persisted when silence descended: a stout bald man reciting from the book of Revelation. It took Underwood a full half minute to realize that it was Enoch Hoseason. Then he started to recognize the others. There were twelve, in all. The mad messiah and his disciples. There was heresy in the very number. Underwood formed his face into a stern mask and advanced.

Frankie dismounted and let her bike fall onto his, her pedals barging into his spokes.

"Hiya," she said, and the awkwardness of it, the fact that she'd never said it before, melted him.

He embarked on a number of sentences that he couldn't complete.

"Are you . . . ? Do you still . . . ? Did you, was it, I mean . . ."

She busied herself with herself, ignoring him. She fussed with her garter belt through her skirt, tugged her sweater back into order, shrugged her coat into shape. Tossed her hair back. Then she looked up at him. Her face was almost expressionless.

"Shut up," she said, then planted her mouth on his and forced her tongue in, pressing herself against him. He was shocked; they'd never snogged openly in a public place before.

"So," Frankie said, pulling away, "here we are. Still alive, just as I said we'd be. Where are we going?"

"This way," he said.

He didn't dare take her hand until they were some way along the beach, out of sight of the cliff-top huddle of fishermen's cottages and gabled bungalows. Despite the enormity of what they were about to do, Frankie seemed to be without a care. She lifted her face to the bright pallor of the sky. She inhaled the sea air like a tourist. The silence between them didn't appear to bother her; in fact, she seemed to want it. His own anxiety was so strong that he thought it might be audible, plangent as cracking ice. At least there was no one else around, he thought. He had no faith in his luck. It would not have surprised him if they'd come face-to-face, at this momentous moment, in this remote spot, with someone who knew him, someone who would report his assignation and bring the world down in a heap.

The gorsy jumble of fallen cliff forced them closer to the low surf. They walked across a springy mat of seaweed, bladder wrack. Its brown blisters popped beneath their feet, which delighted her. She let go of his hand and jumped on them, bursting them childishly, laughing, little squirts of water staining her shoes. He stood watching her, smiling like a parent.

Beyond the landslip, there was a sign on a pole: a pocked and dented skull and crossbones.

Frankie said, "What's that mean?"

"Beware of pirates," Clem said. "Come on."

He took hold of her hand again and led her toward the cliff, where a great slab of concrete, a wartime ruin, angled into the sand. He reckoned that in the lee of it they would see anyone approaching before anyone approaching would see them.

"Will this do?"

Frankie looked around as if she were considering buying it.

She leaned her back against the slab and smiled and opened her arms, which parted her coat, and said, "Come here, Clem Ackroyd."

So he went to her and kissed her and put his hands up inside her clothes, up her back where he could feel the bra strap and the silky shiftings of her shoulder blades. She parted her legs, and although he almost didn't want to, he shoved his shameful hardness up against her. Miraculously, it excited her. She placed her hands at the top of his hips and tugged him tighter in, lifting herself, mumbling his name into their kiss.

He thought, Is this it? Like this, standing up? Is this what she wants?

Then her mouth was smearing away from his, and she was somehow laughing and gasping, "No," at the same time. She pulled away from him, shrugging her coat off. She spread it on the sand and sat on it, leaning forward, her arms wrapped around her knees. Not looking at him. Distant, as though he weren't even there and she was lost in a private moment. He felt something that was the comfortable opposite of hope. Then, as if she were alone and getting ready for bed, Frankie flipped her shoes off and reached up under her skirt. She unfastened her stockings and peeled them from her legs. Such outrageously beautiful legs. She stretched them out and fingered the sand with her toes. She felt under her skirt again and fiddled with something. Produced, like a magician, her garter belt, a flimsy-looking thing like the skin of a small black reptile, and . . .

And looked up at him.

"?" her eyes said.

?

So he took his shoes and socks off, awkward, leaning against the slanting wall of the pillbox.

With her eyes on his, she undid her skirt and cast it aside. Her knickers were pink with a white lace waistband. Her belly curved like a question mark up toward the edge of her sweater.

With unsteady hands, he unbelted and dropped his jeans. He somehow got his right foot stuck and had to hop around to keep his balance. She laughed, and he tried to. While he was still struggling, she stood up and ran down to the slow surf and walked into it.

He didn't know whether to lie on the coat and adopt some sort of seductive position until she came back or to follow her. From this distance, she looked so like a child, in her sweater and pink knickers and her arms held out and the cold, lazy foam separating and regathering around her shins. She turned and called something, words shredded by sea sound and gulls.

So he went to her, his shirttails flapping below his sleeveless sweater, his feet wincing on the stones and broken shells. The coldness of the water was withering at first, then an almost pleasant numbness. Frankie's arms were folded under her breasts now, and she was gazing out at where the blue-gray horizon was silvered by slants of light.

"Frankie?"

It was like waking her up.

She said, "I don't believe all this is going to come to an end, actually. It just can't."

"Yes, it could," he said stoutly. "Right this minute some Russian or some American could be pressing a button, and we wunt know anything about it until . . . well, you know."

She turned her head and looked at him.

"It's not going to happen." She said it brightly and firmly, with tears in her eyes.

His heart went as dead as his feet.

"Ent it?"

"No." Then she smiled. "I love it when you go all pouty. It makes you look ever so young."

She put her arms around his neck and kissed him, the cold gray water sloshing at their legs.

"Come on, then," she said, and took him by the hand and led him away from the sea.

"Mr. Hoseason!"

Enoch seemed oblivious to the vicar's presence. He carried on declaiming the words of Saint John the Divine.

"Mr. Hoseason, sir! What is the meaning of this, this unseemly . . . *exhibition*?"

At last Enoch lifted his eyes and fixed them on Underwood's.

335

The dark ecstasy in his glare made the clergyman flinch.

"'I know thy works,'" Enoch recited, his voice grimmer than before, "'that thou art neither cold nor hot: I would thou wert cold or hot.

"'So because thou art lukewarm, and neither hot nor cold, I will spew thee out of my mouth.

"'Because thou sayest, I am rich and have gotten riches, and have need of nothing; and knowest not that thou art the wretched one and miserable and poor and blind and naked . . .'"

Good grief, Underwood thought. He knows the damned thing by heart!

It was clear that he wasn't going to get any sense out of the blacksmith, so Underwood looked around the circle of Brethren until he caught the eye of Jonathan Eldon, whose denuded head was specked with razor cuts.

"Jonathan, for the love of God! What are you doing?"

"Awaiting deliverance," Eldon said placidly.

"Deliverance? Deliverance from what?"

"Death."

Underwood glanced around the square, uneasily. The crowd, though still small, had increased in number. The expressions on its faces ranged from scandalized outrage to coarse glee. There was, unmistakably, ugliness, or the promise of it, in the Sunday-morning air.

Someone called out from the crowd, "They're waitun fer the Bomb to drop, Vicar!"

There was the kind of pause that precedes laughter, but no one laughed.

Ruth had her hands in the sink, peeling potatoes, when the phone startled her. She peered out of the kitchen window and called George but got no reply. No doubt he was in that bleddy shed of his, with the transistor radio on. She wiped her hands on a tea towel, hurriedly.

"Hello?"

She heard *pip-pip-pip* and the clunk of a coin.

"Ruth? Thas Chrissie."

Which made Ruth uneasy straightaway. Chrissie Slender was a regular visitor, Wednesday afternoons, sometimes Saturdays, but had hardly ever phoned.

"Chrissie? Whassup, then?"

"Ruth, you better come downtown. Thas Win."

"Mother? Whatever d'yer mean? Hev somethun happened to her?"

"I dunt rightly know howter tell yer, Ruth. She're in the square with Hoseason and that lot."

Ruth felt a chill run through her. The hair on the bedroom floor. Oh, my God.

"Whas she doin in the square, Chrissie?"

"She're makin an exhibition of herself, Ruth. They all are. I dunt like to be the one that tell yer."

"Oh, Chrissie!"

"Get you down here, Ruth. An if yer got a spare coat, you bring that an all. Or a blanket or somethun."

"Whatever for, Chrissie?"

She heard Chrissie hesitate.

"Win hent got hardly nothun on," Chrissie said. "I'm worried she might catch her death."

Ruth sat down heavily on the little chair beside the telephone. One of those hot, distancing spasms ran through her, and she clasped her hands on her plump knees until it was over.

When she came back to herself, she thought about Clem. Why hadn't he come back to tell her what was going on?

She felt an inrush of incomprehension, of being excluded from events. She got to her feet and took off her pinafore and went outside to find George.

Frankie and Clem lay down on her coat in the soft shadow of the World War II gun emplacement. Their wet feet had gathered sand, so that they wore gritty pairs of ankle socks. They kissed, lengthily. She pulled him tight to her but kept her legs together. He pushed her away a little so that he could put a hand to her breasts. They murmured each other's names when they paused for breath. After a while he thought she might be expecting him to force her, so he slid his hand down between her legs. This did not have the effect he'd desired. She levered herself into a sitting position.

"Oh, God," she said.

"What?" Clem asked thickly.

Frankie groped under the coat and produced from its pocket a small flat bottle. She twisted the top off it.

"Brandy," she said. "For Dutch courage. Strictly speaking, Dutch courage should be gin, I suppose. Do you like brandy?"

He was fixated on the little display of flesh between her

knickers and the rucked-up edge of her sweater, and the two dimples above her bum.

"I dunno. Never had any."

Frankie took a swig and inhaled through her nose while swallowing, like someone in pain. She held the bottle out toward him. He sat up and drank. His throat and then his chest caught fire, and he coughed, spluttering spit and spirit into the palm of his hand. She laughed and took the little bottle back.

"Do you have any ciggies? I'd like one. The Condemned Woman Smoked a Last Cigarette sort of thing."

"Frankie . . ."

"Please, Clem."

He crawled over to his jeans and fumbled the cigarettes and matches from the pocket. They lit up and smoked in silence for a while. Then she took another swig from the bottle and passed it to him, shuddering.

"No, thanks."

"You must. You have to have the same as me."

"Why?"

"You just do."

He drank, this time keeping the brandy down, and felt a shelf of heat form itself at his diaphragm. When he turned to her, she was smiling and serious. She threw her ciggie away and then plucked his from his fingers and threw it away also. Before he could get on top of her she rolled away, then back to him. Like a conjurer, she displayed something in her fingers that hadn't been there a moment earlier. A little packet.

"Ta-daa!" she said.

Clem frowned at it. "What's that?"

"A johnny." She bit her lip. "Just in case the end of the world doesn't happen."

He lifted his gaze to her face. His mouth was hot and dry.

"Where'd you get it?"

"Does it matter?"

"You didn't get it from Griffin's, did you?"

"Lord, no. Are you nuts?"

When he continued to goggle at her, she put the thing in his hand and lay back on the coat sacrificially, closing her eyes.

"I pinched it from Daddy's bedside cabinet, if you really must know."

She pulled him down onto her.

"If you like, I'll close my eyes when you're ready to pop it on."

We were hopeless, of course. Inept, frantic, silent, shamefully quick. How could we not be?

It's one of life's countless little cruelties that you never forget your first time. So instead of forgetting, we have to forgive ourselves, which is a far more difficult thing to do. I've never achieved it. But I guess that in my case there were special circumstances.

Anyway, we managed it, Frankie and I. She helped me, showed me what to do. And my response was to suspect her: how come she knew?

But what nearly ended it before it had begun, what almost deflated and unmanned me, was the grotesque fact that we were using one of Gerard Mortimer's condoms. Even as her marvelous body gave way to me and let me in, I couldn't help picturing her furious father's moist mustache.

"Dunt drive into the square," Ruth said. "Park round the back of the church."

"I was going to," George said.

He was tense with the anticipation of shame. He parked the Land Rover on Vicarage Street and followed Ruth through the kissing gate into the churchyard. She hurried past the gravestones and the church porch and out into the square, where she stopped, speechless, and put a hand to her bosom.

"Ruddy *hell*," George said.

All sides of the square were now lined with people. It was quiet but not silent. A murmuration of onlookers. A voice rising and falling but not pausing. Ruth recognized her almost unrecognizable mother among the circle of robed figures and almost fainted.

"Oh, George," she cried, and hid her flushed face against his shoulder.

Win's slumped old breasts and belly and buttocks were clearly discernible through the thin white cotton. Her cropped gray head was lifted, and she was smiling bitterly at the sky with her eyes closed. Her mouth was working silently.

"Christ on a bike," George said, and, as if in response, Police Constable Neville Newby cycled slowly into view.

P.C. Newby was a large man who believed his physique represented the weight of the law and therefore ate to sustain it. His uniform was not quite correctly buttoned, and he had the look of a man whose lengthy Sunday breakfast had been rudely interrupted. He dismounted, laboriously, outside Cubitt and Lark's and propped his bicycle against a lamppost. He assessed the situation while removing his bicycle clips, then advanced upon the Brethren, who paid him no attention. He surveyed the circle slowly, nodding to announce that he recognized each of its members. He came full circle back to Hoseason.

"Enoch," he said loudly. "Enoch, what in God's name do yer think yer doin?"

Hoseason continued to read from the book.

"'And he opened the pit of the abyss; and there went up a smoke out of the pit, as the smoke of a great furnace; and the sun and the air were darkened by reason of the smoke of the pit.'"

"This wunt do at all, Enoch. Come along, man. I dunt want to hev to arrest you all."

"'And out of the smoke came forth locusts upon the earth; and power was given them, as the scorpions of the earth have power.'"

"Dunt you push yer luck, Enoch," Newby barked, adjusting his helmet, "and dunt call me a scorpion. You take yer people away nice and decent and get yer clothes back on, and I wunt hev to call Norwich for a van to take yer all away. 'Cos I can do that, you know."

"'And it was said unto them that they should not hurt the grass of the earth . . .'"

Newby hissed his impatience and turned to Enoch's brother.

"Amos, what in hell is all this about?"

"The hour is at hand, Neville."

"Don't you bleddy Neville me," Newby said fiercely. "Thas Constable Newby to you, Amos."

"All office is cleansed away," Amos said beatifically.

"What?"

Amos said (while his brother announced, "'And the shapes of the locusts were like unto horses prepared for war'"), "We're doing nothun illegal. Is it against the law to declare our love of the Lord? Or to surrender ourself to his unimaginable mercy? Strip off the trappuns of earthly power, Neville Newby. Take off thy helmut and stand with us. Even at this moment it ent too late."

By now the constable was so hot with anger that it seemed his abundant nostril hair might spontaneously ignite.

"You ent right in the head." He glared around the circle of saints. "None of yer is."

"'And they had breastplates,'" Enoch declared, his voice rising, "'as it were breastplates of iron; and the sound of their wings was as the sound of chariots of many horses rushing to war.'"

"I'll give yer bleddy chariots," Newby declared. "I'm off to phone Norwich. If yer still here when they come, be that on yer own head."

He strode back to his bicycle, but didn't risk the ungainly act of mounting it in the full gaze of the public. Instead, he marched it back through the square, as if it were a young vandal he'd nabbed by the collar. At the church gates, he caught sight of Ruth's stricken face, and halted.

"I'm sorry to see yer mother here, Ruth," he said. "She dint seem as mental as the rest of that lot. Why don't yer see if yer can't talk some sense inter her?"

He noted the mackintosh over George's arm.

"An see if yer can't get that coat on her. That ent a pretty sight, is it?"

And with that, he plodded on his way.

Ruth looked at the faces around the square. There were none she didn't know, hadn't spent her life among. The idea of them all watching her as she made the long walk to her mad mother, the shame of it, brought her to the edge of nausea, of swooning. She burst into tears, noisily, and stumbled back into the churchyard. Reaching the bench where, in her long-gone age of innocence, she'd shared lunch with poor soft Stanley, she sat down, took off her spectacles, and wept.

George came to her and, after a moment or two of hesitation, sat beside her and put his arm around her shoulders.

"I'm sorry," Clem whispered.

"Don't say that. Don't spoil it."

They were lying on their sides with their arms around each other. He could feel Frankie's breath on his neck. His fingers trembled in her hair.

"It was nice," she said.

"Was it?"

He remembered her short hiss of pain, or anger, her lips pulled back from her teeth. It had shocked him.

The light had changed, brightened. A wind they could not feel rattled the gorse above them. He wondered about the tide, how high it might come, and when. Stupid holidaymakers were always getting cut off by high tides, all along the coast. Having to be rescued. If he and Frankie were . . . God. He quelled a ripple of panic.

She said quietly, seriously, "I expect it's something one gets better at with practice. Like the violin. Or anything, really."

He sort of laughed, or scoffed. He couldn't help it. She lifted her head and looked at him gravely. Her eyes were so dark and liquid and lovely. He forgot this, sometimes, because he thought so much about her other parts.

"What? Don't you think so?"

"Yeah. I spose."

"You *spose*," she said, mocking him. "Well, let me tell you, Clement Ackroyd, we are going to find out. We are going to put in lots of practice."

She kissed him.

"Lots and *lots*. Okay?"

"Yeah. Okay."

She propped her head on one hand. "You don't sound too sure."

He was in a state of sticky wilt. He didn't know what to do with himself.

"Frankie, leave off."

"Or are you one of those boys who lose interest in a girl once they've had her? Are you going to finish with me now that you've made me a tart?"

"Yeah," he said. "You read me like a book, Frankie."

"Or a poem."

"Or a poem," he agreed.

"Tell me you love me," she said.

But before he could speak, she pressed two fingers onto his lips.

"Don't say it if you don't mean it. Don't, honestly. Don't say it just because we've, you know. Had sex."

"I love you, Frankie."

"More than before, or the same?"

"More."

"Good," she said, and lowered her head onto his chest.

He looked up at the colorless sky, where gulls drifted, scolding and mewling.

We've done it, he told himself. We've actually done it. *Yes!*

Yet what he felt was worryingly familiar and childish: something like getting caught stealing fruit from someone else's garden.

They walked back along the beach, making silly dramas of dodging the slow overlaps of low surf.

She said, "We've never done this before."

"I know that," he said.

"No, not *that*. I mean, we've never walked anywhere holding hands. I really like it."

Something, a slight catch in her voice, made him look at her. She was nearly crying.

"Hey," he said. "Hey, c'mon, Frankie."

They stopped, and he put his arms around her, awkwardly.

"Hey. Whassup?"

She sniffled into the folds of his jacket, shaking her head.

"I hate everything. I really do, actually. All I want is to be with you. Everything else is such absolute shit. So *boring.* D'you know what I wish?"

"What?"

"That the world *would* end right now. That Kennedy or thingy, the Communist, would blow us all up. I expect it would hurt. It would be ghastly for a minute or so. But then it would be all over. I wouldn't have to go back to Mummy and Daddy and tell lies about where I've been and then think up more lies so I can meet you next time. I don't want to do that anymore. I really don't. I can't bear it. It's all so *mucky.*"

He thought, She's ending it. Because I was no good.

Suddenly he was exhausted by the very thought of the long ride back. Sickened, as though he'd already smelled the warmed-up and congealed Sunday dinner waiting for him. As though he'd already tasted the lies that he, too, would tell.

Frankie seemed to have read his thoughts somehow.

"I don't want to go home," she said, so childishly, so innocently, that it made Clem laugh.

"I don't," she said more fiercely. "I can't bear the thought of it."

"Nor can't I," he said. "Come on. The tide's coming in."

When they could see the rooftops of Hazeborough hunched at the cliff top, they heard voices. Yells ripped meaningless by the wind and the surf. At some distance ahead of them, an ancient timber jetty sloped into the sea, sand and shingle banked up against it. Two—no, three—young boys, their shapes made indistinct by sea glitter, shouting and throwing stones. As he and Frankie drew nearer, Clem saw that the boys were not stoning the jetty but something close to it, half buried. Something rusty black and spherical with stumpy little legs.

Clem would never be sure if he'd recognized it in that last instant. Whether he'd yelled a warning just before everything stopped making sense, before all memory turned false. Before all that had been separate and different—sea and stones, wind and sand, his and Frankie's place among them—erupted into the same thing: a silent roar with huge rough hands that picked him up and changed him terribly and threw him away. It all seemed to take a long, long time. Something was happening to his arms and legs and face, but those parts of him were far away, floating by themselves. He wondered where Frankie had gone, thinking that he should be looking after her, that she would be frightened.

Then something big thumped into his back and he was still.

Just before he went to sleep, he heard a pattern of sound: *ssshh-tick-tock, ssshh-tick-tock.* Like someone kind, a nurse perhaps, trying to persuade a clock to stop.

* * *

When he woke up, he was dreaming. His head was in a bubble through which he could see the empty sky. The bubble was the glass cab of a big machine, but nothing would obey the controls. He sent urgent blurred messages out to its limbs. After a while he saw, at the corner of his eye, something come alive and lift itself out of the sand. It looked a bit like a hand at the end of a ragged tube. It seemed to be pointing. He looked beyond it and saw a pair of legs, splayed and painted red, sticking up out of a drift of sand, close to a dummy's head wearing a red mask and a black wig.

He could not understand why he couldn't hear anything while at the same time his head was full of noise.

Frankie?

The word came from nowhere.

His eyes refocused on the hand at the end of his arm. Actually, it looked more like a red knitted glove that hadn't been put on properly. Then fiery fingers that were colder than ice pressed themselves against the side of his face and ushered him down into a merciful and fathomless darkness.

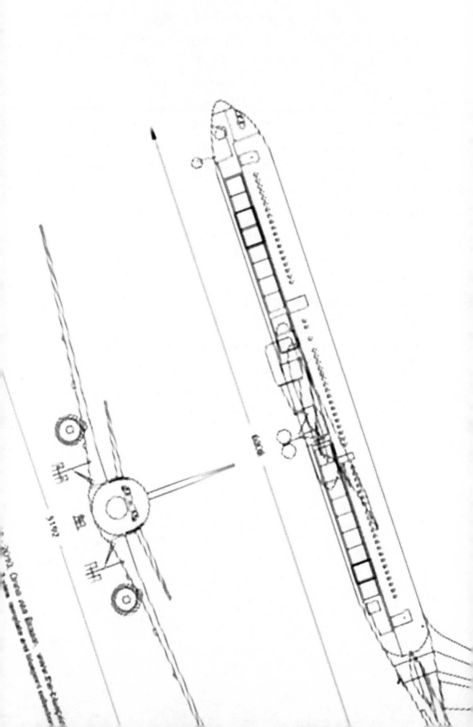

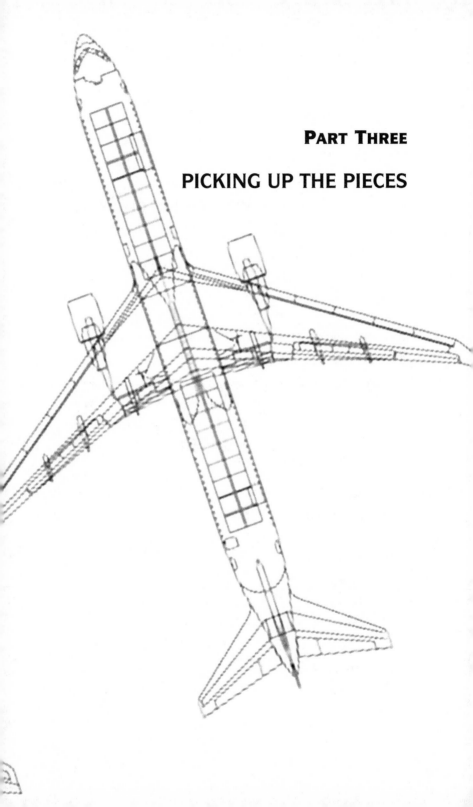

PART THREE

PICKING UP THE PIECES

44

I **AWOKE BRIEFLY** on days five, six, and seven and spoke her name before sliding back under the surface.

Ruth, who'd sat beside me all that time, must have been deeply disappointed. Sons are supposed to call out "Mother!" when Death comes to visit. I didn't.

My first coherent question was, "If she alive?"

Ruth said, "Who?"

"Frankie." It seemed to take the better part of an hour for my crippled mouth to form her name.

"That Mortimer gal?"

"Yef."

"She's alive."

"If she orright?"

"I dunt know," my mother said. "I hent asked."

For which, God forgive me, I never forgave her, even though she'd been crying for a week.

They'd identified me by the label (which I had been at pains to conceal from Frankie) stitched to the waistband of my underpants.

Rule 19: All items of clothing, including socks and underwear, are to be clearly labeled with the pupil's full name.

I don't know how they identified Frankie.

Goz came to see me in Norwich sometime between my second and third operations. Not that there was much of me to see. I was bandaged like a mummy, just the right side of my face—eye, nose, and half mouth—showing. My white-packaged left arm was propped up on a sort of cradle. My white-parceled left leg hung from a wire attached to something like a gallows. Goz, to his credit, didn't flinch. He sat down on a chair where I could see him by swiveling my eye.

"It probly don't look that way to you," he said, "but you are a lucky sod. That mine blew a hole in the beach you could park a bus in. Two buses. You heard about the three kids, I spose?"

I had, yes. George had told me, shakily.

"During the war," he'd said, as though talking to himself, "we'd sometimes put stones in the coffins when we couldn't find all their bits. To make up the weight, like."

Goz said, "You were in all the papers. There was even a bit on the telly."

I knew that, too.

"Frankie," I managed to say.

Goz seemed to see something interesting on the floor.

With difficulty, slurping the words, I said, "D'yer know how sher if? No one'll tell me anyfing. Gof?"

"She's gone, comrade."

"Gone? Gone where?"

"London, so I'm told. Some private hospital. A week ago."

"Yer know how sher if?"

"No," Goz said. "They wouldn't tell me anything, neither. I said I was her cousin, but they didn't believe me."

It was Goz who told me, some days later, about Win and the Brethren. He'd been there, stayed to the bitter end. He hadn't found out about me and Frankie until the following day.

Ruth and George had fled the shameful display in the square and gone home. They'd stopped answering the phone, unable to face any more calls about Win. Just before five o'clock, a police car stopped outside the house and two officers knocked at the front door. Ruth assumed their business concerned her humiliated mother, and it took her some time to grasp what they were telling her. When it sank in, she sank with it. She fainted and fell backward against George, who was unable to take her weight. He also fell backward and was pinned to the floor by his stout wife. After an ungainly struggle, he was freed by the policemen.

During that Sunday afternoon, the square had filled with people. Must have been all of Borstead there, Goz said, and more besides. The piss-taking and joking gradually died out, and it got very quiet. It was like everyone was listening to mad Enoch

Hoseason reading out that crazy stuff about plagues and earth-quakes and Beast number 666 and all of that. But you could see that the Brethren were suffering, getting knackered. Fighting off doubt. Now and again some of them would start to moan, "Let it come, Lord; let it come."

Goz said that the atmosphere got weird. Some of the onlook-ers started encouraging the Brethren to stick at it. Like they'd started wanting the Bomb to drop, too. Two carloads of police arrived to reinforce P.C. Newby, but they didn't interfere. The Reverend Underwood had a heated discussion with them, then stormed off, waving his arms about.

Come evening, with the light going and a thin drizzle fall-ing, the crowd started to dissipate. Goz went home and had his tea and returned to the square. There was still a good number of people there. Hoseason was still reciting, but some of his follow-ers were clearly in a bad way. Doreen Pullen, who ran the Cosy Tea Shop, unlocked her premises and carried chairs out and per-suaded some of the Chosen—including Win—to sit. She also brought cups of tea and rather dry slices of cake, but these were refused. Someone draped a coat over Win's shoulders, and she didn't cast it off. Goz was puzzled that none of us—Ruth, me, George—were there. He went to the phone box at the top of the square and called our house. (He got no reply, of course. By then, my parents were arriving at the Norfolk and Norwich Hospital.) Newby and one of the police cars had disappeared; the remain-ing three officers were enjoying Doreen's hospitality.

There was muted talk of an explosion—another one of them mines—on Hazeborough beach.

By the time the church clock struck eleven, the Brethren were wet, wilted, and dejected. Hoseason and his brother were the only two left standing. Enoch was now on his twelfth recitation of the book of Revelation, and his voice was as coarse as the rasp of a file on a horse's hoof.

At the last stroke of midnight he fell silent and lifted his face to the rain. Some of the few remaining onlookers applauded, self-consciously. Most of the Brethren were now asleep or semiconscious on chairs or the ground. Enoch and Amos went around the circle, shaking them vigorously. Some responded; some did not. Then the two brothers, alone and caring not who followed, walked away in the direction of Angel Yard. Halfway there, on the pavement outside the Star Supply Stores, Enoch stopped dead and fell on his knees and cried brokenly, "'My God, my God, why hast Thou forsaken me?'"

Amos helped him to his feet, and they went on.

Win was left slumped on one of the Cosy Tea Shop's bentwood chairs. Goz was by now very perturbed that we were not there to get her home. Then Chrissie Slender and the poacher, Bert Emery—with whom she lived in sin—stepped out of the darkness and helped her into Bert's van.

Some weeks later, Goz reported that Enoch Hoseason had disappeared from Borstead. The rumor was that he'd moved to the West Country, presumably to found another sect in preparation for the next end of the world.

It was during that same visit that Goz told me he'd heard

that Frankie had gone to America for treatment at some special clinic. He didn't know where.

I progressed from bed to wheelchair (Goz whizzing me along the hospital corridors in defiance of all protocol) to crutches.

I went back to Newgate at the end of September 1963. By then I needed only a walking stick. My new nickname was Frankenstein, and I answered to it, causing embarrassment. (Although, one day a Maggot burst into tears when he looked at me, and that hurt.) Tash Harmsworth and Jiffy and Poke Wilkins gave me extra tutoring. My right hand was undamaged. Writing and drawing were okay. Painting was more difficult then. Too much color mixing, too much changing hands.

I was solitary, dislocated. My few school friends had left at the end of the summer term. Goz was at Cambridge, the first person from Millfields to go to university. And thus getting higher Above Himself than anyone from the estate had ever been before: a working-class Icarus.

The months in the hospital, the surgery, the physiotherapy, the obsession with physical and mechanical functions, had left me emotionally numb. Clumsily robotic. It was as if the last general anesthetic hadn't worn off. But, slowly and surprisingly, school woke me up. I started to feel again, to reassemble myself. Often I wished that I hadn't. At the core of the wreck of who or what I was, there was a vacancy, an absence whose name was Frankie. My rediscovered feelings had nothing to attach themselves to, no purpose. They were like a wardrobe full of a dead man's clothes. My parents treated me with careful circumspection, as if I were a delicate and rather embarrassing alien visitor from a remote star entrusted to their care.

Because I found it difficult to paint, I was not going to do very well at the A-level exam. My portfolio of drawings (many of which featured a stylized girl's body in dark imaginary settings) was good, though. Jiffy had a word with his old art college, and they gave me a place.

I left Norfolk for London without a backward glance, with my paltry possessions in a suitcase that looked like leather but was made of pressed and laminated cardboard. I had fifteen pounds, cash, in my pocket and a council grant worth ten pounds and ten shillings a week. George was quietly outraged. It was pretty much half what he earned, and he didn't get to look at girls with no clothes on.

I loved the late 1960s. We all did. It was like stepping out of a black-and-white movie to find yourself standing on sunlit uplands full of color. But for me, personally, the crucial and life-changing thing was that it became compulsory for young men to have long hair. I gratefully hid most of my face behind Cavalier-style black locks and peered out at the world from between these curtains with greater confidence. In 1969 I was working as a designer for an early "style" magazine near Covent Garden. One of the writers was a very pretty girl who sometimes wore thigh-length maroon suede boots below her miniskirt. Her name was Julie. I was, it seemed, invisible to her, but one day we happened to be leaving work at the same time and she said, "Coffee bar or pub?" It was a hot July evening. The day before, an American called Neil Armstrong had stepped—well, sort of hopped backwards—onto the surface of the moon. This was only slightly less amazing than the fact that Julie Hendry had spoken to me. It was a great deal less amazing than the fact that after a couple of drinks and a meal at an Indian restaurant, she came back to my flat with me.

She was amused that I kept my dope inside the hinged hump of a wooden camel.

"Where'd you get this? Morocco?"

"Yeah," I lied.

The following summer, word spread of a free music festival near Glastonbury, in Somerset. Julie and I traveled down there with a couple of friends in their wagon, an old post office van painted all over with rainbows and BAN THE BOMB signs. The festival site was on a farm. It was a strange scene; "far out," in the parlance of the times. A rural landscape a bit like Norfolk: long low hedges, willow and chestnut trees, gently rolling fields, cows. And winding through it an erratic parade of longhairs: guys in headbands and pastel-colored bell-bottoms and stack-heeled boots, barefoot girls in minis or translucent cheesecloth skirts, their faces decorated with stars and flowers. The mingled odors of dung and hashish, the sound of the Grateful Dead on the wind. As we neared the field where the stage had been set up, we saw, just ahead of us, a merry mob gathered around a bald but bearded man dressed in black. I assumed he was some sort of performer because he was attracting a great deal of laughter and applause. Then I recognized him. He was standing on a sort of dais with a densely lettered signboard in front of it.

"Turn away!" he shouted. "Turn ye away from inebriation and fornication!"

"No way, man," someone called out. "We've come all the way from Birmingham for some of that!"

Laughter.

"Turn ye away, for ye stand at the very gates of Babylon, the Mother of Harlots and Abominations of the Earth! She who sitteth upon the scarlet-colored Beast with seven heads and ten horns!"

Cries of "Whooo!" and "Yeah!"

A blond boy wearing a tie-dyed T-shirt and a top hat turned to the gathering and said, "He's got to be tripping, man."

A girl who was clearly not wearing a brassiere beneath her lace dress reached up to offer Hoseason a drag on her spliff. Someone else tried to tempt him with cider.

I pulled Julie away.

Apart from the reappearance of the Apocalypse Man, it was a great weekend.

Julie and I married two months later at Camberwell Registry Office. Neither of us invited our parents. We were very happy for the first six years and not very happy for the next two and a half. She left me in May 1979, the day after Margaret Thatcher was elected prime minister. It was a pretty rough week all around. I don't blame her. (Julie, that is.) I'd always felt grateful to her for loving me, and gratitude isn't a good basis for a marriage. Feeling grateful all the time will make you bitter eventually. She left me for a charming (and handsome) property developer called Martin. They're still together. We exchange Christmas cards.

I'd gone freelance by then. I was hardly ever out of work. At first I did anything and everything: graphics for newspapers and magazines, cookbooks, album covers, travel guides. Then I started to concentrate on book illustration and eventually started writing, too. Nonfiction. I don't have much time for novels. Two of my books were taken up by an American publisher, and in 1990 I flew to New York to do promotional stuff. I fell in love with the city. By the simple trick of overwhelming me, it relieved me of my emotional luggage, like one of those superb hotel doormen pushing a cheap and careworn suitcase toward the gutter with his toe. In 1992 I sold my London flat and my studio, and I've lived in Upper Manhattan ever since. I have no regrets. I am content.

I don't know whether to call it courage or stubbornness or what, but Win went back to work at the laundry three days after the world had failed to end. I imagine she endured a great deal of mockery as well as pain in her gnarled old feet, although the white hat would have covered the shame of her cropped head. She served out her six months to retirement. When she left,

361

she was given an elaborately written certificate confirming her forty years' devotion to soiled clothes and sheets, a fancy teapot, and a pension of two pounds and twelve shillings a week. She devoted her remaining years to making my parents' life a misery, by means of prayer and eccentricity and a calculated indifference to personal hygiene. She died, at home, in her sleep, in 1978.

A week after Frankie and I were blown up and apart on Hazeborough beach, my father came face-to-face (or maybe side to side) with Gerard Mortimer in the toilets between the men's and women's wards of the Norfolk and Norwich Hospital. Now, you'd think, wouldn't you, that here were two men united in grief who might console each other. Might even defy male convention and embrace each other. Oh, no. They had a bitter, foulmouthed, and furious row that attracted the attention of the nursing staff. They were ushered out of the building onto the forecourt (I'd like to think they both still had their flies undone), where they continued their altercation until the police were summoned.

George got his notice, and his outstanding wages, through the post two days later.

When it was decided that I was unlikely to die, he went looking for work. Eventually he was employed by a small factory in Norwich that produced metal-alloy models of tanks and aircraft and soldiers. He bought a secondhand Ford Popular to travel back and forth in. It was an absolute pig to start in the winter. Ruth had to go out in her dressing gown and Wellies and shove the damn thing, with George pumping at its pedals, until it fired and farted off up the road, leaving her shapeless and breathless inside a small cloud of exhaust.

In 1983, two months before he was due to retire, George had a heart attack in the factory storeroom, where he'd gone for a quiet smoke. Falling to the floor, he dragged a number of boxes from the shelves and died under a scattering of samurai warriors and Prussian cavalry.

Ruth never quite recovered from the double blow that she'd suffered on October 28, 1962. Both Win and I had shamed her. Photographs of our different embarrassments had appeared in the *Eastern Daily Press* and the *North Norfolk News*. Smaller reports found their way onto the inside pages of the more vulgar national newspapers. Illicit sex and spectacular religious mania: not the kind of activities that would enhance your status on the Millfields estate. Especially if you were a family with a reputation for getting Above Itself. So Ruth became more and more reclusive. Conveniently—because she was looking after her mother—it became increasingly difficult for her to leave the house. Fortunately, it was still the age of the delivery van. Butchers and fishmongers and greengrocers and coal merchants and milkmen cheerfully supplied her and took the money she proffered through the half-opened back door. When such tradesmen disappeared from the streets, she came to rely on her neighbors and the telephone. She ordered clothes and shoes from the Littlewoods mail-order catalog.

She spent the last twelve years of her life alone, never

venturing farther from the house than the end of the garden. The telly increasingly obsessed and satisfied her. She planned her week from the *TVTimes* and grew very fat on sweets and biscuits. In 1995, halfway through *Countdown,* her brain choked on an anagram and she fell sideways onto the sofa. Two hours later, a neighbor who'd failed to get an answer from Ruth's phone came to the house and found her unconscious.

I flew back from New York the following day. I was sitting by her hospital bed, drawing her, when she died.

Goz surprised us all by becoming an actor. And surprised me even more by becoming a bit of a star. At Cambridge, he'd performed with the Footlights, then joined a repertory company as a do-anything dogsbody. "Assistant stage manager" is the correct term, I believe. He wrote to me now and again during my years with Julie. I may have replied once or twice; then we lost touch. Years later I went with friends to see a Royal Shakespeare Company production of *Twelfth Night* at the Aldwych. Goz was playing Malvolio. He'd changed his name, and it was well into the second act before I recognized his body language, saw through his beard, remembered his voice, and realized that it was him. I almost got to my feet and yelled, "Goz! What the hell are you doing up there?" He's rather famous because in middle age he got to play, on TV, the part of a melancholic and alcoholic detective who always gets his man but never gets the girl. He has the perfect face for it, a slumped face you couldn't lift into a smile with the help of a crane. Actually, he's just about the happiest man I know. His show is in its sixth series, it's an international hit, and he's loaded. He writes and directs plays, too. Last year he was here in New York, directing and performing in an off-Broadway production of his play *Brethren*. We had dinner at Le Bernardin. He slupped the oysters like an expert. On my increasingly rare visits to England, I stay with him and his partner, David, at their home in Surrey.

And the Cuban Missile Crisis?

Well, it petered out. The truth is that Nikita Khrushchev was not the reckless and brutal barbarian that Kennedy had taken him for. He'd lived through the Second World War, in which more than twenty-five million Russians had died, one of them his son. He was no more eager for Armageddon than Kennedy was. It's clear, now, that he never intended to hand control of the Soviet missiles over to that wild boy Fidel Castro. And, despite all his bluster and huffing and puffing, the fact is that as soon as Kennedy announced the sea blockade, Khrushchev gave orders that no Russian ship was to cross it. He knew the game was up. He argued, of course, that he'd won. He'd given the Americans a taste of their own medicine. Taught them what it felt like to have enemy missiles parked on your doorstep. He'd frightened them. He'd put the hedgehog down Kennedy's shorts. Plus, he'd got Kennedy's word to take the Yankee missiles out of Turkey. All in all, a good result. So, on Sunday, October 28, 1962, Khrushchev ordered the Cuban missiles to be dismantled, crated up, and sent home. When this decision was announced on Radio Moscow, the newsreader made it sound like a moral and military victory for the peace-loving Soviet people. (As he was speaking, two bloodied bundles of rags, previously known as Frankie Mortimer and Clem Ackroyd, were being wheeled through the doors of the Norfolk and Norwich Hospital.)

If the Russians had won, the Americans had won even better. The Soviet Union had backed down. The unwavering determination of the United States and the cool nerve of its young president had banished the Red Menace from the neighborhood. The brave frontiersman had stared down the grizzly bear and dispatched it, shuffling and grunting, back to its lair. So everyone was happy, and the cold war continued on its merry way.

Actually, not *everyone* was happy. When Fidel Castro learned of the Russian "betrayal," he kicked the walls and roared and trashed a mirror. And the hawkish U.S. military men were livid. On that Sunday, the air inside the Pentagon was thick and foul with curses. The generals were psyched up, erect, ready to go. The invasion of Cuba was scheduled for the following Tuesday, for Christ's sake! And the goddamn politicians had screwed it all up.

"This is the greatest defeat in our history," crazy Curtis LeMay said. "We should invade Cuba today."

Much time has passed since then. A lot of blood has flowed under the bridge.

A sniper murdered JFK in 1963, in Dallas. A year later, the hard men of the Kremlin gave Khrushchev the shove; he died, obscurely, in 1971. In 1968 a young Palestinian man by the name of Sirhan Sirhan gunned down Bobby Kennedy in a Los

Angeles hotel. At the time of writing, Fidel Castro is old and sick but still alive. Since the thrilling days of the crisis, he has seen nine American presidents come and go and witnessed, in shocked disbelief, the defeat of Communism. His brother Raúl runs Cuba now.

The Soviet Union collapsed in on itself, like a diseased lung, in 1989. In that year joyful Germans swarmed over the wall that had divided East Berlin from West Berlin; the wall that had divided, symbolically, Europe. Christian capitalist democracy had won the cold war! Rejoice! The world was no longer divided by crazed ideologies! Rejoice!

I lived through all these times, these great events, without caring very much, concerned with my own aging rather than the world's. Most of us do likewise. History is the heavy traffic that prevents us from crossing the road. We're not especially interested in what it consists of. We wait, more or less patiently, for it to pause, so that we can get to the liquor store or the laundromat or the burger bar.

And I lived down all those years with the absence that was Frankie. I grew a coating over it. Several coatings. It grew bearable. No longer a mortal wound but a familiar and manageable affliction. A small ulceration of the soul. A slight tinnitus of the heart.

45.
BAD TIMING

I **WAS UP** and about early on the morning of September 11,
2001. I had a meeting downtown scheduled for eight forty-
five, and a good deal of money depended on its outcome. I'd
spent the last four months on layouts and drawings for a book
with the working title *Fantastic Machines from Fantastic Movies.*
It was to be a large-format volume with hyperrealistic spreads
by yours truly: cross sections, cutaways, exploded diagrams of
James Bond's cars, spacecraft and gizmos from *Star Trek* and
Star Wars, stuff like that. A lot of work, because I'd had to invent
lots of futuristic technology that doesn't feature on the screen,
that gets bluffed with special effects.

There was more riding on the meeting than my nice fat
fee. I'd been commissioned for the job by Val Leibnitz, an art
director I'd worked with several times already. I liked Val. She
knew what was possible and what was impossible, and if she
needed the impossible, she was always prepared to pay extra for
it. She'd just moved to a new publisher, and *Fantastic Machines*

was her first big project there. She really needed it to succeed, and so did I. The trouble was that the budget for the thing was starting to get swollen and ugly, largely because the film companies wanted big greedy slices of the pie. So I knew that as well as Val and the editorial people, there'd be a couple of cold-eyed accountants at the meeting. Which is why I was at my worktable two hours earlier than usual, getting cranked up on black coffee, going through the designs one last time, rehearsing my spiel, thinking about what could be sacrificed when the accounts people asked how we were going to trim the figures.

The phone rang just before seven thirty. I was going to leave it to the answering machine, but picked up at the fifth chirrup, figuring it might just be Val.

"Hi," I said.

There was that little pause you often get when someone realizes they've got the wrong number.

Then, "Hello? Is that Clem Ackroyd?"

A woman's voice with an upper-crust English accent. It spoke my name with a tiny hint of amusement, as though not quite able to believe that anybody could really be called that.

And I knew. Ridiculously, impossibly, I knew. My heart hiccuped. I couldn't speak, and in the ensuing short silence my dodgy hearing played one of its tricks. The faint static on the line turned into an echoic rustling: the sound of time sloughing its skin.

"Hello?"

"Yes," I managed, and cleared my throat. "Yes, it is."

"Clem, it's Françoise. Françoise Mortimer. Frankie."

"Dear God."

"Yes."

"*Frankie?*"

"Yes."

I felt dizzy. (Dizziness when I'm confronted by the unexpected is one of the features of my damage.)

"This is . . ." I said, and couldn't think what the next words might be.

She supplied them. "Something of a surprise, I imagine. A nice one, or horrid?"

"I don't know. No, of course not horrid. Christ, Frankie."

"You don't want to hang up? You can if you want to. If you do, I won't call again."

"No," I said, and there was probably a touch of panic in the word. "I don't want to hang up. I'm, I was just . . ."

"Oh, Lord," she said. "What time is it in New York? Have I got my sums wrong? It's nearly lunchtime here. Did I wake you up?"

"No, it's fine. I was . . . I had an early start."

I was staring down at a penciled piece of nonsense labeled *Android Phase Transformer.*

I said, "Frankie."

Like a child who has just discovered a thrilling word and can't stop saying it.

"Where are you, Frankie?"

"Bratton. The manor. I've been here for some time. Looking after my father. He had a stroke. Then he got pneumonia and died. His funeral was yesterday, actually."

Actually. I was telescoped to a barn. *It's beautiful, actually.*

Her covering the body that I'd drawn. Memory like a keen fragrance. One I didn't want. I'd healed and moved on.

"I'm sorry," I said.

"There's no need to be. He was suffering, and I didn't like him, anyway. I never forgave him. But I thought it might be interesting to play the role of the dutiful daughter for once. Besides, there was nobody else."

"What about your mum?" I asked, and immediately regretted it. *Mum* was a word I hadn't used for years. I was regressing, losing control.

Frankie said, "Nicole died several years ago. They'd separated, anyway. So now I'm a poor little orphan. That's not true, actually. I'm a terribly rich middle-aged orphan."

I couldn't cope with it. I didn't want to hear this. For almost forty years Frankie had dwelled like a pearl in my chest, oystered in my heart, something to be dug out and examined when I was wheeled, beyond speech and explanation, to my postmortem. On this morning it was grotesquely inappropriate. I was alive and had stuff in the present tense to deal with.

I looked at my watch. I couldn't read it. The numerals were blurred because I was freshly full of ancient loss.

Somehow, I said, "How did you find me?"

"It wasn't difficult. I came across one of your books. Months ago. On the back flap, it said, *"Clem Ackroyd lives in New York City."* I rang Information, and guess what? There were only two C. Ackroyds listed. One was an upholsterer. So the other had to be you."

"You looked for me."

"Yes."

"I didn't look for you."

"I know."

"I'm sorry."

She said, "You were always apologizing, Clem. I thought you might have grown out of it by now."

"I'm . . ."

I stopped myself, and she laughed. I laughed, too, sort of.

I said, "I'm . . . It's amazing to be talking to you, Frankie. It really is."

"How damaged were you, Clem? I never really knew."

Like introducing a normal topic of conversation, such as, *How's the weather where you are?*

I took a breath and said, "I lost most of my left ear. Left side of my face pretty screwed up. Skin grafting was still a primitive science back then. I look pretty good, right profile. Left profile, more like a map of the Norwegian coast. A pink glacier sort of a thing. I lost two fingers of my left hand. Also, I've got a gimpy left leg."

After a small quietness, she said, "You married, though. Julie."

"How'd you know that?"

She made a humorous sound before she answered. I saw her, imagined her, lift her shoulders and smile.

"Borstead is still the headquarters of the Norfolk CIA."

"Right," I said, then, not wanting to, afraid to, "How about you, Frankie?"

"How much do you know?"

"Not a lot. They flew you to America. After that it was just, I dunno, wisps. Rumors. Nobody would talk to me."

I sat, quietly cracking up and worrying about the time, while she told me her story. Her tone was droll and matter-of-fact.

She'd spent ten months in a clinic in Los Angeles, then another year in California as an outpatient. Nicole had stayed with her all that time. Her father had flown out for both Christmases, and on three other occasions. The doctors and cosmetic surgeons had done a great job, and it had cost a fortune. Unfortunately, they hadn't been able to save her eye.

"Oh, no, Frankie. No. You lost an eye?"

"Yes, the right one. It's okay. One gets used to it. The fake I wear these days is rather brilliant, in fact. You wouldn't be able to tell, unless I'm watching tennis."

She hadn't thought that anyone would be interested in her. But was surprised by how many men seemed to find a girl with a glass eye and a limp attractive. When she was twenty-four, she married "a rich chump" and for nine years went by the name of Françoise Chamberlain before leaving and later divorcing him. They had a child, a daughter, now twenty-eight, a textile designer, living in Paris. Her name is Clementine.

Frankie paused after telling me this, as if waiting for me to comment.

"I don't have any children, myself," I said eventually.

Her parents' marriage was, according to Frankie, a late victim of what she called "our accident." Nicole had not wanted to leave California. She'd liked the climate, hadn't wanted to return to the twin bleaknesses of Norfolk and her marriage. She used Frankie's "condition" to make excuses for delaying their departure.

"Besides," Frankie said, "I think she had a little thing going on, if you know what I mean."

"Really? A man, you mean?"

"One of my surgeons, believe it or not. I don't know. Maybe I was imagining it. He was a lovely man. I was a bit in love with him myself."

And, at last, a worm of jealousy stirred in my chest.

Gerard had issued an ultimatum, then another. All the same, it was another year before Frankie and her mother returned to Bratton Manor. Things turned nasty almost immediately. For reasons Frankie couldn't understand at the time, each of her parents blamed the other for what had happened to her. And they both blamed Frankie.

"So there was this triangle of blame, Clem, you see? We couldn't get outside of it. If one of us did get free for a while, the other two would drag her back in. Or him. Because that's the only way we . . . it was the only relationship we had."

"So, uh, how were you at the time? Like, physically, I mean."

"Oh, I was fine. Well, I was fine with myself. I didn't particularly want to meet people, you know? I rode a lot. Hey, d'you remember Marron?"

"Yes, of course."

So anyway, Frankie said, after eighteen months of triangular hell, Nicole went to Montreal to visit her parents. She never came back. She wouldn't allow Gerard a divorce on the grounds that she was a catheter.

"Christ, Clem, did I just say *catheter*? I meant *Catholic*."

I thought, *She's been drinking*. What time did she say it was in England?

I said, "Interesting Freudian slip."

"No. Catheters have been a major concern of mine, these last few months."

"Right," I said.

So Gerard had soldiered on, pretending that the separation was temporary. His wife's parents were unwell and needed her. She was looking after their business interests over there. The story varied, then became uninteresting. Gossip and conjecture moved on elsewhere. Gerard started drinking heavily.

"Wait a minute," I said. "Your mother didn't take you with her?"

"No. She left me, too."

But, Frankie said, that was okay. She wouldn't have wanted to go back to Montreal, anyway. As it turned out, Nicole moved to California within a year. Frankie had, she said, married the Chamberlain guy so as to put an end to "the boomeranging back and forth across the Atlantic" between her parents. Then, when Clementine was three years old, Nicole had died in a road accident near San Diego. In her will, she'd left everything to Frankie. A lot of money. Much more than Frankie had expected.

* * *

I checked my watch again. Oh, my God, five past eight already. I tucked the phone between my shoulder and my ear and started fumbling drawings into my portfolio.

"Frankie, listen, I'm sorry, but I have to . . ."

"I've thought about you a lot, Clem," she said, out of nowhere, stopping me in my tracks. "More than you could imagine. Especially since being back here. Revisiting the places where we used to meet."

I felt myself welling up again, like an inconsolable child.

I said (*why*, for God's sake?), "Have you been to Hazeborough?"

"Yes."

I waited.

"I . . . I didn't recognize it. I didn't remember it. I can't remember anything about . . . about that day. Actually, that's not quite true. I do remember that morning, cycling down the back lane away from the manor. I can even remember what I was wearing. Then nothing until I woke up in the hospital. I wish more than anything that I could remember. I thought that going there might bring it back."

"It doesn't matter."

"It does, Clem. It does to me."

There was a sort of challenge in the way she said it. But there was no way I was going to respond, even if I'd known how to. And time was pressing.

"So, Frankie, what will you do now? What's next?"

"I'm staying here, of course." She sounded surprised by my question. "The estate is my responsibility now."

"And is that a responsibility you want?"

"Oh, yes. Very much so. In fact, that's why I called you. Or, rather, it's one of the reasons I called you."

"Really? How so?"

I heard her take in a long breath and let it out.

"I intend to restore it, Clem. Make it beautiful again. Put everything back."

"Uh, right. What does that mean, exactly?"

She started to talk faster, more urgently. For which I was grateful.

"You know what my father did to this place. He, he *scoured* it. Leveled it. Trashed it. Turned it into a prairie, a wasteland. It's ugly. I hate it."

"*Our* fathers," I said. "Fathers, plural. Yours and mine."

"Yes," she said. "George bulldozed everything Gerard pointed at. But I'm going to put right what they did. I'm going to replant trees, hedges. Copses. Woods. Dig out the ditches and ponds they filled in. I'm going to bring birdsong back to this place before I die. I don't care if it costs every penny I own."

"Frankie . . ."

"I'm going to re-create Franklins, Clem. I'm going to plant pines up there. I'm going to rebuild the barn."

I took hold of the phone again. I sat down.

"*What?*" I sort of gurgled the word, I think.

"You heard me."

"Frankie . . ."

"What? You think I'm crazy?"

"No. No, I . . . But, you know. You're talking about turning the clock back, Frankie. I don't think it's possible."

"Yes, it is. I'm very rich, and it's what I want."

"Yeah, okay, but . . ."

"Listen, Clem. Since I've been back here, in between poking pulp into my father's mouth and wiping it off his chin, I've been working. Doing research. Looking at old maps. Old photographs, old prints. Talking to old people. Trouble is, there are fewer old people than there used to be. We are the old people now."

And here I got a first glimmer of what she wanted. I blinked it away, though.

She said, "I've got a picture, a model, in my head of how the estate used to be in my grandfather's time. When I was a girl. What I haven't got is someone to share it with. Someone who remembers it the way I do and who cares as much as I do. Someone who's as sentimental as I am."

I was not, absolutely not, going to rise to that.

"Look, Frankie—it's incredible, wonderful, to talk to you. To hear your voice again. And I feel terrible saying this, but it so happens I've got a meeting in half an hour. It's important, and I'm going to be late."

"I'm sorry. I won't keep you. But will you think about it?"

"Think about what?"

"About coming home, Clem. About helping me remember. Being my artist again."

I was stunned. That's a cliché, I know. You can only be stunned if you've been whacked aside the head. I was stunned.

"You can't be serious," I managed to say. "You don't know what you're . . ."

"Yes, I do know what I'm asking. What I'm *not* asking is that you give up your brilliant career or anything. You could do your own work while you're helping me. The Garden Cottage is vacant, and we could make you a beautiful studio in one of the courtyard buildings. All rent free, naturally."

"Frankie, for Christ's sake, it's not the money."

"No. It's the love."

I said, "Pardon me?"

"A code word for anything truly valuable. A child's life, for example. Or the place you belong."

"Frankie, please. I left a long time ago. And I never belonged there."

"We'd be a great team. Three good eyes between us. Three ears. Two good legs. Nothing could stand in our way."

I tried to laugh.

"I'm strong, Clem, but I'm lonely."

"Please, Frankie. Don't. I have to go. Look, I'll ring you back."

"Will you? Do you promise?"

"Yes," I said. "I promise. Later today or tomorrow. What's your number?"

I wrote it down.

"It used to be Bratton Morley 239," I said, sort of absently, while I was writing.

"Fancy you remembering that," Frankie said.

There was an *aha!* in her voice, as if she'd caught me out.

"So, okay," I said.

"Go," she said. "But think about it, Clem. Think about it very seriously. Think with your heart as well as your head."

"Yeah, sure. I'll do that. Bye, Frankie."

"And Clem? Losing you hurt a lot more than losing my eye."

She hung up before I did.

I sat in the crowded, southward-racketing subway car with the awkward portfolio of drawings between my knees. I was angry more than anything else. After a lifetime—a lifetime of hurt, of wondering, of remembering, of erasure—she'd chosen *this* morning, of all mornings, to reach out of the past and mess with my head. *Damn* her!

I hate being late. Punctuality is one of my obsessions. I looked at my watch again. No way was I going to make it to Val Leibnitz's office by a quarter to nine.

I tried to focus on *Fantastic Machines,* on my pitch to the skeptical accountants.

It had taken me a long time to master the American art of boundless enthusiasm. That innocent, volcanic bubbling about almost anything. It went against my grain. During my early years in New York, I'd lost a number of jobs by being understated, apologetic, ironic. British, in short. It was Val Leibnitz who'd taken me to lunch one day and laid down the law, revealed the commandment: *Thou shalt believe absolutely in whatever shit you're selling. Because if you don't, why the hell would anybody who's buying?*

Obvious, of course. All the same, I couldn't quite do it. It didn't come naturally.

Then I read an interview with some actor, can't remember who, who said, "It's bull, that stuff about finding the character within yourself, identifying with his motivation, all of that. What you do is decide what kind of clothes he wears, what he likes to eat. Then what you do is put those clothes on, eat what he eats. Walk the way he walks, all of that. Sooner or later you start to talk like him. And that's it. Acting isn't a matter of truth or honesty. It's a matter of impersonation."

It was my Road to Damascus moment, that article. A revelation. I couldn't do the foamy, heartfelt, swept-away-on-a-tsunami-of-conviction stuff. But someone who looked like me, behaved like me, dressed like me, had the same name as me, could. So I sat in the subway car, trying to become him, my impersonator. Checking that the cuffs of my stonewashed blue denim shirt came an inch below the cuffs of the sleeves of my gray Paul Smith jacket, that my black Peter Werth pants were free of lint, that there were no greasy streaks on my pale buckskin Timberland shoes. Looking sharp is important if, like me, you have the kind of face that can distress people.

"Come home," she'd said. *Home!* Hadn't she realized what an insane idea, what a ridiculous term that was? It had been years and years, a whole lifetime, since I'd thought of Norfolk as my home. Or anywhere else, for that matter. And I was glad of it. *Home,* for me, is a word with stifling, subterranean connotations: badgery burrows, premature burials, walls that edge closer

when you're not looking. Norfolk had squeezed me, exploded me, had fired me into the world like the shell from a gun. Did Frankie really think that I would, or could, reverse that trajectory and worm back into the dark breech called *home*? Absurd.

And her, her . . . project, was, well, deeply eccentric. Or actually mad. Time simply will not be turned backward. Things cannot be what they were. We can't have our childhoods back, re-create those worlds. And even if she *could,* she'd never live to see it. Those pines at Franklins had been at least a hundred years old.

Sane people do not refuse to grow up.

I wondered if perhaps she was, in fact, crazy. Rich people often are.

I wondered what she might be worth. Several millions, presumably.

"I'm going to rebuild the barn."

"Be my artist again."

I squirmed in my seat, remembering my clumsy efforts at drawing her. The heavy-handed way I'd scribbled and scratched at her litheness, her lightness. If only I'd been as good then as I am now. Now I'd be able to do her body justice.

Get a *grip,* Ackroyd, I told myself. *Fantastic Machines from Fantastic Movies.* Focus!

Over the years I had, naturally, tried to imagine an older Frankie. To imagine her as ravaged by time as I was. I'd done it to bury her ghost. To banish her. I'd packed weight onto her hips and belly. Turned her hair gray. Thickened her ankles. Pulled support stockings onto her legs. Now, to complete this grotesquery, I could add a glass eye and a limp. Maybe a walking stick. Yes.

But it wouldn't do. It wouldn't take.

Instead, she swung her hair away, descending to a kiss.

Biting her lip, bare-breasted, kneeling over me.

Pulling me down, sand on her fingers, the sea heaping itself onto the beach with a sound like *yes, yes.*

She would stay young, sixteen, for ever. Unless I went back.

So I would call her, and say no. Yes, I would call her. Later, or maybe tomorrow.

"I'm strong, Clem, but I'm lonely."

At least I hadn't said, "So am I."

The train whined to a halt. The doors opened. I'd lost track of where we were. It didn't matter; the WTC, my stop, was the terminus. Peering through the press of bodies, I saw that we were at Chambers Street. Then the throb of the motor died. A tinny voice said something I couldn't make out. PA announcements — at airports, railway stations, sports events — are among the things beyond the limits of my hearing. But the other passengers responded with the resigned truculence that New Yorkers specialize in and started to leave the train. Clearly, we were going no farther. I got to my feet.

Mass indecision took place. A great many people stood on the platform, thinking that there was a good chance that the problem would be fixed. Others headed up and out to the street.

It was eight forty-three. Damn! Val's office was, what, four, five blocks away? Ten, twelve minutes at a fast limp. There goes your credibility, Ackroyd, I thought, climbing the stairs. Late for a crucial meeting. What does that say about your commitment? And where the hell is my enthusiastic impersonator? Thank you, Frankie, for coming uninvited out of the bloody past and making me late.

I turned onto West Broadway and called Val on my cell.

"Val? Hi, it's me. Look, I'm sorry, really. I'm gonna be just a tiny bit late."

"Clem, hi. So where are you?"

"Chambers and West. Don't worry. I've got the work, and it's good. But I had a call from home, you know? And I had to take it. Then the damn subway . . ."

Val said something I didn't catch because a loud plane came overhead. I remember thinking it was unusual; planes don't come in low over Lower Manhattan as a rule.

I stopped walking. I looked up at where Val's office was, maybe thinking, stupidly, that she might be looking back at me from her window on floor 102 of the North Tower of the World Trade Center.

"Sorry, Val, I missed that."

"I said, don't sweat it. Right now we're just going through some figures here."

Something silvery, a fleck, like a fault in the clear blue sky, appeared then disappeared behind the twin towers.

I said, "Sounds like fun. I'll—"

I pulled the phone away from my ear because it tried to savage me. A noise came out of it like . . . I still can't say what it was like. Immensely brutal; the war cry of some huge primeval beast concentrated into a single second. Then silence.

And as I watched, the North Tower split open and extruded an impossibly vast orange-and-black flower of boiling flame and smoke, which, as it blossomed, spat out seeds of fire and steel and stone.

When the sound of it rolled down over us, we in the streets, the Spared, the Elect, began to shout obscenities and the various names of God.

AUTHOR'S NOTE

Clem Ackroyd is an unreliable historian. In concocting his narrative of the Cuban Missile Crisis, he has used (and sometimes abused) material from the following books:

The Kennedy Tapes: Inside the White House During the Cuban Missile Crisis, edited by Ernest R. May and Philip D. Zelikow

One Minute to Midnight: Kennedy, Khrushchev, and Castro on the Brink of Nuclear War, by Michael Dobbs

Thirteen Days: A Memoir of the Cuban Missile Crisis, by Robert F. Kennedy

The Cuban Missile Crisis: A Concise History, by Don Munton and David A. Welch.

There is some evidence that he has also accessed the websites of the National Security Archive and the Cold War International History Project.

Finally: there are still approximately seven thousand nuclear warheads in existence. More than enough to blast the planet into a perpetual winter. I assume there are people who know where they all are. But we don't talk about them much anymore. We have other things on our minds.

HL - 820L
AR - 14
BL - 5.6

DISCARDED

Richard Sugden Library
8 Pleasant St.
Spencer, MA 01562